VĀ

STORIES BY WOMEN
OF THE MOANA

VĀ

STORIES BY WOMEN OF THE MOANA

EDITED BY SISILIA ETEUATI & LANI YOUNG

Published by TATOU PUBLISHING, New Zealand / Samoa, 2021.

Copyright: Sisilia Eteuati and Lani Wendt Young, 2021

ISBN : 978 982 9175 23 6

Editors: Sisilia Eteuati and Lani Wendt Young

Copy Editor: Lynne-Marie Eteuati

Cover Art: 'Blueprint' by Lalovai Peseta, 2018.

Cover Design: Lani Wendt Young and James Quizon.

Interior Formatted by

emtippettsbookdesigns.com

Mo tamaita'i uma o le Moana, e le mafai ona taofia lau tala, e le seua lau ti'a, e sa'olele lava le folosaga.

For all the women of the Moana, with stories in their hearts, no-one can stop you telling them.

TABLE OF CONTENTS

THE GIRL WHO SAW THE MOON'S SICK

By Rebecca Tobo Olul-Hossen

Natu just had to see the moon's sick when Mama was away overseas for a training.

To make matters worse she had not even realised that she got the moon's sick. Tata was the one who commented on the spots of blood on one of the only skirts she owned. The skirt she normally wore to Sunday School. The one with the large black elastic waist and the pale green-pink-blue stripes running down it.

"Is that blood on your skirt, Koko?" Tata asked softly followed closely by, "Do you have a sore on your bum?"

All this while Natu was running past in hard pursuit of her fat black and white cat, Fluffy.

Natu stopped in her tracks.

"Whaaat…?" she stammered whirling around to try to look at the back of her skirt. "I don't have a sore on my bum. It might be an old stain," Natu said.

Natu prayed hard in her heart that one of her sores from allergic reactions to grass had opened up again and was bleeding. The blood rushing through her veins was so loud in her ears that she thought she could hear her heart thumping.

"Koko, I need to talk to you," Tata said quietly. "Do you remember your mother talking to you about monthly period?" he asked softly.

1

Natu looked around to make sure her two brothers were not within earshot. After all, she was the girl who at nine years old knew about the sick of the moon and where babies came from, all thanks to a midwife mother. Her friends could not believe it when she told them. So many bad things happened in the area around a women's vagina.

"Yes . . .", she replied quietly.

"Go to the bathroom and check your underpants to see if there is any blood, okay?" Tata said.

Natu nodded. She turned quietly and went into the bathroom remembering to lock the door behind her this time.

Sure enough, there was blood on her underwear. She has the dreaded sick of the moon that Mama had been telling her about! And at only 12 years old too. Could the dratted thing not have waited a few more years?

Natu spent the longest time in the bathroom. Just sitting on the toilet seat. Perhaps if she sat long enough it would go away. Maybe it was only a dream. She pinched herself. It was painful.

"Tata, I think I have my period," she said quietly, when she finally found the courage to come out of the bathroom.

"That's okay, koko," Tata said, tears filling his eyes. "Stay here. I will go to the shop and get you some pads."

After what felt like ages, in which Natu prayed even harder that none of her brothers would come into the room looking for her, Tata came back with a package wrapped in last month's newspaper. He asked if Mama had taught Natu how to wear a pad. Natu nodded mutely.

Natu went into the bathroom and wore the pad with fresh underpants. She removed the much-loved stained skirt and scrubbed the blood off with soap and cold water. Letting the evidence slowly get swallowed by the drain.

Then the dreaded phone call with Mama when she cried, "My daughter is all grown up now!" Of course, Tata told Mama before Natu got the chance.

And Kaka Ken sending a pig from Tanna for her kaliku. Mama had explained what normally happens when a girl first sees the moon's sick in Tanna kastom. It was bad enough that Mama and Tata knew she had seen the moon's sick, but for the whole world to know if she were to have the kaliku – Natu thought she would die! No, she could not.

2

Imagine how those highly decorated girls in the village in grass-skirts with bodies (including budding breasts!) well-oiled with coconut oil must have felt when the women, men and everyone are hitting each other with the banana stalks and suckers on the way down to the beach for her first swim. The whole village knew that she had seen the moon's sick. The elders in the village were eyeing her for marriage to one of their sons.

Natu almost died when Tata brought the pig home from the wharf. She hid in her room, hugging Fluffy tightly, wanting it all to go away. She wanted things to be normal again. She wanted to climb trees with her brothers and the other children, play le loup and robbers and police.

Somehow, she knew that things will never go back to the way they were before. She was not allowed to touch food when she sees the moon's sick. This was taboo. She would have to be careful with how she sat and try not to run around so much like a boy.

But when the moon's sick left her, for a little bit of time, things almost felt normal again. Natu ran with her friends, played le loup in abundance and robbers and police.

Just like the times before she saw the moon's sick.

KOVITI AIKAE

By Lani Young

A m afraid. Make that, terrified. In big bad worst way. But not for me. For parents. There is worldwide pandemic, Koviti, and germs trying very hard to come to Samoa. Koviti very bad for old people. Especially old people with weak lungs. The father is seventy-five. The mother seventy-three. Both parents used to be smokers. They quit when we teenagers, but now they get pneumonia and bronchitis whenever they catch flu. Koviti will be like one spray of Mortein on a mosquito and kill them for sure. Is me and Big Brother Siaki's job to stop it.

Or else.

Is scary big responsibility.

Every Samoan knows importance of fifth commandment – 'Honour thy father and thy mother'. Commandment so important it's one of only God rules in entire Bible that gives reason for observing it. 'That thy days may be long on the land that the Lord thy God has given you.'

Bible very clear. Unless you want to die early, probably painful lonely death, then honour your parents. No disclaimers or qualifiers. Fifth commandment drilled into us even more than 'Thou shalt love thy neighbour.' Because screw the neighbours. Samoans know priority ordering of ten commandments is little bit incorrect. Because number one before neighbours and all others, is parents. They right up there next to God in list of who needs obedience and respect. So what if your parents mean and fasi you often? Never mind if they tell you every day you useless and stupid waste of their love. Still not exempted from honour.

We fortunate our parents are not the fasi type. Yes, the mother used the salu a few times. The seevae kosokoso. Maybe she threw a pot at Siaki's head once. But doesn't count, since he ducked. And yes, she is skilful at soul cutting with words. But then, what Samoan mother isn't? She never needed to take us for stitches because she cut our heads open with the axe handle. Or to the fofo because she threw boiling water on us. No, as a Samoan mother goes, she was moderate. The father even more so. He never hit us girls. Only Siaki. When he deserved it. And he probably should have hit Siaki a lot more because if being honest here, Siaki doesn't live like someone taught to walk straight and narrow. When not selling joints to his friends, he's sleeping with all the girls I once went to school with. (Because he already slept with all the girls *he* went to school with.) Can't see it myself, but women find Siaki dangerous attractive. He sings in band at the Mountain Club. It's little bit famous band. They have songs on iTunes. Some CDs selling at the flea market. All up, with the dope selling, the CDs and the girls who give him expensive gifts, Siaki makes more money than I do, even though I have university degree and am teacher. Which makes me resentful sometimes, because feels like somebody somewhere lied to me about why I should not smoke dope and have sex with all the boys at school. Which would make me pa'uguku. Is not fair. Life not fair.

But this not about me. It about Koviti. And parents.

Is tiresome fact of universe that even when you grow up, get old and fat with too many kids of your own – still must honour parents. God said so. Moses wrote it down. Jesus never cancelled it. Samoan parents carve it into your head and heart over and over. *HONOUR THY MOTHER AND THY FATHER!* And honour includes keeping them alive in pandemic. World Health Organisation and all expert pandemic scientists don't need to convince us we must protect the old people from Koviti. We already got the word from God. (Thank you Moses copy and paste skills.)

Right now, every Samoan in the world everywhere is saying, *Koviti aikae! You'll have to bust a way through us before you can get to OUR parents.*

Me and Siaki determined. We got this.

We make a plan. We will build wall between parents and outside world. Bigger and better than Trump's shitty wall against Mexico. Wall made from disinfectant, hand sanitizer, masks, our ferocious dog Whiskey, and our chain-link fence with the barbed wire on top. A no visitors policy.

We will do all shopping for parents. Do all errands and driving to town. Buy their food. Pay their bills. I make roster and Siaki agrees to it. Because of course he agrees. He is good son even if he is dope head and slutty sex machine. We certain that with all these things, Koviti and anyone carrying it, will not reach the parents.

I feeling good about our plan, the brilliant roster with colour co-ordinated highlighters.

Then SHE calls. The Dragon in Wellington. Also known as oldest child of the parents. Our many years older big sister Falute. Phoneline crackles sharp and loud with her words. Instructions. What to do, how to do it.

She wanted to come home herself you understand. But she has to stay in New Zealand and look after her five kids. Her palagi husband who has diabetes. (Type One he's always reminding us. The kind you're born with. Not the kind we Samoans get with our bad food choices and lazy-ass ways.) And she very busy with her Very Important Job at the Ministry of Pacific Affairs. Where she is single-handedly preserving all of Samoan culture and language in the entirety of Aotearoa. (She reminds us of this frequently.) So many important things. Chaining her there. When she REALLY wants to be here in Samoa. To protect the parents, order me and Siaki around from day until night, and clock up her blessings in heaven and longevity days for honouring parents.

Me and Siaki listen. Like we always do. We don't tell her we already have plan and roster and wall construction. No point. She is old. We are younger. Hierarchy is important. And she must assuage guilt of Samoan daughter conscience. So she gives orders, everything about how to keep parents alive in apocalypse.

'They mustn't go to town. They must stay home. They mustn't have any visitors. They shouldn't go to church. They should eat more fruit and vegetables. Drink nonu juice with turmeric and ginger. And get them multivitamins and Vitaimn C with Echinacea. They should go for regular walks though, keep fit and active. Get some exercise videos so they can do Zumba at home. Make them wear masks, gloves.'

On and on she raps out her list. Then she tells us she sending money for them as per usual. Which is only information we actually care about.

Honour thy father and thy mother looks like weekly trips to Western Union.

I want to say to Falute – *children who don't live here should only send money and keep mouth shut*. But I don't say it. I am only youngest child. The Little Sister. I must not argue or be le mafaufau. Is my job to keep mouth shut and be obedient on the outside.

While saying bad words on the inside.

I remind self. One day when I travel the world and get magical job in faraway place like maybe Dubai or Japan, I must remember, my responsibility to honour parents will be to only send money and to shut up. Because I know what the parents are like.

They don't want to eat fruits and vegetables. Or drink nonu juice. Which is not surprise, since that stuff is foul. Makes me want to vomit. The father doesn't believe in vitamins, the 'palagi's big con where they make you pay money for useless pills that do nothing.' The mother would rather stab a fork in her eye before she ever went for a walk. Or Zumba'd to a Zumba video. Forget that!

But is no point telling the Dragon. She hasn't lived at home for twenty years. She won't understand. As long as she sends the money every week, we endure her haranguing. So me and Siaki do what we always do. Nod, agree, be meek and humble.

Yes Falute. No Falute. Kiss your ass Falute. Goodbye Falute.

Then hang up phone and roll eyes at each other.

The Prime Minister announces State of Emergency. Rules and regulations for everything. We are like people of Old Testament. The more rules the better. Rules that make very much good sense. Like close schools, outlaw public gatherings, no funerals and everybody wash your hands a lot. Shut all nightclubs and bars – which is good news because Siaki won't have excuse to disappear all night and then sleep all day. Ha.

Then there are rules that make nothing sense. Like no swimming on Sunday? Is Koviti scared of the water? And why only on the Sabbath day? And why shut bread shops on Sunday? Does Koviti only infest bakeries every seven days?

But rules about old people very sensible. Top A-plus rules. We like very much. Me and Siaki nod head emphatically in agreement.

Prime Minister says, those over age seventy must stay home. No outings to public places. They should only go out for essential reasons. Like to the hospital for check-up. As disincentive, government removes all senior citizen travel benefits. No more free rides on buses or ferries. This very excellent news. Now we will have legal backing to make the mother stay home and not roam about to faikala with other old lady friends. The father won't be able to go to Savaii every weekend to visit plantation and lecture cousins who look after the koko.

Except we much over-estimated the parents' willingness to be good citizens.

The father says he going to barber shop. For haircut.

Siaki tells him, in nice way, that he should stay home. Because Koviti.

The father says, "But you just had a haircut at the barber last week. Why can't I go to the barber?"

I tell him. "Koviti is more dangerous for old people. The Prime Minister said nobody over seventy years should ride on the bus or go to town. You should stay home and be safe."

But the father unconvinced. He says, "That's stupid. The Prime Minister is over seventy. But he's still going places and even talking on the TV! Why's he trying to lock us in our houses? You call up the Prime Minister and tell him he has to stay home then. Bossy old man. Go on, call him."

Am little bit proud the father thinks I important enough to have the Prime Minister on speed dial. Then am back to frustrated. Again I explain. With patience. Koviti is contagious disease spreading all over world, killing many people. No cure. Yet. Is especially bad for old people. That's why government said all old people must not go to public places.

The father frowns. Then gets shifty gleam in eyes. "The barber is my friend. His shop is downstairs in his house. So I'm not going to a public place. I'm going to visit my good friend Malo. And while I'm there having a chat, he can cut my hair."

The father is triumphant at the brilliance of his rationalization. I spend next half hour arguing with him about why Malo's barber shop is classified public place. Finally, the father concedes. But only because is time for his favourite radio programme. He has big smile as he sits in lazy boy chair and turns volume up loud. The father enjoys a good debate. I won argument, but sure don't feel like it. Am exhausted.

When I come back from work that evening, there is cream donuts on kitchen table. The mother's favourite. From Diana's Bakery in town.

"Did you buy these?" I ask Siaki.

"No. I thought you did."

We exchange confused look.

"Your mother bought them," says the father. "When she went for a ride to town with Salaneta. But I'm not supposed to tell you."

I confront the mother. "You went to the bakery!"

A shrug. "Me and Salaneta wanted to get a few things."

"But you're not supposed to go into stores. Me and Siaki will do your shopping for you."

Airy wave of her hand. "We walked fast. And we didn't let anyone cough on us."

"People will think you have no children to do shopping for you."

"I want to look at the pastries and choose for myself."

"Did you go anywhere else?" I ask. Softly softly. Popo i lalo calm down the voice inside me that wants to demand.

"Only to the pharmacy," says the mother. "Salaneta needed to fill her prescription."

"The pharmacy?!" Both me and Siaki burst out at the same time. "The worst place for you to be. Where all the sick people are!"

"But you stayed in the car, right?" asks Siaki. He looks as harassed as I feel. He totally going to smoke a joint after this. I know it.

"Oh no, I went in too," says the mother. "It's so hot in the car. And besides, there's lots of nice new stock at the pharmacy. They got some new lipsticks. You should get a new lipstick Mara. Your face always look so serious. That's why you can't find a husband."

There are words inside me. Boiling words. Rising, pushing, fighting to scream free.

I DON'T NEED ANY FUCKING LIPSTICK. I NEED MY MOTHER TO STAY HER ASS AT HOME.

A neon sign flashes in my brain just in time. A siren wails that only I can hear. *Children, honour thy mother and thy father…*

So I swallow the bad words.

The mother turns up the television volume with the remote. Announcing to me and Siaki that the conversation is over.

Is only Day One of lockdown and already I tired. Is very difficult to be good children to elderly parents when they stubborn. How are we supposed to keep them alive in Koviti apocalypse if they won't listen?

Next day I make several phone calls. To the bakery, the pharmacy and to the mother's favourite grocery store. They all know the parents. I ask them nicely for help. Then I make Siaki call the mother's bestie Salaneta and ask her with all his usual suave charm to please not invite our mother on any outings anymore. Thanks to his gift with wheedling women (it works even if they are very old) Salaneta is happy to co-operate with our Wall plan.

I exultant when I go to work. *Aha, the parents will be safe at home today!*

Am in middle of marking essays when phone rings. The mother. She is angry. Oh, so angry. Spitting words that leap through phone to slap my face and fuki my hair. I am disobedient, cheeky and ungrateful. A curse to my parents. A waste of her love. And worstest of all, I am FIAPOTO.

Why? Because she went in a taxi to the Happy Foodtown grocery store and the security guard escorted her outside. Because the owner (apologetically) explained that they are enforcing the government's directive about old people not going to public places. And the reason why they are enforcing it is because my mother's daughter (i.e. ME) called and asked them to. My fiapoto-ness has publicly shamed her.

Is no use my pointing out that getting into taxi with stranger and their germs was bad choice and directly opposed to Koviti battle plan. Is no use reminding that we trying to KEEP HER AND FATHER ALIVE THROUGH PANDEMIC.

No. Instead, I listen with humility and patience as she berates me. I even apologize for my wrong when she pauses for breath. Because that's what you do when you Samoan and you trying to obey fifth commandment. You be meek and penitent always. Or at least you pretend that you are.

I leave work and go pick her up. She is standing outside Happy Foodtown with handbag clutched tight to her chest, rigid and angry angry angry, like she ready to run into walls, be human battering ram. When she sees me, she marches towards car. Child vendors selling car air freshener sidle out of her way. They know better than to ask her for a sale. I brace self. Ready for her retribution.

Suddenly, am struck by just how little and wrinkled fragile she is in her voluminous red floral dress. And how fierce is her spirit still as she clutches tight to all the freedoms that make up her daily life. I humiliated her today at favourite grocery store. I did that. Shame rips through me. I am sorry for real. I get out of car to go greet her.

But then she pauses and turns back. Uh-oh. What she doing?

In the glaring sun of the afternoon, she shakes her fist and screams, "AIKAE!" At the security guard with his mouth gaping open in shock. At Happy Foodtown. At the sky. At the State of Emergency. At the Prime Minister and his Cabinet's rules. At the pandemic. At the death and suffering in faraway places showing on the TV every night. At the unfairness and misery of it all. "KOVITI AIKAE!"

Then she brushes past me and gets into car. Slams door. Hard and loud. Everybody in the world still reeling from her AIKAE flinches. Including me.

"Hurry up Mara," she snaps. "We go now."

We drive in silence. Because Samoans don't say sorry. Or I love you. Even when we are penitent for real. Instead, on the way home, I stop at Diana's Bakery. We both go inside so she can choose her favourite pastries.

But we put on masks first.

Close Encounters

By Lehua Parker

An oil slick of rotting fish guts and slaughterhouse blood stretches out behind the dive boat for a quarter mile or more. Immersed in the Dive Master's pre-encounter briefing, shark cages prepped and waiting, nobody even looks up as a zodiac roars alongside and a twitchy man with an AK-47 boards.

Nobody except Captain 'Aukai.

Captain 'Aukai charges out of the wheelhouse, hands flapping.

The gun goes boom.

Blood and brains spatter the wheelhouse wall like a Rorschach ink blot. Captain 'Aukai's body tumbles over the railing, hitting the water like just another bucket of chum tossed overboard by the deckhand.

Twitchy-with-the-Gun has everyone's full attention now.

Standing in her wetsuit with the rest of her tour group, Claire wants to hide from the unnatural way the Captain's body moves in the ocean, tugged this way and that like a rag doll in a washing machine. But she knows showing any fear will draw Twitchy-with-the-Gun's attention like blood in the water, so she presses her lips tight and watches as piece by piece, the Captain disappears inside dark shadows ringed with teeth.

It doesn't take long.

As the last ghost of blood dissipates in the sea off the Australian coast, the Dive Master crosses himself. On the back of his hoodie is the great white shark logo and tagline of the dive charter: Close Enough to Count Teeth.

Twitchy casually—too casually—slings his AK-47 over his shoulder like Huck Finn's fishing pole and barks something at the First Mate. Claire doesn't know the words, but the meaning is clear.

Mine.

All mine.

Over Claire's shoulder, a German lady tosses her wedding ring. It bounces along the deck and rolls along smooth planks to rest against Twitchy's combat boots. He smirks and kicks it overboard, screaming something incomprehensible.

The First Mate holds up his hands, speaking rapidly.

"What's he saying?" asks a Brit. "Anyone know what he wants?"

"Nyaope," whispers the Dive Master.

"Nyaope? Drogen? Ist er hoch auf Drogen?" asks a voice in the back.

"Ja, Drogen—drugs, heroin," says the Dive Master. "He sees the cages and thinks we work for the syndicate. The First Mate is telling him he's made a mistake—we're a dive company offering shark encounters—but he's not listening."

Twitchy stomps along the deck, cursing and shaking his fist, sweat rolling down his face and staining the collar of his flak vest. His pants pockets and gun belt bulge with extra mags. There are only two of them, Twitchy and the man waiting in the zodiac, but the AK-47 makes the numbers irrelevant.

Twitchy whirls, raising the rifle off his shoulder, and fires into the air.

A voice shrieks.

Twitchy's eyes lock on target.

The girl is young, no more than fifteen, with long hair swept up in braids cascading down her back and pink manicured nails peeking from the sleeves of her too big wetsuit.

Twitchy points at her and then at his feet.

Come.

"No," says the Dive Master, stepping forward.

Twitchy grins as he spins the rifle, cracking the butt against the Dive Master's forehead.

The Dive Master drops to his knees.

Twitchy doesn't look back, just steps over him and whistles to his partner.

The zodiac roars to life and pulls alongside the dive boat's gangway.

Twitchy points at the girl, then the zodiac.

A woman in a ball cap pushes the girl behind her.

Twitchy raises his rifle.

Claire looks toward shore.

Two miles or more.

She calmly zips her wetsuit, lowers her head, and charges.

Wrapping him in a bear hug, her momentum carries them both over the railing and into the water.

Bubbles like silver coins burst around them.

Holding her breath, Claire pushes Twitchy away.

Twitchy flounders, air exploding from his mouth as he screams, the weight of his ammo, boots, and flak jacket dragging him down.

As she rises to the surface, Claire only has time to see the first shark nose him just before the second takes off his head.

It's everything the dive charter promised.

ON "LIVING THE DREAM"

By Karlo Mila

We are wearing linen these days. Our taonga, exquisite, orbing at our throats. Or lunging between our breasts.

We wear comfortable shoes these days. They can be heels. But they are cushioned. To absorb the shock.

We buy our lingerie from Lonely. It would shock you. How gorgeous it is. How expensive it is. The quiver of deconstructed lace, well-thought through, designed by a girl from Palmy (a friend of a friend - gone international) on our curving, aching bodies. That can still be beautiful, naked.

Our nails are well-kept these days as part of a self-care routine that goes flashy, or neutral, shiny, or matte. As our mood dictates.

We are good at being women with money. Give generously to give-a-littles that catch our eyes. We buy ethical. We buy art. We buy handmade, homemade. We buy from friends. We buy fair trade, trade aid. We buy organic. We buy free-range. We drop our spare change into good causes. We make our own fucking money. We make thousand-dollar deposits into the accounts of friends in trouble. All that "girls can do anything" we grew up on.

We've left our husbands. Even if they were *good men*. Older women *tut tut* *tsk tsk* at our choices.

"You *educated* women" an older Tongan woman says to me... in an expression that could be contempt or disbelief or envy... but educated equals stupid regardless of tone.

I have those days I regret it. I have those days I don't. Yes my husband had multiple degrees and did the washing and the dishes and yes he never beat me, not once. Not one violent incident ever. I know. These older women wished they married my ex-husband. Hoped to raise sons like him.

I know.

I grew up reading Alice Walker and Mary Oliver and I truly believed in "that one and wild precious life - what will you do with it?" I buy my own jewellery these days.

Semi-precious.

Thought through for the properties of the stones, just as much as the shine or colour of them.

I look it up in a book, on the internet. I research the meaning behind my bling.

I look at the tiny diamond on my engagement ring from Michael Hill jewellers, and whether he was a Satanist or not - as the rumour once went - (lol), it is everything that is wrong with the world. When I stare into its sparkly eye. The jokes on you, blood diamond. You have been found out.

I buy fresh flowers for myself. It is the epitome of middle class. Jesus. Who buys flowers for their own house? I grew up in a household that would not dream of this. My mother would never do this. Even though she can afford it (now). It makes me some kind of hedonist. My ex-husband, who rarely bought me flowers - would raise his eyes. My sons raise their eyes.

"You can't eat them Mum."

"What's the point?"

Beauty. I think. Bringing beauty into my house. The fragrance, I think. To bring fragrance into our house.

Just because. I think.

I can.

And because. I think.

I'm a feminist.

And because. I think. I don't have a lover to bring me flowers. And because. I think.

I just can.

I'm in an airport. And I see you lady. And I see myself. I see us. This new breed. On our iPhone 11s in our favourite colours. Sprawling ourselves without any shame, legs up on the ottomans, defiantly, making ourselves at home, everywhere the fuck we go, thank you very much. Pulitzer Prize-winning novels by women of colour in our carry-on luggage. Demanding / commanding good service from white people who try to intimidate us with their "can you afford this" attitudes. We demand / command excellent service from these snotty motherfuckers working minimum wage, looking down at us.

It's so interesting, how life works out.

How, now, we both have contempt for each other.

No. Not takeaway. I'm here to stay. I'm here to sit down and drink all your view has to offer. I'm here for the comfortable seats. Thank you. And three glasses of complimentary sparkling water. And can you tell, that I give zero fucks that for some reason, this is making you awkward.

Yes. I see you beautiful brown professional successful woman applying your MAC lipstick. You who broke through the glass ceiling because you dared to shine bright, bright like a diamond... all the letters after your name. You, who the government tries to woo, on advisory groups and panels. You who NGOs send letters to, asking you to sit on their boards. They are all trying to solve a problem, that somehow you, by existing, have solved by living your own success. Somehow you, make it the fault, of those who haven't, because you have. The system doesn't need to change if there are more of you everywhere. You stop accepting invitations.

Your privilege is more than a poem. It is a novel.

It is the rest of your lifetime. Activism becoming more and more important. I mean really... can you believe this shit going down. These dumb decisions. *Really*? Our tongues getting sharper, more impatient, more entitled, more angry.

Do you think, like me? Now we've won this world over... the way we were supposed to do. All us brown girls "with potential".

What the fuck do we do now?

This. is. not. enough.

HOMESICK

By Steph Matuku

David Howe was our boss, a white guy in his forties who imagined himself as that guy at the end of the Breakfast Club film, fist held high, marching along to an iconic Gen X theme song. You could see it in the way he dressed, the expensive plaid shirts open over grungy band tees, the bone carving replacing the tie at his neck, the smooth kicks on his feet on Fridays. He had Pasifika-style tattoos up and down his arms which he showed off when he rolled up his shirt sleeves to indicate how hard he was working. He greeted us with a kia ora which was nice, even if he couldn't roll his r's. He tried.

The last few years had been good to people like him. He had a title now; he was an *ally*. He was a useful cog in the wheel against racism. He said he was going to start te reo classes as soon as his schedule allowed it, which was pretty much never, but at least he tried.

He had hired Te Rangi and me, the only two brown faces in a sea of white, apart from Dana who was Chinese, by way of Henderson. There was Paora too, and Terry the Samoan who both worked in the basement in Packing, but Te Rangi and I were the only tangata whenua upstairs in the office. We knew we were the diversity hires, but we didn't mind. If the business managed to tick a couple of boxes – women, check, indigenous, check - and we were those boxes, what did we care? At least we were getting paid.

Of course, it kind of sucked getting hauled up the front whenever visiting managers came, to smile, smile, smile and show off our keen browness, and it sucked when people came to us in a flap wanting to know how to do a pepeha because they had a work course and everyone had to do a pepeha, and would it be okay to sing Ten Guitars afterwards?

And it really sucked whenever some politician or broadcaster would be all over the news pontificating about Mowrees being losers and druggies and ungrateful for the pittance the Government gave them because they couldn't find work or whatever, with no mention of how colonisation was the creation and the cause.

Our colleagues would discuss the latest tirade in the staffroom, their words floating around and stinging our brown flesh with careless venom. Whether they agreed or disagreed, or thought it was okay because it was free speech, and wouldn't it be worse if we weren't allowed to say whatever we wanted, they didn't seem to understand that it was still Te Rangi and me who were the loser, druggie, ungrateful people being discussed. All Māori get sliced and stabbed by racist rhetoric, no matter if it's specifically directed at them or not. The words find us. They cut us. They force us to heal with a thickened callous. They make our souls harder.

And because we both had long wavy black hair and brown eyes and brown skin, people would mix us up, or assume we were related.

"I'm Ngāti Porou," Te Rangi would hiss at them. "Can't you tell?" and she'd jerk her hips from side to side and wiggle her bum at them, and they would back away, eyes wide, not knowing anything about the infamous Ngāti Porou hips but not wanting to admit it, and not wanting to be caught staring at that juicy bum of hers in case she slapped them with a Me Too hashtag.

"If you've got the hips, what I am supposed to be known for?" I grumbled.

"Your triangle head," she replied. "Just like your koro."

She meant my mounga, of course, Mounga Taranaki. I loved that first glimpse of his white topped peak emerging from the clouds in greeting whenever I flew home to visit. He made my heart leap and brought me home. My hand crept up to my head to check the bones of my skull and Te Rangi laughed, a booming chuckle that made me laugh too, and soon we were screaming and clutching one another, because our existence isn't entirely pain and struggle. It's joy too. So much joy.

It was our monthly staff meeting. The guys from Packing came upstairs, blinking under the flourescents like little owls in daylight. David Howe always had piles of fish and chips delivered for the meeting – he said it was the only way he could make sure we all turned up – and we appreciated it, even though the cloying smell would linger in the office for the rest of the day.

After we'd tucked in, scoffed the lot and thrown away our paper plates into the big garbage bag – "not the office bins!" trilled Sandy, one of the bossy admin staff who thought she was running the Dow Jones or something – David called on the heads of department to brag about whatever they'd done over the past few weeks, and then asked for any other business. Somebody said something about parking in the garage, and someone else said it was the last day to put your name down for the indoor netball team. A couple of the lads glanced surreptitiously at Te Rangi, and I could tell they were imagining those Ngāti Porou hips bouncing around the court. No one glanced at my triangle head.

When silence finally fell again, David said, "And to finish up, I'd like to make mention of a very special piece of art that's been donated to the office by the Woodruff family. As you know, they started the business a hundred years ago and as part of our centennial celebrations, they're donating a piece of greenstone named – "he squinted at a piece of paper – "Tea Ah-tah-fy. Very old, very special. We'll put it out in reception later today."

And he pulled Te Atawhai out of a shopping bag and put him on the table where the remains of the fish and chips lay so that we could all ooh and aah at the chunk of rock lying in a glass box.

Te Rangi blanched, and swept to the front of the room. I could see her lips moving, perhaps in a karakia, more likely in a stream of inaudible invective, and then she took the box up in one smooth motion. "I'll put him in reception now."

David Howe looked after her in some bemusement, but no one said anything. Māori people doing strange Māori things, you see. The rest of the team dispersed, lips still greasy, stomachs bloated. Sandy tsk tsked and threw open a window, waving her hand around as if she was magically disappearing the miasma of fish.

I went out to reception along with Terry and Paora and a couple of others and we watched in silence as Te Rangi carefully laid the pounamu on the shelf that held the awards the business had won over the years, another trophy to add to the rest. Then she said a karakia, for real this time, and Terry sang a song, but only a short one because he was due back in Packing.

"Kia ora, Koro," I said. "We hope you'll be happy here."

"Would you be?" said Te Rangi. "In a box?"

No, I wouldn't.

We leaned forward, our breath misting the glass. Te Atawhai was a clear forest green on top, with a webbing of yellow and white across the middle that traced his arteries and veins. The base was darkest green, like the deep, deep sea. He looked like a mountain, but not like my graceful ancestor. This mountain was stumpy and squat, stoic in his existence, all crevices and slopes and sharp valleys. When I looked closely, I could see the figure of a lizard, a taniwha, in the grain of the rock, crouched beneath winter tree branches.

"He'd look good all carved up," said Paora.

Te Rangi gave him a wink and a poke in his soft belly. "So would you."

I greeted Te Atawhai every day after that. It was automatic. Say hello to Jillian the receptionist, check for messages, say hello to Te Atawhai, go to office. At the end of the day, I would say goodbye to Te Atawhai and then to Jillian and punch the button for the lift down. Sometimes I would brush my finger over his glass box as I passed, an affectionate caress to keep him happy in his prison. I wished I could touch him. If he was carved and worn around my neck, he would feel cool at first, and then warm under my touch, like a standoffish person thawing from attention. He would remind me of the sparkling tingle of flesh being dunked in cold mountain streams. He would hold whispered secrets and never let them go. He would bring comfort when I held him at night, and in the day, he would be a guardian against the sting of scathing white stares. He would hold the carver's essence too, a meaningful message in every line. The glass box didn't feel like that. Glass was impersonal, cold, rigid.

Te Rangi saw the taniwha in Te Atawhai's grain too. She said it looked as though he was crying. The speckles didn't look like tears to me. They looked like rain, or water dripping from the branches above.

"Those are tears too," Te Rangi said. "Sky tears. Mountain tears."

She coughed and pulled out a tissue to wipe her mouth. She was always coughing these days, and very quick to say it wasn't Covid, she'd been tested. I didn't know if that was true or not, but it didn't sound like a viral cough. It sounded like a cough that came from deep within her, as though something was trying to get out. She threw the tissue in Jillian's bin, and beckoned me over to the trophy shelf to stare at the chunk of pounamu.

"He hates it in there," she murmured to me. "He wants to go back home."

"Don't we all," I replied. I liked Auckland, liked the sunshine and the busyness and the air of possibility in each new morning. Home wasn't like that. Home was a sleepy provincial town with smothering parochial pride, but it had its charms. The endless black sand beaches, the stirring wind, the cheap parking, and of course, my mountain.

"Look, he's crying again," she said, pointing at a mark on the greenstone that had the gloss of moisture to it. I looked closer. It did look like liquid was seeping from the stone.

"Condensation?" I said, tentatively.

"If you say so," said Te Rangi.

We went back to work, but I made a point of stopping by Te Atawhai several times that day, to check if more tears were falling.

The next day, Te Rangi's face was flushed with fever, her eyes dull. The coughing had worsened to a hacking bark.

"You can't work like that," I said to her. "Take the day off, stay in bed. You'll make everyone sick."

"I've got that contract to do," she said, but David Howe walking by caught the tail end of our conversation. He sent her home then and there, and gave me Te Rangi's contract to finish instead. I didn't mind; he said I could get a bottle of wine from his fridge afterwards.

As soon as they had all gone home, I went into David Howes' office and perused the contents of the fridge as if I was supermarket shopping. I wanted a nice Pinot Gris, an expensive one, but there was only a row of Sauvignon, clearly ones that no one else had wanted, so I took the 6 pack of craft beer at the back instead. I wasn't a connoisseur of wine or anything, but the only way I would ever drink Sav would be if someone had poured it down my cold, dead throat.

25

I finished up my work, gathered my things, turned off the computer and the lights. Everything was very quiet with just the humming of electrical things doing what they had to do.

I went out into reception and put the keys in the office drawer. Jillian had long gone and when I turned to say goodbye to Te Atawhai, he was gone too.

I wondered about that as I went down in the lift. Perhaps Dave had moved him to another office. Perhaps he'd taken him home.

Perhaps someone else had taken him home.

Te Rangi lived in a suburban villa with a rotating group of flatmates. Right now, there was Wendell in the front room, Theresa and Sonya out the back in the sleep-out, and Doors in the tiny room off the kitchen that was supposed to be a mudroom or pantry or something. He only paid half rent because his room had no windows and the cooking fumes made all his things smell, but he didn't care. He was saving for his OE, although with the pandemic, it was unclear where exactly he was going to go.

I could hear Te Rangi coughing as I made my way up the stairs, armed with a bunch of flowers, the six pack, and a thermos of the previous night's boilup. There were no bones, but there were still bits of meat floating in it and I'd added some fresh baby spinach to wilt in the heat. I pushed open her door and found her, not propped up in bed with a mountain of tissues on the bedside table next to her, but sitting on the floor, untangling a shoelace knot in a hiking boot. She was dressed in black tights and a big hoodie. A heavy backpack was lying next to her.

She started when she saw me. Her skin had a greenish cast to it, her eyes feverish and yellow.

"Where are you going?"

"For a walk."

"With boots and backpack?"

"To the bus station. To the airport. Then to Christchurch."

I blinked. "What the fuck's in Christchurch? They don't like brown people in Christchurch. I brought you boilup."

"Thanks."

I handed her the thermos and she stuck it in the front pocket of her bag.

"When are you coming back?"

"As soon as…" her voice trailed off and a look of guilt crossed her face. She didn't have to tell me. I knew.

"Jesus, you didn't."

She unzipped the bag and dug around inside, taking out a colourful parcel, a soft scarf wrapped around a hefty weight. She gently unfolded it and I reached out a hand and stroked Te Atawhai's cool head.

"You stole him."

"They stole him first. I'm taking him home."

"How do you even know where he's from?"

"I don't know. I just know."

"He's making you sick."

"Yes. That's why I'm taking him home."

I nodded. Took out my phone. Dialed.

"Who are you calling?"

I shushed her as David Howe picked up. "Hello?'

"Hi, David? It's Ana. I think I've caught Te Rangi's cold. I'll be off a few days." I added in a cough for good measure and said goodbye.

I hung up, smiled at her. "I'll drive."

My Ancestor in a Museum

By Momoe Malietoa Von Reiche

After a long Journey
They put him in a glass case
At a London Museum
People came to stare
At his big wooden genitals
One professor said,
"Some romantic notion
Of the past eh what?
Or is it cannibalism?"
The other said,
"Perhaps it is the savage titillation of holding
Evil in the hand, no doubt!"

Every night he turned to face South
The direction of home
Every morning they
Straightened him again
To face the west
With fear in
Their pale eyes

SANDPIT

By Gina Cole

Your kid brother, the accused, stands marooned in the dock. Hands gripping the bar. Beechwood rubbed shiny. You imagine misty, sea battered headlands, sanded smooth and pocked with caves.

Your family is absent, braving the tsunami swamping you all including the dry drowning victim, your whanaunga.

You question why you're here bearing witness in this foggy courtroom. Open mouthed, staring people bob against you. His lawyer dives in, says he is sorry. Spit flies from her lips adding to the oceanic haze. The crown lawyer crosses her arms, turns away, utters a cascade of evil. Hisses her words like sea spray.

The judge sums up your kid brother's case, tells him the crimes he's committed, lectures him, digs deep into the paper dunes piling up across her bench.

'I sentence you to ten years in prison with a six-year non-parole period.'

His shoulders drop, his chin sinks towards his heart.

All these words suffocate you, fill your ears, nostrils, eyes, mouth. The same way dry sand smothered you when you pitched your four-year-old body headfirst into the hole in the sandpit. He played close to you in the sand that day. Tipped himself into a shallow dip, performed a wobbly headstand. You copied him, his happy freewheel. But you dug a much deeper hole for yourself.

Sand collapsed around you, fell into your nostrils, eyes, mouth, ears. Your arms pinned to your sides. Unable to escape, frantic, you choked and kicked. Tiny hands pulled your legs until he dragged you free. You ran into the house, tears tracking your face, grit between your teeth.

He turns to you now, lifts his chin as guards lead him from the sand-coloured box. He's dug a deep hole for himself. A chasm. You cannot drag him free. He disappears into the mist. Waves of people carry you out. You let the current take you.

THE VUNIWAI

By Mere Taito

Aunty K (short for Kijiana) thinks it is in my best interest to make new friends. What gave her that impression? Was it the long hours I spend in my room reading up on the Spatial Bayesian Networks (SBN) analysis of Leptospirosis in Fiji? Maybe she caught a whiff of my anxiety as she held me at the Nadi Airport arrivals lounge. Nothing frightens me more than the awkward silences that slide into the polite talk of strangers.

Politeness is a weird thing. It is a cunning ally – a veiling of truth through careful word choices, flashing of teeth, and softening of tones. Why do we not engage full-frontal? Cut the crap? Get to the chase? Whoever you are next door neighbour, please do not ask me about the weather in New Zealand. If you do, I will find ways to poison you. I am a doctor.

I check myself to see that I did not say that out loud. I do not want to offend Aunty K. She has been very kind to me.

- *it is good to know the people who live around you. especially on days when you need a cup of sugar or when your power goes off and your freezer leaks. meat must never rot in the hot sun.*

Food wastage here is like torching a warm house in front of a street sleeper. It is cruel and they do not do cruel here. It will do me good to remember that. And perhaps make an effort at being polite. It would not hurt to flash some teeth and lower voice tones into peace range, surely Franky. This note-to-self

33

comes off a little too patronising for my liking.

-   *and besides, your Mum said to take good care of you while you are here on your 6-month international medical exchange program.*

Aah yes, my mother. Mother with all the stereotypes of an absentee parent with a rich new partner. Mother who sends child to boarding school in the South Island because motherhood is not a good look with Dolce & Gabbana heels. Mother who deposits guilt money into child's back account on birthdays. Mother who never calls. Mother who does not attend milestone graduations that mark the successful end of medical school. Mother who calls sister to do her dirty work of watching over sheltered adult child in host country. This mother. And they dare cast light on absentee fathers.

-   *Sefeti will take you. Are you ready?*

Aunty K is a retired school teacher. Her need for punctuality nudges me to quickly fill my water bottle and grab my wide-brimmed khaki sun hat. The midday sun in these hills can turn skin like mine into human crackle.

Sefeti Aisea carries more than his weight around the house. He does not keep his mother up at night with midnight singalongs under the Mango tree with the hood boys and their cartons of beer. His day job as a bank teller puts warm bread on the table every morning. The electricity and water bills are paid on time. Their home in Vosanilevu is one of three in this semi-rural patch fitted with a Sky antenna. But Sefeti had not been a kind nor a handsome child growing up in the barracks. His runny nose and scabies were feeding spots for flies. Sugar lollies destroyed his adolescent teeth before they were ripe enough to fall naturally. His whiplash tongue and grisly imagination frightened his cousins and the neighbourhood children. He knew the game of pouncing-on-your-broken-English like a pro.

When nine-year-old Losa screamed, 'Toff the light!' in a game of hide and seek, Sefeti gripped her shoulders and demanded she say it correctly. The English Language God was listening in the Baka tree outside. He would come in the night and break off all her toes and feast on them at the foot of her bed. Then he would seek out all her horrible English teachers who failed to teach her proper English. If the English Language God was still hungry, he would come for all of them and then all the Mapiga-s and Bubu-s in their town. Did she want that? Did she want the blood of severed toes to be on her hands? Losa ran home howling. She felt vulnerable and unsafe because the English Language God hanging upside down in the Baka tree like a bat, was Sefeti's friend. Not hers. Sefeti's toes would be spared.

Today, Sefeti is a good son. He does as he is told. He puts on a fresh T-shirt and combs his hair. He has a full set of teeth and the scabies are gone. The flies no longer scavenge his legs and arms for a feed. Introducing Franky to the Koro-s next door should be easy. The two kilometre walk to the Koro-s is manageable for returning relatives, even those visiting for the first time. They should be back home in time for the live coverage of the All Blacks and Irish test match at 8.00 p.m.

He checks to see that Franky is wearing comfortable walking shoes.

Dear Lord. We have been sitting cross-legged on the Koros' veranda floor for the last hour and then some. This 'pop-in' is not turning out to be a quick-hello-meet-my cousin-from-overseas kind of a meet and greet. I should have paid better attention to Aunty K's crash lessons on social calling. 'Pop-in' in this place is not a friendly knock and a stand-up exchange at the door or a quick hello over lemonade and biscuits. 'Pop-in' is a long stay. 'Pop-in' is to listen to Sefeti and his friend Lemeki rattle off in their local codes. Meshed-up English and local words shoot out of their mouths in unintelligible spurts of air. Sefeti does not speak this way to Aunty K. He is almost unrecognisable. How bizarre. I pull my hat lower over my head and send word to all my invisible travelling guardians to come at once and carry me back to the comfortable armchair in Aunty K's home. If Mr and Mrs Koro had not travelled to Suva for the birth of a new grandchild, this 'pop-in' would have been far more inclusive and civilised.

-   *set, set. we mix early today. us gang mix when the falla come back with the grog cloth eh. mix early so we finis early.*

Hold on. Did I hear that correctly? Did Lemeki just say the word 'mix'? Aunty K once explained that 'mix' is the word to signal that Kava will be prepared and consumed. Like a verb. But it can also be used like a noun as in 'a baby mix' to mean a small bowl of Kava that is often drunk in a shorter amount of time. At least one to three hours. Oh God no. Kava or 'yaqona' as the locals call it, looks like sewage water – the devil's runny diarrhoea, infested with E. coli and Streptococcus, no doubt. I clear my throat but Sefeti ignores me.

- *you kno ga. gettin ole and can't sit long on the bakside. me mada ga got one boil thea man. the thing painin like hell wen I sit down like this. the docta say from sittin on the cement. he say the cole in the cement go into your arse. trues up!*

Sefeti keels over. He does not seem to be in a hurry to steer the conversation toward some sense of propriety. Nope. No urgency there. I pick up on the 'arse', 'cold' and 'boils'. How dreadfully inappropriate. Against my will, I begin to imagine the anatomy of Lemeki's anus and the placement of furuncles around his sphincter. They are visibly distended with yellow pus, straining to burst. The rupture will soil his undergarment and stench-up his posterior. Who is his long-suffering GP, if he has one, doomed to a life of odorous anal examination? Poor sucker. This is also an odd moment to recall Olei Bomboki's infected anus in Epeli Hauofa's book Kisses in the Nederends but I should know better. The brain is a spectacular trigger-happy organ firing indiscriminately at stored memory. It's a shame that mine does not have the superpower to strike these crass buffoons in front of me into epileptic silence.

- *i thot the docta foolin me but he say the cole is very dangeraas. what kain this reh?! very soon to this cole in the cement. sa siosio ga this cole in the cement. weilei lewa! how you can stay in Nui Silan??!*

They are both looking at me now, clearly amused. I hear 'New Zealand' but I'd rather give myself a myocardial infarction than engage.

- *jeepez! the cole there is like one what!!! man, you must have lots of boils in your arse eh.*

Lemeki is waiting for an answer, barely holding onto himself from splitting wide open. Jesus Christ. Did he just call me a 'man' and point to the possibility of me having furuncles in my anus?! What is this place?! Breathe Franky. Breathe. Deep Breaths. One stethoscope. Two stethoscopes. Deep long breaths Franky. I look away, pretending to be bored. Will my lips to stay together. Play deaf.

- *eh! you speak Englis or no? i think you need Kava eh to open your mauf*

eh. we wanna hear your fansi talk

He chuckles and punches Sefeti in the arm. This bona fide savage. The sudden desire to urinate in Lemeki's mouth comes without warning and is strangely satisfying. This fantasy brings on the urge to empty my bladder. I turn to Sefeti.

- *can you graciously ask your friend if I may use the washroom, please?*

The convenient buffer of a familial interpreter gives me time to collect myself. Hold a moment of reckoning with my fast-growing contempt.

- *chi chi! hear the fancy Englis. sa yawa Sefeti, your cousin sound like a*
  posh!

Urgh. Whatever that means.

- *bro, kerekere, can my cousin use the toilet?*

- *kua ni leqa, the toilet inside. but no toilet pepar. only the Fiji Sun. tell*
  your cusin toilet pepar cos plenti money, so we use the Fiji Sun. cheaper.

'No toilet paper'? And there it is. The legacy of this man's hospitality. The scarcity of soft 2-ply toilet tissue. The scarcity of manners. God help us all.

- *ok seto! the falla here with the grog cloth! now we mix.*

The *Fiji Sun* is inked butchers' paper that is thick enough to bruise and tear a urine-splattered vulva. Franky chooses to harm herself this way rather than clean herself with her fingers. Before she crumples a section of the front page, she looks at the picture of the man holding a mic. He is the Attorney General. The caption describes him speaking to school children in a rural town about the importance of budgeting. Squatting over the toilet pan, Franky scrunches the Attorney General's face and presses it to her vagina. She winces at the coarseness of the paper against her soft skin. No one will ever hear of this humiliating toilette, she vows.

Franky can hear her cousin and his friend outside the toilet window. They are speaking their bastard English and cackling in a way that would shame a gaggle of wild geese. The demonstration of hilarity thus far has been quite marked in their favour. From this squatting position, she does not understand a word they say. As a final gesture of revulsion, Franky yanks up her jeans and scrubs the blank ink marks on her fingers and hands with her nails and soap, desperate to erase all evidence of Fiji Sun use. She gives thanks to her lucky stars that she did not walk into this lavatorial space to do a No.2.

-   *eh, bro, your cusin Franky from Niu Silan like one stuck up Queen Sheba man.*

Lemeki holds up a muslin pouch while Sefeti pours the powdered Kava in.

-   *isa, vosota. yu kno ga, these vuniwai from overseas eh. sumtaims, they think their poo poo don't stink!*
-   *oi! she a docta? she got one boyfren or no?*
    weilei bro. she gonna eat your balls when you sleepin. qarauna. don go thea. i hea plenti men leave her. say they sked. she like to bite when they bajang.

Lemeki yelps like a wounded mongrel. The idea of a woman biting and drawing blood from his ear lobes in the heat of foreplay is both thrilling and terrifying. Sefeti laughs at his friend as he dips the pouch now fat with Kava, into a bucket of water and squeezes. The Peace Corp who visited last year said Lemeki was like a people whisperer. He had a natural way of putting newcomers to this town at ease. He had warmth and the promise of lasting camaraderie. It is unfortunate for Lemeki that the-Docta-Franky-Queen-Sheba-from-Niu-Silan is having none of this people-whispering shit.

The profanity-spewing Kijiana Aisea is an experience privileged to a few. Of course. It is *always* the referee's burden to bear. His lack of sharp observation in pinning down and penalising spear tackles:

-   *vicai ref! vicai!*

His indecisiveness in extracting crucial information from the Telegraphic Match Official and consequently erring in judgment:

-   **'taụ 'uạt patpat!** -

His failure in monitoring forward passes and enforcing penalty swiftly and purposefully:

- *'saali kutia! maichod!*

Her late husband Futfiri was always entertained by her ability to stage a damning multilingual response to flawed refereeing decisions. Yet, it is the inaccuracy of calling offside play that brings out the Queen Mother Medusa in Kijiana. No one quite understands why this judicial error upsets her the most. In tonight's live match between the All Blacks and Ireland, there are many erroneous offside calls. Gross incompetencies that have transformed Kijiana's voice into a static and untune-able vintage radio station. Hoarse frequencies of raw yelling. If Futfiri, by any chance, is hovering above her coffee table doilies in amused suspension, her game fervour is generously on full display for his friendly ghost.

She is beside herself at final whistle, and quite unaware that her child and visiting niece are not home. The All Blacks lose heavily.

A veranda away, a different kind of yielding is unfolding. Franky is trying desperately to lift her confused jaws off the floor. Clear the fog in her head and pinpoint the exact moment she cupped and clapped her hands in acceptance of a bowl of Kava. What about the infestations of E. coli and Streptococcus? Nothing makes any sense this evening. No sense at all. Not even the mosquitoes that have come on this Vosanilevu night to drill their proboscis into human flesh, as they have done since the beginning of time.

It. Is. Hard. To. Be. A. Doctor. Today.

Each word takes a swipe at me as I work through my list of patients. The scent of colonial antiseptic in this 1950s-built, timber-clad clinic is overpowering and very difficult to snub. The descent of moisture and humidity from the arrival of the hurricane season is even harder to ignore. Cuts and grazes can blossom into raging sores if not tended carefully. For a diabetic, this 'flesh rage', as I like to call it, can be life-changing. I slowly unwrap Mr Nuku's stump and carefully look for infection. There is red swelling and abscess. Dammit. I must act quickly. Review post-amputation antibiotics plan. Reassess wound care. Check monitoring of sugar levels.

Shanti has a phobia of pill-swallowing. She is convinced that the 500 mgs of amoxicillin capsules prescribed three times a day for a severe ear infection will catch in her throat and choke her. Because they have a mind of their own. Because they know her little secret of diving for kaikoso in the Qele river with her friends. Because they know that this youthful defiance flooded her ear canals with muddy water. I scribble an urgent note to her exhausted parents to hide these fearful capsules in her food. Now. Today. As soon as they get home.

The arrival of the hurricane season also marks the arrival of the festive season. The Tivaknoa-s are usually run off their feet in the town's only bottle shop during this time of the year. There is no shortage of customers for the purchase of Benson and Hedges cigarettes, Bounty Rum, and the favourite - Fiji Bitter, long-neck 12 in a carton. When Tutu Viliame tells me 'vuniwai me nomoa smoko', the wheezing and rasping noises in his chest and cough show me that he is lying. Tutu Viliame is not the only one lying during the hurricane season. Mrs Hanfakaga's claim of 'moa bele now, no mit no booze ok docta' is inconsistent with her worsening gout. Her limping dobs her in. Her limping tells me she has been indulging in regular weekend BBQs and alcohol binge parties.

I play with the idea of showing them graphic images of advanced stages of their pathological afflictions. A soot lung for Tutu Viliame and a monster foot with heavy tophaceous deposit malformations for Mrs Hanfakaga. Then stand back and hope to Dear God that the show-and-tell scares the living crap out of them into action.

I do neither. It is cruel. This version of cruelty is not part of these hills either. We do not remind sick adults of their looming death. They have their bones to tell them that. Aunty K has taught me well. We do not waste food. We do not speak ill of neighbours who cannot afford toilet paper. We do not hold grudges against neighbours who introduce us to the relaxing effects of Kava-

- *VUNIWAI FRANKY!*
 URO LEVU!!

What the hel -

- *SA LONG TIME NO SEE!*
 WHERE YOU BEEN HIDIN MAN?!!

The screamer T-bones into my consultation room with his muddy boots and filthy overalls like a megaphone-wielding protester fighting for a cause.

-   *WAWAWAUUU!*

    SA VERI FANSI YOR WHITE COAT!!

    PUPUPUUUUU!!

It is too late to draw the curtains. Too late to scuttle into the sterilising room next door. Too late to duck into the Staff Toilet and stay there until all is clear. Too late to ask the Matron for cover. Too late to conspire with the Nurse to keep a look out for a loud obnoxious man. Too late for *any* defensive action of avoidance.

-   *BOSSO LEVU O IKO!*

    PAALA PAALA!!

Each word takes another swipe at me, and this time with sting.

It. Is. Double. Hard. To. Be. A. Doctor. Today.

I brace myself for the loud disorder of Lemeki Koro.

The town of Vosanilevu is a punishing five-hour drive from the coast. During the hurricane season, the roads are treacherous but the villagers do not care as they make the butt-numbing bus ride into the hills.

It is a little price to pay to see the doctor.

There are many versions around the circumstances of Franky Steven's residency. Some people will tell you that the village clown Lemeki poisoned the doctor's Kava bowl with black magic and put three children in her belly against her will. That she laughs like a cyclone and lets her hair down because Lemeki feeds her with the crazy fish that no one eats during the tamboo season.

If Sefeti Aisea was alive, he would have rubbished these stories. There was no black magic, he would say. No forced impregnations. No crazy fish from tamboo lagoons. Only a woman. And a man. Numbed by loneliness.

Kalofae/ Ka alofa i ai / I feel love for them

By Sisilia Eteuati

Back in Apia we love a good wedding. Invitations optional. Really, if they wanted it to be exclusive, they should have had it in Niu Sila. Obviously. Even then, maybe not in South Auckland, where Apia rules still apply.

Of course, "By invitation only" was gold embossed on my cousin's invitation. And, of course, there would be an aunty or two checking those invitations at the front. But that means nothing in Apia, where everyone knows you or should know you. No one would stop us walking in in our second best puletasi. Best was for lotu and God.

Really, it's embarrassing for them if the bride and groom's family forgot to invite you. Definitely nothing to do with the bride and groom themselves. We all know the bride and groom have no choice in anything important. We've seen the bride's three dresses. All ugly. The two cakes - one for the bride's family (twenty-five tiers), and one for the groom's (twenty-six tiers) - clearly trying to outdo each other in ostentatiousness. Malosi outou!

No one cares about that stuff anyway. We are there for the food. The groom's family is Aiga-i-le-tai - his father the sa'o of their aiga. The seafood needs to be next level. It won't be enough for them to have the standard oka and sashimi. The ula need to shine red, flesh sweet white; and needs to weigh down at least half of a big banquet table. The pa'a, drowned in rich coconut cream, better weigh down the other half. They need to have the rarer seafood as well, like alili and fe'e - and they can't overcook it so it is tough. They need to have tuitui so fresh that it was like you had just pulled it from the coral yourself and ripped it open. Otherwise, what's the use of being people of the sea? We will know the richness and strength of their whole village by how well they feed us.

Surely their Savai'i side will have butchered at least ten povi, and hopefully they are not just going to use them for si'i. If they don't have at least a vilivili povi and a vilivili pua'a next to the hotel swimming pool, we will know their family doesn't have enough sway to make sure the hotel made an exception to the strict hotel rules for them. Kalofae! What shame for their family who are so fia tagata around town. Also their Niu Sila family surely has sent them boxes and boxes of mussels and oysters. Or money to buy boxes and boxes of mussels and oysters. Surely the aiga from Pago has turned up with turkeys and hams. Naturally, this should be in addition to the food the hotel itself serves, and they should have had it catered for five hundred at least if they invited the standard two hundred.

If at least four large plates of food aren't run out by a subservient child to my car boot as I leave the wedding we weren't invited to, we will all know that their aiga is not all it makes itself out to be. They will know it. I will know it.

And of course it will all be discussed in detail. In the office, at lotu, at the Marina Bar. Samoa will KNOW it. Then even though I may have eaten a tiny piece of dry fruit cake, not because I wanted to but as a blessing to the bride and groom, we will all know they are doomed. If they don't come from proper families, what hope do they really have?

Now we are in Niu Sila and lockdown life is very, very hard. Oka it has been over 90 days. I never ever get to go to weddings. Invited or uninvited. So I sit here and reminisce instead. I have stayed home and saved lives like Jacinda told me. O a'u ou ke savali i le kulafono! I walk with the law as I tell everyone . . . because in a way I am the law since I am a Justice of the Peace and Community Magistrate. I tell all of my friends to stay home and I would have even put one of those "I got vaccinated for Aotearoa" frames on my facebook profile. Except I didn't get vaccinated for Aotearoa, I got vaccinated for my aiga.

I'm lucky because I have lots of my aiga living with me. I brought over my parents when Covid hit. They didn't want to come but I told them, "What is the point of the family home here in Aukilani AND my sacrifice being away from Samoa just to pay the expensive rates and lafo aku kupe if you don't come over when there is a deadly pandemic? We all know the hospital there is where people go to die (even though the doctors there are very smart)," I say in case my parents think I am disloyal to Ana, who was my best friend in Kolisi and went back home after she got her medical degree in Otago to serve our people, as I had wanted to do. "What will happen if you die? You know your grandchildren will not even be able to come to your funeral and they will never be able to recover." Then I put my children on the phone to seal the deal because they are their grandparents beloved pele youngest grandchildren. My parents came over on the next flight. My cousin going to Auckland Uni lives here too. She is skolasipi of course because our family is very academic, as everyone in Samoa knows, and she is good at helping with feau and I am hoping that my kids will see a proper Samoan girl and it will rub off on them.

It is good having lots of people in your aiga. I feel sorry for palagi who have small families. Who do they talk to? - just each other. I look through my kitchen window to my neighbours. They don't even have children. Just one of those designer dogs. I don't know what that dog would do if a robber turns up, it probably couldn't even bite my little toe.

It is still very lonely here with my small Samoan aiga of eight. I only get to catch up with everyone else from afar on facebook. My friends and I try to keep each other up to date. Their faifeau had a birthday party in the middle of the pandemic. Outrageous. They sent me a video on private messenger. They didn't go themselves because they, like me, know the rules - but, can you imagine, the faletua did a live feed. I counted the people and there were definitely more than the twenty-five allowed. And they weren't even one metre apart. O kagaka kogu a la ka'u valea ai kagaka Samoa. This is why I have to look at the paper and see it is Samoans who are getting the covid! Ka igoigo e! And I thought "oh the faifeau must be so old and maybe it's his last ever birthday", but I saw the cake (only two tiers - how are they even going to kufa it?) and the number on the top said 34. I mean, really? That's not even a special number, and eleven years younger than me! Also they filmed the food and the only seafood was mussels. Pandemic isn't a reason not to kausi fa'alelei le feagaiga. If you are going to break the rules, at least do it well. I was so embarrassed for them. It's like they came over here and forgot their culture. Or maybe they're NZ born.

I mean they aren't a real lotu. They are one of those new lotu patipati happy clappy churches so that's probably why. My own lotu EFKS has been really careful and are doing all of our lotu on zoom. Aoga faifeau zoom, aufaipese zoom, komiti o tina zoom. My eyes are very tired of zoom, zoom, zoom. And really seeing all of everyone's faces that up close and personal is not good for anyone's eyes. I also have to be careful that only my picture of Iesu is in the background, so people know that even though we are in Niu Sila my faith hasn't slipped at all, not even a little bit.

People always say that it is hard for Samoans who migrate here which I know is lapisi because I got a great job as soon as I came over to look after the family home, and ten years later I am a Justice of the Peace and Community Magistrate. The work just comes naturally to me. Of course I did work for many years at the Ministry of Justice back in Apia. There is so much good work here if people want to find it. Me, I was willing to start from the bottom. But I didn't need to. Of course.

I am not going out at all and we are even getting all the groceries delivered because I am careful.   Yesterday Countdown delivered what was at least $400 worth of groceries contactless at my door. My dad sees them left and brings them in. My cousin was in the back doing the laundry. The kids should have done that and I would be shamed in Samoa if anyone knew I let my dad, who is a very important matai in four very important villages, do menial tasks like bring in groceries. I am a matai too, but I am still a daughter, and I was working and didn't even know about it until after 5pm when he tells me the order had arrived. Lucky we live in Ponsonby and all our neighbours are palagi anyway.

They don't even count.

I give my kids the side eye, so that they know they haven't performed as expected. It is hard bringing up Samoan kids overseas. You have to make sure you oke them enough so they know how to act and don't bring shame to your whole entire family. But, most of all, they don't bring shame to you. I am always telling them - A fa'apea e fai le mea ga e fa'apea kagata e leai sou kiga. People will think you have no mother if you act like that. It is the worst insult because, of course, the mother is the most most important person.

"I didn't make that order."

"Are you sure?" My dad asks, like he suspects I may have been grocery shopping under the influence. I really have no idea why he thinks these things. "It's that same strange beer you ordered a while back," he says. I know what he is really saying is, "Remember the night you and your cousin drank all that beer and didn't even do the dishes but left them in the sink like animals."

I try to summon outrage as if that has never happened. The drunk ordering or the drunk anything. "Yes. I definitely did not order more beer," I say. Because while I am forty-five and a matai and a community magistrate, most of all I am a good Samoan daughter and I understand the subtext. I understand all of the things not said.

"YUM! LOLLIES! CHIPS," the kids clamour.

"O oukou gi manu?" This is another favourite one of my sayings when the kids are acting like I haven't taught them how to behave. Ask them if they are animals. When they were younger they used to cry out gleefully "Cheetah! Monkey! Taika! RAH!" as if it was a game. They didn't even know I was shaming them! Before covid I always used to send them back to Samoa at Christmas so they could be useful to their grandparents and learn how to act. It's been two years without travel for all of us and somehow they have magically forgotten everything. I blame the tv and am going to throw it in the bin tomorrow!

"Tu'u! Aua e ke kago fua i ai. That's not our fa'akau!"

"Well can we keep it anyway?" they ask. Definitely manu. I make a mental note to myself that they need an intensive aganu'u class and I wonder if my dad should be teaching them how to folafola meaai because the nine year old, at least, should know how to do it. Imagine if someone showed up and my child didn't know what to do. I breathe deeply . . . at least in lockdown this is not something I have to worry about, because we are obeying all the rules.

"Of course not. We have to do the right thing and tell Countdown." I am a very good parent who has Iesu up on my wall and I want to be sure my kids know we have morals. Te ara tika as I like to say to my colleagues . . . mostly to see if anyone else has learnt our work values in te reo. Most of them look at me blankly. I have been a great champion for tangata whenua since I arrived in Niu Sila. Some Samoans look down on them for losing their land but I definitely don't. I've even encouraged my kids to do kapa haka. I tell them that Maori are like our cousins, and I joke to my Maori friends that they are the ones that got banished from Samoa. We always laugh together. And joke that even our hyena laughs are the same.

I go online and chat to the Countdown bot Olive who is supremely uninterested. "It sounds like you need to call the Countdown call centre" pops up in chat. Oka! This is the type of Customer Service I expect in Samoa - where everyone makes sure you know they are doing you a favour by deigning to serve you. I imagine her painting her nails. Slowly.

So I call the call centre. Twice. Because we get disconnected. They need to talk to their managers, call the shop. Finally, they advise because it is level 3.2 they cannot pick up the groceries. I should keep them. Sorry about the mix up. My children overhear on the speaker phone. They don't yell "Party time" or say anything at all, as they understand well that this will affect their ability to fall on other people's groceries as soon as I am off the phone.

"Ok, you can both choose one thing after you kapega those groceries," I say to the kids. Because it's Friday and I am a fun mum. A fun mum who has gotten a lot of free groceries.

My dad looks on as the kids become very industrious, "Why didn't these people order milk?" he says.

My father and I proceed to bond while watching the children put away the groceries. "Oh, it's the fancy grass fed meat. It's the fancy dairy free ice cream. Oh, they bought bagels like they were in New York. Oka se fia Amelika," we say, fully intending on eating it all. It is almost like being at a fa'apoipoga. Eat and judge, judge and eat.

Today the palagi neighbours text me, "Did you guys happen to see our shopping dropped off yesterday?"

"We did have shopping delivered to us that wasn't ours. I rang Countdown. They said to keep it because it was level 3 and they couldn't pick up. Sorry."

"Oh, no worries," they say, "we got reimbursed. No need to worry about it. Unless there is anything you don't want / can't eat there."

"Go and take all that shopping to the neighbours," I instruct my kids. "We can't have them thinking we can't buy our own groceries." The kids look crestfallen. They had just eaten the bagels with gusto and asked if we could put them in our next order. Ummm…. o lea ga fesili valea? At least they know not to open their mouths and complain. One day in the future I will have to organise their weddings. As they start moving the shopping bags that are left I wonder if I should start encouraging them to elope to Paris.

My kids come back from contactless dropping off and said they talked to the neighbours at the front door, but they were definitely more than two metres away.

They tell me the neighbours are lactose intolerant.

Kalofae!

A - W A K E – (E) N D

By Audrey Brown-Pereira

know in time how much

too much

wanting more than can give or hide
or show hide

hiding

hidden more
with less of me

knowing
there is/more/are/multitudes/multiplied/hidden/buried/contained/bottled/
brewed/canned/tinned/stored/frozen/ and/screwed/lid-tight/sealed/
vacuumed/separated/from/air/to/preserve/reserve/use/later/in/times/
of/hurricanes/ cyclones/ and/ flooding/when/feet/lost/eyes/can/t/see/
through/mind/and/sea/and/rain/fight/against/ land/ to/ drown/you/lift/
the/roof/from/us/tearing/into/i/and/me/with/out/you/ no/more/we/only/

i /as/ in/the beginning/
lie

lying lied too many times to me to
mine
not mine not yours

wanting more
knowing will/ may/ might
n o t e n o u g h
by t a k i n g h e r
s t e a l i n g h e r back
s o s h e
can breathe again b e s h e
reclaiming/h e r/i /a m/m e!
nana speaks to *h e r* through the window of baby's eyes

'no more waiting for the storm!'

EARTH, OCEAN

By Shirley Simmonds

They met at a café.

She drove by the day before, paused across the road, peered out the window at customers coming and going, couples meeting and greeting. Were they meeting for the first time too? There were seats and tables arranged in the garden. It was humble and cosy, it looked like a place that provided good, wholesome, satisfying food, served by staff with warm smiles.

He knew the café, was the one to suggest it. It took exactly thirty-five minutes to get there from the coast, over the mountain range. He arrived just before 1pm, expecting she would be late, ordered an orange juice, and sat at a table that would allow him to watch the café entrance.

She parked outside the café, after circling the block one more time so as not to arrive too early, not to appear too eager. She spotted him straight away, his head down, thumb busy with his mobile phone. Texting, perhaps? Or just appearing occupied so that he didn't seem too eager perhaps?

"Kia ora."

A slight pause before he looked up.

"Oh. You're here. Kia ora."

(not the spark of the first meeting, not the tingle all over, not the skip of a heartbeat, not the intuitive gut feeling that he was *the one*).

She fixed her smile. They kissed cheek to cheek. They ordered, they talked a bit. They ate, they laughed a bit.

He talked of his work with the rangatahi, and their waka ama club on the coast. From beneath her eyelashes, she observed him as he spoke: his face, his mannerisms, gestures, expressions.

His shirt was taut across his chest. She watched it move as he moved, slacken then tighten. She envisaged running her palm across that chest, following the curve to where it dipped in the centre. She would curl her hand there and feel the warmth, tuck her face in that hollow and listen as the heart gently patted her cheek, as he whispered into her forehead -

The shock of her thoughts jolted her back to this reality. She surprised herself with the strength of this physical lure. She hadn't felt anything like this in a long time. She felt a stir, an awakening. She grasped for something to talk about, to cover her thoughts. She spoke of the bumper crop of tomatoes she grew this summer. Of chutney, relish and warm jars of pasta sauce.

He noticed the shift in her and wondered at it. He observed her while she chatted. A quick smile, a true laugh. Her hands talked when she talked; palms splayed then clasped, a dismissive flick over the shoulder, a waving finger to punctuate a point. When she listened, her chin rested in one of those hands, fingers curled, and he felt her entire focus in his direction, and it was thrilling. Her nails were short and she wore no nail polish, no rings or jewellery. He noticed a scratch on the back of her wrist and envisaged taking the scratched hand from her chin in both of his and drawing it to his chest, pulling her near. The impulse surprised him. He liked to think he had good control over his physical desires. He shifted in his seat. Sought something to talk about. He spoke of early morning trainings, fundraising activities, trips to regattas.

It was three o'clock. The lunch had been 'okay', the conversation 'okay', but she wasn't sure if it was enough for another date. Wasn't sure what he thought either.

"How 'bout Thursday?" he said.

"Thursday? Thursday would be great," she replied.

She had to admit she knew that they would sleep together at this, the next meeting. And she knew that he knew. But they both went through the day pretending that the evening and all it entailed wasn't approaching. She didn't know if she felt thrilled or apprehensive. Excited or afraid.

They took her girls to the beach. She glanced around. He'd gone further up the shore to chat with someone. She unwrapped her towel to her togs underneath and eased into the water, gasping at the cold, but revelling in the chilly tingle all over her body. She glided in the shallows to where her daughters were paddling. The water felt great, sensual, the waves buffeting her gently.

While catching up with his cousin, he watched her from behind his sunnies. She was comfortable in the water, at ease. More than he was. He preferred to be on the surface, riding the waves and the surges of the ocean, easing his waka with the currents of the sea, turning with the wind. He wasn't that keen on being in the water itself. Too exposed. Too vulnerable. She wore togs. Most women he knew wore shorts and t-shirt in the water. He could see each ridge of her spine, skin sparkling with seawater. Found himself wondering what it would be like to run a finger slowly down the centre of her back . . .

They got pizza and ice-cream for the girls, and iced coffees for themselves. She watched his hand lift his coffee to his lips, fingers curved around the glass, and found herself wondering what it would be like to feel a finger run slowly down her spine . . .

Back at his place she put the girls to bed; sandy, exhausted and sun-kissed. As they drifted off, the aroma of grilling steak wafted in from the kitchen. She slunk out of the room, closing the door gently. Steak, salad, red wine. They ate fast and silent. Then he was behind her chair and his lips were on her ear, her cheek, her neck. Then she was off the chair and leading him by the hand, and they ran up the carpeted stair to his bedroom. She undressed. He undressed. God, he was beautiful. His skin was dark and glossy. She could see the definition of every contour in the dim light. Her eyes roved the intricate detail of his tā moko, chest, shoulders, hips, thighs. The whorls and patterns indented in his skin. She wanted so much to trace it with her fingers, her tongue. Beautiful. So sexy.

Their bodies came together, her thighs, his thighs. Her breasts, his chest. They kissed, desperately. And she inhaled, burying her face in his neck. *Hā ki roto*. Long and slow, taking him all in. She smelled through the layers of his life, detected boot polish, something like baby lotion. The fresh sweat of the day, salt and seaweed, hot sand and barbecue smoke.

Then the deeper, manly musky smell. He reached a hand to her breast. For a moment she resisted, holding his arm at bay, her heart thumping. Then relented, and nearly cried out at the touch. They tumbled onto the bed, their bodies already entangled. She burned for him. Yearned.

She knew she should be sensible, but – oh! She couldn't stop.

He tried.

"Are you on anything? Do we need to be careful?"

Oh damn.

"No, I – "

"Shall I – "

"Yes."

With some effort, he got off the bed and delved around in a drawer. Handed her a little silver packet.

"You do it."

"No you do it."

"No, you do it. It's more sexy if you do it."

Gah. She hated putting condoms on, could never do it right. She tore the packet open and stifled a laugh.

"What?" He said, catching the edge of her giggle.

"Blue! Why do you have a blue condom?"

"Well, I don't know. They were freebies."

She giggled some more, and tried to unroll it. What was that? She sniffed delicately. *Bubble gum!* He had bubble gum scented condoms? Wait a minute – on impulse she put out the tip of her tongue to the blue rim. They were bubble gum *flavoured!*

Her laugh burst out as a snort, then overflowed, uncontrolled.

He was mystified, embarrassed. "Well, they were freebies," was all he could think of saying.

She hiccupped and tried to swallow her laughter and it took a massive effort. She only managed it because she so dearly wanted to go there now. Wanted his body on her body. In her body. Ached for him now.

Loved him even.

She let herself in the front door of his house, with the key he'd given her. At one and the same time feeling familiar, yet intruding. The girls tumbled in after her, running around to explore their surroundings. Lifting this and that, climbing on furniture, pressing buttons. She hefted them onto a stool each and plonked a plate of crackers in front of them, then busied herself with dinner preparations. She had promised to cook for him, something special. So she fished out the precious package of whitebait from the chiller bag, barely defrosted.

She was whisking eggs when he came home.

"Hey girls!" He went to each of them, a kiss, an awhi, all the while, his eyes darting in her direction. He came up behind her and nuzzled her ear.

"Hey you."

She tilted her head to the side to tuck her face into his neck. Inhale. Boot polish, baby lotion, that musky manly smell. She breathed deep. He pulled back a little and looked into her face.

"You look happy. But - "

She ducked her head quickly before he could see into her eyes. Buried her face back into his neck. Inhaled again, now so familiar. Salt and seaweed, sand and smoky barbecue.

"I'm pregnant."

She didn't mean it to come out like this. Not with the girls so near, despite the whispered tones. He pulled back again to look into her face.

"How do you know?"

"I know."

"Yes, but how?"

"I just know."

"But *how*?"

She knew. But to satisfy his need for evidence, she did a test the next morning. Then a second test. Both results positive. Now *he* knew.

They lay on the bed of the upstairs room, moonlight through the open curtains, gilding the edges of their bodies, still glistening. It was hot. She couldn't sleep, and knew he didn't either. They had talked it out all they could. What to do? Where to live, his town or hers? She couldn't imagine him ever leaving his rohe. She couldn't envisage herself ever leaving her garden. *What to do?* She needed to think of the girls. How would they react? Would they understand? She knew this whole situation had rocked him, his routine, his life. She knew he had plans that needed him to be free, available. To travel. She knew that deep down –

- he really didn't want this.

She lifted up onto one elbow. Feeling her eyes on him, he stopped pretending he was asleep, and turned to her. Did they need to talk about it some more? They'd been round in circles. This was heavy stuff. He didn't know what to do. He felt trapped and cornered. He needed to think about his plans, his mahi. He couldn't envisage leaving his home, the coast, but maybe he'd have to. He was acutely aware that they had known each other for just a matter of weeks, but he knew she would make the best of this, despite being unexpected. She would dote on this child as she did her girls. He knew deep down that –

- she would love this.

"Sooo . . . " he cast around for something to talk about.

"Sooo – do you do any sport?"

She frowned slightly. He was avoiding the Big Topic. Okay. "Nah, not really."

"Oh."

He thought of his world of rugby league, marathons and half marathons, basketball, paddling. Early morning runs and damp training shoes, sweated t-shirts and liniment, gym workouts and the clink of iron. The shriek of the whistle and the roar of the crowd. He thought of the paddle in his hands as he dipped and pulled it through the water and the waka scudding along the surface, rising and tilting with the surge of the ocean.

"I've never been sporty," she said. "Although I used to run a bit. Not for a while though, not since the girls."

"Oh. Um, and … you've got a big garden at home?"

Sheesh, this was starting to sound like an interview!

"Yeah, I love gardening."

"Yeah?"

"Well, it's so satisfying, pulling up a carrot, or digging up spuds, chopping silverbeet that you know was only tiny seeds a matter of weeks ago. The girls love it too, hanging out with me and looking for strawberries and worms, eating flower petals and collecting caterpillars." She thought of her trowel plunging into the fertile, fertile soil, and the pleasure of the sun on her neck, the ache in her arms from pruning, cutting, hauling loads of clippings. She thought of the thrill of the first blossoms on the fruit trees after Matariki. Of unearthing taewa or picking plump tomatoes, snapping beans from their vines and snipping a lemon from the tree. The smell of fresh earth, damp compost, orange blossoms, the hum of bees and the scent of pollen on a warm spring day.

"Never really gardened myself," he said. "Can't say I've got green hands at all."

She smiled into the night at his misuse of the phrase. What a mental image! Green hands, blue condom.

"Hey, what are you laughing at?"

"Nothing." She swallowed a giggle.

"Yes, I can see your teeth!"

He tackled her and tickled her, and she laughed outright. He laughed too. They loved.

Afterwards they lay again, a new sheen to their glow in the rounded moonlight. She sensed him start to drift off, his breaths deepening. She whispered softly, lightly into the depth of their night:

"Are you not even a little bit excited about it all?"

His breath stilled. So long that she thought maybe he hadn't heard, maybe he slept. Then, "Yeah I guess. Yeah, a bit." He paused, breath held. Then, "But it's a very tiny bit."

His mouth set in a straight line. Did she imagine the slight upcurve to it? Did she imagine it could have almost been the edge of a smile?

The following weekend she went back to the Pā, looking forward to the peace and stability that returning to the marae always brought for her. Although, a part of her was apprehensive. They weren't 'telling' anyone yet. It was the sensible thing to do, to wait till around the twelve-week mark. But would anyone see? See it in her ahua? This was her whānau. They knew her well. Surely someone would know something was up. Those nannies, they had a way of detecting these things. She felt fake, false, nervous. Heck, no one even knew she was going out with this guy!

On the morning of her cousin's wedding, the dawn covered the marae ātea with a blanket of unseasonable mist that gently burned off to produce a glorious day - filled with the aroma of hangi and steam pudding, kids running in and out of the wharekai, waiata and hoots of laughter. Her cousin beaming and radiant, a bride happily, heavily pregnant with their first child.

She sat on the cool grass in front of her whare tīpuna and watched her cousin pledge her life to her love, and she cried behind her sunnies. Cried hot tears that streamed straight down her cheeks and dripped to her chest, her breast. Tears of unfettered self-pity. She felt a twinge below her puku, noticed it but thought nothing of it, dismissive.

Then later a spot. Then more spotting.

She travelled home. The next day there was more bleeding, and now she was certain.

That night saw her waking suddenly at around eleven, with an urgent need to go to the bathroom. The strangest physical sensation came through her lower belly, and as it came out, she cupped her palms around it, and held it close. She felt a curious detachment, a numbness, yet a sense of protectiveness. With an odd clarity, she noted sharp irrelevant details: the blue-grey patterned lino, the ingrained dirt in her cuticles, the healing scratch on the back of her wrist, the *smallness* of it, this thing in the palm of her hand, the absence of blood (now, was that strange?), the slightly tacky, visceral feel to its membranous wrap.

She may have even slept for a brief moment, curled up right there on the blue-grey lino, for the world closed in and went dark, then she woke, and *ached* and wished she slept still.

With a cruel polar irony, she recalled the first detection of her oldest daughter's heartbeat, the muted *whump-whump-whump* of the ultrasound machine. She remembered blinking back sudden tears as the words arrived in her mind: *I never knew I was lonely until I realised I was no longer alone.*

And now, crouched here, cupping this small sad bundle in her hands, her body centred around it, she felt so utterly, *utterly* alone.

After a time (how long?) she rose. She thought of Maui, once swathed in his mother's hair. She wrapped the tiny bundle in a soft muslin lavalava, one of the ones she used to once swaddle her girls in, round and round. The gentle folds of muslin made it almost substantial. She tucked it snug into the front of her waistband. Nearly where it should be. Then got a torch and her garden trowel, pulled her dressing gown around her and stepped out into the night, one arm curved protectively, tenderly, around her middle. The moon was nearly full again. At the bottom of the garden, she dug in the nearly full moonlight. In the fertile, fertile soil. A small hole in the earth, a small hole in her soul. She piled a heap of rocks over the area.

Two strands of whakapapa, joined for a moment. And then . . . nothing. She felt empty. Stood and paused, feeling that a karakia should be said, but nothing came. So she returned to the house, crawled into bed between her two girls, who automatically wrapped themselves around her.

She slept.

He felt a numbness. Her words on the phone last night lay like rocks in his soul. He felt he had lost something he didn't know he'd even had. He felt lost.

She drew a deep breath. Sat on the edge of her bed and knew she needed to do *something*. Something to shake this feeling. Something to lift her.

He drove down to the shore, hefted his waka from the roof rack and readied it. Paused to look out across the bay. Across there, the mountains. The other side of the mountains, *her*.

She spied the tip of a running shoe at the bottom of the wardrobe. Pulled them out from beneath the pile of fallen clothes and shoes, rummaged around for socks. Sports bra, shorts, tank top. It had been so long, years even.

He dragged the waka to the water, clipped on his lifejacket and positioned himself in the seat. Steadied the canoe with his paddle. Took a deep breath. One more glance across the bay, then in a deliberate motion, turned his back towards the mountain range and began to paddle in the other direction. Steady, even strokes. Faster, smoother, swifter. The waka skimmed across the ocean.

She let herself out the front door. Down there, to the right, was the little mound of lonely rocks. She lifted her gaze to the mountains. The other side of the mountain range, across the bay, *him*. Then, in a deliberate motion, she turned to the left, turned her back to the pile of rocks and the mountains,

and began to run.

THE ROAD TO FAA'IMATA

By Caroline S Fanamanu Matamua

'Iuna opens out the window, the fresh morning breeze brushes her face as it rushes into the kitchen. She closes her eyes, taking in the fresh dawn.

"Tūlou ki he taano tōfa he Langi tupu'anga." She utters her respects to the sacred dusts of the dead, her ancestors that rest in the skies.

She slowly opens her eyes, and follows the clouds brushed across the red sunrise. She knows it will rain. She welcomes it. Her prized 'Falahola' is parched amongst the flora. She remembers the day it was planted. It was her thirteenth birthday. Moimoi paki lau he Funga Fa'atoto, your permeating fragrance koē mātanga kakala 'o e loto. It begins to rain, the euphoric place of my heart.

'Iuna walks out to her garden to check on her falahola. It has been a lifetime since she was thirteen years old. Her falahola plant has done so well on its own and kept her company all these years. Her falahola had seen her through puberty. No one listened better to her confusion and fears. It kept her company when she missed her Ball. Everyone at her school went, but not her. No one understood why she couldn't go. She didn't understand why she couldn't go. It wasn't a place for a young Tongan virgin to go, she was told.

How did she not see her falahola dying, neglected? Her best friend. 'Iuna's tears are soaked in the raindrops running down her face.

She had been so busy maintaining the new flowers. 'Oh, nothing exciting about falahola,' her town friends would say. It will always just be around.

These introduced ones are harder to grow. Everyone had said so. Everyone on Tongatapu at least.

She had so carefully cultivated that which was never meant to grow here. She imagined how she would beam with pride as people looked over her yellow roses and white Brisbane Lily. And though the soil was foreign to those flowers, it was rich. And they grew and grew like weeds, spreading, propagating with every praise heard. Whether it was deserved or not. 'Thank goodness you left that old falahola alone,' they would say, 'that big bulky tree doesn't belong in this new clean garden, with everything in neat tidy rows.'

They grew over her own Kakala. They crowded out her own worth. She had forgotten the sweet fragrance in the garden was from her falahola, not those foreign flowers. She found herself reading instructions on the back of small seed packets how to till and plant in her own soil. She began to doubt the knowledge born to her, that which had once been natural undermined by prescribed lines that spoke about Winter and Spring.

'Follow the instructions because those papalagi people wouldn't have printed it out if it wasn't absolutely true,' they say. 'Iuna forgets how she used to garden with her grandmother. They would plant the night before it rained for natural irrigation, water the soil according to the colour of the sky and wind direction.

'Iuna straightened up, standing tall, her head slowly sweeping the landscape of the garden.

Eden had grown out of control.

When did the name even change to Eden? This garden was once known as 'Api', named by her grandmother. The tall breadfruit tree looking over the garden, the kuava trees her mother lined along her bedroom window facing West for fresh breeze. Mum had planted so many beautiful flowers and plants. The falahola they planted together had stood between the Heilala and Patiale. She remembers as a child looking through her bedroom louvres, her heart swelling like the sea as she watched the sunrise roll over her Falahola, Patiale, Heilala, her beautiful Pua. She remembers her mum cutting those flowers to decorate the church. The missionary's wife had sniffed at them, as she tried to put them into arrangements that would be pleasing to the Lord. "'I am the rose of Sharon, the lily of the valley" that's my favourite verse Fasi,' she had said to my mum. 'I can help you have roses, just like in the Bible.'

'Iuna reaches down and begins to pull out those introduced flowers she had once held so precious. They do not come easily. They cut her hands. They are stubborn now. The garden's soil is too rich to leave. They have been thriving off the veins of 'Iuna's kakala for so long, too long! She kneels on the wet mud, and carefully hollows out around her Falahola, gently bringing it up by its roots. Holding the precious plant in her hands she exhales. "Ngananga ho le'o 'i he loto ngōue," she promises. "Your murmurs reside in the garden. Never again will I ignore your Upe. Your poetry belongs here."

She burrows a hole with her hands. The soil is warm, ready. It was patiently waiting. 'Iuna gently places her falahola back into the Fonua. Her roots instantly stretch and spread, coiling its veins into the earth. A burden is lifted. Ngungulu 'a e mapu 'a Tangaloa, the gurgling sound of Tangaloa's whistle. 'Iuna can hear the sounds of home again.

She looks up to see the introduced flowers she had pulled up fading away. Pōpoaki mei Pūlotu ki Langi, sentiments from the underground to the heavens, one that was almost lost has returned! Fakafeta'i! fu'ifu'i' mana mei langi, her mana is nurtured and gifted from Langi. It is a promise that her falahola will never die.

Na'e holo e vaitupu 'i he matangi, the water well was damaged from the strong winds, the garden once occupied by Eden, will be remembered as a passing storm.

Bathed now in familiar fragrance the Fonua is alive once again. Sweet fragrant young flower buds scattered on the ground. Ka koe fala 'a e To'a, the mat of a warrior who won the war of salvation.

All roads lead to Faa'imata.

FAMILY PRIDE

By Nicki Perese

Tick-tock. Tick-tock. Tick-tock. The clock pulses three beats slower than my heart.

Today is the day every young tamaita'i Samoa dreams of. It is a day to showcase status. To show irrefutably- that you (and your whole family) are marrying down, he (and his whole family) are marrying up.

"Smile and shut your mouth," my mother's words are piercing me. "That's what you get if you don't listen."

I stand in this pure white dress, white pure white denying my truth. "Would they notice?" Silently I stare out the windows. A pig shuffles past, nose to the ground. "Would they know?" The whispers of the faitatala women in my family, village and church, echo, echo, echo, and seem to bounce off the old cracked concrete of the room where I stand.

The sun is shadowed, dressed in white clouds. Nana Sai's old curtains dance in sequence while the wind gently brushed my wavy hair against my cheeks.

"Smarty pants Lucy," my family call me. I had seen myself as the true definition of a tamaita'i. I was destined to pursue big things in life. I would be a doctor or maybe a lawyer. I was an only child and my parent's pride and joy. Lucy - their poto daughter. Lucy who was laden down at prizegiving year after year. Parents would gaze enviously as my mother flaunted gracefully across our school hall stage, pushing anything in her way, chanting and singing as she tossed ten tala notes towards where I was dancing.

Every Thursday, we three watch the boys' rugby games. Well, more accurately, Tanya drags us along with her to go watch the rugby. Salina, a pastor's daughter from Savaii, was the first friend I met during orientation week. We both got lost on the first day of classes, which is how we found each other. We automatically clicked because like me, she has all sorts of rebellious fire bottled up inside that we never dare to let out. Tanya is a petite fa'afafine from Apia whose daily mission is to outshine every girl at the National University. She is loud while me and Salina are too meek and quiet to even be called her entourage. All eyes are always on Tanya: the way she walks, the flamboyant outfits she wears, and how she flicks her long silky brown hair while holding a cigarette in her other hand. Even though it is strictly no-smoking on the NUS campus.

Tanya always wants to make an entrance and today is no different. She pauses to fold up the bottom part of her shorts that are already quite revealing, and tie a knot in the side of her oversize tee shirt to show off her flat stomach and the snake tattoo on her lower back. Then like Naomi Campbell on the Paris red carpet, she strolls barefoot in front of the spectators' stand to the front seats. While we scuttle along behind her.

"Kagia pa'umumuku!" one girl calls out. This doesn't faze Tanya at all.

"Haters gonna hate. . . Look at me. Look at them," she whispers to us, followed by a wicked laugh. She always finds daggers aimed for her heart amusing. The name-calling and mimicry of the way she walks only makes her more confident, knowing that she has everyone's attention.

The games always bring a big crowd of screaming supporters. Some come to watch the rugby. Others just come to see Tanya's side show, as she calls out to the players by name, describing their dream future together. "Pepe! I can cook for you and look after your mother!"

A tall, broad-shouldered player runs out onto the field. He is bare-chested, his rugby jersey in one hand. Sunlight gleams on his muscled six-pack. Tanya squeals in excitement and leaps to her feet.

"Gooooooo Masiiii!"

He looks over to where we are sitting, looks right at me – and winks. That couldn't be right? Maybe he caught something in his eye. Then he grins and mouths my name, "Hey Lu," before running to join the rest of his teammates.

Tanya nudged me, "Auuuu go girl! I think he likes you."

Beside me Salina whispers that Masi is studying towards a Bachelor of Science. "He can study me ALL day," Tanya laughs. "Se Masi, I sacrifice my body for science," she screams across the field at his broad back. I melt into the stadium floor, hoping he knows Tanya is the one yelling for his combination of abs and brains.

The next day Tanya says, "Girls conference at the back of the Fale Samoa at 3pm sharp."

"E iai lo'u vasega," Salina says, always the good one not wanting to miss class. Tanya rolls her eyes. "Girl, pule a oe, but you are not going to want to miss this." I get there early at 3pm sharp. Because when Tanya says 3pm sharp, she means when she feels like it. I look at the sinnet that binds the Fale Samoa poles. This Fale Samoa was built about ten years ago but the sinnet still looks strong. Salina shows up at 3.30. Tanya makes her grand entry five minutes later and looks at Salina and nods. "Good you came." Salina shrugs, "Mr Tavanu didn't even show up, so we were lecturing ourselves on Othello, but you know the boys in that class - all clowns."

"Speaking of clowns," Tanya says with a dramatic wave of her hand, "Makua'i fia alu Masi ia oe Lucy."

I laugh.

"No seriously," Tanya stamps her foot to show me her body is in accord with her mouth and we all need to be serious. "He is super in luff for you girl!" She looks around to check if anyone is around. Like "Fia kisi to you girl. And you know what? He is so faithful! I told him to just close his eyes and pretend I was you and he swore at me." Tanya laughs. "Popole fua Lucy. I wasn't trying to steal your man."

"He's not even my man," I say.

"But he could be," Tanya sing songs, waggling her brows suggestively. "He asked me to ask you to meet him tonight."

"What? Does Masi want me to die?"

"Salina can come and fa'agoi your parents for you." Tanya has it all worked out.

"A'e, why me? Salina complains.

"Duh! Her parentals won't say no to the pastor's daughter."

It is the night of our N.U.S graduation. Tanya, Salina and I hit the clubs. We are dancing together when I feel someone behind me. I turn around as strong arms slide around me. "Congratulations baby," Masi says nuzzling my neck. "I'm so proud my girl is a graduate."

Abruptly, someone yanks my arm. "Sai, Sai, so this is what they teach you at University?" Uncle Ryan calls me by my grandmother's name. "No, what?" I'm confused, but I see Masi bunching his fists and I say urgently, "Ku'u, it's my uncle."

"Pa'umumuku! Get in my car, I'm dropping you off home." I start walking, quickly shaking my head left to right so Masi knows not to follow. I'm not walking fast enough. Uncle Ryan grabs my arm and drags me to his white double-cab Hilux pickup. I'm lucky it's not by my hair, I guess. Tanya and Salina follow. But what can they say? He is my mother's brother. It's his job to protect my honour. Our family pride. His breath stinks of alcohol and his eyes are bloodshot red with darkness. He is still my uncle. He drives and lectures about life and the wickedness of men. He is very passionate on this subject. I am mortified. He pulls up the car. Wait! This isn't home. "Ae ga e ke fia pa'amumuku solo," he says.

Later he drops me off home and threatens to tell my parents how I was being a slut in the club.

I slowly feel changes to my body. My mother, hawk-eyed, notices the changes too. She suddenly starts insisting that Masi and I get married.

"Lucy, you both need to get married now," she says firmly. There is no other option. "If the village knows, oh the pastor, this will be the downfall of our family." My father tries to intervene and calm her down but she raises her voice louder. "You would think that with your degree you would be smarter, but it looks like you are stupid. And then people will think I am stupid. That our whole aiga are stupid!" Her voice rises and rises. And then the kicker, "Do you love him?"

"Yes, mother," I nod with my head facing the floor. Because what has love got to do with it? That yes is all it takes. Tears stream down my face and taste bitter on my tongue. "Pregnancy hormones," My mother says and arranges everything. Marriages are between families and his parents had come twice with Masi to fa'amalamalama to my parents, but my mother has always turned them away. "My daughter needs to finish her degree. And get a job." Now with my body beginning to curve and round there is no time for such niceties.

The wedding day was arranged in one week. Our families have been up all night. Everyone has their own set of tasks to do. Tanya is in charge of all things that needed beautifying - the church, the hall, and now me. I stare blankly at the fresh white teuila flowers with silver fern leaves mixed with artificial white roses interwoven into the teu that I will hold as I walk up the aisle. Tanya brushes foundation into my skin. I never wear make-up, and as it dries it feels like a mask. Salina readjusts the comb for the veil. She looks over at Tanya who seems to have taken in her dress so it skims tightly over her skin.

"I can't believe you even made Tanya a bridesmaid," Salina says. I want to tell her to shut up in case Tanya starts stabbing her with the eyeliner she is carefully drawing across the lid of my eye. Tanya stops and tosses her hair and recites her famous lines, "Sis, look at me and look at you, Deeeee!" For a second, I am in the moment. The heaviness of my heart lifts and I am truly thankful for the sisterhood we share.

As I walk down the aisle on my father's arm, I look in the pews - so many people that I don't know. I think that they are all from Masi's side and I'm sure Masi's is assuming they are all from mine. None of these people are friends. Aiga only in such a short time.

Later that night Masi holds me on the dance floor and no one has any right to pull me away. We are married now. I almost feel safe.

It is too early to feel a kick.

I will never tell Masi that I do not know if this child is his.

There are some things one has to hide. For family pride.

I Am Clothed

By Filifotu Vaai

The tapping of the 'au still
                        rings loudly in my ears
Rhythmic, like the beating of my heart, thudding with pride
As it pumps blood through my veins, each tap reminding me

That the lifeblood of my ancestors
flows through me

The black of the lama is etched on my thighs
Leaving permanent imprints
on my body   and in my mind

Of Warriors, of Goddesses
that walked this path before me
Braving uncharted courses, forging towards open horizons
Showing me the way

I am clothed in measina.
With each tap, each tear of my skin
I feel their legacy

Their alofa rising in me, deep within my bones
I am clothed in alofa

I bear the patterns of lineages past
on my skin
I wear their stories as

I create my own

Finding belonging in the land of the long white cloud, Aotearoa

By Rebecca Tobo Olul-Hossen

In Rebecca's mind a "P.I." was equal to "Private Investigator", meaning "detective" or "sleuth". Similar to those in the Nancy Drew and the Hardy Boys books that she grew up reading. The books that normally have long lists of bookings even before they arrived at the school library at Malapoa College. A sanctuary that Rebecca spent lots of her out-of-class time in.

Then Rebecca went to New Zealand for high school in an all-girls' school and was told that she was a "P.I.". That P.I.s were naturals at singing. And that she must join the P.I. choir. To be honest, she was not considered that good a singer back home in her local church. She was told that she was a Pacific Islander. She did not identify as Pacific Islander. She was ni-Vanuatu through and through. She was Melanesian, yes! But a Pacific Islander she was not.

There were three other Rebeccas in her economics class. So, the teacher said for them to decide who will be "Beeks", who will be "Beeker", and who will remain Rebeecca. She was "Beeker" and sometimes "Beeks". It reminded her of being in Mr. Kampai's year nine science class at Malapoa College, and being introduced to Bunsen Burners and Beakers. That gave her a bit of a giggle.

The English teacher in sixth form (this is what they call it in New Zealand, not year 12 like in Vanuatu), Mrs. Yelash was a peculiar woman. She had the most luscious head of grey hair you'd ever seen, which surrounded the palest skin and intense blue eyes. The class secretly thinks that may be why she used

"Bush" as her penname for her novels.

One day she said to Rebecca, "Now tell the class, do people in your beautiful country still live in these lovely houses made of grass and wood?" Rebecca was dumbfounded. Lying in her bed in the dormitory later, she made up all kinds of responses. Her favourite was, "Yes they do. Some still live in caves. And still eat people! Especially white ones."

She cackled every time she imagined Mrs. Yelash's eyes going wide. That would teach her. Why could she not have just asked Rebecca to describe how communities traditionally live in Vanuatu. Rather than jump to conclusions about how people lived. Just like how she was not asked what she identified as, and instead just given the label, P.I.

Her best moments were when she made the second XI soccer team. She travelled in the school van to other towns to play against other schools. In Vanuatu she would never have even made any of the soccer teams. She was usually the last girl picked for any sports and games. Although she did well in track and field events and enjoyed long distance running, especially cross country.

Being in a crowd of girls dressed in purple gear bought from various Op Shops in Nelson, faces painted purple, and hair braided in neat corn rows with purple ribbon, yelling out from the bleachers in support of the purple house was exhilarating:

"Thunder, thunder, thunderation
We are Whangamoa delegation
When we fight with determination
We create a thunderation"

She had chills running down her back every time she thought about it.

She was just a seventeen-year-old girl who missed home a lot. All her pocket money was spent on phone credits so that she could call home to speak with her parents.

She loved History and how the teacher makes lessons come to life with actual footage from WWII. Mr. Kirby was the best Geography teacher, bringing scree slopes and other landforms found on the pages of textbooks to reality through excursions to the Kaikoura Ranges. The long hike up in the morning and the run down at the end of the day was definitely not for the fainthearted.

The photos and little bits of wood, rocks, and plants she picked up on the excursion found a home in her journal with photos of the excursion.

And just like that Rebecca had found a home in Aotearoa, the land of the long white cloud. She could never pinpoint an actual moment in time when she started to feel at home.

She loved coming home for Christmas with her family, but after the New Year's she starts to pine for New Zealand. It was her second home. Whether she liked it or not . . . it was a part of her.

HĒNINUKA

By Denise Carter-Bennett

My kūpuna Hēninuka
Hair dark and wavy,
Tongue accented with Oʻahu
A child of only 17
With babe in arms and husband away
In a foreign land but not foreign at all
Kuia cradling you while you cradle your own
Faces that remind you of your ʻohana but tikanga not of your own
Kūpuna, tūpuna, tīpuna
You share the same
Waka hourua made a home here
Your canoe to this foreign place was cold, destitute, unwelcoming
Your husband with his alabaster skin and Yiddish ways
Your belly swollen with the ache of love forbidden
Jane is what I will call myself. My husband will call himself John.
Kāo. Hēninuka. HĒNI
The kuia say you are one of us
Kūpuna, tūpuna, tīpuna
We share the same

Hone, you shall call him Hone
This child of yours hair dark and wavy
Skin like alabaster but golden when loved by Tama-Nui-Te-Rā
Why does he sound like one of those haole?
His reo speckled with Oʻahu and tangata whenua
He's going to marry a Māori girl
A chief's daughter
Her hair dark and wavy
Her skin golden like Rā
Her reo haole, tangata whenua, mātauranga Māori, love
Kūpuna, tūpuna, tīpuna
They are the same

You see her in your dreams
This child of 17
Her dark and wavy
Her skin golden for Rā
You reach out but space and time deny it
She sits there drowning in her darkness
Crying out for Hinenuitepō
Screaming out for Rohe
Oh sweet Moko, I am here to cradle you
Do not jump off!
Raʻiātea is not ready
Your tiare apetahi still forming
Her reo filled with pain and whakamā
I AM NOT MĀORI she spits out

Kanaka, Māori, kaikamahine Moana is who you are
Fiery like Pele, born of her
You weave a kete of aroha, discovery and acceptance
You put it on a waka hourua and set it out onto the moana
Over time and space it will reach her
Kūpuna, tūpuna, tīpuna
I am her and she is me.

The Bumble Fumble: a Super-Bowl Sunday misadventure

By Filifotu Vaai

The humid Honolulu tradewinds whispered noisily through the damp February evening along my quiet Central Oahu street. Apparently, some game was happening before or after the JLo & Shakira concert, I'm not quite sure. My neighbors are calling it Superbowl Sunday? I exaggerate how little I care about American traditions not because I'm above capitalist, overhyped holidays, but because my brand of colonialism is British and so I prefer rugby.

It was otherwise, a fairly regular Sunday spent eating and laying on my couch taking intermittent naps. I'd just returned from a business trip the day prior and my tired, no-boyfriend-having-ass was enjoying the unusual calm on the street which was silent aside from the occasional scream from the neighbors yelling at their flatscreen TVs, "THAT WAS A FUMBLE REF!" Nobody cares, bro. Take a seat.

That afternoon, my Dad, who was equally unenthused by Gridiron, and I spent some time grilling steaks and arguing about my life choices over a glass of Pinot. It's usually a retelling of my origin story as a girl from Motunui with the hopes of my ancestors on my shoulders, the key message being – don't fuck it up. As my Dad reached his third glass, about the stage where he started to once again implore me to reconsider my decision to divorce my ex-husband, I resorted to distracting myself with chatting with some insta-model looking guy on the dating app, Bumble.

Enter, Dino.

Dino was thirty-five, ripped, profile teeming with smoldering selfies and perfect lighting. Disgustingly and sickeningly hot, in that B grade celebrity kind of way. Like, he's good looking enough to maybe be famous, but probably as a back-up dancer, or maybe he did a Target catalogue campaign once. Not sure if it was the washboard abs, or the note on his profile that said, "casual only" that made me feel emotionally safe enough to entertain the nonsense that would soon ensue.

He claimed to be an "entrepreneur" from Maui. He said he was stuck in Oahu overnight, staying at a swanky downtown hotel called the Modern. As we were chatting he said he was watching the Superbowl at a soiree in Park Lane which, for those who aren't acquainted with the Honolulu real estate market, is basically a boujee downtown Honolulu apartment complex where rich people and their rich friends live. I know, so relatable . . . right? His pics were vain and filtered. Now granted, so are mine. But he had an almost cartoon- drawn six pack flexed in every pic. I mean, my type, obviously. The chat we had was not particularly substantive, so naturally, I kept it going. While we're talking about weekends and #gymlife, it crossed my mind that he probably had core muscles strong enough to work out the kink in my back that was bothering me after my eight and half hour flight from Dallas the day before. Just saying, right?

He seemed smart and nice enough, talking about business meetings and expensive whiskey, and when he suggested that we should "meet, order room service and watch the stars", I rolled my eyes and played coy, because by "stars" I knew he actually meant, "this ass".

"Sounds fun," I responded and proceeded to ignore his invitation until, as I was getting ready for the gym around 10pm, he messaged me and asked, "You coming through?"

On a whim, I thought. Why not? I realize now that this is kind of a slut move. But also, I kind of don't give a shit. So that's grown woman slut to you, Judge Judy.

So, then it's 11pm. There I am, looking cute and smelling fresh. As I parked my car outside the Modern, I text my friend to let another human know where I was because rule number 2 of the Hoe Handbook (coz if you're gonna be a hoe, you'd better do it right and follow the handbook) states, Pro tip to staying alive to hoe another day: Before you go, Let another hoe know. After my friend responded with, "Ok Thotiana, be safe," I walked into the lobby and texted Dino I was in the vicinity. He told me to meet him in his room, gave me his room number and said, "Come up, don't worry, I'm no serial killer. Haha"

Um, that's not a funny joke, sir. Also, no.

I text back, "Meet me in the lobby" (Mo fo!)

He sends me some laughing emojis and says, "Ok."

A Caucasian man with sandy blond locks and a fit, trim frame approaches me, he reminds me of a blond Peter Andre from his Mysterious Girl video, definitely cute but back-up dancer bod so shorter than me. I do a double take and realize, oh yea, it is him, catfished by camera angles I have to think quickly. What's my move? My inner thoughts race as I level set with myself.

"Um ok, it's no biggie." (see what I did there?)

I'm tryna be open-minded here. "Think positive, girl he's still cute, stay for a drink and go from there. Looks like there's still abs under that shirt and maybe he has that big dick . . . energy so, stay for the drink, let's see where this goes."

After a pause, I smile, and offer a "Hi."

Then he spoke, and out of his mouth comes the world's most annoying voice. He had this terrible flat, froggy tone that made me want to instantly tell him to shut the fuck up. Ugh. I should have walked out right then and there, but of course, I didn't.

He hugs me, and even though I can feel he's got cut abs underneath his paper-thin shirt, he's kind of petite and I feel like the man in this hug. Lol. " I need a drink," I think.

I order an Old Fashioned, and half way through my glass, I relax a little. Dino's got jokes and with some help from the whiskey and my Oscar worthy active listening skills, he easily draws a laugh from me which he follows up perfectly with a compliment about my smile. Okay, Peter Andre. Shots fired. He's a little self-absorbed talking about his busy schedule and flying private like he was the only one who could, but his confidence makes me curious. So , fair play, I'll allow it. I pretend to listen attentively while keeping an eye on the time. He eventually invites me to his room and I decide, okay, let's see about these stars, shall we?

As we leave the bar, we're chatting about the hotel, the people at the bar, and the Superbowl while we get in the elevator.

Me: (doesn't watch, let alone care about the Superbowl)

Also Me: "How 'bout those Chiefs tho?"

The Modern is a 5-star hotel, but I'm surprised by how few emergency exits there are as we're walking down the hall. Rule number 11 in the handbook: Scan for quick escape routes. I find myself humming the tune to Mysterious Girl as he's fiddling with the key, because, involuntarily, my brain has decided that's the roleplay we're going with this evening. As we get to the door he asks me, "Are you a Mormon?"

I pause. Strange question, but okay. "No, I'm not," I respond.

He says, in his slightly high-pitched tone, "Oh, I grew up in Utah, and a lot of my friends growing up were, uhh, they were, um, uhhh Polynesian." He looks me up and down, "You're Polynesian, right?"

In my head, I'm thinking, did you forget the word, bro? I decide I won't choose this moment to educate this man that Polynesia is an outdated concept introduced by white colonisers to put us in boxes they could remember.

"Yes, I am," I say.

I realize he's trying to relate to me, and his only reference for a Samoan is some brown missionaries he grew up around in Utah. LOL. Oh boy, I sure can pick 'em. I'd better put us both out of our misery.

"Do you have anything to drink?" I ask.

He looks around blankly and says, "Um, no." Ok. Awkward.

"I'll go and grab us some from downstairs," he offers.

I offer to go with him, and he tells me to stay and relax in the room, he'll be right back. And then he pauses with a wry smile and says, "Oh, but I have something for you," and he looks at me with what I now notice are bloodshot eyes and uncovers a line of white powder on a key card, on the dresser.

Ugghh, I know that shit ain't icing sugar. Fuck! Be cool. Be cool.

I try to look casual, relaxed, "Oh, I'm ok, thanks."

He smiles, "Have you ever done coke?"

There is a lump in my throat. "I haven't," I say.

After what felt like ten years, he blurts out, "Okaaaaaay, you don't have to if you don't want to," and he puts the key card with the line of coke back on the dresser.

"Ok." My heart is pounding.

Then he laughs awkwardly and says sheepishly, "Sorry, I know, I'm out of control," as he walks out.

My mind is in some kind of trance as I flip through the room service menu blindly as I try to process what is going on. I call the front desk and the cheery attendant informs me that room service is closed, "But you can download Uber Eats." Five stars my ass, this is some dive motel bullshit, I think as I hang up the phone.

Once I hang up I kind of snap back to reality looking at the line of hard drugs in front of me as I ask myself, "What the actual fuck are you doing here? You tryna get drugged bitch?"

I text my friend, "Uh, I'm kind of in a sitch right now. There's an actual line of coke in front of me right now."

"Get out of there, bitch."

Without a second thought, I grab my shit, get up and book it out of there like I was Flo fucking Jo.

My phone rings twice as I'm walking out the door. I don't answer.

He texts me, "No room service?"

I text him that something came up and I had to leave.

He responds with, "I understand."

The fuck you do, Dino.

I drive my ass home recounting the night's events thinking, what the actual fuck just happened? I mean, it could've been just fine, but also, aren't you lucky you're still breathing and not at the bottom of some dumpster. And all for what? Some dusty ass dick? Holy fuck. This wasn't in the handbook. Also, what a waste of gas.

I get home, I have a hot shower, and pour myself a hefty glass of leftover Pinot. My Dad asks how my night was. "It was ok," I respond. "You were right. I should have stayed home."

I'm scrolling through my phone while I sip and I discover that unsurprisingly, Shakira won the Superbowl. I then read an article about the hazards of online dating including one scenario to beware of where drug dealers will match with women, give them drugs and essentially have them become regular drug users and buyers. I think about Dino. "Entrepreneur" my ass, you mean Drug Dealer!

Kefs. For a second I miss being married. But just for a second before I recoil from that thought, and come back to the present moment to think about how lucky I am to be enjoying this glass of wine alive. Shit, I think. It's hard out here in these streets.

I don't think this is what my ancestors meant when they wanted me to come to the land of milk and honey. Then again, it's probably them that saved my ass tonight. Probably disapprovingly, I imagine them plucking me out of danger's way tonight, with a loud okegia, "Aikae loa i le fale." But I'll also dare to believe that they'd want me to have whatever the fuck I want.

I change into an ie lavalava and crawl into bed. I exhale deeply trying to shake off the night's events as I drift off to sleep with thoughts of drug dealers, dodged bullets, disapproving ancestors, and dancing Shakira swirling in my mind.

Oh Shakira, Sharkira.

Her hips don't lie. But don't worry, men on Bumble sure will.

HANBOK

By Tanya Chargualaf Taimanglo

Older Brother tells Younger Brother, "We should wait for Big Sister to get here before we decide."

"Omma will like it." Younger Brother says, "Agreed. Though wait for Big Sister."

I do like the hanbok. Spring colors, cherry blossoms, and petite birds. My three children are so worried about what I should wear to church. This is a rare time of agreement and a conciliatory tone I witness occasionally, mostly on holidays.

Big Sister arrives from Oregon. She hugs Younger Brother and Sister-in-Law and settles in the backseat of the warm truck. Her mind drifts to decisions and choices. Has it really been five years since she was in Guam? Is it right to leave her three children in Portland? Routine, school, friends are what matter to them. A grandmother they met twice is a faded melody of a TikTok trend. How will Omma handle all the visiting friends and family? Can I survive these next ten days? Big Sister thinks.

"How was your flight?" Younger Brother asks. Big Sister thinks his long black hair fastened in a topknot makes him look like a character in a Chamorro legend their father repeated often. Younger Brother is grown, and marriage suits him.

"Easy. The next two weeks will be rough." Big Sister sighs.

"True. I'll drive you to Omma's house before church."

Big Sister hums in agreement.

Big Sister steps into the cool home after placing her running shoes on the bamboo shoe shelf. She surveys jars of pickled vegetables, cute knickknacks, a calendar marked with Korean writing, and framed pictures of her and her brothers at different ages. She wonders what she will take home to the Pacific Northwest. What will brothers want? Her eyes are drawn to the hanbok.

"Hi, Omma." Big Sister calls out. Big Sister believes in spirits.

My daughter is a beauty, unknowing, unwilling to use this power. She always preferred a muyo' and an intelligent answer to get her through life. This combination has sent her six thousand miles away from our island. She is surgically detached from me and her father. She left the island as soon as she finished college to a life I barely know and grandchildren who probably don't know my full name, Kim Mi-Young. I learned anything about them through the lens of Facebook. Why is Only Daughter like this, I do not know. Much changed during her middle school years and I have been grasping at her retreating figure since.

Younger Brother and Sister-In-Law share a smile and carry in Big Sister's single gray suitcase. Big Sister stands in front of two outfits, one traditional Korean dress-an electric pink jacket, lined with green accents, and a long flowing excess of snowy white material-nature scenes dotted along the bottom. Too warm for Guam, Big Sister thinks. The Pacific Ocean of Guam dances with the Philippine Sea and East China Sea and kisses the coast of Korea she muses; but this dress does not fit Guam. The second outfit is a storm cloud gray linen dress with straight lines and no adornment. No shape, and too warm for Guam, Big Sister thinks. She feels the gray material with her right palm, but scans the hanbok. I would choose the gray for myself, she thinks, but Omma deserves vibrance.

I certainly love the hanbok. My own Big Brother hand carried it from Korea for my Little Son's wedding five years ago. I withstood the heat and henpecking relatives then. I think I can do it one more time. I hope Only Daughter choses well.

"Sister, we'll be back in an hour or so. We need to check on our puppy." Younger Brother punches Big Sister's arm. She responds instinctively with a kick to his back side, which he responds by overdramatizing its power. They laugh. Sister-in-law rolls her eyes, smiles, and says, "Why can't you hug like normal siblings?"

This is more like it. My children acting like they always do. Wrestling, kicking, punching at each other lovingly. It makes me miss their father, the referee and fight promoter of our family. The children have not had him in their lives since their high school years.

The church is large and cavernous. The bright lights annoy Big Sister because she can be seen by everyone and anyone. She hugs Older Brother, First Sister-in-Law, and Nephew, and plants herself between Brothers securely before mass begins.

"Is that Bad Uncle?" Big Sister whispers to Older Brother.

"Yes. He came in from California."

"Why?" Big Sister tenses and continues to glare at the man in the opposite cluster of pews.

"Something about our parents. He wants to meet with us."

Younger Brother watches Big Sister's hands grip the missal and follows her sight line to Bad Uncle. He places a hand on her shoulder. A warning and a calming squeeze. She sighs, and melts back into the pew.

Bad Uncle. The twin of my husband. Younger. The man who asked for my husband's land at his funeral. The man my children will need to thwart. I hope the kids can work together. I believe they can protect their heritage. One acre to unite my three children. An acre that blessed us with papaya, iba, coconut, red peppers, and star apples. An acre that yielded memories.

"You chose well." Older brother says to Big Sister. "Omma looks lovely, even if she is wearing neon pink."

"It's electric pink." Big Sister pushes into Older Brother. "It would have been what she would have wanted. I know it."

"You're correct. And she would want us to work together to deal with Bad Uncle." Younger Brother whispered.

Only Daughter found it. The piece of paper that will prove our land remains our land. My sons do not know yet, but she will reveal this when needed to thwart Bad Uncle.

"I hate funerals." Big Sister tells Brothers. "I don't know half these people."

"That's Omma's best friend from the Senior Center." Younger Brother nods to the woman with stiff white curls and a billowy purple dress.

"That family there is from dad's side. The good ones from Agat." Older Brother adds.

Big Sister's memories are vapors from the 1990s that are like a dream she vaguely recalls. She scans the room, always ending on Bad Uncle's watchful eyes. She resents him for sharing her late father's face. She resents him for not having her late father's heart. The heaviest stone of resentment is locked in a black crate tucked away in her mind. Unknown to everyone in this church.

Bad Uncle circles the seafood delicacies of the buffet. Then, makes his way to his Only Niece. Brothers flank her as protection.

"Hey, girl." Bad Uncle jerks forward for a hug, but Big Sister steps back as if repulsed. "Boys, so grown."

"Hafa Adai, Uncle." Oldest, most kind Brother adds.

"Is this a good time to talk?" Bad Uncle asks. He picks his teeth with his pinky, dislodging a piece of crab meat, inspecting it, and eating it.

"About?" Younger Brother asks.

"You know, your mom's house and the land." Bad Uncle laughs.

Big Sister pulls out a brown envelope from her satchel. She can't meet his stare. Brothers notice his traveling gaze on their sister.

"What's that, Big Sister?" Older Brother asks.

"Deed." She finally looks at Bad Uncle.

"That's not legit." Bad Uncle raises his voice. "That land is my father's."

"This says otherwise." Big Sister steadies her stance. Memories, sensations, smells flood her mind and heart. "And you will never be on the land you stole from."

"Stole what?" Bad Uncle sneered.

"Me," Big Sister says in a small voice. One Brother hears her, the other does not. One tenses, the other looks from Bad Uncle to Big Sister.

"ME." Big Sister says louder. "You took me. And my childhood."

"I don't know…" Bad Uncle staggers back.

"The papaya trees…" Big Sister squares her shoulders, "…You know what you did in my Papa's orchard. And he knew too, and his way of making it up to me is this deed."

Bad Uncle looked at the watchful eyes of relatives. He could not swallow his food, and placed his unfinished plate on a green folding chair. The warm breeze brought in ocean air and washed away this bad man.

Brothers followed Bad Uncle to the parking lot and Big Sister returned to the church. She sat in the cool retreat alone. She thought of how beautiful her Omma was in pink. Her hanbok perfect for this day.

GROWN GIRLS GET THE BROOM'S SICK

By Rebecca Tobo Olul-Hossen

Nawalak's *Mama* tells her the funniest stories of growing up. Imagine thinking that grownup girls get the broom's sick!

But then Nawalak did grow up in a much more progressive household. She knew where babies came from and that girls see the moon's sick when they become women and no longer little girls.

Mama told the story of being in the village one day.

One of the older girls, Mariana, had come around to visit *Mama* and *Kaha Patan*.

Mariana was in the outdoor bathroom taking a shower, completely naked, after fetching her water from the well with a bucket, when Mama walked in on her.

For the first time ever, *Mama* saw a young woman, not quite a woman yet, but no longer a girl, stark naked. Her tiny budding breasts pushing out for the world to see. And what is the black triangle between her legs?

Mama was horrified! She ran screaming into the kitchen to *Kaha Patan*.

"What is it, *koko*?" *Kaha* asked.

"Mariana has the sick of the broom!" Mama gasped when she had the time to catch her breath. "Mariana has the sick of the broom!"

Kaha burst out laughing after Mama explained what she saw.

"All girls get that when they are growing up," explained *Kaha*.

Imagine Mama's horror that she too will one day get the sick of the broom.

Mama explained that it was only hair.

Not long after Mariana came sheepishly into the kitchen, smelling of lux from her bucket shower.

TURUKAWA

By Tulia Thompson

It begins with Turukawa, the hawk goddess who is mother to the first humans. On the first day, the day of the implantation, Mere ubers to the fertility clinic by herself, and ubers home by herself. She has had two previous implantations. This is her last embryo created in an IVF cycle which has cost her $25,000 - an amount she finds almost unimaginable. There is no way she can afford another go if this fails. She feels a moment of self-pity in the uber - of not having a partner to go with her - but admits to herself that it feels easier than involving others.

She thinks of Turukawa, the hawk goddess with her expansive blue-grey wings and orange eyes. The feathers on Turukawa's chest are pale pink, like the sky at dusk. In the forest, you could sometimes hear her distinctive call, ki..ki...ki...

The narrative usually starts with Degei, the snake god. Sometimes they are friends. Sometimes they are lovers. Some stories say she is a dove from Tonga, but Mere feels sure she is a powerful hawk. Degei finds Turukawa is missing, but returns to her nest to find two eggs. He nurtures them, and when they hatch, they are human.

In the operating theatre, the Pakeha doctor calls Mere over to a screen and says she is very happy with the embryo, which is healthy and doing the right things. Mere looks at the small circle which looks like a textbook diagram of a cell. It looks like a silver moon, covered in craters. On one side, the outer shell seems to be breaking apart. The doctor points this out to Mere and explains that the embryo breaks free of the outer shell to latch onto the uterine lining.

Mere tries to comprehend that this is the first image of her future child. She wants to feel love and maternal instinct, but her future child does not look human. Interesting but somewhat alien. She feels the burden of self-pressure in front of the doctor to respond appropriately, and show maternal care. This is a child she has fought hard for.

"Oh, wow!" Mere says. "Will it move around in my uterus?"

"Ah no," says the doctor, with a concerned look at needing to state the obvious. "Your uterus is not actually empty space. It is more like a jam sandwich." Mere feels mild shame, and realises she never properly understood the medical diagrams she saw in high school. She thought her uterus was a cave.

After the procedure, the doctor takes a photo and prints an image of a tiny speck of light. She explains the speck of light is not actually the embryo - which is too small to see - but an air bubble they use as a marker.

Mere feels elated at the tiny speck of light. She realises that even if it doesn't take, this might be the closest she gets to being a Mum. The embryo is five days old, and so there is a 10-day wait until she can do a blood-test to find out whether she is pregnant. A jolly Scottish nurse hands her a paper bag full of medications. "Sometimes positivity is all it takes," she says enthusiastically.

In the hot afternoon, Mere and her sister Adi go to the small Fijian bakery in Onehunga. Adi has a mocha layer cake and Mere has a lamington, and they chat and gossip with the owner. Adi gets a call that she has got the job she wanted, and she says, "We are both celebrating!" It seems possible to Mere that good luck works in doubles, that maybe for both of them sweetness is igniting and spilling out.

It is a turning point, like seeing young Turukawa through dense forest. Turukawa with a pale yellow and brown pattern on her chest, like fine weaving. Turukawa with yellow eyes and mid-brown wings rising 1200 metres above forest and searching for prey. Mere looks up information about the Fijian goshawk on her phone and finds her fossil bones were found from 'Eua in Tonga. Ha! The dove from Tonga story was true!

On the sixth day, Mere goes to her cousin Olly's house and eats fried dumplings and watches stand-up comedy on Netflix. Her abdomen and lower back are uncomfortable. Olly asks what is going on with her.

"Not much, cuz," she says, because there is no way to say, "I might be pregnant", or "I've been trying to get pregnant", without straying too closely to language too personal to say. She drinks sugary tea instead of beer.

When she gets home, she knocks over the tiny, heavy silver frame given to her by her Mum. She lies in bed thinking about mother-daughter relationships. Her Mum Lily was a tiny blonde Pakeha woman, beautiful and expressive, who could also scowl and find cruel words that cut, and redouble and bind, words that rise in the dark. She could be strangely obtuse to her daughter's feelings. Once, she had gleefully boasted, "The women in *our* family are always petite!" in front of her six-foot, broad-shouldered and plus-sized daughter. It was as if she hadn't adapted her frame of reference to see the daughter in front of her. Mere feels perpetually unseen by her. And yet, Mere felt a kind of grace in how her mother was excited for her to have a child. Lily, a devout Christian, did not even care that Mere was single. She was delighted at the prospect of a grandchild.

On the seventh day, Mere catches the train to Otahuhu, her lower back now aching like an inconsistent sea siren, calling, calling. She goes to the small, warm yellow art gallery where plastic mats have been laid out on the floor. She is there for a talanoa by an artist who is friends with her brother Epeli. The artist is down-to-earth and lives in a tiny house, and gardens. Afterwards they sit around talking, and it is 11 o'clock.

In the dark-blue Lexus on the way home, Elin turns to face Mere from the front seat and says, "Epeli says you are pregnant!". Elin has long pale-blonde hair and pale blue eyes. Epeli and her met in France, but she is Swedish. They are here for a short visit before returning to Paris. Mere is not sure what Epeli will have told her. She likes that Elin is so direct, but also caring. She isn't sure what to say. Around them the dark streets look deserted.

"Yes," she says tentatively. "I will find out on Friday if it's successful - but I'm not three months yet!"

On the ninth day, Mere gives an 8 am lecture, but after feeling tiredness passing over her in waves, she goes home to bed at 11 and sleeps until 2. She tells herself it is her body working hard to support this pregnancy. She tells herself she is soil for a small, turning seed, burrowing and burrowing. Her breasts are sore too, and she feels relieved.

She thinks about her journey as a feminist; not to define herself by her body, and how she does not believe that biology is destiny. And yet here she is, stuck in this place where her uterus unexpectedly matters to her self-identity, because she is prepared to do anything to be a mother. She is prepared to retell her story to strangers. She is prepared for the ongoing stream of internal exams, medications, wait times and mild disappointments. Her long, loping body feels like mangroves at low tide, the reach of it. She thinks that maybe her biology is a love-bind, making her pin her heart on biology, like a lover you can't trust. For the desperate dream of having her own child.

Mere is cooking pizza. Her friend Maia wearing large, gold hoops in her ears and a loose, brightly coloured kaftan, sits on a kitchen stool and sips a glass of wine. Mere wants to distract herself with rolling dough and caramelising onions, but she finds it hard to concentrate. Her mind kicks into overdrive trying to prepare herself for the potential for loss.

"You know you could always try hooking up with a guy," Maia teases. "It would probably be easier".

"True," says Mere doubtfully, "But you know my luck with men."

Actually, Mere couldn't imagine putting herself through that again. Her past love affairs had devastated her. She felt panicked thinking about it. Her thoughts flicked to the last two Fijian men she had tried to have relationships with.

She remembered how her lover had gently called her "kai loma" while they were lying in bed. It was the first time she had heard kai loma as an endearment, and not as an insult. She had wanted to find safety and sacredness, as a counter to dealing with mainstream Pakeha racism and white privilege. Instead, she felt profoundly betrayed when he used her and left. Fiji guys acting like they are Degei, who are more snake than God. It was the same for all her friends, constantly dealing with the toxic masculinity of their men, which itself was a damaging, psychic consequence of colonisation. Maybe kai loma was always intended to sting.

Late at night, Mere watches YouTube ASMR healing videos of people giving reiki or energy healing or even crystal healings. She listens to fertility meditations where you imagine your uterus blooming like a lotus. The moon shines through her open window. She is wanting to hear the flow of positivity of people talking about healing light. She feels that there is a psychic cost to this viewing - that she is putting aside her actual scepticism and disillusionment, but she really wants to hear people say things like "I am imparting my healing to you".

Mere grew up with Christianity, her Fijian Catholic Dad and her evangelical Mum. She wonders if the need for healing language is because night was a familiar time of prayer. She doesn't want to pray, exactly. She wants to believe in something bigger than her, that isn't global warming or neoliberal capitalism. She doesn't want to go back to believing in God, but sometimes she misses believing in God. Mere remembered how praying in bed at night felt like building a bridge between herself and the immensity of the universe, and her imagining of a powerful sentient creator. It makes her feel deeply sad, because who wouldn't want a powerful being they could rely on? Who wouldn't want God on their side? Maybe even a small embryo in a jam sandwich.

Mere put her laptop down beside her bed. She sipped the glass of water on her bedside table, and listened to the night sounds of insects. Last year she visited her Uncle Silikeli in Suva. They sat in a small, white-washed eatery, waiting for black tea with ginger in it. Uncle chose this place because it has nama, not like cafes for Westerners. Mere is visiting Fiji for the first time without her dad being alive to interpret everything for her. She had not understood this would be difficult.

"We have a curse in our family," Uncle said, eyes twinkling.

"A curse?" said Mere. She cuts her dalo with a plastic fork.

"Lots of the women in our family do not marry or have children."

"Hmmm," she says noncommittally. She really doesn't want to go there with him.

"I think that is why you have not married or had children," he said, "because of the curse".

Mere allows herself to have fledgling imaginings of what it would be like to have a child. She imagines taking her child to the Auckland Central Public Library. She imagines a playhouse in the garden, little planter boxes where we grow crinkled lettuces and giant sunflowers and tiny, bright strawberries. She imagines taking her child home to Fiji, and saying, "This is our vanua," and showing her the fine woven thread of their ancestor-gods, and how it connected her to these pale aqua waters and the bright, branching corals, and string-rays gliding beneath.

On the morning of the blood test, Mere made porridge and then lay touching her lower belly with her palm. She remembers touching her sister's pregnant belly, and how hard it was, and how hers feels soft like the belly of a small, defenceless animal. She catches the bus to the lab testing place, and afterward she feels at a loss to know what to do with herself. She feels alone.

She gets a call in the afternoon while she is standing in the garden. She stands watching a bee slowly travel between lavender heads,

The Scottish nurse is upbeat, "Hi Mere, how are you? We've got your test results."

Mere vaguely registers that it must be good news, because the nurse sounds so positive.

"I'm good, thanks," she says numbly.

"It's not good news I'm afraid," says the nurse, "The blood test shows that you are not pregnant."

Mere is plunged into another bodily state, suspended above her own body. She cannot yet feel the grief that she knows will come. Some psychic forcefield is holding it at bay.

At night Mere goes to the kitchen to have something to eat. She eats as if she is carbo-loading for some invisible event. She just wants to shovel food into her mouth. Everything she eats tastes stodgy and not salty enough. She wishes she could eat the Fijian food she grew up with, kokoda and crab curry and dalo. The food her dad would make. There is no one she can call.

It is a warm night, and Mere walks down the road to the small reserve she often reads in. Moonlight falls through the silhouettes of nikau and ponga. She sits in the empty field. Alone, in the dark, she can feel the shape of the loss, pressing inside her. She feels the full weight of her uncle's talanoa. She feels cursed. The physical pain in her chest. Tears stream down her face, rough as cyclone seas. Her body convulses. The immensity of this tiny loss that robs from her ancestors.

Mere thinks of Turukawa. Her piercing eyes and talons. She remembers how Degei found Turukawa missing and raised the human children without her. The truth of Turukawa was that she left, alone.

She imagines Turukawa, a solitary hawk rising into the clear sky.

I DON'T NEED TO REMEMBER

By Kiri Piahana-Wong

I don't need to remember
How everything hurt
And the sky lifted up

The way he would run on the sand
Holding both of our hands at once
And how his small body curved into mine,

Saying, 'Mama, Mama'
And keening like a bird
That has fallen from the nest

We were up so high, is the thing
And the sun burnt us brightly
I don't need to remember

ALL KINDS OF BAD THINGS HAPPENED DOWN THERE

By Rebecca Tobo Olul-Hossen

Mama had always warned Louise about staying away from boys.

"If you stand too close to boys you will get pregnant," was Mama's stern warning.

It wasn't hard for Louise to stay away from boys. Or girls, for that matter. She grew up pretty much on her own.

Even though Mama and Tata were John Frum followers and believed in kastom, this did not stop Tata from making sure that Louise got a good education.

At the tender age of seventeen, Louise fell pregnant. She had not realised until then that standing close to boys had nothing to do with getting pregnant.

That there was more to it than that.

Louise also had not realised that getting pregnant and having the baby of this boy man who promised you the world did not guarantee that he would want to be with you. Or that his mother would accept you.

Louise blamed a lot of this on the kastom of kaliku. She had seen her first period and there was such a public display that everyone in the village knew that she was now ready. It seemed that literally overnight she became marriage material. Literally like a butterfly emerging from the chrysalis, she transformed from a girl into a woman. Or so it seemed.

But she was not ready for what that meant.

Bad things happened down there. Blood flowed from down there. And now this baby. This baby that she was having was coming from that same place.

Already Louise knew the father of the child, Jocklie, did not want her. Jocklie's mother, her dear kind aunty, has sent word that she was not to bring this child to her doorstep. It was not her beloved son's child. How did she know this?! Was she there when the 'standing close' happened?

Now Louise cast disdain on the kastom where Aunties tell you that there is more where it came from when you say that you like the nawanangen. All the while saying under their breath that their sons were there also.

Louise wished that she did not get pregnant. That she had not stood so close to that boy. Ha! If only it were that easy. Why did Mama not tell her fully what would happen?

It took more than standing close to a boy for her to get to where she was at that point.

And this baby who was soon coming out from down there certainly did not come from standing close to a boy.

Louise's son was born. He was the most beautiful thing she had ever seen. She fell in love and named him after Tata.

Maybe not all things bad happened down there.

BLOODY ISLANDERS

By Lani Wendt Young

"Bloody islanders. There he is again."

Frank stood at the kitchen window looking out at the man shuffling past on the sidewalk.

Alice sighed where she sat in her chair, knitting. A quiet sigh though. One that Frank couldn't hear. She didn't bother getting up because she knew what she would see. An elderly brown man in grey sweatpants and a Manu Samoa rugby jersey, with a rumpled green hat that flopped over wiry grey hair.

"Now he's in our yard. What?!" Frank opened the window, almost spilling his coffee in his haste. Leaned out to bark. "Oi, get out of our garden. Piss off!"

The old man looked up at the palagi in the window. Smiled and waved. Then went back to what he was doing.

Frank was incredulous. "Alice, he's not leaving! Come look. Alice. Alice!"

Alice knew from weary experience that her husband would just keep saying her name until she responded. Like the children used to do when they were little. So with another sigh she put her knitting down and heaved herself out of the chair to walk over to the window with ponderous slowness. Peered out. "Yes, that's him. He comes by most days."

"But what's he doing?" demanded Frank.

"Weeding probably," said Alice. "Or picking up rubbish. He'll be on his way soon enough."

"That's unacceptable," Frank spluttered. "We can't have strangers in our yard. It's trespassing. Just because they've got no concept of private property in their country, doesn't mean they can go wherever they like when they come here to ours."

"He's not doing any harm," countered Alice. "He's being helpful."

"Helpful? Bollocks he is. He's probably seeing what he can nick. Y'know these people are like that. They don't understand other people's property. Think they can just take stuff if it's lying around. He'll be walking off with my weed whacker. You watch. Gonna go out there and give him what for."

"No, look Frank, he's leaving," soothed Alice. "See?"

The couple looked out at the old man as he shuffled back through the gate, this time with a handful of weeds. He turned and waved cheerily at the couple before continuing down the street.

Alice went back to her chair and her knitting while Frank paced. "How can you be so calm about these things? You let that behaviour slide, then before you know it, they're taking over the whole neighbourhood. I'm going to see if anything's missing from my tool shed."

He stomped out while Alice shook her head. She winced at the slam of the door.

It had only been a few weeks since Frank retired from his job at the office. He was finding the adjustment difficult. Alice had suggested he get out a bit. Maybe go visit his mother at the retirement home? But Frank hadn't liked that idea. "I see her three times a year already. At Christmas, her birthday and on Mother's Day. What more do you want from me?" Then he had launched into a familiar spiel about how hard he had worked for forty years, "supporting this family! All I want now is a break. Some rest. Is that too much to ask?"

Alice knew it was pointless to reason with him when he got like that. She didn't begrudge him his rest, but she did wish Frank would find somewhere else to have a break. He was upsetting her schedule. Peace and quiet was getting harder to find.

******

Frank was watching cricket on the telly when he heard the scrape of a wheelie bin on concrete. He turned the sound down. Listened. There it was again. Someone or something was fiddling with the bins outside. Maybe the neighbour's dogs?

"Alice!" he called out. "Alice. Check the bins."

No answer. Alice was in the back yard, hanging up the washing.

The noise came again. Frank grimaced, muttered to himself as he got up, swore as he accidentally knocked over the cluster of empty cans beside him. He poked his head out the window. It was the old man again. This time he was tugging at the handle of their bin that Frank had put out the night before for rubbish day.

"Fecking bugger, stealing my bin in broad daylight. He's got some nerve."

He leaned out the window and bellowed. "I see you! Thief. Stop. Leave it be!"

The old man paused in his tugging and waved at Frank. A huge grin on his face. He pointed at Frank's garage and said something that Frank couldn't make out.

"I don't care whatever it is," shouted Frank. "I'm coming down there. You'll be sorry, old man."

Alice came inside the back door with her empty laundry basket, breathing heavy with exertion. Puzzlement on her face as Frank stormed to the front hall, stopping first to put on his boots, before he threw open the door.

"Frank? What is it? What's going on?" She followed him, worried.

"That bugger's stealing my bin!" said Frank over his shoulder, as he looked around wildly for the bin thief.

"No," protested Alice. "He's bringing it in."

"Whaddya mean, bringing it in?" Frank's question died away as the old man finished tugging their bin back up to its usual spot by the garage. This close up and Frank could see the toothy gaps in the man's smile. There was a red lanyard hanging around his neck.

He had a tattoo on his left forearm. Probably gang-related, thought Frank.

"All finish!" the old man announced as he patted the bin and waved at the couple.

Alice waved back. "Fay-fee-tai," she called out. To Frank she said, "That's thank you in Saa-mo-wen. Try it dear."

Frank snorted in disgust. "I bloody well will not. We're in New Zealand where we speak English."

The old man tottered off to the next house where the neighbour's wheelie bin was left lying on its side, half on the road.

While Frank watched in bemusement, the old man hefted the bin up and started pulling it along the neighbour's driveway. The bin was nearly as tall as he was, but the old man persisted. He whistled an unfamiliar tune as he worked, a smile of satisfaction on his face when he finally got the bin next to the neighbour's garage.

"See?" said Alice as she turned to go back inside. "He takes everyone's bins in on rubbish day."

"Must be a mental case," scoffed Frank. "Something wrong with him alright."

Frank didn't like it. Not one bit. Alice was far too trusting. Always had been. Too naïve that woman. He stood there for a long while and stared after the old man. Watching him as he fiddled with other people's property.

He's up to something. I know it.

"Nanny, can I have a biscuit?"

Alice looked up from her knitting at her grandson Philip. He was already holding the biscuit tin, in anticipation of her answer.

"Yes. You know I bake them for you."

"Can I take two?" asked the little boy.

From behind his newspaper, Frank grunted. It sounded like a *NO*. Alice ignored him. Their grandson spent the afternoon with them every Friday while his mum went to yoga. Alice looked forward to his visits and always made a batch of his favourite chocolate biscuits.

"Of course," she said with an indulgent smile as the boy lit up with glee. He took two biscuits (or it could have been three?) and ran back outside to play in the yard.

"Be careful," cautioned Alice. "Stay away from the road."

Frank rustled his newspaper, took off his glasses so he could glare at his wife. "You spoil that boy. Feeding him too much. Getting a bit podgy there. isn't he?"

Alice ignored him. Just kept on knitting. Their second daughter was pregnant and Alice was making booties. A different pair for every day of the week.

"Well?" demanded Frank. "Did you hear me?"

"You could try playing with him," suggested Alice. "Throw the rugby ball around. Since you're so concerned about his weight."

Frank went back to his newspaper. No comment. Alice smiled. A secret little smile to herself.

The slam of the door as Philip came running back inside, went straight to a drawer in the kitchen, rummaged around and then headed outside again.

"What did I say about slamming doors ay?!" shouted Frank.

"Sorry Grandad," the boy called back, the sound of his footsteps clattering on the front steps. He didn't sound sorry at all which annoyed Frank immensely.

Quiet in the living room again. Only the soft click clack of knitting needles and the tick tock of the wall clock. Alice liked these times best. The house was clean, a load of laundry was drying on the line, there was a stew for dinner simmering in the slow cooker, her grandson was happy playing in the yard, and she was making rainbow booties with love for grandchild number two.

Contentment.

Frank put his newspaper down. Frowned. "What did the boy get from the kitchen? Huh?"

Alice shrugged. *I don't know.*

"What's he doing out there anyway?" asked Frank. Irritated. "Why do his parents think it's alright to leave him here every week? We already did our part raising our own kids. This is our time to relax. But instead, we have to check on this boy." He huffed a loud huff of annoyance and stood up.

"He's fine Frank," said Alice. "Philip's a good boy."

Frank shook his head. "I'm going outside."

Alice was glad to see him go. Now maybe she could knit in peace. It didn't last long though. A loud shout from the yard startled her.

"Oi, what are you doing? I knew it. Alice, get out here. ALICE!"

Frank was yelling loud enough to disturb the entire street. Alice bundled up her wool and hurried outside. "What on earth is going on?"

There were three people in the front yard. Frank, Philip and the old Samoan man. Frank held his grandson in a tight grip on his shoulder as the little boy struggled to break free. The old man was kneeling on the grass, looking up at the both of them, a look of puzzlement on his face. In his hand he held a pair of scissors.

"Let me go," cried Philip, fierce and indignant. He saw Alice. Appealed to her. "Nanny, I was HELPING."

"I caught him with this," said Frank. He was triumphant as he waved a pair of kitchen scissors at Alice. "Out here with this old bugger. The both of them. Now, I ask you, what's an old man doing with a child, huh? Probably interfering with him ay?" There was a world of meaning in his tone as he looked at Alice knowingly. "I say we call the police."

The little boy protested. "We wasn't doing anyfing bad Nanny."

"Oh yeah? So why did you have scissors then? Why's he got scissors then?" said Frank with a jerk of his head at the old man who still knelt on the lawn.

"That's enough Frank," said Alice. "Let him go." She pulled Philip away from her husband's grip. Soft concern as she inspected him. "Are you alright?"

The boy nodded, breathing heavily, more from frustration than fear. "Yes. But Grandad is scaring my friend."

Alice looked over at the old man who did look afraid. Confused and afraid as he held up his pair of scissors and said, "I cut?" He gesticulated at the lawn. "Grass get long. I cut. See?" Then he bent over and started snipping at the grass.

"See?" said Philip. "Me and Mika, we're trimming the grass. He was doing it with his scissors, so then I got some. But first I shared my cookies with him. Mummy says sharing is good. Isn't it Nanny?"

Alice tugged the boy into a hug of reassurance. Relieved to make sense of the situation. "Of course it is. Your grandad was just confused, that's all." She glared at Frank. "He didn't understand what was going on."

Frank threw his hands up in disbelief. "Confused? I don't think so. Who cuts the grass with scissors? Nobody." He moved to stand in front of Alice and Philip, a shield between them and the old man. Puffed out his chest and talked loud and firm. "Now you listen here mate. You can't go roaming around the neighbourhood with a weapon like that. Coming into people's property. Interfering with little boys. You're a danger to society. A menace."

Alice had had quite enough. She pushed past her husband. "Oh, don't be ridiculous Frank. Nobody's been interfering with anyone. They were trimming the lawn together. That's all." She turned to the old man. "I apologise if my husband frightened you. But really, you don't need to cut our grass. And especially not with scissors."

The man looked up at her, puzzled, even as he nodded his head. Eager to agree. Eager to make peace. He took a yellow packet of chips from his pocket. Already open and half-eaten, he offered some to the group. "Banana chips. Best chips from Samoa. You have some?"

Philip went to take a handful of chips and Frank grabbed him back. "No you don't," he hissed. "Keep away."

The boy was resentful, opened his mouth to protest but Alice spoke first, always the peacemaker in the family. "No thank you, Mee-ka, is it? Do you live around here? I see you walk by every day."

The old man smiled as he sat cross-legged on the lawn and ate a handful of chips. Crunch crunch. Then offered the packet to them again. "Banana chips. Best chips in Samoa. You have some?"

"I told you he's a mental case," said Frank. "We should call the police. Before he flips out and hurts somebody with those scissors."

Alice ignored her husband. Spoke to her grandson instead. "Philip, how did you know his name?"

"It's on his name tag," offered Philip. "See?" To the old man, "Mika, can Nanny see your tag? On your necklace?"

"Yes, yes," said the old man. He stood up, brushing grass from his sweatpants, bobbed his head up and down in a kind of bow at Alice and proudly displayed the card on his lanyard.

Alice read it from a careful distance.

My name is Mika. I have dementia. If I am lost, please call my wife Luama. 021-3745201.

"Oh Frank," said Alice softly as she shook her head at her husband. "He's not well. And there you are shouting at him."

"Told you he's sick in the head," said Frank. Belligerent in his insistence of rightness.

"He shouldn't be roaming around the place. Could hurt somebody."

There was a kind pity on Alice's face as she spoke to the old man. Loud and slow. In case dementia made you hard of hearing.

"DO YOU WANT TO SIT DOWN ON THE VERANDAH? WE WILL CALL YOUR FAMILY TO COME GET YOU. OKAY? DON'T BE AFRAID."

She told Philip to go inside and get the phone for her. Then she called the number on the card.

Frank wasn't happy about the old man sitting on his verandah. In close quarters, Mika smelled like grassy sweat and an undertone of stale urine. Frank's mother smelled a bit like old pee too because she wore a diaper. It always turned Frank's stomach and he wrinkled his nose in distaste at the old man.

Frank didn't like it when Alice brought Mika a glass of cold cordial to drink. Or when Philip sat next to the old man and chattered to him about school and his friends and did Mika play Xbox because it was Philip's favourite thing and he wished his mother would let him play on school days instead of only on weekends and wow that was a super cool tattoo and one day he Philip wanted to get a tattoo too, probably of a robot, or a Spiderman tattoo, and had Mika been to Rainbow's End? Because Philip was going there next week on a school trip, a reward for all the traffic patrol kids and he really wanted to go on the roller coaster but his mum said they wouldn't allow him to because he was too short and that was really stink unfair ay?

Mika just listened to the boy talk, nodding every so often and smiling. He didn't look annoyed in the least about having to listen to a seven-year-old prattle on. Whenever there was a pause in the chatter, Mika offered Philip some chips. "Banana chips. Best chips in Samoa. You have some?"

The two of them shared the packet of chips as everyone waited for Mika's family. Crunch crunch.

It didn't take long for a beat-up old van to pull up in front of their house. It was crammed full. Frank had never seen so many people exit from one van before. It was by far the most islanders that Frank had ever been surrounded by. It didn't feel safe.

The driver, a big man who looked like a younger version of Mika. Not shuffly and frail like the old man, but hefty and with slabs of muscle straining at his shirt sleeves. His wife, carrying a sleeping toddler, she had to waddle up the verandah steps because she was heavily pregnant. Well, Frank hoped it was because she was pregnant. Otherwise, it was because she ate far too much. Like his grandson.

Several teenagers, still in school uniform. Quite sloppy too, thought Frank. Whatever happened to school rules about neatness? Another young man, possibly another of Mika's sons? Covered in tattoos. Definitely a gang member concluded Frank. A little girl in a fluffy Princess dress who ran to hug her grandfather with a squeal of delight. And Luama. Mika's wife. All of them together were a tidal wave of concern and alofa as they surrounded the old man, gently chiding him for his wandering, patting him on the back and joking with loud laughter about his scissors and banana chips. Mika welcomed them to Frank's verandah like it was his and introduced his family to Philip and Alice. While Frank stood back and glowered.

A greying soft woman wearing track pants underneath her long bright floral dress, Luama apologized effusively for her husband. "He like to go for walks," she explained. "First it only one walk around the block, in the mornings. But then he start forgetting he already do his walk, so he going again. And then another walk again. But longer and further to different streets. Most time, he find his way home no problem. Only a few time he getting lost. So that's why we put the ID card on him."

"Papa always worked hard all his life," added the big son with proud affection. "Worked on the rubbish trucks. And on weekends he had a second job in a yard cleaning crew. Even now, although he's sick, he always wants to work. We try to make him stay home and relax. Bought him a new flat screen TV with all the channels and the Netflix. A karaoke machine. A massage chair. But no. He still wants to go outside and work." To his father he said, "A ea Papa? You very busy working all the time, keep all the neighbourhood tidy."

Mika smiled. "Very busy. Take the bins. Pick the rubbish. Weed the garden. Cut the grass."

"You should see our neighbour's gardens," said one of the teenagers. "Papa keeps them all weeded and cuts their grass. Cleans up the rubbish everywhere."

"Yeah, Mama makes us go help him when we get home from school," said the second teen with a wry smile and love in his voice, so you knew it wasn't a complaint. Not really. "Everyone on our street knows Papa and looks out for him."

"I see," said Alice. She was apologetic. "My husband may have startled him a little bit by shouting earlier."

The big son waved her worry away. "'Ae, Papa won't remember. Sure he's forgotten already."

Alice continued, "Frank was just concerned when he saw Mee-ka carrying scissors about. We didn't want him to hurt himself. Or anyone else."

Luama was understanding. "Of course. He is sneaky and take my scissor when we not looking. He used to do the grass with the sapelu…" She stopped and looked to her grandchildren for help, "What do you call it in English?"

"Machete," said one of the teenagers helpfully.

"Ah yes," nodded Luama. "Machete." She pronounced it with an emphasis on the 't' so it sounded like ma-shitty, and the young people snickered. Luama ignored them. She was used to their teasing of her English. "But we worry Mika get hurt, so we hide the ma-shitty. That's why he take the scissor when he going around the places to trim the grass."

"You haven't thought of perhaps getting some help with him?" suggested Alice. "Putting him into a good care facility?"

"A home for the old people?" clarified Luama. Horrified, she shook her head. "Oh no. Why he go for a place like that when we all here to look after him? No. He very happy with us." She turned to her husband. "Okay Mika, we take you home now eh? You finish work?"

Mika nodded. "Yes. Finish work. Go home now." He went and shook Alice's hand, bobbed his head up and down like before. "Fank you." He shook Philip's hand. "Fank you for your help to me with the grass." He went to Frank who didn't want to shake Mika's hand but everyone was looking at him so he had to. "Fank you."

"Oi I nearly forget," said Luama. She snapped at the teenagers in Samoan who immediately went to the van and came back bearing a massive pot that they placed on the verandah table. A strong odour of soy sauce, garlic and ginger wafted along with it.

"Some meaai for you," said Luama. "A mealofa to say fank you."

Alice tried to protest that they didn't need a gift, that the pot of food was far too much for them to eat.

"It's only sapasui. My son was cook it for the dinner and when you calling about Mika, I tell him to grab it and bring for you. If I having more time then I make you some tray of panipopo. Coconut buns very nice. You like. Everybody like panipopo. But since we coming quick, can only bring this sapasui." Then Luama stepped forward and clasped Alice in a hug. It was an embrace that smelled of chop suey, coconut oil and chocolatey koko. It surprised Alice that she found the smell strangely pleasant.

"Fank you for looking after my Mika. I'm worry about him every day. You are a good lady," Luama whispered hoarsely. Alice heard the soft press of tears at the edge of Luama's voice and so she hugged the other woman just as tightly. For some reason she couldn't explain, Alice suddenly wanted to cry.

Frank found it all very disturbing.

The Samoans fitted themselves back inside their van and called out more THANK YOU's as it reversed down the driveway.

Philip had a big grin on his face as he waved to the visitors. "They were nice people Nanny. I hope Mika comes visit again one day."

Alice agreed. But quietly. So her husband wouldn't hear.

Frank watched the van drive away and shook his head. "Bloody islanders. Can't look after their old's properly. They should put that man in a home where he belongs."

Red Flags

By Dahlia Malaeulu

Your nose and toes are so skinny, unruly frizzy hair tamed and straightened, lucky to be born with a natural acceptable tan, normal sized calves even. You're too pretty to be an islander.

You speak so articulately, know so many words you must have been the first educated one in your family. Don't sound or think like an islander at all.

Wow, your name is super long and unique, okay unusual - can I just use your initials? Say mine precisely, I'll remind you each time that you don't, at the end of the day a name is just a label for us humans. And I'm a real humanitarian at heart.

German, French and Chinese blood? Okay I knew you were more than just an islander. Good mix. You should totally start with that.

Take the help on offer. You islanders do get heaps. No judgement here, we've been trying to help you for so long. It must be pretty hard with an overcrowded house, always getting loans for your church donations and twenty-first birthdays - and all that fast food! Now I know you eat with your hands, because you've had such a, broke-village, high cholesterol, tough kind of life.

Honestly, I really didn't even think you worked here, but lucky you aren't lazy like the rest of them. You're so different! Plus I know you will get along with Kalani, are you related? Because you are both from one of those Pacific Island places. And you both stand out. What do you mean you can't swim? I know you weren't born in the islands, but isn't the ocean your thing? Like how Moana in the movie says, it's inside of you. Islanders like to survive. Off the land and stuff, I guess it helps when you're used to living with not much.

You totally must know how to dance and sing. Go to church all the time, even though your dad bets on horses, your mum goes to housie, how do they do it with so many part-time jobs?

Because you know it would be easier if they set themselves the goal of getting full-time factory jobs.

Shhhhh . . .Not so many questions, don't be so difficult, you don't need to fully understand, all you need is to go along to get along. Your people are at the heart of what we do. Welcome to the round white table. No need to share your brown ideas. We've got it sorted. Just agree and smile.

Between me and you, I've actually caught on to your funeral tricks. There's no way someone can have as many aunts, uncles, cousins, grandparents, adopted family members - as actual relations. But if you do, I would recommend becoming an island instead of an islander – I thought that up myself, good one aye? What about when you're too bright and loud? Flower headband thingees and flower necklaces. It's A LOT. We get that it's your culture, but there is a time and a place. Like we fully support one off once a year events. Not before or after. Because it's only fair that we use English. So everyone feels included.

Otherwise it's a bit rude really.

Honestly it's a safe place here. I just don't like having conversations about touchy subjects that make me feel uncomfortable. It's just the way of the world. Why I should put time and energy into learning more about you when it won't benefit me? Look, life is hard for everyone.

We are totally equal, have the same opportunities. No need for the race card to be played here because I don't see colour at all, meaning I don't really see you for you. You are kind of better off as one of us, and I am not a racist. My sister is married to an islander. I'm sorry for my ancestors, especially for those Dawn Raids. I had nothing to do with any of it. It's so sad that your islands are sinking. There's nothing we can do really, probably best for you to get over it because you really don't know how lucky you are.

To call New Zealand (not Aotearoa)

Home.

HAIR

By Nadine Anne Hura

I found a clump of hair on the bathroom floor. I leaned down to have a closer look. It definitely wasn't mine. I'd remember if I'd cut my own hair. I picked up the strands and held them to the light. Too straight to be pubic hair, too fine to be the contents of a hair brush. I risked a tentative sniff. Nothing. No tell-tale scent.

I stormed into the lounge.

"Who's been cutting their hair in the bathroom!"

Denial from all quarters. Nana, watching TV and knitting, didn't look up. I eyed her suspiciously.

"Mum, you asked for scissors the other day, what did you use them for?"

Nana held up her knitting needles. "It w...aasn't me!"

I turned to the boys. They shook their heads, smoothing slick hairstyles down with practiced fingers. It couldn't have been them. They were too vain to cut their own hair.

I was still troubled when I got into bed that night. Could a burglar have broken in?

Unlikely - nothing was missing. Anyway, why would someone break into the house, take nothing, and give themselves a haircut?

I fell into a fitful sleep, dreaming my hair was falling out in thick, bouncy fistfuls, like the stuffing used in hobby-craft projects. I woke in a cold sweat and googled 'what it means when you dream your hair is falling out.'

Face aglow in a harsh blue light, I read the unwelcome explanation:

"Hair loss in dreams signifies the loss of sexual virility, seduction, sensuality, vanity, and health."

Fuck the internet. I lay back in the dark, thinking and thinking. Just another sleepless night. Chalk it up. Who needs sleep, anyway?

I wondered if it was time to shave my head. God knows, I've considered it often enough. What is hair but a crown of vanity? A lifetime of creams and oils and sprays and scars from hair irons, and underneath it all you're still the same person you started with.

It made me think of the make-up artist that came to the house on the night of the sixth form ball. I was the last of my friends to sit down, blushing when I took my seat in front of the mirror. "Gosh," the make-up artist said, blotting my face with milky foundation. "You're exotic-looking, aren't you? What have you got in you?"

I didn't know how to answer. I thought of my father, whose dimples I inherited even though I only saw him from a distance when he came to collect my brothers. And I thought of my mother, whose green eyes matched mine.

I looked at my reflection in the mirror and tried to see beneath my pale skin and masses of thick, frizzy hair.

"I'm a half-caste," I said to the make-up lady.

"Ahaa!" she said, as if accepting an apology. "Well, let's see if we can give you a cupid's bow anyway, shall we?"

The cat began sinking and prising its claws on and off my chest. I pushed it off with a thud, imagining it was my ex. He always joked that the hardest thing about living with me was sharing a bathroom. He used to say that if I ever left him, he wouldn't miss my hair clogging the plug holes.

"That'll teach you for testing fate," I hissed to the cat. "Clean plug holes aren't all they're cracked up to be."

Then again, I thought, turning over to watch the moon beyond the window, maybe the solution was to love my natural hair. It sounded radical, like the applied version of decolonisation theory. I thought of the prick of the needle the first time I received tāmoko. I'd blabbered incessantly while the artist worked, but of all the things I said, I omitted the one closest to my chest:

I wanted tāmoko to make visible externally what I had always hidden inside me. A tāmoko, I believed, would let everyone know - without doubt, without shame - who I was.

At that precise moment, my hair, which occasionally presented with a personality and a voice, erupted in laughter. 'Bro, stop burning the shit out of me with a flat iron and wear me free! One look at these wild curls and everyone will know what we've got inside us!'

I felt like I was approaching a great revelation, but I was too tired to make the necessary connections and I fell asleep, dreaming of a drain choked with sixteen years of hair, and make-up artists dressed as paramedics.

When I woke I felt better. I opened the curtains and saw that the sun had risen on a new day and this knowledge filled me with comfort. I yawned, stretched, then went into the bathroom.

There, on the floor at my feet, was a fresh clump of hair.

'For fuck's sake!' I yelled. 'Who's been cutting their hair in the bathroom?'

MANUMEA

By Lily-ann Eteuati

Parents are always right. They know best. Always. Especially the Samoan ones. I would know because mine are. The typical, ancient, kua back ones. They know everything, I tell you. Everything! And we cling to their every word the way fat inquisitive beads of sweat cling to our backs, sliding slowly down, refusing to fall off our skin unless wiped or shaken off as we labour the family plantation.

Tama said it is the fruit of their parents' hard labour, and their parents' parents. And so on and on and on. We were to be thankful to them, and thankful we were. I seemed to show the most gratitude of all my eight siblings. There is only one way to do that.

Saying thank you is meaningless.

I work, and work and work. I show the most gratitude by doing three times more than the others. Ou ke le komumu. I don't complain. Ever. Because I'm the quiet one. I carry feau and blame willingly.

That is how you show love.

I do it willingly. I do it with a heart like a manumea, wild and free.

Truly. Until I wasn't, and my whole existence was suddenly just an empty shell in the middle of the moana sausau, slowly but surely sinking into the abyss.

"You kids sleep too damn much! La'a uma le aso kou pogaua! Paie!"

Ah. The sweet, sweet sound of our beloved Tina. We did not need a Koa to wake us. We do not need a Digicel phone to beeeeeeep at us, like Falole had, courtesy of her older brother who went as a seasonal worker overseas. We don't even have the money to pay for the cash power to charge a phone. And anyway, we have our very own talking, walking alarm. Cost you nothing except maybe a couple of eardrums. And a few salulima marks if you're not as fast as Koko, the stray dog that has claimed our umukuka out back as his scavenging terrain.

Koko too has also been a victim of Tina's morning wrath. Not anymore though. At some point he started syncing his barking with Tina's morning tirade. And Tina wouldn't mind him anymore. It's as if they discovered that their agaga was aligned. Either that or they agreed that they weren't the problem, it was really us...the paie kids. And by kids, she really only means me. Because everyone knows the four younger ones are her favourites, and the four older ones she's up on.

I always considered myself quite special. My fall from grace has been spectacular. Having come from gentle, grateful goodie-two-seevae-kosokoso to disgraceful, disobedient and defiant daring. Out of the blue. Or so they say.

Everyone loves a mystery. Why did it happen? How did it happen? And so they talk, talk, talk about me. I'm unbothered when I hear the whisperings of the village, telling their versions of why and how one changes drastically overnight. They do not notice me walk by on the side of the road as they sink deep in their own concoctions of lies and lies and more lies under the ulu tree. Completely neglecting their own daughters to the preying eyes of the men drinking and whistling from across the road. Every evening there is a new version of my life. And even I've gotten invested and look forward to hearing the updates. Nicely mixed until colourful and so very shocking.

"Maleka! Maleka?!" Round two. Salulima round. Tina's bellowing whooshes up the ie, hung up as a curtain to make something of a room. I spring up from the fala laupapa that is my bed, having no feeling in my back. For once I'm grateful for the concrete floor and its numbing effect. It saves me stings and marks from the long, freshly shaven 'ie'ie trussed kuagius of a salulima that has become Tina's extra limb. Because that's what makes contact as I make a run for and jump the wooden puipui of the fale, a few seconds too slow.

The tips of the salulima may be soft, but Tina's whips are a force to be reckoned with. Especially these ones specifically for me. The first swing catches me mid-air as I fly over the low wooden puipui and I fall flat on my face. I lie there my rough cheek against the rough ground. Skin beat by the merciless sun has become tough. The taste of blood is in my mouth.

"O le sasa o le alofa," she says, and swings the salulima onto my back

My back is no longer numb. I feel the first sting of the obedient kuagius. Obedient, unlike me.

"Aia!" I finally shriek as I flail off the ma'ama'a but only to give Tina another side of my stubborn thick taugauli skin to fasi.

I fight the urge to dodge a hit. It would just enrage her further and she would almost certainly upgrade from salulima to the pole leaning against the mango tree. That's an unwritten and unspoken law. Dodge a hit, earn another. I stay as still as I can and do not make a noise while she shrieks. In all honesty, it doesn't hurt as much now. The subconscious squirming is just habitual after years of this exact routine.

As soon as Tina is satisfied with her hits and turns to walk away, I stand up to dust myself off and wipe the dripping blood from the corner of my mouth. I let out a sigh of absolute le salamo and I almost regret it. She definitely took that as kaufa'alili. Her head whips back at me with a look letting me know that today might finally be the day I meet Jesus.

I stumble backwards as she flips the salu over so that the hard handle is pointed at me. But before she's close enough to swing at my face, a taxi pulls over just in front of Tina's pa aute and she instantly turns her head to look. In case it's an unexpected guest that she needs to appear nice for. I turn also to look with hopes of a saviour emerging out of the vehicle. It's Tama.

"O lea foi laga mea ua fai?" I hear Tama ask Tina what I have done. Because, of course, I must have done something with my le fiu le usika'i amio. Always the problem, always asking for more hidings. I stay standing there. Not exactly sure why though. I usually walk off and let them exchange the usual list of how I've been such a pain in their muli.

"Ma'imau alofa!" she sobs about their wasted love. I feel an unfamiliar tug at my heart for a second. Before I'm reminded of my still bleeding mouth.

"E fasi aku, ae pei fa'alili mai! Ua le koe iloa se makua. She no longer even knows her own parents," she says in between sobs.

My shoulders slump and I turn to walk away. Tama notices and calls, ""Mareta. Faasaga mai."

"What happened to you? Se'i e fai mai sa'o po'o lea le mea ua fa'apea ai lou olaga?" he questions. And is that a hint of…pleading in his voice? I feel hope creeping up.

"If you no longer want to listen to us or do any good for this family, alu ese loa la ma igei. Get out!" he says.

I turn around and face him and really truly look him in the eyes. For the first time I really look at my father's face. Rough skin with hard eyes and nostrils that flare slightly. I look a lot like him.

"Mareta, Kali mai lou gutu," he demands that I use my mouth to answer.

I think of Tina and Koko. Koko, too, has been a victim of Tina's morning wrath. Not anymore though. At some point he started syncing his barking with Tina's morning tirade.

And Tina wouldn't mind him anymore.

"E le o a'u se maile!" I say.

I bring my little finger to my mouth. I bite from the first joint. Clean through. I spit the bloody joint at their feet. I do it willingly.

I do it with a heart like a manumea, wild and free.

O SE MEAALOFA TAUTELE

By Niusila Faamanatu-Eteuati

O la'u tifa i le atuvasa

E iloga lona 'i'ila mai

E taomia e 'amu, figota, ma'a ma otaota

O le loloto o le moana ma le souā o peau laga

O afā, timuga, lōlōga, mafui'e

E lūlūina ai le 'ele'ele ma lōfia vaiālia

E solo ai mauga ma fa'avae papa

E ogotia i le la, ma magumagu pei se mutia

Ae le punitia e le loulouā ma le loloto

E gagana mai e i'a ma lā'au

Taili mai e le matāmatagi ma le vaito'elau

Momoli mai e le faata'uta'u o afa fulifaō i le laumua

Le ausa o au talosaga

E le muta ou faiva mau

O le fanaafi o afi mo mālama

Auā mātua, 'āiga, aulotu

Tamateine, tamatane, tausala

Fanau a fanau, fanau a fanau a fanau

O le va'atu'umatagi o le ola

E so'oina le atuloaloa o le vasa

Mea manū oe sa e tu i matagi'olo

Po o penei e le faitauina ni o matou aso

Faafetai tina o oe o se meaalofa tautele!

- Dedicated to my mum Kueni Tuao'i Ianeta Asiata Iakopo – Utuga Famanatu Faaaliga on her 80th birthday.

Nanaʻue

By Lehua Parker

Maiden
Kinohi Loa

In the murky, silver-coined depths of the reef, the lesser ocean god Kamohoʻaliʻi lurked. In the shape of an octopus or curl of a wave, he watched for a decade, waiting for lelekawa, that moment each day when I fearless leapt from the rocky shore of Kuiopili on the island of Hawaiʻi and sliced deep into the ocean, splashless and perfect.

It took him a year from our marriage to confess his ten year obsession. He told me I'd caught his eye when I was still slender as pili grass, slipping eel-like through the currents and swimming circles around my cousins. Admiring the bold way I trapped sunlight in my lungs diving for conch and lobster, he waited for me to grow round in hip and strong of limb.

The young are fearless. The aged know better.

But looking back, I couldn't have known that the rogue wave that swept me off the bluff and into the sea a year ago was sent by the handsome stranger who rescued me, Kamohoʻaliʻi himself.

Safe again on shore, I collapsed, heaving. Forehead against the sand, water gushed from my nose as I coughed the sea from my lungs. My long hair clung to my face and body like jellyfish tentacles.

Ugly, but alive.

Blinking away the salt, when I turned my head the first thing I noticed was the shape of his instep, how it curved to his ankle, the pale under-sole stark against the darkness of his skin. I followed his leg all the way to his face where the sunlight framed a halo around his head.

"What is your name, woman?" he asked, his voice resonating like the downbeat of a pa'u drum.

"Kalei," I stammered.

"Kalei." He smiled. "You will be my wife."

My sister rushed to my side. "Kalei! Are you all right?" As her hands searched for bruises, our cousins ringed close.

"I'm fine," I choked. "Thanks to—"

But he was gone.

When the moon turned, it brought both the Makahiki season and the stranger to our village. Head raised, he approached our chief with a basket of ulua so fresh that the gills still fluttered.

Charmed, Chief Palinui welcomed him to our celebration. Each night for a month the stranger returned bearing gifts from the sea and easily won every competition, dazzling us with his skill at wrestling, spear throwing, and konane. A master of riddles and puns, he also enthralled us with stories of great ocean voyages and ancient battles.

Each morning, as dawn streaked palest pink on the horizon, he would beg Palinui's permission to leave. Once granted, he hopped into his weathered canoe with its threadbare sail and disappeared over the horizon. Each morning Palinui's permission to leave came more reluctantly.

All Makahiki he never spoke to me, but I felt his eyes caressing my shoulders, hips, and thighs, the heat of his gaze hotter than Pele's fires. His return during sunset was the reason I lost count in the oli and faltered in my dance, and the reason I was beaten by the kumu hula for dishonoring the gods.

While Mother hid her face in shame, the stranger only laughed, saying, "Nothing so beautiful could ever be offensive."

Annoyed, the kumu hula again raised the bamboo switch, but Father said mildly, "It's only practice, Kumu. Tomorrow at the ceremony her hula will be a perfect offering to the gods."

"There can be no mistakes," the kumu hula growled. "The eyes of the gods are everywhere. Offended gods spare no one."

"I will watch," said the stranger, "and when it is perfect, we will marry."

Before Father could answer, Palinui shouted, "Hoʻomaikaʻi! Our village needs strong and clever men."

With the barest shake of his head, Father stopped Palinui from giving me to the stranger right then and there. "But we must not presume," the chief said.

Father stepped forward. "During Makahiki you proved yourself a worthy competitor, but my daughter requires more than someone who can throw a spear or answer a riddle. What do you offer?"

The stranger held out his arms. "All that I have is hers."

My uncles chuckled and nudged each other. Uncle Lohe whispered, "A battered canoe, an empty fish basket, and the malo around his waist. Our Kalei will have everything!"

A warm body next to mine, I thought. *Rain and lehua blossoms.*

"Especially if she wants to wrestle." More stifled laughter.

"No land, no people, no way," muttered Uncle Pono.

Father tilted his head and crossed his arms to shush the village. Mother placed her hand on my shoulder. *This is what's real,* her touch said. *Our family always protects its own.*

Softer than a feather cloak, Mother's words enveloped me. "You hold out your arms and say that all you have is hers, but I see nothing that will fill the bellies of my daughter or her children," she said to the stranger.

"Food? Is that what concerns you? Food is nothing," the stranger said, turning to the sea. "Fish," he called. "Come."

The surface of the sea roiled like lava in Halemaʻumaʻu crater as an ahi leaped like a dolphin from beyond the reef to the shore. We stood transfixed as the great fish flopped against the sand, his scales shimmering in the twilight as he pushed himself ever closer to the stranger.

Cousin Alama raced to sink his dagger deep into the fish's eye. "Uncle!" he called, "This ahi is as big as four men!"

Palinui said, "Surely such a fisherman will keep his family and village fed!"

Father drew breath to speak, but Palinui didn't pause. "If you agree, my wedding gift will be the portion of land that juts into the sea and a newly planted taro field. In exchange for this fish, the village will build a hale for you and your bride."

"I thank you for your offer," said the stranger. "Be sure to carve a fine fatty slice of the belly for yourself, my chief."

"You will be one of us?"

"When Kalei offers her perfect hula to the gods, I will marry her and live among you."

My stomach trembled. Fear and excitement are much the same.

"As you speak, let the gods hear," said Palinui.

Father took one look at the village's joy in the fish and closed his mouth. Later, when he walked me to the women's sleeping house, he said, "This is unusual."

"He is very sure of himself," I said.

"If you are opposed—"

"He is handsome. And capable." I wrapped my long hair into a bun and tied it on top of my head.

"You want him?"

"There is something exciting between us," I said.

"I know. The whole village knows. I just wish—"

"You worry that he is a stranger. We don't know his people."

Father stopped before the hale door. "Exactly. Chief Palinui wants him, but he isn't the one marrying him. He just thinks of fish, Kalei. Palinui believes if the stranger marries you, when famine roams, it will never call our people home."

"And you don't?"

"He came from the ocean during Makahiki. What's to stop his return?"

"Love," I said.

My father nodded. "I hope that will be enough." He hugged me tight. "Think about it. If you are unsure—at all—do not dance perfectly tomorrow."

"Father!"

"I mean it."

"The gods—"

"Will understand," he said, brushing his lips against my forehead. "Sleep on it."

The next night I stood in the torch light, the line of my neck graceful as a palm tree, my arms reaching out to the sea in the form of Hiki'aka calling her lover home.

With the last 'uwehe, my ti leaf skirt slowed and came to rest against my thighs. Heart pounding as the oli faded into the darkness, I slipped to my knees and kept my eyes to the lauhala mat.

Chief Palinui stood. "It is done."

"Perfectly," sighed the kumu hula.

"Come, Wife," said the stranger, taking my hand and bringing me to my feet.

I didn't dare meet his eyes. "What is your name?" I whispered.

He paused. "Call me Nalukai."

Startled, I looked up. His brown face was unlined, as smooth and as perfect as water in a calabash bowl. *Nalukai? Ocean Wave is an odd name for one so young.*

When I look back at that moment, I cry. Nalukai wasn't an ocean wave; he was a tsunami.

A year later, I was round as breadfruit with his child when he finally told me. I knew something was odd in the way he arose every day from our sleeping mats, flinging off the kapa sheets just before dawn, and disappearing in his canoe until sunset. He always returned with fresh fish, 'opihi, or sea urchins—as Palinui hoped—his nets so full, he fed the entire village.

As the baby turned in my ōpū, Nalukai returned one evening carrying great armfuls of crisp green limu harvested from the reef, salty-cold and tasting of the wild sea.

But with our child nearly here, the honeymoon was over.

"Kalei, my love, I have to leave you," Nalukai said.

"Oh? Does Father need you? Is the taro ready for the imu?"

"Put your weaving down, Kalei. My father needs me, not yours. I've tarried too long."

"We're going to your family? That's wonderful!" I looked at my baskets of half-finished kapa and lauhala leaves, twists of coconut husks and kukui nuts, hoping that I had enough time to create fine gifts for his parents. "When do we leave?"

He placed his hands along my cheeks and tilted his head down to mine. Foreheads touching, we honi, our breath mingling and becoming one in our lungs. "Forgive me," Nalukai whispered. "I didn't mean to love you."

"Nalukai, you're such a tease. How many canoes are we taking?" I trailed a finger down this arm. "We can't leave until I make lei and pack gifts of poi and salt. Does your mother prefer roasted crabs or dried ʻopae? Oh! Just think of her excitement at our baby."

He smiled, but it didn't quite reach his eyes. "Our baby." He caressed my belly, and I felt it kick, strong and sure against his palm. "Kalei, I have a confession. Nalukai is only one of my names. My parents call me Kamohoʻaliʻi."

I slapped at him, no more serious than a child. "Oh, Nalukai! If you want to role play, fine. Call me Hikiʻaka, and I will dance—"

He caught my wrists and held them to his chest. "Kalei. Look at me."

I thought of the fish, of his leaving and returning, of his confidence and ease with the chief, and his casual conversations about gods and their pleasures. The space behind my heart burned. I shook my head.

"Kalei." The voice of a god. I had to obey.

In that moment I thought I understood what I had lost, but no one can imagine Milu's pit who has not fallen in, and I wasn't even close to the underworld.

Not yet.

"No," I pleaded.

"Our child will be different."

"No."

"He will be dual-natured. Like me, he will be able to change his form. He will be a shark who walks on land. You will have to protect him."

I tried to pull my hands away, but Nalukai held them tight. I raised my shoulders to block my ears from the awful truth, but like all gods, he was relentless.

"Hear me, Kalei. Our child will incite fear and jealousy. The chief will see him as a weapon. The priests will want him for their temples. Others will kill him simply for being different."

Deep in my womb our child rolled, stretching like an octopus until I thought my skin would split, spilling him out into the world in a sea-tide of blood and water.

I shuddered and held my breath until the pain passed. "Nalukai, our child comes."

He tipped my chin so our eyes met. "To keep him and the others safe, you must never feed him meat—none of any kind. Only taro, banana, and sweet potatoes—things rooted in the land. You must teach him to be humble. Your lives depend on it."

"Our lives? But you'll—"

He shook his head and raised my captured hands to his lips. Gently, he blew on my knuckles, his cool breath shattering me like stones. "No. The only way our child lives is if I return to my father, the great ocean god Kanaloa. It must be now, before the child is born. A child such as this is forbidden by kapu. If I know of his existence, I must kill him."

I bit my lip, but the word slipped out bitter as 'awa. "Why?"

"Why?" he mocked. "Why? Because. That's all you need to know."

"The great Kanaloa decreed." I snatched my hands from his and pulled them to my hair, working swiftly to unbind turtle shell combs and cowry shells. Nalukai watched with hooded eyes. "What you haven't said is that Kanaloa's kapu means death for you, *Nalukai,* if you fail to carry it out. It's your life or our child's."

He sat back. "You love me that much? You'd rather I killed our child than leave?"

I shook my head; combs tumbled to my lap as hair fell like water across my face. "Your leaving on the eve of our child's birth will have the village gossips whispering. Is that what you want?"

He sighed, and his god's breath shook the hale. "The choice is yours, Kalei," he said. "I stay and slaughter all our children as they come. Or—"

Freed at last from a wife's knots, my hair cascaded down my back, brushing the floor like a maiden's. "Go," I said, dropping the hibiscus flowers I'd worn over my left ear into his lap.

He brought the love token to his face, rasping delicate petals against his chin before tossing them one by one into the fire. The flames flared as they ignited, the taste of hibiscus ashes thick in the smoke. He stood. "I watched you," he said, "for a decade in the sea. I waited because I loved you."

"No," I said, watching the last petal curl and blacken. "You really didn't."

I never saw him again.

Sometimes in my darkest hours I wish that I had chosen differently. The aged know what the innocent cannot.

Grandfather

Hānau

Swaddled and oiled clean, my daughter Kalei held her newborn son to her breast. "No," she said.

"Kalei," said her mother, my wife.

"No."

"Kalei," I said. "You know he doesn't belong to us. Look at his back. He belongs to the gods."

"The gods?" Her face twisted in the candlelight. "The gods gave him to me. He's mine."

Her mother touched Kalei's brow. "No fever," she said. "That's good." She lifted Kalei's wild hair away from her face and ran her fingers through it, smoothing the snarls and pulling bits of rubbish from the strands. The fire snaps as my wife hummed, working her way down to the ragged ends. "Shall I braid it for you?" she asked.

"Leave it," Kalei said. "I'll never bind my hair again."

"The baby," I said, reaching for him. "Give him to me. It's time."

"This is his father's responsibility," Kalei said.

"She's right," said her mother. "Nalukai should be the one to do it."

I sigh. "His father isn't here. As the grandfather the kuleana falls to me. You know the law."

Kalei turned the baby in her lap and laid his stomach against her knee. She lifted away the swaddling to expose his back. "Look how tiny it is. It's less than the length of my little finger."

"He'll be crippled. Weak. The village cannot bear this burden."

"He grows strong. His appetite is good."

I shake my head. "An open wound in his back will fester."

"It doesn't bleed," she said. "I think it will heal."

"It's a lifetime of pain and suffering. Is that what you want?"

"Let me try," Kalei begged. "I will keep it covered."

"How?"

"He'll wear a cape."

"The villagers—"

"We'll tell them he has his father's kapu—a kapu that requires his back and shoulders to be hidden from the sun."

"Chiefs have kapu. Is that why Nalukai left during the day?"

"Yes."

My daughter raised the baby to her shoulder and rocked him. She smoothed the swaddling over and over, but didn't look at me. This is how I knew she was lying.

She said, "I'll rub his skin with coconut oil and bathe him at night in the sea. No one will ever know."

"People always find out."

"But by then he won't be a sickly infant. He'll be strong. I will call him Nanaʻue. He'll be a fisherman like his father."

I frown. "You don't name a child who is about to be returned to the gods."

"Naming is also a responsibility of the father," said my wife.

"He is mine." This time she met my eyes. "I decide."

"Where is his father?"

Kalei shrugged. "Somewhere at sea."

Grandfather
Paʻi Punahele

Five years later, my daughter Kalei stood outside the men's eating hale, holding Nanaʻue's hand.

I reach for Nanaʻue. "It's time," I say.

Nanaʻue's father should be here to greet him as he moves from the eating house of women and babies to the world of men. He should be the one to bring him to his place on the lauhala mat. He should be the one to slip him the choicest bits from the platters and calabashes, but the kuleana again falls to me as Nanaʻue's grandfather.

Inwardly, I sigh. Nanaʻue was a pale and spindly child, barely able to carry two coconuts. Damaged. The gods gave us laws for a reason. I should've returned him to the sea.

Kalei bent to adjust the bottom of Nana'ue's kapa cape. "You remember the rules?" she asked him.

Nana'ue nodded. "Taro and bananas. Sweet potatoes and luau leaves. Breadfruit, bananas, and coconut."

"No meat. Ever."

"Yes, Mama."

In the men's eating hale, for a skinny and sickly child, Nana'ue was ravenous. Next to me on the lauhala mat he ate all the bananas and more than a chief's share of poi.

"What's that?" he asked, pointing the succulent and glistening platter.

"Roast pig," I said.

"Meat." His face fell.

My brother Lohe picked at a fish bone. "Eh, Nana'ue, why so sad?" he asked.

"My mother says I must not eat meat."

"That's not meat, it's pork," Lohe teased. "Food of the gods. Women can't eat pork. Men can."

"I can't," Nana'ue said.

"You're with the men now, right?" Lohe said. "Men eat meat." He handed him a rib; the succulent flesh shiny with fat.

Nana'ue looked at me. I couldn't fail him again.

"Eat it," I said.

I watched as my grandson eats like a man and grows big and strong.

Mother
'Ōpio

One day Nana'ue brought a massive koa log from the rainforest down to the shore. "I am making a canoe," he said. "Father had his own canoe."

My eyes swept my son from feet to head. *How tall he is and strong,* I thought. "And you are very like your father," I said.

Nana'ue's smile blinded the sun.

All morning he worked, carving a deep groove down the length of the log. When it was ready, he built a fire and tucked coals into the groove. Each time he bent to add more coals, his cape slipped.

"Oh, this stupid thing!" he said, flinging it away.

"Nanaʻue!"

"I know. Just give me a minute."

"What happened to your back?"

"What?" He looked over his shoulder, twisting this way and that.

"Stand still." I knelt and examined the slit along his spine. *Was it bigger? And what were those boney ridges along the edges?* I ran a finger along them.

Nanaʻue laughed. "That tickles!"

"You felt that?"

"Yes. It makes my mouth tingle!"

"Nanaʻue, have you eaten—"

"Yes! But I'm starving. Do you have any breadfruit?"

"You're hungry?"

"All the time. Let's eat, Mother."

"I don't—"

He swung his cape over his shoulders and turned to face me. "It's all right. Once I have my canoe, I'll never be hungry again."

Whistling, he sharpened his adze.

Grandfather
Uʻi

I was heating stones for the imu in the cooking shed when Lohe hurries over. "Have you seen ʻAma?" he asked

"He went fishing with the boys."

"They're back, but he's not with them. They said ʻAma headed down to Kuiopili to dive for lobster. I was hoping he'd brought his catch to you for the imu."

"I haven't seen him." We looked toward the point just in time to see Nanaʻue paddling his canoe to shore. "Nanaʻue! Where have you been?"

"Near Kuiopili. I was diving for lobster." He held up two fine fat ones, their claws waving angrily in the air.

"Did you see ʻAma?" Lohe asked.

Nana'ue shook his head. "No."

"He wasn't there?"

"No. I was alone." Nana'ue beached his canoe, dragging it above the tide line. He moved slowly, as if in great pain. His ʻōpū was distended, and when he brought me the lobsters, I saw that his neck was bruised and swollen.

"Are you okay?" Lohe asked.

"Yeah. Just a little tired," he said.

Nana'ue handed me two full baskets, more than enough lobster to feed the village. "For the evening meal," he said.

"That much diving is hard work. You must be hungry." I broke two bananas from the stalk hanging in the cooking shed.

"No, thank you," Nana'ue said.

"What? Since when do you pass up bananas?"

"I think I'm going to lie down for awhile."

"You better. You must be sick if you're not hungry!" Lohe teased.

"My stomach hurts. I think it's something I ate."

"Go rest," I said. "But if you see your cousin 'Ama, tell him his father is looking for him."

Nana'ue burped. "Okay," he said, walking along the path to the men's sleeping hale.

Mother
'Ike

'Ama.

Mahi.

Nalani.

Ehu.

Nohea.

Five children swallowed whole by the ocean in a single year. No one dared to fish or swim or even comb the reef. No one except Nana'ue. Without the fish he caught in his canoe, hunger would've stalked the village when the taro crop failed.

"It's a shark," said Uncle Helewa. "And a big one."

140

Father shook his head. "A shark doesn't hunt like this."

"Nana'ue," said Chief Palinui, "what do you think?"

I watched my son sit taller when the chief addressed him. *He's so big and strong,* I thought. *He's a man grown. He's settled. He knows who he is. He's not so anxious all the time.*

"I agree with my grandfather. It's not a shark. We would've seen signs—my fish traps would've been empty or a hooked ahi would've come up half-eaten. I've seen nothing that hints to a big shark in the area."

"No seals have washed ashore with bite marks. The dolphins still settle each night in the bay," said Father.

Uncle Pono raised his chin. "Were they stolen, perhaps? Is some village kidnapping our children for offerings or slaves?"

The priest shook his head. "All of our neighbors are our friends. They are family. They are as concerned as we are."

"But no children are missing from their villages," said Chief Palinui.

"That we know of," said Uncle Lohe.

"Maybe someone should visit them," said Nana'ue. "Learn about their children. Get to know them better. See what they may be hiding."

"Yes," said Chief Palinui. "That's a good idea, Nana'ue. Priest? What say you?"

"It's a sound idea. It's always easier to trust those with whom you've shared meat and poi."

"We must keep the villages united against this threat," said Uncle Helewa.

Chief Palinui stood. "It is decided, then. Nana'ue and 'Umi, you'll leave tomorrow. Nana'ue, travel to the east; 'Umi, to the west. Ask questions, but be gracious. We don't want to provoke a war with baseless accusations. I know you can do this."

Nana'ue beamed.

Grown. And how like his father he is. Full of aloha and pride, I reached out and placed my hand on his back.

Through the cape I felt it.

The sharp edge of a shark's tooth.

Nana'ue reached back and captured my hand, squeezing it tight. "Just think, Mother," he said, torchlight dancing along his skin, "There will be so many new people. So much poi and meat."

ROLLER COASTER

By Gina Cole

Moana faces the accused. A white flash whizzes past the courthouse windows, diverting her attention. A roller coaster train carrying screaming riders, their arms flung high with careless freedom. Always at the judge's back, muffled roller coaster carriages holding muted shrieking people.

'Hemi didn't rob the dairy. You did, didn't you?' says Moana.

The roller coaster framework twists and turns in bright summer light, awaiting his lies.

Moana remembers taking her infant nephew to the amusement park next to the courthouse one summer. Made the mistake of taking him on the underground mineshaft train. Fun for adults, but not for toddlers. How could she have made such a misjudged decision? The train rocked and bucked and threw them around in dark tunnels. She will never forget his terrified face. She spent the whole ride in a state of emergency. Holding onto him tightly, his small head knocking into her ribcage at every sharp turn. He stepped off the train clutching her hand, lips parted, dazed eyes questioning her. She thanked God he'd survived. Took him to the children's section, to the more sedate crocodile train snaking around in an easy loop at ground level with other infants onboard. She hoped to replace his terrifying experience in the mineshaft train with safe crocodile ride memories.

The accused shifts in his seat, lies under oath, offers a constructed alibi through quivering lips. Tries to deliver his hollow fabrication with an air of truth.

'I wasn't there. Went to the cemetery, visited mum's grave. Ask the homeless woman at the gate.'

'The homeless woman saw you the next day. There's camera footage,' says Moana.

The accused squirms in the witness box, grips the wooden rail in front of him, his alibi crumbling. The judge inhales, looks at her papers, writes a note, struggles to keep her hands down.

Silent roller coaster wagons fly past the courtroom windows. The passengers ride high beyond the courthouse, holding on, yelling in utter horror. The judge sits beneath the Queen, blind to the amusement park at her back. Moana stands tall before everyone; the roller coaster riders, the sombre judge, the pasty lying accused. All seated, all throwing their hands in the air.

Searching the Heart

By Sylvia Nakachi

Dad was striding ahead along the dirt road, as we headed towards the direction of Beizam village, the main location for the people who belong to the shark clan. They represent the sharks found in the water's zone. These sharks are their totems and their augud, the god of their worship and belief. In our Island of Zau, it is told that the ancient zogo le of the Beizam clan surfaces or appears to his clan members on their outings on the seas. Aule Beizam is told to be larger than a normal shark. His skin is said to be darker than normal, with huge black human-like eyes as he swims near his people, making his presence known; that he is always watching and protecting them.

While I paced behind Dad, I was admiring all the huge rocks that laid on each side of the road, so perfect and neat as they stood like warriors on such a thin and narrow dirt road. I wondered who had the job of placing these huge heavy grey rocks that paved the way for our direction?

Dad still didn't say a word. Walking behind him seemed enough to reassure him that I was with him. As we drew near to Beizam, I began to get curious, as I realized that there was no person, young or old, in sight.

'How strange,' I thought.

All the huts stood a good distance from each other, but still there was no movement or noise. Then up ahead I saw a man signaling to my Dad. We made haste and came near to where the man stood, in front of a hut, much larger than

145

the others in Beizam. The man in front of the door was very tall. He had thick broad shoulders, and the sun's heat caused sweat to be pouring down from his face and arms. His hair was short and tuff. He had a strong jaw line and piercing dark eyes. In a humble manner, he embraced my father, then without a word, he moved the coconut mesh for us to enter.

In the hut, the intensity of the heat greeted me. It was stuffy and dark. No sunlight. No fire. I ran my eyes around the dome shaped hut, made of neatly woven grass. At the center of the hut roof, was a very tiny hole that someone had made for the sun to come through, the size of a cuttlefish bone.

I strained my eyes and tried to focus beyond the edge of the dimness. I saw shadowy figures of the men from Beizam village, big and small, all sitting in the formation of the hut. My feet could feel the texture of island mats, the smell of musky pandanus leaves floated through the air. These mats were freshly made and were brand new, indicating the importance of the occasion. The atmosphere was still and quiet.

Sweat slowly dripped from my forehead and down the sides of both arms. A soft voice spoke.

"Come in child."

That surely was not my Dad's voice.

"Warem come in and babbook, Ara's boy come, come my warem and sit with me," said that voice again.

A shiver ran through my body from that voice. Being our traditional custom and showing great respect in front of any adults, I humbly lowered myself, as I bent my back forward to walk towards my dad. He was sitting cross-legged, beside a fragile old man, laying on his own mat. Both of the old man's hands were clasped together on his bony chest. His head rested on a small mat that was rolled up to be his head rest. The old man's body looked very weak, like a helpless turtle ready to be slaughtered,

"Sit down," instructed my Dad.

I immediately squatted next to dad and crossed my legs. Sitting down, my view of the old man was much clearer. His wrinkled face and shimmering white silver hair of wisdom looked still, and his breathing was faint. His chest moved slowly and it seemed like a very long time for his rib cage to move in the up and down motion.

His eyes slowly opened and he stared in my direction.

"Ara I see he has grown to be a fine young man ah," said the old man.

"Wa Au Papa this is him," Dad replied.

"Long time, we never get to see him, you always keep him, but safely my son," the old man spoke again.

Dad just nodded his head, showing respect as he acknowledged what the old man was saying.

"Come warem, come, come. Come next to this aule," said the old man.

Dad indicated for me to sit next to the old man. Slowly I got onto my knees and moved closer. I positioned myself near to the old man's head and I crossed my legs. The old man stretched out his right hand for me. Quickly I looked over to dad, who gave me a nod. Immediately my hands met the old man's.

"Ah big boy, au warem, yes you are different," he said.

He had these piercing black eyes. His eyes spoke of his calmness, as did his touch. There was a connection, as our hands remained together. I was being drawn to him, drawn to his presence. His strength and wisdom drew me to him. Even though his eyes spoke of weakness in his body. Even though his ragged breath told of his fight to hold on to this life.

"Ara" said the old man.

"Yes my Au Papa," replied dad.

"Please leave me alone with your son. Let me speak to him," said the old man.

'Me left alone with this old man?' I thought. 'Why would he want to speak to me, a boy? Dad is more important than me. Besides, what would an old man expect from me anyway? Not that I was afraid of him, but why me?'

"If it pleases you my Au Papa, then me and the other men in the hut shall leave," said Dad.

"Au Esauo my son, Ara, let this old man capture and visit your son's heart," replied the old man.

Dad signalled for the other men in the hut to move out. Quickly and quietly, the men started moving towards the door of the hut, until dad was the only one left. He placed his hand gently on the old man's left shoulder,

"Aule, may we meet again as the totems or stars that glow in the sky over us. Aule watch over our people, guide the generations to come. Give them signs, help show their destination," said my father.

Dad's voice was different. It was soft, calm and caring, as he stared at me with an unusual look on his face. Then he stood and headed for the doorway. Complete quiet and stillness flooded the empty hut. It seemed huge without the men. The air was lighter, more breathable.

Then to my amazement, the old man sat upright and looked straight at me. He stared into my face. My heart raced fast and pounded hard against my chest. My insides felt stirred up, and a strange feeling ran up my back, making my hair stand on end. His old wrinkled face, transformed into that of an ordinary man, similar to my dad, as his hands gripped mine with a strength that startled me. I was afraid.

"Ah Ara's son, you give me strength. Child, never be afraid of me, never be afraid or else you will miss out on your destiny." His voice was strong with authority.

"Now look at me, without fear," he said, 'You know fear searches for you. You draw fear. It awaits lurking, prowling like a shark, ready to attack and rip its prey. Like a shark, it only has to smell one drop of your fear. That's when it grabs a hold of you with those strong jaws and sharp teeth that will shred you to pieces. Fear is always searching for his next prey. Kara warem fear is always hungry. Its hunger never stops, it feeds, it lives. It breathes and suffocates its victims. Remember kara, blood fear attacks the spirit man, these are the laws of the spirit world. If you have fear of your enemy, you will get killed; like many great warriors get their heads cut off in the battle field because of fear, Kara werem! Fear is always at war; it has its own battlefield. Once fear kills the spirit, our body stops working."

My heart stopped racing and I felt at peace. It was as if something was travelling through our joined palms. Something was coming from his old hands into mine. My eyes fixed on his, the old man looked very different. His skin drew tight, some sort of light shone and glowed around him. I could feel my insides being drawn to his black shark eyes. He had this presence about him.

His grip tightened further. I did not move.

"Son, many many moons from now, there will come a time where those who are not ours will come. They bring change, and it will change us forever.

Kara son, you are different to Ara, your heart speaks with great love. It is your love that will guide you, it will conquer fear. Man become cruel, mean and corrupt when they have fear. Remember kara son follow the voices of your nerkep. Listen to that inside man, let the deep call and guide the deep."

His words were strong and clear. I felt light, as if I were floating inside the hut. Then it was over. He fell back onto the mat and transformed into the old man I had first seen when I came into the hut. He closed his eyes and spoke in a small soft voice.

"Go now, Ara's son. Go."

His hands slipped from mine. I arose from my position and headed to the door. I faintly heard him speak one more time.

"Remember kara warem. Remember."

I pulled the mesh door open. The sunlight hit my eyes. In the distance I saw my father and the same man who had been standing at the entrance of the hut when we arrived. They were sitting in the shade of a small coconut tree. I went to him, and my father, without any indication or word to me, ended his conversation with the man and headed on the path that led to the main road back to Nam village. I followed.

As we continued our walk home, there was a great silence between us. My mind thought still of the old man transforming before my eyes. I could still hear his voice lingering in my ears.

Then I heard a great wailing from Beizam village behind us. I did not turn back to see what was going on. I just kept walking. I followed my father. As we walked through the huge rocks that lined the thin and narrow dirt road, so perfect and neat as they stood like warriors.

SNAKE

By Sisilia Eteuati

Oh Australia
Even
Cheap labour
    Even
            our strongest
                proudest
young women and men
    Can't pick fruit
    Shrivelled
    on the vine.

We
    are survivors.
And even
    when the ocean
overwhelms us
We will   Find a way.

But it won't be
Picking your

Fucking fruit

We
       Will watch
       From waka
As you
       In all your
       Arrogance
try to
eat coal
ripped from
stolen lands

And a rainbow snake
Hot and angry
That you have

fed
And fed
And fed

But never believed in   Anyway

Devours you.

BREATHE

By Laura Toailoa

Another Sunday evening and I find myself on the bedroom floor. Wonderful. I reach for my phone and unlock it: 6:42pm. Ugh. Is it really that time again? The night before Monday? All I can think about is tomorrow's to-do list—meetings, looming deadlines, uncooperative clients, and empty office chit chat about the dull weekends of my colleagues who get paid more than me to do half the work.

Oh shit, it's not pay week this week but I agreed to dinner with Anna on Wednesday. Maybe I could ask mum for $40. Wait, no, she asked me for money for a fa'alavelave last week, I think we're in the same boat. I'll ask dad. I start typing, "Hi dad!" No, this sounds happy. Backspace. "Heeeey." Too hesitant. Backspace. "Hi dad, sorry to ask, do you have a spare 40 I can pay back next week? All good if not, not urgent." Send.

I hope he doesn't worry too much about me.

"Are you okay? Have sent 100. No need to pay me back. Love you."

Good going shithead. You have a full-time job and you're asking your parents for money instead of sending it to them. Why did you shout everyone KFC when you knew you couldn't afford it? Oka sou fiamimika. Riley's gonna see how bad you are with money and break up with you...

I do this every Sunday. One small worry reminds me of another worry, that reminds of a different worry, and on and on it goes. Until it snowballs into a universe of stress, and I have no idea what step to take to get out of it.

I sit on my bedroom floor and attempt breathing exercises, but they only make me feel inadequate. I can't breathe without thinking about the half-finished work waiting for me at my desk. I inhale, and worry about a possibly offensive and unfunny remark I made to an acquaintance I only see every two years.

I exhale, and notice how my clothes have been getting tighter lately.

I breathe in, and wonder why I said yes to training the new person at work when I knew other people had a much freer schedule.

I breathe out. The week hasn't even started and I'm already too tired to socialise. With every breath I am reminded how I can't even do a simple activity to calm myself.

My futile attempts to get centred are interrupted when I hear the door squeak open. "Hey, what do you feel like for dinner?"

Riley's voice, that is normally so soothing, is grating on me. Strange.

"Whatever you want, I don't mind."

"For real? This won't be like the last time you "didn't mind" but shut down like, five suggestions?"

"When did I- Ugh. Never mind. Whatever... I mean, no it won't be. I don't care. You choose."

His brow furrows, he takes a sharp breath, seemingly about to say something. But all that comes out is a deep exhale.

"Babe, do you want to talk about it?"

Of course not. "No, no, I mean it—I don't mind, you choose."

"Not... that," the last word sounding more like a sigh. "We'll order curry and samosas, that's easy. I've been having a craving since I saw Vita's insta review. But do you want to talk about..."

"I'd rather not."

Another exhale.

"Alright then. I'll let you know when the food arrives."

"Cool."

He backs out, I close my eyes, and I don't even hear the door shut.

Inhale.

You always do this to him.

Exhale.

He doesn't deserve you.

Inhale.

He just wanted to know what you wanted to eat.

Exhale.

You always treat him like trash.

Inhale.

Why can't you just say what's on your mind?

Exhale.

You're always making him work for it.

Inhale.

One day he's gonna see that it's not worth the effort.

Exhale.

He's going to leave you.

"Hey, babe, wake up, food's here."

My eyes shoot open. Wait, is it tomorrow already?!

"What's the time?"

He rubs my back. "Hey, ssh, it's alright. It's only 7:30. I think you fell asleep for about half an hour."

"I didn't mean to sleep." I rub my eyes and push myself up from the floor.

"I hope your back is okay."

I snort, "Oh well, if it isn't."

He furrows his brow again, this time only for a split second.

"Do you want to eat? Sorry, should I have left you to sleep?"

"No, no, it's alright, whatever, let's eat."

We walk to the kitchen and plate up our food. We plop down at our dining spot, the couch, and turn on Bob's Burgers.

We eat and watch like we do most evenings. Riley cracks up a lot during the episode and with every laugh I can see his head turn to see if I'm laughing with him. I can't stand the surveillance.

I wolf down my food and finish eating before the episode is halfway through. I stand up to leave. "Thanks for dinner. I'm going to sleep."

I hear a quiet sigh. I don't know if he meant for me to hear it. It pisses me off. Oh, I'm sorry - is *my* sadness hard on YOU? WHY DON'T YOU TRY LIVING IN IT!

I pause, and without turning around I manage to squeeze out, "Sorry."

"You have nothing to be sorry about."

A classic bullshit "kind" response. I continue to the bedroom and shut the door behind me.

He doesn't follow me in.

Oh there you go again, pushing away someone who actually gives a shit about you. Wonderful. Grand plan you have there. What are you gonna do when he gets tired of your shit? Notice how he didn't follow you? He doesn't want to be anywhere near you, he just pities you and doesn't know how to break up with you.

You should take mercy on his poor soul and break it off so he doesn't have to be the bad guy. We know it's you.

I don't know how long I've been crying, but the soaked pillow case, hyperventilation and throbbing headache tells me it's been a while. He didn't follow me to bed. I *knew* he was getting sick of my bullshit. Any second, he's going to walk in and tell me tha–

The door opens, painfully slowly.

"Hey, are you okay?" His voice is so gentle I'm not sure if I really heard it. I glare at him. "Okay, I admit, I asked the questions already knowing the answer." He approaches and sits at the edge of the bed. "I love you. I hate that you're in pain. I wish I understood."

But he never will and this is too much and he needs somebody who communicates her feelings better and he's going to pack his stuff up tomorrow.

"A mate of mine had really bad anxiety and recommended this psychologist. I don't know if what you experience is the same as them. I don't even know if what you need is a psychologist or a psychiatrist. Shit, I don't even know the difference...I mean, I don't know if you want to hear this now. Sorry, I know I always jump to solution mode when you just need me to be present."

He remembered.

"I just wanted to say, I'm here... when you're ready. No rush."

He leans down and kisses my forehead - lightly, deeply, and I feel, at last, air to my lungs.

Modesty Tasi, Lua, Tolu.

By Nafanua PK

Tasi. Skinny Dip
they take your hand they pull you to sea they stop.
- why bother with clothes?
- those people are miles down the beach - only dogs and gulls can see
[that]
their   pale   skin   is   free
and yours is not.

Lua. That No One is Watching

is never true
because the fish
the molluscs   the seaweed   the sami

carry your nakedness in their shimmer and guts,
shell and sucking cups
through green brown blue-black waters

give you over
to the backs of turtles, stingrays and whales

passing Goddesses, Gods
in underworld gaps
to lap up onto your family's beach

 ten thousand holograms of you naked
will wash up in foam
at Falealupo   at Satufia   at Aleipata
to be stomped on
by white-clad aunties
and behatted mamas
because of course, it's Sunday.

and they'll cut your hair
take you to church
and throw you at the floor
to be prayed upon

they might even
send your image packing
down into Pulotu
summon the serpent aitu to come and feast
tau-sami on your flesh.

Or, a palagi man may find you
with his red swollen face and raw disease in his folds
settle his bright eyes on you
and shame you
out of your skin
                              [he might slap his skin onto yours]
and say, you don't know any better
and say, you should not have tempted
and say, you are his now anyway

so you cover up.

[how his ancestors taught yours?]
because if creatures recognise your
flab   crevice
      malu   coarse hair

they get to claw
your goodness
right out of your being
and spit it back into the sea.

That no-one is watching is never true.

***Tolu*. Lavalava Lost**
you dive
deep   [into your element]
greet Atua   [wet kindred]
who wash   [off the white ash]
and watch you
swim   [your freedom]
beyond your skin.

Napina Reclaims

By Rebecca Tobo Olul-Hossen

I

He beat her up again tonight.

It was date night. Napina's iarman, her man of almost a year, had scored tickets for boxing. It was a chance to get out after being cooped up in the house with a breastfeeding three-month-old.

Napina relished the chance to feel less a feeding machine and more her own self – a twenty-seven-year-old young ni-Vanuatu woman.

It had been eleven months since Napina finished working at a nongovernmental organisation, choosing to do more short-term work. Working at home meant that she had very little interaction with anyone.

This, coupled with having a baby on an island where she barely had family or friends, meant her life centred on Baby Tamalu and her iarman. He worked full-time but she paid for most of the bills including the expensive rental.

"I got us tickets to boxing, honey," he said with a smile that stretched to show his even white teeth against charcoal skin.

"Oh thanks," Napina responded with a grin, thinking about what she was going to wear.

Two hours later they were ready. Kaha Licha was there to babysit. Instructions were dished out.

Napina was dressed in a fitting red camisole slip dress, a touch of sophistication. Probably overdressed for boxing, but who cares. She relished company and a drink.

He, in his long-sleeved white shirt that said Afro-American with just a touch of island, giving him that air. The air she first fell for.

She recalled the first time they met. He appeared to know what he was talking about. Worldly, unlike the young men she was used to.

He knew how to worm his way into her life. She did fall for it: the veneer of charm and worldliness fooled her.

Fast-forward six months, she found out she was pregnant. She took a second pregnancy test when the first showed positive. Still pregnant.

It was at 10.35pm when Napina noticed that he had gone quiet. It felt like he had been quiet for some time. Watching.

She was having fun. A couple of glasses of bubbly and catching up with old friends.

Her breasts felt heavy with milk. "It's time to go home," Napina said close to his ear, so he could hear over the din. He did not seem to hear.

She touched his arm. He turned to her. "It's time to go home," she mouthed at him.

He turned away sharply. "When I am done!" he said, tossing the crushed beer plastic cup into the bin.

Grabbing her hand, he yanked her through the crowd towards the exit.

Outside the boxing venue, Napina saw an old university friend she flatted with the year before graduation. She called out to him waving with her free hand.

Too late she realised that he was in one of the photos her iarman burnt in a fit of rage three weekends ago. Her acid-free black album where she pasted memories writing captions in white pen. She brought her right hand down. The hand with the index finger forever deformed when he crashed the laundry basket down aiming for her head and she'd raised her arm instinctively.

Napina's attention was caught by a flash of movement across the road. By the Chinese store opposite the Parliament House was a dilapidated lean-to with corrugated iron roofing. Under a blue tarpaulin strung across the front, a dull yellow light beamed hopefully on a congregation of men. Napina knew it was a nakamal. The men were drinking kava.

She imagined she heard guttural sounds of spitting and the fresh rooty smell of kava made her choke back a vomit.

A taxi pulled up. Napina's iarman shoved her in. It was when she was inside that she realised it was Tawi John's taxi, her iarman's cousin. He must have phoned him.

Napina turned around to face her iarman and found her face forced down on the seat of the taxi. He boxed her face and head with his balled-up fists.

She looked at the fake red leather of the taxi's seat. It too would soon be stained with her blood.

"How could you!" he said. "You embarrassed me," Napina's iarman continued.

Napina realised he was talking about her waving to her friend. She knew very well that he hated feeling like she defied him.

Napina cried for help as the taxi pulled away and headed for home.

"Tawi, please stop at the police station," cried Napina. "He will kill me," she said, pleas muffled by the taxi seat.

Tawi John did not help. It was their domestic issue.

Napina heard the thud! thud! thud! of her heart like the pounding of a dull axe against a nakatambol tree through the pummelling of her head.

"Sori…" Tawi John said averting his eyes in the rear-view mirror.

Napina was a cornered animal, pinned down in the back of the taxi to stop her calling out for help to passers-by.

Napina's mind furiously ran through options. The catch was her three-month-old son. She could not run and leave a breastfeeding baby.

"Get out!" he said through gritted teeth. Napina realised she must have blacked out.

He pried her fingers loose from the taxi door, carried her into the house and threw her on the bed. Napina's thoughts were of Kaha Licha and Baby Tamalu in the spare bedroom.

Coming back into the bedroom, he grabbed his black Nokia mobile, and started dialling numbers. "I am going bring her here and fuck her on the bed next to you," he ranted.

She knew this was not going to happen. Not right now. But tonight, she wished it did. This would spare her from more beating.

Napina felt a stinging sensation on her face. How was she going to hide a black eye tomorrow?

"I am sorry," she whispered through swollen lips, a mantra to keep her alive. Napina's tired brain had gone into shutdown mode. Like the first grey Acer laptop she owned.

When she forced open the painful slits that were her eyes, it was daylight. She was alone. Napina breathed a sigh of relief. She was alive. Everywhere was pain.

The door swung open. Napina tensed. Her iarman came in with a red ice-cream container and her fluffy white face cloth – her flannel. She liked flannels. They made her feel feminine.

"Good morning, honey!" he said cheerfully. Her iarman had come to clean up the mess from last night. "I am going to clean your face with warm water. Then Bubba will breastfeed," he announced.

Her iarman wiped her face tenderly murmuring about how sorry he was. "I love you so much," he said.

"I love you," Napina said. "Thank you for cleaning me," she added. "I'm sorry about last night."

Napina found that she thought in Tannese or English whenever she was angry or hurt. Nolkeikeiian, love, could easily be used to talk about an object with no feelings. Had she become a mere thing? Love, the most overused word in any language.

His benevolent smile lit up the room. He left to empty the now bloodstained water down the white porcelain sink in the bathroom.

He returned with a wriggling bundle – her baby, Tamalu. Napina could not turn on her side to breastfeed him.

Her iarman arranged a pillow for Baby Tamalu to lie on so he was able to reach her breast. He latched on eagerly and started to suckle. Napina's eyes filled with tears of pain.

Napina breathed in his sweet scent – a mixture of talcum powder and baby wipes. The scent of a clean baby. Napina suddenly felt unclean.

Napina looked into Baby Tamalu's eyes praying silently, "Don't remember me like this, little man . . . "

He graced her with a smile.

II

There were moments of clarity. Moments when Napina knew she should leave. There were times when she left and then returned.

"Why are you still with him?" demanded Napina's friend, whose house she sought refuge at one night with her son. "Please don't tell me you love him after all this!"

Napina's friend paused in her pacing across the earth floor of the house she was renting to glance at her in disgust. She pointed at Napina's battered face to stress her point.

"Go and see your mama," she said. "That'll teach him to try to do this to you again."

Napina sat resolutely patting her baby's bottom willing him to sleep. She must prove to her mama that she could make it work.

"Do we have to talk about this right now?" Napina asked. "It's late and baby is sick . . ."

In a twisted way Napina guessed she still loved this man.

Okay she should have listened to her mama. Napina's mama did warn her against him.

"Koko, there are some good men, like your father. But there are some men that are bad. There are men who lie," her mama had said to her that Sunday afternoon after church.

But thinking she knew better and maybe, to an extent, to defy her mama Napina pursued the relationship.

"But you don't know him, mama," Napina responded. "He is a good man.

He loves me", she added.

And now she cannot go to her mama. That would be admitting defeat. And Napina has too much pride to admit that she was wrong.

Her mind goes back to the time he hit her on the beach close to his family's home. Baby Tamalu would have been less than two weeks old. She was still weak from the caesarean section.

He had held her face into seawater for the longest time. She flailed as she fought for breath. He released her finally. Gasping for air, she realised her face was all cut up by the reef.

"Let's go home," he said. They walked back in the rain together. Napina looked around at passers-by. She wondered if any of them noticed the cuts on her face. Everyone was averting their eyes. Were there cuts on her face?

"What happened to you?" asked his maman. Napina started to respond trying to hide the tears rolling down her nangalat-stung cheeks. "Why is your face bleeding?"

"Oh, shut up, maman!" he retorted.

His papa came running in from the bush kitchen where he was creaming sweet yams for dinner.

"What did you do to her, son?" he asked sharply. "She doesn't have family here. What if something happened to her?" he added.

Napina felt unseen. Why was everyone talking about her like she was not there?

"It's her fault. She never listens!" he said shortly.

His maman held Napina, rocked her like a baby and cried.

"You have to learn to listen", she crooned. "Don't make him angry because then he hits you", she scolded.

Napina nodded mutely. Her tears could not come.

His maman boiled some water in a kettle on the open fire for Napina to have a bucket bath in the outdoor wood and black canvas shower stall.

She bent to scoop water to wash her body and hot water steamed up over the stall's black canvas walling as it started to drizzle. Tears mixed with drizzle flowed down her cheeks. Towelling off, Napina stepped gingerly onto blocks of bricks not wanting her feet to get muddy.

Napina felt clean. His maman made Napina a sweet smelling pamplemousse leaf tea and put her to bed.

III

He had been cheating on her the whole time. Napina felt the fool. Everyone knew about it. The town was too small – a mere fishbowl.

Ping! Ping! Ping! Her laptop started to ping as soon as she got into her office and it connected to the internet.

"Shall we plan for the next weekend she is away?" said the first message.

"Yes, honey, let's do that," was the response from her iarman.

Napina did a double take. This was not her own messenger. He had been on her laptop at home and had not logged out. She realised the conversation was carrying on. Napina felt like an outsider looking into her own life. Like someone looking into a fishbowl.

Long after it ceased, Napina guiltily scrolled through the messages. He had been talking to this woman for some time. There were rendezvous. There was history. There were many other women it would seem. All being called names she thought were reserved for her.

Napina felt hot and cold at the same time. The whitewashed walls of her office were caving in on her. She struggled for breath.

Napina heard a gravelly new edge to her voice when she spoke to him.

"I gave up all this for this man," she cried bitterly to her sister. "I took the beating and tried to make the relationship work for what…?" she added.

Her sister just listened then shook her head.

"I don't recognise myself when I look in the mirror," Napina cried pointing to her battered face. "I am so ashamed. I hate feeling so weak," she sobbed.

"We don't recognise you anymore," responded her sister bitterly. "We hardly see you. Don't you see how he is stopping you from seeing your friends?"

Napina kept her head down – silent tears dripping onto her lap creating circles on her cream skirt. She gripped her hands to hide her deformed finger.

"You are a fighter. You can do this. I am here to support you," her sister assured her.

Napina did not feel like a fighter.

"You have to do what is right for you and baby," her sister added quietly.

"You made me do this," he said mockingly when she confronted him with the evidence of his lies over seven years of their lives.

"If only you were much more of a woman," he said. "You need to be more respectful," he added.

Napina could not believe what she was hearing.

"How can you expect me to respect you when you have no respect whatsoever for me?" she retorted.

"That's exactly what I am talking about!" he shouted. "Everybody talks about how proud you are. You think you know everything just because you are educated. If I ever left you, no man would take a second look at you!" he exclaimed storming out and slamming the door.

She recoiled as if slapped. This was a fight that was not going to end well.

IV

Six months later, on a Monday night at 9.52pm, he put a bush-knife in her hand.

And told her to cut up their nine-month-old son.

Six months had passed since Napina found out all his lies. The tension between them was as thick as ever.

Napina had just started working for a nongovernmental organisation. She felt a lot more like herself. She did not care about his comings and goings. He could come home at 3am if he wanted to. She was getting out of the house more. She met her girlfriends for lunch. She felt a lot more connected to the outside world.

Napina stood at the bedroom door trembling with terror as silent tears coursed down her face. Who was this monster that she lived with?

Her baby was crying in his bed. His legs were kicking in the air. He demanded to be lifted and held.

She felt an intense hatred for this beast her iarman rise threatening to choke her. Control, control she told herself.

She felt herself calm down. As if in a dream she heard herself say, "I'm sorry . . . I'm sorry . . . I'm sorry". That was all she could say. Napina did not know what she was sorry about.

There was immediate transformation.

He took the bush-knife from her, put it on the floor, hugged her and said, "Honey, you know I love you. I am only doing this because you hurt me."

Her body sagged with relief. She squeezed him tightly.

Her eyes angled over to the forgotten bush-knife. For a moment, she thought what sweet relief it would be to pick it up and hurt him with it. She must not let go before he does.

As soon as he let her go, she picked up her baby and held him close to her. He gurgled and stopped crying. Soon enough he started cooing as she nursed him. He bit her nipple with happiness. She barely felt it. The pain in her heart was greater.

She hid her growing revulsion and disgust well. She fake-moaned during sex, marvelling at the ceiling's peaceful pastel colours.

She had to find a way out.

Her way out came in the form of her sister and angels disguised in human form. Although she was not highly religious, she believed in a higher being.

Her face was a mask. She was no longer booted in the ribs or thrown against the wall. But the hurt and betrayal grew bigger still.

She recalled the night before her father died. She couldn't remember what set her iarman off. Napina dodged his punch. His arm hit the bed's headboard cracking his wrist. It was almost comical that she burst out laughing.

Days after, whenever friends or family asked him what happened, he would supply them the story that he slipped and fell. Napina could feel a smug grin taking over her face when he said this.

Napina knew the time would come. When it came it seemed to creep up silently. She wrote him a note, packed her baby, and left the life she had tried to make work for seven years.

Telling the taxi driver to stop by the waterfront on her way to her mama, Nipina took something out of her bag and threw it into the water. She watched as it was washed away by the waves, flashes of red appearing now and then. She wondered if someone would see her red camisole slip dress and think that it was a dead body.

Then she got back into the taxi and went home to her mama.

Dedicated to women who remain silent and those who have not found a sympathetic listening ear

IVI

By Sisilia Eteuati

I do not need
philosophy. I would not waste one more
thought.

Keep the platitudes. I want no zen. I choke on trite.
I want poems that snarl
       that bare their teeth

I want the howl of them.
I want poems that rip
at the very flesh
       of us.
that sink in
and tear away
bite by bite
till the bone flashes white

At least a bone
a white white bone
is
Clean.

Sunday Fun Day

By Filifotu Vaai

"Malia, kakou e loloku gei," my dad says firmly from across the breakfast table.

I can tell this is non-negotiable. It has been three months since I moved to Honolulu from American Samoa and I haven't seen the inside of a church yet.

"Dad, I've been so busy with work," I say. He has just arrived and it's probably the jet lag that is making his face look so dismayed I tell myself.

"Oi, e ke faigaluega i le Aso Sa?" Dad asks.

Yes. I have been working on Sunday, I think to myself. On my tan. I bite my cheek. Sunday has been funday here in Honolulu, and by funday I mean none day. Nothing but blackout curtains and Chinese takeout that is . . .

Humidity and expectation hangs in the silence as I try to think of which church we can go to. My mind draws a total blank. I mean, just because I am Samoan, and I moved here from Samoa, what does he expect? That I would actually know other Samoans here and have joined a church already? I look at his face. That is definitely what he expected.

"Dad, ou ke le'i masagi i gisi i igei," I say, "But finding a church was definitely my next top level priority!" I want to sound convincing as I hit my cell phone screen trying to pull up Dr Google. Where is Dr Google when I need him?

"Makua'i e kaea kele! Su'e se loku," my Dad says. His tone holds all the how-did-I-raise-my-daughter-this-way sternness that tells me he loves me.

The nearest Samoan church is about a twenty-minute drive away. I search online for information on start times and find only recordings of their Lotu Tamaiti service from two years ago, showing a well costumed Jesus semi suspended on a life-sized cross with fake blood dripping around his face. Oh they, *extra*, extra, I think. I text a Samoan friend of mine that lives in the same area as the church to ask her what time church starts. She responds with the LMAO emoji. Another text pings "Girl, you know my sinning ass ain't been in that church for years. Pray for me" OK, I should've known my atheist, Jesus needing friends wouldn't know. Maybe my Dad has a point.

"Dad, maukigoa e amaka i le sefulu, I'm sure it starts at 10am," I say based on nothing other than that has been the start time of every Sunday morning EFKS church service I had ever attended. I say it both in Samoan and English because that will definitely make it more true.

"Ok," he said. "We'll go at 9." Ua lelei la eager beaver I think, as I say "Ia ok, se'i fa'asaugi kamaiki." My six-year-old rolls her eyes, safe in the knowledge I can't igi her auaga with her Papa already grumpy at me and in severe doubt about my Godliness.

When we pull up to the church, the parking lot is half full. The service hasn't started but the pews are filling up and soft organ music is playing. A young boy in a white ie faitaga at the door hands me a printed program and the italicized Times New Roman font and the familiar stock image picture of Jesus on the front page gives me instant nostalgia. I notice the start time is 10.30am, and today is Fa'amanatuga. Everyone in the building is dressed in head to toe white. I, of course, am wearing a lavender top and a black skirt, I might as well be wearing a sheer, blood red ball gown, judging from the scornful looks of the ladies a few rows up. We exchange tight lipped smiles and nods. "Hello in the name of the holy spirit to you too, sis," I mutter under my breath.

The agelu children of good churchgoing Samoan mothers sit quietly up front, each with their own pese and highlighted bibles. I, on the other hand, quickly pummel my kids with snacks and muted cell phones as we settle into our seats because Lord knows they don't have the fear of God, and Lord certainly knows who ALL the other Samoan moms will blame for that. I can't tell if it's the judge-y looks, or the excess of white lace and tulle, but I feel strangely at home.

I exhale and smile as I take in the impressive assortment of church hats on display in the choir pews near the front. There are diamantes, sequins, and beads in every color. Tuff le competition. The Melbourne Cup can take several seats! After a careful ten minute review on my part, I silently award the headpiece of the day to a lady strategically seated in the center pew of the front row. Her ivory hat had a brim as wide as Africa with what looks like a full spring bouquet made of chiffon and glistening bead detailing on her head. It was really more of a Mother's Day hat rather than a Fa'amanatuga hat, but go off sis. You better werrrk.

Everyone springs to their feet and the choir starts to sing the opening hymn. Only then do I notice there is an entire band to the side of the pulpit. A drum set, guitars, standing mics, lights on a trellis, the works. Where are we? Coachella? I think of the barefoot conductor in his crisp white suit and the rinky dink old Casio keyboard in our village church and I wonder if my Dad is finding this very Amelika love-in-the club set-up as peculiar as I am right now. They break out into a lively rendition of the opening hymn. "Ua so'ona olioli nei, lo'u loto ia Iesu..." Dad's familiar tenor sings out beside me in perfect harmony. My own voice joins in of its own volition.

My six-year-old looks up from her phone and asks me, "Mom, is this a church or is this a party?"

"Wait, is this my party?" my two-year-old asks, her eyes widening and she cranes her neck out to see the band out front.

I laugh. "Shhh pisa," I say, as if anyone is going to hear the questions over Samoans singing pese lotu. Like that's even possible. I give her a look that says, fair question, little one. If it's not, it should be. She seems to agree before returning her attention to Peppa Pig.

We take our seats, and the pastor starts off the service with his opening prayer. "Lo matou Tama e, Silisili ese, fa'afetai mo lou alofa… matou te iloa e na o oe e mafai na e puipuia i matou mai puapuaga ma faigata o lenei olaga.... Tama, puipui mai matou mai le ISIS."

Wait what? Did he just launch into asking for protection from ISIS? I didn't know ISIS were active on the West side of O'ahu and an imminent threat. Jokes about sleeper cells fill my head.

"Ou te valaau atu ia te oe tama mo lau tausiga ma fa'amanuiaga mo

President Trump ma le First Lady Milania." I open my eyes and look around, not one flinch across the land. Alrighty. I guess we really are in the heartland.

Even while making jokes in my head, the eloquence of the Samoan language and its cadence and sway is moving me. Something in the words, the tone, the feeling of hearing it just resonates in me at a primal level. As the pastor's sermon booms across the congregation, I breathe in deeply and the words of my favorite poem roll through my head, "learn to speak Samoan, not so you may sound Samoan, but so you can feel the essence of being Samoan." Gratitude swells in me for my messy life, for my kids who are messily eating goldfish crackers beside me, and for my Dad who cares enough about my slipping chances of entering into heaven to bring me here today. I whisper my own prayer of thanks in my head.

My thoughts are interrupted by the pastor's voice, "I don't want to preach, that's not what the pulpit is for."

'No, seriously. What's it for then?' I think.

"I just want to talk to you. In English. Some of the younger ones don't speak gagana Samoa," he says. His accent is fresh as, so I can tell he just wants to show off his excellent English. "We must keep this great nation great." Profound, I think. "And that is why I strongly encourage our church aiga to make donations towards our fundraiser towards our new hall."

Pulpit mystery solved. I look over at Dad who is looking pointedly at my purse. I try to figure out if I have any cash left over - who even carries cash anymore? I hope that God is taking credit I think as the choir start singing the last pese. The stained glass window panes hang on for dear life as the choir sopranos sing *the hell* out of the familiar closing notes of "Aaaaaaaameenee!"

A gust of cool air fills the church as the wide doors are pushed open for the sea of white to pour out, people chatter and greet each other with handshakes and kisses like they didn't just side eye each other during the hymn.

I'm in the mix too, nodding and smiling in response to the perfunctory, "Malo!" and "Ua a?" that meets me as we slowly file out. I corral my children towards my car and we're half way through the parking lot when I hear someone yell out my name. "Malia!" I turn to see a smiling face, Bible in one hand, the other holding her hat as she walked quickly towards me. She looks vaguely familiar. "Malo Suga, I thought that was you. How's your mom?" she asks.

"She's well," I smile back and we have an entire five-minute conversation asking about each other's families like we grew up together. Then I realize why she looks familiar. I recognize her from the Samoan source of truth, second only to the Bible, Facebook. Pretty sure our moms are second cousins. Or something. I remember her name and confidently offer a, "Great to see you Lusia!" as we exchange numbers and part ways.

As we drive away, I look her up on Facebook and realize her name is Atalina. She must think I'm an asshole. Eh. Wrong 'cowsin', sis, sorry. This is the problem with being related to half of Samoa.

'We have taro at home, a ea Malia? It's not toona'i without taro," Dad says to the girls who jump up and down. "Tammy's, Tammy's," they sing. I automatically start driving there.

"O ai Tammy?" Dad asks. "Oh, it's our local Filipino owned Samoan food store," I say. I can tell Dad is shaking his head in my peripheral vision, but buying Samoan food ready cooked is not as serious an infraction as not finding a lotu. And so we ride on without another oke.

Arriving at the store I lead the way in as I know these aisles well. "We can get anything you like Dad." Out of the kitchen, a head pops and a voice yells out, "Komisi!"

Two ladies from Dad's village in Savaii rush out of the kitchen. They embrace Dad and tears flow down both their cheeks as they talk about their mutual connections, people that have passed away, who has moved away and who's still in the village. Their eyes light up and they listen enthusiastically as Dad tells them about the latest court case dispute over titles, and which party was the favorite to win. It's a family reunion up in here.

"Oka Malia ua e lo'omakua ma e lapo'a!" Aunty one says laughingly, looking me up and down.

I know better than to say anything so I just smile and say, "Malo Aunty."

"Avaku la'u gumela lea," Aunty two says.

Fresh from the Luisa incident, I decide to use all my diplomacy and tact, but mostly a podcast I heard a month back that said if you didn't know someone's name ask them to spell it. I'm thinking I'm slick as I take out my phone and say, "Sipela mai lou igoa fa'amolemole, Aunty."

She looks at me and laughs "You don't know my name a ea? Ka igoigo e!

T.A.S.I!"

All three of them burst into laughter. My dad's rings the loudest. And I just laugh along with them, because if you can't beat them, join them. If you're not being roasted by your aunties whose names you can't remember. Are you really Samoan?

"Ia se'i makou o, ae kakou koe fekaui," Dad says.

The aunties busily hug my children and heap extra of everything onto our plates while saying "Seriously watch your figure suga."

As we drive along the freeway heading home, the Sunday sun beating down, my Dad humming pese lotu, and the smell of warm taro and luau wafting through my car, I realize that for the first time since I moved to this country, I feel a little bit at home.

Taking my grandmother's name

By Kiri Piahana-Wong

In memory of Sylvia Te Hiri Hiri (Piahana) Wong

I changed my last name so that
I could see the world through
my grandmother's eyes

I felt her presence as I stirred
the milk in the morning, her
sweetness in the tea

The swish of her long black skirt
Her gentle fingers running
through my hair
I am six years old again—

This is how you stir the milk
so you don't get a skin on it
Yes it's good on the weetbix
on these cold mornings

Eat up, eat up, you get big
and strong, strong big girl!

Your Dad, he could eat 12
of these, āe those boys

Then I grew up,
my grandmother was gone
But walking the old road past Judea
was like reaching back and touching
her face with my fingertips

And when I have to spell my
name, every time, to the pharmacist,
to the jeweller, at the bookstore,
to every government department
I hear her spirit laughing

You know when I married
your grandfather I changed
my name to 'Wong', dear
Everyone understand that
name

PUTAUAKI

By Ashlee Sturme

It is just a post, a lonely soldier in the sea of grass. Smooth, light. New. The earth is still drying at its base, upheaved worms desperately wriggling away from the autumn sun. The spade has just gone, the surveyor's tracks marked by flattened grass.

"It would be a rectangle, quite simply, if it weren't for the extra 10 metres tacked to this border. Why? Why couldn't it have been done properly?"

Dad rubs his beard. The spiky short hair is ginger, and gross, and I want to tell him that they did studies and found faecal matter in beards, and besides, it makes you look old. Shave it off. But I've learnt to pick my battles, and right now getting answers on this land is more important than getting that beard off his face.

"I guess it just happened," he says, surveying the land that he must know intimately in his heart, with his eyes closed, in his sleep. "There was so much else going on and…"

I've heard it all before. "Can we change it? If we just move this post…" but he is shaking his head. It's a done deal.

My grandmother is waving her arms at us, doesn't stop until we are right in front of her. "I made you coffee," she says, and then peers into my face. "Except you don't drink hot drinks. I have a juice for you."

I don't want a juice either, but I'm too polite not to drink it. I smooth my hands over the tablecloth as my father explains how the new fence will go up. "Around that post?" my grandmother says, and I notice the way she is shaking her head slightly, quick jerks.

"Yep, that post is the new border," he explains.

"Did I tell you that Truus has sold their farm," she says, and doesn't notice that Dad and I look at each other.

"I heard that," Dad says to her, "the family got a good price, didn't they?" but she tells us anyway.

Truus and her family are moving in three weeks. I look out at the post in the paddock and wish for another three years.

"I guess I'll have to sell sometime soon," my grandmother says. "Not until you are ready," Dad says, and I say, "Nope you don't have to do anything you don't want to." Her head stops jerking.

"Oh yes, I was going to tell you something. Did you hear that Truus sold the family farm?"

I look into my empty glass and wish that I didn't want to cry.

Other than this paddock which is now being divided by a rectangle AND an extra ten metres, the rest of the farm is divided into relatively even paddocks, with no distinction between this farm and the ones it sits next to; a stranger couldn't see the borders, define the neighbours.

But I have walked those boundaries, and in fact nearly every square metre sometime in the last thirty-two years. When I was brought here from the hospital, our kainga, our home, was on this farm. I was brought home to a white cottage surrounded by a hedge, with a lawn and a huge lemon tree. The tree was not pretty like you see nowadays, with glossy fruit and clean shiny leaves. The lemon tree had puckered leaves that curled slightly, a dirty green. The fruit was more round than oval, balls of white pith that were often thicker than the yellow inside. They were not the best fruit to zest, really, blemishes from insects, and uneven almost mossy skin. They made great cricket balls if you were too lazy to walk around the hedge to retrieve the one lost in the grass. But they were plentiful and pancakes were nothing without them. You didn't have a sniffle on this farm without drinking lemon honey.

There were stained glass windows and a toilet outside in the laundry. Today the house still stands, but it is no longer white, no longer proud, and no longer easily accessible, hidden in tussocks. The stained-glass windows are dark, manky, uncoloured. The forgotten lemon tree discards its fruits into an overgrown lawn in front of a door that is slouching on its hinges.

I should make pancakes.

There is a massive row of trees, one side Japanese Cedar and the other Poplar, that line the driveway to the old cottage, bordering the paddock the main house sits in and casting shadows at dawn. They were planted by my father and my grandfather, so close that the branches have knitted together and tangled in their growth. Below them in springtime, there is a pretty good chance of finding a fallen nest of tiny little blue eggs. The rest of the year there is usually a rusting piece of tractor machinery, perhaps a rake or a mower, buried under the fallen leaves and waiting for the summer season of haymaking.

Beside this driveway that is framed by the tunnel of trees, is a paddock, a bit smaller than the others on the farm, and it is the separation between the house and the cowshed. This paddock is a historical sea of blood, the slaughter site of many many cows destined for the freezer. It was a non-event on the farm, a single shot, the butchering, the packing. A few months of excellent steak dinners, and then months of being inventive with mince.

Last month it was time for the next generation to learn the facts of life. I stood with my back turned to my father, clutching the arms of my children as they watched. I flinched at the shot, crouched to console the children. "Can we go see?" they cried excitedly. I turned as my daughter helped to hold up the head, tongue lolling lazily from the side. "You can eat that," Dad was telling her. My son watched the butcher pull out the liver. My stomach churned. Once, I told them, the butcher found a little calf in a cow that was supposed to be empty. It looked like a dead newborn puppy.

Talk about spontaneous biology lessons.

I don't think anyone was listening to me, and once my husband and father started up the chainsaws, I stepped over the puddle of blood and walked back to the car alone.

"Did your dad shoot those cows," my grandmother asked.

"Yes," I told her, looking carefully at the way her hair stuck out to the side, one forgotten curler tangled on the top. A bra strap peeked from her top. "They did that last Saturday. They got two into the chiller. My kids thought it was

185

exciting."

"Oh yes, I can see that would be very interesting for them."

"Would you like some meat when it is cut?" I ask her.

"Of course not," she snaps at me, and she begins to rub her fingers. "I don't eat meat anymore. I think I'll have a cup of coffee. Do you want one?"

I shake my head but she is already talking. "Oh no, you don't drink hot drinks."

The silk tree is my favourite. You can run your fingers down the stems of the little branches and open your palm to reveal a handful of natural confetti.

The delicate pink flowers filled our paddling pool in summer, turning into a brown rotting mess. In winter, it was nothing, stripped, fallen, bare.

Stark and naked on the roadside, the For Sale sign was nothing too.

Walking the herd of cows into the shed on hot sticky afternoons as the cows batted their tails against the flies, in near dark on fresh mornings with the dog for company watching the stars fade into the reborn sun, and on cold winter days when there was a wonderful thick ice on all the puddles.

Right now, my heart feels like the shards of ice after my boot went through them.

"What happens next?"

Dad is tugging on that bloody beard again. I'm starting to think he likes it for something to do. Perhaps it is a replacement for work. I could get him something that reads, *I retired and all I got was this beard*, as if he's been to Vegas and brought back a shitty overpriced tee.

"I think I'll like being retired," he says.

"No," I say, nodding at her house in the rectangle plus rectangle paddock.

"We'll notice good days and bad days. Hopefully the medication means more good days than bad."

And then?

"Eventually she won't remember how to get dressed. She'll forget who we are."

After we broke the ice on the puddles, we'd run to the troughs of water and smash them too. The ice was thinner and would quickly melt away in the darkness of the concrete bottom. That's where my breath is right now, empty, deep.

I only had two poor attempts at learning to ride a bike – one resulted in a crash into the hedge, and another that resulted in my dropping the heavy bike and being unable to lift it again. After that, I was happy to walk.

I've walked the whole farm. Every paddock and every race. Some paddocks send shivers up my spine, raise the hairs on my neck. I don't know why. I imagine the ground being trodden with the heavy feet of moa, or soaking up blood from the land wars. Who was here before me?

I was proud to be a farmer's daughter, but I know now that our freedom came at a cost we will never understand and never repay. Acknowledging privilege has become a daily routine.

I ask my grandmother about her experience of war. My son sips at his hot chocolate, bored.

"Oh, I don't remember," she says, but she has said this for my whole life, so I know this is not memory loss.

The summer soundtrack was Bayrock station blasting with old-school heavy rock from dusty speakers, settled on the rafters of the brand new cowshed. The cows would parade in, necks were adorned with necklaces on which green transponders and electronic numbers were threaded.

There was no time. It was row and then row and then it was only a few left and then it was wash up time. Whooshing of the machinery, clicks as water pulsed through the tubing. We'd lock up the cows, and I'd press my face to his warm back, my arms around his waist, holding on as we bounced on the motorbike home, him and me.

One Sunday afternoon a man roared into our driveway, dust swallowing the car, his horn beeping. He was breathless when he ran to the door shouting. "Call the fire brigade!" There were shouts. Then all the adults rushed out, leaving me alone with my sister. I picked up the phone, twirled the cord in my fingers as I waited for someone to answer. "Fire, fire!" I shouted at the man.

Can I have your address please? And then the phone cut out.

Flames owned the computerised shed. The phone line melted away my connection.

Mobile phones were bricks back then. It took the fire brigade forever to arrive. We stood on the lawn, listening to the fire station alarm, and then the truck siren, watching the smoke rise and plume above the farm.

The stand of trees marking the east border thins every winter.

"Did your dad plant these too?"

"Nope," he says, looking up at the towering branches. "Maybe we shouldn't stand under this one," he says, backing away. "Those branches don't look too stable."

"Who planted them?"

They were already here when my grandfather bought the farm. There must have been over a thousand, Dad guesses. Planted to help drain the Plains, turn the marshes into fertile land (food, life, independence, money, big business, like everything). The storm that sunk the Wahine, he tells me, destroyed half of the forest.

I cannot speak. There can't be twenty left today. A thousand? Imagine.

He works hard, today is no exception. As the chainsaw dwindles the fallen logs, I sit on one and survey the farm again. How much space did a thousand trees take up? That paddock, the one beside it? But the rest of the farm had none. What did it look like without all of these trees in those paddocks to the east? What did my grandfather see when he bought this landscape, bare and green?

Did he turn like I am doing now, and sighting a thousand blue gums contemplate felling them, or mirroring their towering presence into the rest of the farm. He had a vision. I wish I knew what it was.

Did he imagine the shelterbelts, the orchard, the hedges, the single trees in his plan? He must have planted over a hundred. One lonely but thriving walnut tree. My father's green walnut chutney is amazing on sourdough. There was an avocado tree on the lawn of the cottage that we grew from a pip, despite Dad insisting that it would never produce. It took nine years, and then suddenly, one autumn, there was a knobbly green fruit hidden in the trees. That was the only fruit we ever saw, and the year I left home, a late summer storm knocked it over.

I called my grandmother to let her know I was running late. "Sorry, I've forgotten something, and I had to dash back home to get it," I puff as I unlock the door I had just locked. "I'll be at your house in ten minutes."

"That's fine," she says.

She's not fine when I walk into her house. Her eyes are red. "Why am I going? I don't even like these people."

I used to smile for her bluntness, but now I want to cry. "I'll bring you home as soon as you've had enough," I insist. "It's nice to get out."

We walk outside, she refuses my arm. She fumbles with the keys. We turn towards my car and she stops.

"Where are we going again?"

I draw in my breath. "We're going to see your brother-in-law. He's looking forward to seeing you. Just a nice coffee and I'll bring you straight home."

She refuses my arm. I strap her seatbelt around her. "I really don't think I should be going."

I kiss her on the cheek. "It will be fun."

The Barn (with a capital B) stands on a lean. One side is filled with towering piles of hay. When we were little, our summers were spent in fields of hay, cut, turned, baled, stacked. The tractor and the loader are long gone. They were replaced by an air-conditioned cab and a baler that has a counter on. 267, 268, 269 bales. And the bales are huge now, so its unsafe to play in them. My children don't get to play like I did, making tunnels and bargaining *that pile over there is your house, and this little dip here in the hay is my house.*

There is one iron piece in the wall that is newer than the others. Chickens, a tangy bite to the nostrils, finding the eggs all along the rows of straw nests. Chasing them along the raceways in the sun. I don't remember them taking the coop away and replacing the wall.

There was a pig pen, the old fashioned 'insinkerator'. God they were scary, those beasts, and did you know they kill their young? Before I left home, Dad and I turned that pen into a very successful vegetable garden. He taught me how to prick out the tomato plants to produce more as the mosquitoes fed on our legs.

"It's just terrible," tears are welling in her eyes. She covers her mouth with her hands. "Terrible. I just can't think straight. I can't remember." Her head is jerking, tiny little spasms.

"It's okay," I say to her, and rub her back. "I'll make you a coffee."

"It just feels, it just feels," quiet mews of anguish.

The kitchen bench is covered in little pieces of paper. Take medicine with breakfast. Billy rang. Earthquake in Japan. Need washing powder. Roundup causes cancer – news.

Sticky labels on the jar of sugar, the drawer with the spoons. I open the fridge to get the milk and find a torch.

I watch the steam rising from the jug as it boils into a cloud. It just feels, alright.

We had a plastic milk billy with a lid and a blue handle that we trundled to the shed many, many mornings, on a mission for fresh cold milk from the vat. The billy was replaced with the milk jug, a large red Tupperware pitcher that was harder to fit against the milk vat outlet and usually resulted in us returning home somewhat damper. Always destined for milkshakes, cereal and custard – oh, Dad makes a mean chocolate custard. And then the doctor diagnosed my dairy allergy.

I didn't stop drinking milk until I left home, nine years later. It's hard to see the wood for the trees sometimes, isn't it? On the last day of milking I did sneak a billy of milk, and reminded myself that it was worth it as I scratched my raw and swollen skin.

On the last day, I stood under that row of entangled trees, the late autumn sun streaming through as the sun set, and took one last photo. Later, I saw that in it, Dad's shadow is reflected on the ground.

Yesterday I drove past. Three men were felling the Wahine trees, the eucalyptus towers. There was just one left, a single solider in the paddock, tall and proud and surrounded by fallen comrades. I turned up the music on the car stereo so that the children couldn't hear me crying.

One thousand to zero.

There are so many holes in my heart, I can't understand why I am not leaking blood. Puddles of red tears. Dad seems happier.

There was a rubbish pit on the farm. Imagine trying to do that now. When it got full, someone would light a fire in it, then use the tractor to cover it up. Dig a new one beside it. One day we walked in that paddock, and we found a glass jar, lid tightly screwed on. Mayonnaise, expiry date readable. And inside, in a little puddle against the lid, a spiderweb of white thirty-six-year-old mayonnaise.

I toss the mayonnaise jar into the box, it's nearly full and doesn't expire for seven months. They're not glass jars anymore, plastic. So much plastic in the pits of this Earth now. 100% of sea turtles, 100% of birds, plastic in the gut.

The mustard follows, full, unopened, but the nearly empty jar of tomato sauce is hurled into the rubbish bag. In the next room I can hear Dad boxing up the serving set. It hasn't been used in, oh, at least eleven years now. In another house, another life, I would have wanted a serving set.

Dad comes in and hands me a cake server. He runs his fingers down his beard, and I run my fingers over the carved silver. I can almost taste the apricot flans, the custard tarts, shiny latticed pastry tops, slivers of just-picked kiwifruit on hand-whipped puffs of whipped cream. Memories are carved upon the heart and it is all ending, as all good things do, but sadly, and finally.

I stand up and arch my back, rub my neck. I really wish that she was here right now, boiling the jug, asking me if I wanted a cup of coffee.

Oh, no, you don't have hot drinks, she would say.

A DRESS FOR MOTHER

By Audrey Brown-Pereira

the wind is moving strangely
the trees are blowing everywhere
and yet the red bloom of flamboyant   remains calm

                        stop
                                start
                        stop
start   the girls are looking at colours and patterns of dresses
                                            blue
                                                    turquoise
                                        aqua   green
                                                and
                                        white

she's breathing   heavy now
                            heavy
        can't recognise her voice
                    her mind everywhere
                                    but here in our conversation
she's not hungry
appetite eaten   all of her   she wears

193

        her red beret and smile   on her skinny legs

        now made for imaginary mini-skirts   she laughs

in and out

      about the party for her 70th

      with family from her childhood   no one knows

              seen or heard

her breathing

      it's real heavy now

too heavy

it's slowing down the wind

          the trees appear s t i l l now *if* only for a moment

      as the wind carries seeds

      to a new place

      to grow

the girls decide

their mother will wear red

AN ARRANGED MARRIAGE OF SORTS

By Rebecca Tobo Olul -Hossen

It was Tata who first pointed out the teacher from a foreign place to her. From that time Iakangim tried really hard not to appear to be looking at him. It was hard not to look. Especially when all the women and men in the village remarked on his unusual unmanly ways.

Men on Tanna did not cook. They did not wash clothes. They spent most of their waking time, if not in the garden tending to their yams or feeding the pigs at Nipang Lawahtani, sitting in the imaiim (nakamal) talking about the village's business with other men – a sanctity that women were not permitted to intrude on.

Tabi was different. In the mornings he comes outside to empty out pots he used to cook his dinner furiously scrubbing the fire-blackened pots clean with ash, coconut husks and water. During weekends he spent lots of time methodically washing and hanging out his weeks' worth of clothes to dry on the line by his house.

This was completely unheard of according to the men. In fact, it rated as scandalous according to the women in the village.

Too often is the remark about food being unclean if cooked by men. Men touched their penises. Any food they touched cannot be eaten. Just like when women see the moon's sick, that they are not to handle food.

Tata, being the man that he was, decided to take matters into his own hands

- to make a man out of Tabi. For a start he invited Tabi to the imaiim for kava.

From that time Tata spoke in earnest to Iakangim about Tabi.

Iakangim had a good job as a nurse. She was better educated than many of the village girls. She was raised very much on her own. That is until the twins came along. Iakangim was her father's princess.

But there was only one thing that darkened all of this. Iakangim was a single mother of a little boy. The baby's father and his family did not want anything to do with Iakangim and the boy, denying the boy, throwing their belongings out of their house, and telling them to leave.

No man in the village would be able to take care of her and her son like Tabi could, Tata said. From the beginning, Iakangim felt fated to be with Tabi. She often wondered if Tabi felt the same way.

Due to Tata's promptings, Iakangim finally worked up the courage to speak with Tabi. She begun to get to know this soft spoken and gentle man. A man who did not think it was women's work to cook or wash clothes. But a man, nonetheless.

Iakangim and Tabi decided to get married.

When Tabi came home to get permission from Tata to ask Iakangim to marry him, Tata spoke at length of Iakangim's status as his princess and her place in the village. He talked about Tanna kastom. That there would not be any bride price like the foreign kastoms in the north. But that there will be a kastom exchange. Anytime anything happened between the couple, Iakangim belonged here and will return to the same treasured place.

Eventually with all negotiations complete and the agreements in place, Iakangim and Tabi were married in a quiet ceremony at the Presbyterian Church in the village with only two of Tabi's brothers there to witness it.

Even on the day of marriage, Iakangim was sure the men in the village were wondering how she was marrying such an 'unmanly man'.

She smiled quietly as she said, "I do". She knew that the women, despite their mutterings, were really envious in their hearts. They knew only too well that Iakangim would be well taken care of.

Tata had tears in his eyes. His princess was being married off. In his heart he knows she is going to a secure place, just like the one she had in the village.

For my Yaca

By Emmaline Pickering-Martin

"Yaca!"

She ran up the hill towards her voice, the raspy tone of her Yaca calling her to the house. Jumping across pineapple plants and hearing her Papa behind her, muttering something about food and feet, she ran faster, knowing a vidi behind the ears was close by. Turning left past the tall banana palm she reached the top of the hill. The blue verandah beckoned her out of the sun and into its cool concrete shade.

"Yaca! There you are luvequ! Mai!"

Her Yaca was standing in the garden, next to the pawpaw tree, Papa's favourite one that would wake them up dropping fresh pawpaw onto the roof over Papa's bedroom sometimes. She was wearing a white singlet, the thin one, with baby powder under her arms, and a brown sulu that said Sheraton Fiji in white writing along the bottom. Her cousins worked at the Sheraton and her Uncle played the guitar in a band there. She had been to listen to him play a few times. It was always so much fun. The adults drank grog and Fiji Bitter, and the kids got chicken flavoured potato chips after swimming in the hotel pools. Yaca smiled at her.

"I want you to go to the shop and pick up one five-dollar bag of grog, 1 packet of blue hax and 1 BH 10. Give Mrs Rakkha this, see? Then when she gives you change, you buy sweets for you. Okay?"

She nodded, eyes wide open and salivating at the thought of fresh red jalebi and hot peanuts in the shell from the shop by the park. She loved the warmth of the shells in those small white bags. They reminded her so much of her Yaca and the late nights grogging at the family houses.

"Don't forget to wear your shoes, you know the glass bottles smashed at the top so put your shoes on!".

Yaca was always reminding her of the little things. If it wasn't the glass at the top of the stairs, it was the neighbours' dog who enjoyed chasing little girls to the top of the street, then waiting for them to return to chase them back down to the house.

She took the money, found her flip flops and skipped out the door. The house was built by her Papa and Uncles before she was born. It was all she had known. You had to go down steep stairs from the road to the house and then down a steep hill from the house to the plantation. She always thought that was part of the magic. Living halfway. Roadside above and plantation and creek below. Some of her most bestest memories above, below and inside the house.

As she stepped up the first step a voice trailed behind her …

"Yaca! Sogota na katuba kerekere!"

Whoops! She slipped back down the step and quickly shut the front door. Yaca and Papa deeply disliked having the wire door swinging open. The flies annoyed them. With that done, she began the ascent up to the road. Twenty-nine. That's how many stairs her Uncle had made from leftover wood and concrete. Each time she would count every single one and take giant steps to try and skip one or two, but eight-year-olds don't have long legs like their Uncles. So she always ended up at twenty-nine.

At the top of the stairs by the roadside she stood breathless. She grabbed at her shorts pocket and found her pump. Fumbling a little she took two puffs. Her asthma always seemed a little bit worse in the heat. She stood under the banana palm at the top of the stairs. Across the road she could see the neighbours' gate was open. Pink bougainvillea lined the top of the gate, her eyes followed the beautiful pink plumes, until she noticed the dog. The one that liked to chase little girls to the top of the street and then wait for them to get back and chase them down again.

Taking another two puffs of her pump and shoving it in her pocket she turned and pretended she hadn't seen the dog. Picking up her pace she passed one driveway on her side of the road. There were three left before the top of the street. She could hear her heartbeat and the blood pumping in her ears. Breathing gently, hoping the dog didn't hear her footsteps, she carried on and upped the pace. A small growl came from the street behind her.

Her pace quickened to a run and she was off. When they said Fijians were born wingers, they weren't lying. She sprinted like her Uncle Serevi chasing that final try for the win in a Fiji rugby match. At the top of the road she turned around and saw the dog sauntering back home in defeat. She knew he would be waiting patiently for her return.

She went on, breathing heavily. Mrs Rakkha's shop was over the bridge and two driveways down. She crossed her street to the other side and then walked along the bridge. The rails were thick metal pipes and partially covered with more bougainvillea, both purple and pink. The water underneath flowed down across her street and down a big drain on the side of their house. When it rained the drain would flood, and she would rain bath and float boats she made out of sticks. She stood for a little while and watched the water flowing quietly under the rails.

She went on. Kicking small rocks and looking ahead to see if anyone was at the park. 'Au sa via lai quito i na rara,' she thought as she strolled. Yaca would be waiting so she couldn't, but the thought was there, lingering. 'Segai Lewa! Sa Kua!' kicking a bigger rock as she got to the shop.

Mrs Rakkha was kind and caring. She knew everyone's names and who you belonged to. She could say all of her cousins' names off by heart when they were all together. It was amazing. Mrs Rakkha always gave extra sweets, and sometimes she would let her have a cola if she promised to drink it at the shop and not tell her Yaca. She always told her Yaca anyway, and she would say "Weilei Mrs Rakkha always spoiling you gang". It never made her angry; she always smiled when she said it.

The shop was a little building with lots of signs and big metal bars across the front windows. Sometimes the door was closed and you had to order through the door. Other times it was open and you could walk in and order at the counter. There were still big bars inside over the counter, but you could see all the sweets when you walked in. The door was open. She went in.

"Bula Yaca! When did you arrive?" Mrs Rakkha was always so excited to see her. She knew she lived in Niu siladi now and always asked how the weather was there.

"I arrived on Tuesday," she replied.

"Weilei it's been too long mai mai my girl". Mrs Rakkha walked around the counter and gave her a big hug. She picked her up and took her to the back of the shop. "Raica, pick whatever ones you want!" she gestured to a table full of JALEBI! Fresh hot red and orange Jalebi.

Eyes wide with delight, she grabbed three red and two orange jalebi and stuffed them into a bag.

"Now what did you want my dear?" asked Mrs Rakkha.

She stopped, the excitement clouding her memory. What was it Yaca asked for? Think. Think. THINK. She stared at the ten-dollar note in her hand.

"One bag of grog, one packet of blue hax and …" she stopped. What was it? She knew it was important. What was it? She looked around the shop hoping to jog her memory. Then she saw it. The sign she was looking for. A gold sign with black lettering. 'Benson and Hedges'. "And one BH 10 please".

"Weileiiii!" Mrs Rakkha laughed. "Tell that Yaca of yours she needs to quit". She handed her a small black plastic bag with one bag of grog, one packet of blue hax and one BH 10 in it. Then she gave her one dollar and eighty cents change. "Don't worry about paying for the sweets, I missed you Yaca. You can have them because I missed you. Keep those coins for next time." Mrs Rakkha then turned around and handed her one last item. A warm bag of fresh peanuts still in the shell.

Squealing with delight she skipped out of the shop, and started her journey back home. Across two driveways she stopped to look at shapes on the ground.

"Isaaa na boto sa mate," she whispered as she passed several boto frames on the driveway.

She walked past the purple and pink bougainvillea and listened quietly to the water making its way back down the hill to her home. She stopped there for a while and cracked a peanut shell. Eating the warm contents and throwing the empty shell into the water, hoping she would see it later down in the creek. It floated leisurely away. She took a deep breath as she crossed back over her street.

There he was. The dog. Sitting there like a small soldier defending precious treasures. Except there were no treasures, just her and her bag full of Yaca's stuff. She took a deep breath. Looked at the ground and started walking down towards her steps. Three driveways. She had to cross three driveways before she was there.

One. She walked briskly, hoping the dog found something else to do. Halfway to the second one and he came sprinting. A bark so loud that it made her jump into a run as she was passing the second driveway. Running fast, but she sees the dog in her periphery, snarling and running alongside her.

"PLEASE DONT BITE ME. PLEASE DONT BITE ME," she thought, but not uttering a word in case he did BITE her.

Just before she reached the stairs she heard a loud booming voice "GWWWWWWONNNNN !!!"

A voice she knew all too well. Uncle!!! Of course he was there, home from work. Her favourite. He was always there. Every time something scary happened. Every time something sad happened. Every time she was getting in trouble from her Na. He was there.

He scooped her up in his arms and yelled at the dog again, "GWON!"

The dog stopped chasing and sauntered back to his gate, turning to give her his, 'We will meet again' look.

She giggled and snuggled into Uncle's sweaty neck. He had on his bright orange overalls. He gave her a big kiss. "What have you got in there baby?" he asked.

"One bag of grog, one packet of blue hax, five of Mrs Rakkha's jalebi and some hot peanuts in the shells," she said, smiling at his scrunched up nose touching hers.

"Is that all?" he enquired.

"Oh and one BH ten for Yaca."

LEDGER

(For my twin sister - and our accountant mother)
By Nafanua PK

I'll make an account of our cells one day
        use bone pen, blood ink to carbon receipt
a sum split even and balanced away

I will have earned enough words by then, you see
and with the small change of languages-three
I'll make an account of our cells

Double lines ruled, a margin of veins
on a ream of red light
where we once reigned
as a sum cut rough
        two folds of wet clay

In quickening stretch and salt mother tongue
        where time goes unmarked
except by the sun
there,

                I'll make an account of our cells, one day

See, there's You, Me, and She
the inspired damp where life longs to be
       but a full sum, complete
no debt in its way

With binder clipped
       tight band snapped,
bone-bond paid
and bloodclot wrapped

I'll make an account of our cells one day
a grand sum of two
no halves in our way.

BROTHERS

By Lehua Parker

Drifting in our small fishing boat off the coast of the Big Island, Hawaii, I look toward the Naʻiwi shore. Our family's tents are on the campground above the sand, but I don't see my cousins Haley, Kade, or Jace. Uncle Jeff took them cliff jumping. Too dangerous, my parents said. Come fishing with us. We'll catch something good for dinner.

I don't even like fish. It's so unfair.

"Kekoa," Dad says. "Why aren't you wearing your life jacket?"

"Hot," I say. "Itchy."

Mom says, "You know the rules."

"In a minute," I say, leaning over the safety railing.

On shore, I watch my cousins Roxi and Maile practice hula in the shade. While Tutu and the Aunties talk story and play cards, Uncle Josh tends the grill. Fat dripping and juice sizzling onto keawe coals, the smell of the huli-huli chicken reaches all the way to the boat.

So ʻono. And I'm so hungry. I want to go back to camp where the fun is. Where the food is. We haven't caught anything all day.

"Do we really need to catch fish? Uncle Josh is cooking chicken," I whine.

"Put your jacket on now, Kekoa," Mom says. "Stop stalling."

But before I can, a breeze steals my hat.

"No!" I swing my arm to catch it, but it falls into the water, the current teasing it just out of reach.

Dad says, "I'll get the net."

"No, I got it, Dad." I jump up and rest my thighs against the rail. Balancing with one hand on the boat, I stretch out like I'm playing first base. My fingers brush the brim.

"Kekoa," Mom warns.

Just a tiny bit more—

I fall.

I don't even have time to scream.

Underwater, I sink like a stone, my shoes dragging like anchors. My ears pop as the ocean sucks me down, down, down. Water swims up my nose. I open my eyes and blink through the salt sting. Bubbles escape my lips, tickling as they rise.

I kick and kick, but the ocean won't let me go. Down I sink, faster than I can swim. I cover my mouth with both hands, trying to keep my breath in.

Drowning.

It's a terrible way to die.

Out the corner of my eye, something flickers.

I'm not alone. The hair rises on the back of my neck. I spin in the water, trying to spot the new danger. Rising fast out of the darkness and spiralling like a torpedo, death comes.

It's a shark.

He's big—at least six feet long. He circles past me; his alien black eye peering into mine.

I kick harder and swing my arms like I'm climbing a ladder, but I'm not going anywhere. My bubbles race past me to the surface.

Only ten yards away, the shark shakes his head, flashing his teeth.

It's no use. I can't swim away. I make a fist and face him. I'm not going down without a fight.

He rounds in a tight circle and charges. I pull back my fist. The pressure wave hits a split second before I swing, a moment when time slows and I can count each gaping tooth. I punch and punch until his head snaps back, eyes wide. He jerks away.

Holy cow. That worked.

I tip my head to the surface. The boat's miles above me. I ditch my shoes. Anchors gone, I start to rise. I swim, pulling my arms and legs like a frog.

Twenty feet more. I'm going to make it.

WHAM!

The shark hits me in the back, propelling me through the water like a rocket. I reach back and rip at his tender gills. He jerks away again and circles to the front. He lowers his head.

He's not giving up.

My lungs burn. The ringing in my ears is louder than the recess bell. I'm dizzy. Around the edges, my vision blurs. There's no way I can make it to the surface now. I shake my head and try to think.

If I breathe in water, it will end. Just one giant breath of saltwater, then darkness, no pain. But my lips refuse to open. My lungs won't swell. I can't bring myself to do it.

I'm not giving up.

This time, the shark comes cautiously. As he sidles along my stomach, I punch and punch, my knuckles tearing against his sandpaper skin. To him my fists are nothing more than the buzzing of a fly to a bull. When his nose nudges my ribs, I screw my eyes tight and scream my lungs empty. I feel him thrash, burrowing his head.

For an eternity, I wait, but I don't feel teeth.

Maybe you don't feel what kills you.

The shark flicks his tail, once, twice, three times.

Faster than the bubbles, I rise.

My head breaks the surface. Gasping, I open my eyes, expecting to see red lehua blossoms of blood in the water, but all I see is my shredded tee-shirt floating around me. Thirty yards away in our boat, Mom and Dad frantically scan the water. Dad's about to jump in. The shark nudges me one last time, then turns away.

"Mom!" I yell, but my head goes back under.

"There!" Mom points.

"Kekoa, I'm coming!" Dad says.

"No!" I scream, flailing to stay at the surface. "Shark!"

The shark's dorsal fin cruises to the boat and passes alongside. Mom looks down. "Oh, Ke Akua, look at the stripes! Kamalei! It's Kamalei!" she shrieks.

The shark wheels and circles toward me. The boat's too far. Dad's too far. Treading water, I brace myself. This time I'll go for the eyes.

Mom shouts, "Kekoa! Grab the shark!"

Grab the shark? Is she crazy?

"Do it!" Dad yells.

As the shark brushes by, I grab his dorsal fin. In an instant, the shark glides over to the boat. Dad reaches down, pulls me out of the water, and dumps me on the deck. I cough and cough all the water out of my lungs, but Mom and Dad don't hug or scold me. They don't even hand me a towel. They're both leaning over the railing.

"Mom?"

She turns to me, tears in her eyes. "Come," she says.

I peer over the side to see the shark resting alongside our boat. Mom leans down into the water and strokes his back. Dad's crying, too. Mom takes my hand and places it on the shark. Along his back are delicate stripes of black, gray, blue, and red, checkered and crisscrossed like sunlight through water. I've never seen anything like it.

Mom whispers in my ear. "Kekoa, thank your brother."

I whip my head at her in disbelief. She's not joking. Dad kneels next to me and puts his hand on the shark, too. He says, "It's true. Before you were born, Mom and I went camping at Naʻiwi." He gestures to the shore.

Mom says, "I was seven months pregnant."

"Wait. You had a baby before me?"

She nods. "The doctor told me everything was fine. The baby was strong and healthy. But in the middle of the night, I went into labor. Your brother was stillborn." She takes a deep breath as the memory slides across her face. "I named him Kamalei for the star that shone when he was born. In the moonlight, I washed my firstborn in the sea and wrapped his body in a checkered blanket." She traces the shark's stripes with her finger. "This pattern. This towel." Beneath sandpaper skin, shark muscles twitch. "I'd know it anywhere."

"But—"

Dad says, "Just listen. In the morning, we dug a grave near the beach and buried Kamalei."

"You left him? Is that even legal?"

Dad smiles. "Naʻiwi is a beautiful place. Peaceful. No matter who owns it, it's been our family's land for generations. It seemed like the right thing to do."

"Dad and I spent three days watching the tides and stars and telling Kamalei how much we loved him. We knew he needed to meet the rest of his ʻohana, so we left for a few hours to bring them."

"Everybody came—the entire ʻohana. Grandparents, great-grandparents, aunties, uncles—everybody. We brought a stone to mark the grave, but when we got here, something had torn open the ground. The blanket, your brother—everything—gone."

"Gone? I don't understand."

Dad caresses the shark as his tears roll into the ocean. "We failed our son. We left him alone to be eaten by animals."

"I couldn't bear it," Mom says. "My precious baby was gone, and I didn't even have a place to lay a lei."

Dad says, "But then my great-grandmother Tutu Kalamaonamano told us not to cry. 'We are people of the sea,' she said. 'Look with your ancestors' eyes. Feel with your ancestors' hearts.' She took your mother by the hand and showed her the trail in the sand that led from the empty grave to the ocean, saying, 'No animal dragged him from his grave. See? Don't mourn. Your child born early and bathed in the sea simply returned to his ocean home.'"

Mom says, "And, as a shark, your brother remembers his ʻohana still."

Dad pulls me close. "And loves us, too."

Blue Cake

By Gina Cole

'Stroke! Now!' yells Whetu. Our inflatable raft rushes into white water. I dig my oar into the river and pull hard. The raft wraps around a rockface, mid-stream.

'Hold on!' Whetu shouts. We huddle into the raft's pumped-up seats. Surging water pins us against the boulder.

'Over to the right!' The raft flips; curls out from the rapids in slow-motion.

We're tossed upside down. My feet fall out of the soft rubber foot cups. My girlfriend Aroha screams, clutches my elbow. I grip her arm. We tumble into the rapids together. Icy water engulfs me, shocks the breath from my lungs. Swimming against the cascading torrent, struggling in the headlong flow we lose hold of each other. The current takes me. I join the race to the sea. Downstream, Aroha's head bobs to a safe patch of slow flat water. Whetu runs along the riverbank, following me, her shouts echoing against rocky cliff faces.

I gulp air. A wave dumps on my head and sucks me down. I am caught underwater unable to break free. The river holds me submerged, rushes into my face, pulls and tugs me in every direction.

My lungs are bursting. I'm going to die here. Whetu appears above me on a boulder. She reaches for me, yanks my life jacket, tries to pull me clear. The Velcro strap rips open. Whetu sways, loses her hold on me, falls back. I'm trapped beneath a blue triangular rock.

This can't be happening. My mind travels back to my third birthday. I ate too much cake. Vomited a perfect blue cone of regurgitated sponge cake in a pile on the wooden floor beneath my chair.

Whetu tugs on my life jacket, pushes my shoulders. I sluice free from the rock. My head breaks the water's surface. I gasp and gulp. Whetu grabs my blue hand.

ECLIPSED

By Arihia Latham

Kiri checked her message app again. She had to search his name because she'd archived their chat already. It told her he'd been active at 3pm that day. Still no contact with her though. Sixteen days. Sixteen days of silence since he got up from the couch and said, 'I can't do this anymore'.

Tonight she is curled into her couch cushions watching the slow blood moon eclipse out the window. The darkness creeps up incrementally from the hills creating a tiny frown of ochre at the top. This is what happened to his face that night. He sat across from her, not beside her as she'd motioned to him when they started their talk. And as she sat there watching him, he seemed to be detaching, slowly darkening the glow of her.

His silence was the muffled pull of blankets in the night, his mouth the downturned crescent of the sheet. She thinks of this expression on his face as he leaves often. It's not the one she wants to remember. He made himself mean, she thinks, when he was just afraid. This could, of course, just be her tendency to psychoanalyse every situation in her life. To put everything in two neat categories of love or fear. Act from one or the other, people, she thinks. She wonders about Rona on the moon and if she loved it there, or was afraid.

The Māori astronomer is telling her in a live video that the blood moon is Whiro trying to squash or darken Hina. The image of a dark scallop shell pinching closed around the full glory of its pearl rests in Kiri's mind. She feels her belly cramping, as if her ovaries have decided they too have a pearl on offer tonight. God, why is everything so fucking connected? Can't she just exist outside of time and space and planets and gravity and tides and feelings and global pandemics? But, of course, the moon resembling a red light was not lost on her, as she was trying to understand what the new normal at her job would be. Checking people's passports at the door of the art gallery, and internalising her own anxiety about having to now be alone if the country goes back into lockdown. She starts looking up flights to her sister's place. Her heart beats faster at the thought of going home. Her belly upstages her heart again but, instead of getting pain relief, she scrolls through old photos of the two of them as a couple. Looking for a shadow in his love. Was it creeping over them back when they could still travel to Auckland, and they stayed in a fancy hotel and ate Japanese food. Was he eclipsing her slowly as they went to watch Pacific poetry at the theatre? Was it all the exhibition openings she'd made him pour the drinks at for her work?

For a moment the moon looks like a chip with a scoop of dip on it, and she laughs to no one. Laughs with the cushion pressed into her belly. She tries to tell herself that nothing is connected. It's just a random series of events that you can cry over, or you can just laugh. Laugh like she is sure Rona did when she finally accepted she was there on the moon to stay. Probably just to lie around and eat chips. Oh, for the luxury of moon life.

'I can do this. I can do boundaries. I can pretend I am enveloped in space - light years away from everything, and not text him . . . again. Of course, it might get a little lonely out there.'

Kiri is chatty. He once said she was 'the most honest, communicative person I have ever encountered.' as he'd tucked her hair behind her ear. It had been a rare burst of speech for him, and she held it close. Treasured it. Normally, his silence was like the dark sky. She would ask him a question, and it was like time had been put into slow motion, as minutes ticked by before he would carefully answer her. She used to practise counting in her head, so she wouldn't shout 'answer me' at him. She is a comet rushing through with so much light and time and ideas and hilarity. She is laughing, alone of course, because he'd walked out with the night sky like a cape around him, and now she can't even message him, because she did that three days ago and he was still silent. 'Answer me!'

she shrieks up at the moon. As it furrows further into the frown of the eclipse.

She had so many things to say to him. Nowhere for them to go. She knew if she sent them to her mates they would get worried about her. She diligently decides to write him letters, just small ones in her notes app on her phone, just the things she would have said to him if he was there.

As she dresses for the day, her generous butt and puku curve out of the new underwear she'd bought online a month ago. It had arrived in the mail yesterday and she realises he won't even see her in it. Sighing, she snaps a selfie in the mirror for incaseys.

Taku tau.

What are you doing?

I feel like you should really see me right now. I have matching underwear on. I feel that's an area we could work on, you actually noticing my underwear, and how I have made an effort there. I'm wondering if you saw the eclipse last night and whether it felt like your face!?! Does the moon give men cramps too? If yes to the last question . . . Where? DO YOU FEEL ANYTHING?

Kiri scrambles off the bus and jogs to work in inappropriate wedges. She glides into the gallery seven minutes late with sweat beading on her upper lip beneath her protective mask. Her boss raises one manicured eyebrow as she manoeuvres her rigid blonde bob and impeccable red lips back to the painting of the new show she is observing. Kiri smiles the kind of smile that gives a 'you know how it be - we're in the same club' look which isn't reciprocated. She stuffs her mask in her bag till customers arrive and manoeuvres it and her coat into the overstuffed storeroom. She checks the app one more time for when he was last active. 8.08am. But still no response. Fingers hovering, she quickly opens her notes instead;

Bebe.

I miss you and wonder if I can unravel myself from the safety net I thought we had been knotting. Slowly, surely we were rolling muka in our fingers. Or, maybe, like your ancestors it was Sisal. Maybe that's the problem, we were working with different materials. I can see your long brown fingers now knotting slowly and methodically in that practical way you have. Your eyebrows knotted in concentration too. I want to smooth you out, I want to uncrumple you. I want to untie you.

The day stretches out like tough chewing gum before her. She emails out the curated invitation list for their socially distanced exhibition opening, and fields inquiries from the press. She flicks between these and social media where, of course, he hasn't posted anything, because he never did. Leaving her stuck in the dark. Leaving her thoughts in a non-consensual bind, stuck to him like gum to a shoe.

So, hey.

The cramps in my belly remind me that we never talked about children. I thought about what our babies would look like most days. Did you? Should we even consider having children anymore? In a pandemic and at a time when the carbon levels of the atmosphere are set to rise instead of fall to the safety of 350ppm where it may no longer be safe for children to actually live out our hopes and dreams. Hello? Did you ever think of me round as a full moon, contractions eclipsing me? Everything inside of me is knotted.

After work Kiri meets Sera, her best friend of all eternity, for a drink. Sera is definite.

'No, you *cannot* message him. I mean, what kind of fucking cock leaves this queen on seen?' She preaches, motioning to Kiri with her free hand.

'But . . . what if he isn't okay? Like, have I left a depressed person in their time of need?

'Girl, look at me. You were there with him every step. He's the one that isn't letting you be with him. Remember that. In his time of need! What he actually needs is his ass kicked." And she orders shots and fries.

My love

Surely it's time to drop this. I know you are an introvert. I know you were feeling off with life in general. I am not the enemy. I have been reading a lot about the drama triangle and I wondered where you saw us in that? Was I always the persecutor? Did you see yourself as the victim? I want to rescue us. If mouth to mouth would do it, you know we had magic in our lips. Remember we'd say our lips found each other like waves finding the shore. Or maybe it was just me that said that, and I thought when you kissed me, it was agreement.

The next morning a photo of an eight-year-old in book day dress ups is waiting on her screen. His eyes, effervescent as cola, happily dressed as Māui, shapeshifter. Her shapeshifter. Shifting out of her body into her sister's arms. She, like Taranga, cut her hair in mourning, wrapped him in it for eternity, sending him across the ocean as she did what she had to do.

The thing is, I'm not really that honest. When I pulled away sometimes. When you touched me and I froze. I can't rescue you, because I couldn't admit I needed rescuing. I dreamt of carrying your babies because I know what that feels like. I have a child. Just not one stemming from love. My child is loved like a black pearl. They are living with my sister as her own. You never met that side of the whānau I know. I hid them on purpose. Tāku tau I am unravelling and all the knots are loosening. Your silence is like oil. Slick in the night, on the ocean, carrying my dreams. It is sluicing the knots I have carefully tied around me and filling my eyes, my taringa, my mouth, my tara. Filling the spaces of me with aching quiet. My love, it is like time has become an endless thread. The fibres are oiled in my fingertips. Time has become the only thing I can accept as both real and incomprehensible.

The weekend. The time that usually meant they could wrap tight around each other, it was just for them. The time now is saggy, worn. Minutes tick by into hours, and Kiri stays in bed procrastinating and writing notes furiously.

I forget what we fought about. I forget why you left. I have forgotten all the reasons for the world in the darkness. They have found a new strain of the virus and named it to sound like a Greek robot. You and I would have laughed at this, and talked like R2-D2 and C3PO with sheets wrapping around us and leaves on our heads as a weird mash-up of robotic Aphrodite and Adonis. We'd feel smug about having each other in a pandemic. We could have felt so smug

217

together, wrapping limbs over each other like Kamokamo vines. When you tried Kamokamo for the first time, you didn't respond like I needed you to. I should have seen the future in this. I carefully mashed it in butter and spooned it to your grimacing mouth. I ate the rest and didn't enjoy it as much as I should have beside your ambivalence. I rub my soft belly, a shell without a pearl. You could have met my son who is now my nephew. You could have heard why I gave him to my sister who already had two children and a dog. You could have judged me and eclipsed me then anyway.

Kiri drags herself out of bed and faces the low cloud and incessant wind of the day. It felt fitting for her mental state. She forces her body into active wear, scrambles for mismatched socks, becomes distracted.

I scroll through social media again and your photos are only ones others have posted of you, because you never engage with such narcissistic pastimes. Your self-loathing stops my camera enough as it is. Your photo feed is like a graveyard of your girlfriends who have tagged you in their photos. They stain the story of you, and you do nothing to scrub it clean. You say nothing. You say nothing.

She throws her phone at the bed and leaves the house. Then comes back for it, because what sane woman running alone wouldn't want music. Her thoughts dictate messages and her feet type each word to the ground.

I went running today because I needed to run from my past. I needed to run from this stagnating want for you. I needed to run because my son is running a race today at the other end of the country. So I put in my ear buds and played the songs that make me feel like there is more than just this empty feeling. You told me before you left that you couldn't ever see us moving in together, you would never marry me. Your rejection isn't new to me, see. You're just coming in and picking at an old scab. It's almost black with dried blood. I won't bleed for you taku tau. Because time is something that wraps around us like a korowai. I won't roll it out like an aisle to walk down. I won't cry for the confetti because there are Karo and Poroporo flowers and Whau's tiny white stars falling in this brutal wind. They are swirling around me. I need no minute pieces of coloured paper when Tane's children celebrate me thus.

Tarata is staining the air with its scent like sunlight soap and skin fresh from a swim. The wind is wanting it to be inside my pores. It is asking me to breathe it in, and I somehow feel like I am breathing out your rejection as my lungs move like stingrays. I am running down the aisle of my own self-worth and, unsurprisingly, you are still not here. Unsurprisingly, I am alone with my feet cupped by Papa, dark soil pushing each foot back toward Rangi. Like good parents they are giving me space, but softening the blows. Wind is blowing all the thoughts from my head, and my chest is filled with the feeling of being alive, which has nothing to do with your ability to commit to me. My feet move so fast that sparks fly into the sky. The blooms of all the trees are leaving their roosts for the wind. Together we are flying, travelling so fast that we can't hear a thing. There is no universe that has time to check archived messages. The light out here is just too beautiful to move my eyes away from.

My love. I am my love. I am turning inside out and casting new wishes across my mind sky. I am wrapping time around my shoulders and freeing myself. I am flying past your silence and I am heading for the moana. Because this moon has ever pulled waves to the shore like hungry children, they are beating their hands in rhythm on the rocks and I am joining them. The sounds of the earth are filling me with their love. The sounds of shells making pearls is resounding. My lungs billowing like stingrays, are breathing lifetimes of forgiveness. I am floating. Letting fear wash to the shore, remembering that love is trusting this water to hold me. Trusting this time to pass.

Taku tau

You have eclipsed yourself and I hope that the light comes back for you. But I am Auahi Tūroa, I am a comet, I am flying past. I am too quick, too quick, too quick, I have always been too quick. For the dark of you.

MOANA

By Sisilia Eteuati

Now I know

I can't unknow

                   I can't unknow

                                      I can't unknow

You reclaimed
You did the spade work
As we laughingly used to say
back at Uni

when we were young, foolish and wise
                         All at once.
You
Brought in heavy machinery
To build up that which
was not true

And
shored it up with

large boulder lies

And I'm no innocent

But I almost believed
It might be sure enough
shore enough
to build on

Ah but I
am of the sea
of the salt and of the deep
And no tears will I weep
as the sea

comes
wave upon wave
to claim
me.

As it washes me/ you / me away

It whispers

He was sand
Insubstantial
Crushed reef

You are water
Goddess
And he

Dissolves.

Te Rerenga Wairua

By Gina Cole

Shelley married Dick the lighthouse keeper. After postings to three different lighthouses and birthing three children, Shelley liked to get away from Dick. He always picked an argument.

Their house sat on a hill near the lighthouse tower, where the oceans meet and souls take flight.

One morning while the children made hand paintings in their tiny school, Shelley walked a track to the lighthouse, descended the cliff to the sea, stepped onto a rocky ledge - black, shiny, slick with ocean spray. Waves heaved in and sucked out in monstrous king tide sweeps, arching their backs.

Shelley sat daydreaming beneath the ancient Pohutukawa tree, her nylon fishing line wound onto a plastic reel, a bucket of bait, lead sinkers, and shiny silver hooks at her feet. The rogue wave crept up on her, rolled over the rocks, swamped the platform she rested on, lifted her up and dragged her into the moana. On the out swell she remained calm, reached into a forest of giant bullwhip kelp, large waving fronds, fleshy olive blades anchored to submerged pink rocks, their air-filled bladders slithering on the surface.

Salt water streamed into her eyes. She clung to the seaweed with all her might until the wave receded, leaving her dripping, and choking. She pulled herself along slippery kelp stalks up onto the rocks.

Plodding up the cliff face, she leaned into horizontal wind shear threatening to blow her over.

When she reached the lighthouse, she ran all the way home.

In the kitchen, Dick asked, 'Where have you been? You're all wet.'

'Fishing off the rocks. A wave swept me out.'

'That'll teach you for running off.'

She stared at him. 'I nearly died down there.'

He met her gaze, folded his arms. A wind gust rattled the windows. He moved towards her. She reached out her hand. They embraced.

'S'pose I'll start dinner then,' he said. Light.

She drew away from him. He wiped a tear from her cheek. 'Alright. I'll get the children.'

RACHIELI

By Tulia Thompson

Rachieli heard raised voices. Someone was shouting 'Fight! Fight!' She turned to see a crowd gathering. She could recognise some of Tomasi's army mates, tanked up on beer and laughing boisterously. Switching into doctor mode, in case medical assistance was needed, she pushed through the dance floor, saying 'tulou, tulou' to the people blocking her path. There was a loud thump, and shouting and clapping from the crowd. When a girl wearing a tight gold dress moved out of her way, Rachieli had a clear view of Araj staggering, as though he'd been hit.

'Araj!' she shouted, striding through a swarm of sweaty bodies to get to him. The pulsing blue and yellow lights made it difficult to see. She felt as though she'd been plunged underwater. Before she could reach him, Araj crumpled and fell.

Profoundly afraid, Rachieli knelt beside his prone form, the concrete hard and cold beneath her knees, and tried to rouse him. She shouted to Alipate, the tall bartender with long dreads, to call an ambulance. Araj was breathing and his pulse was okay, but he was non-responsive. She took out her iPhone and used the torch to shine light over his pupils. He was unconscious. For a second, she fought the urge to panic, darkness biting like the teeth of a shark. Then she felt Alipate's big hand on her back, asking her what he should do to help. It jolted her out of it.

'Get people to clear a path so the ambulance officers can get through,' she said. Around her, people were calling out their opinions about what had happened.

'Shame,' said a drunk teenager. 'That Indian boy got knocked out by that fulla – one punch.'

Rachieli felt a rush of anger at how Suva locals talked about everyone, people they knew nothing about. People here had a harsh humour. Tomasi sat hunched on a bench a few metres away, holding his hand to his nose. There was blood on his hand. Under the coloured lights, the blood on his Fiji Sevens shirt looked like blotches of ink.

It hit her that her brother Tomasi was Araj's attacker. Tomasi sat still, resolute, like a carved figure. In the dark, it was hard to see why Araj was unconscious. There weren't any signs of a serious blow to the head or chest. She'd need to check his body for a serious bleed.

'Where did he get hit?' she called out to the crowd. One of the guys imitated the punch, pointing to his mid-back. Jisu. It could be kidney trauma.

Rachieli didn't want to leave Araj, but she needed to check Tomasi. He was drunk. Apart from his bleeding nose, he was fine — although clearly too shit-faced to talk. Sweet Jisu, this kid that she had looked after a hundred times. She gave $50 to two of Tomasi's friends to take him home. Then she sat holding Araj's limp hand, waiting for the long notes of the siren, counting seconds and recalculating the probability of serious injury.

In the ambulance, the fluorescent lights made the danger more real. Araj's body was clammy, and his pulse was slowing. Rachieli wished she was just his girlfriend, and not a doctor who could see through the cheerful small talk of the ambulance drivers. She knew that a serious kidney bleed could kill him.

Please Jisu, she prayed silently. Let Araj live. To her relief, Shabeena Patel was on duty at the emergency unit. Shabeena took his vitals and ordered an urgent ultrasound to see whether there was internal bleeding. It seemed likely from Araj's pallor and weak pulse. When the orderlies went to move Araj to radiology, jolting and rattling his trolley, Rachieli was surprised she had never noticed how loud they were before. She cringed as his head jostled against the white sheet. Rachieli went to follow and Shabeena put her hand on her shoulder.

'I'm sorry my love, you can't be the doctor today. You need to wait in the waiting-room.'

'Of course, sorry. That was stupid.' Shabeena's tone had been kind, but Rachieli felt numb and clumsy.

'It's very different being here when it's someone you care about. What's your relationship with Araj?'

'He's my boyfriend,' said Rachieli, and wondered if Shabeena would react.

'Okay,' said Shabeena, her expression unchanged.

'We'll let you know what's happening as soon as we can.' Rachieli had said this line herself many times, like rote, but she knew letting the family members know was often their last priority. The hospital waiting room seemed more desolate than usual, even though she walked through it most days without a second thought. The fluorescent tube-lighting was flickering and buzzing, casting the room with an eerie green tinge. In one corner the tube-light was missing entirely. The plaster on the walls had been repainted over several times in different shades of white. Moths and flying insects drummed against the glass sliding doors. Rachieli looked at her phone. It was just after one. She knew she needed to call Achala Singh. Earlier that evening, Araj had said he'd argued with his mother, but he hadn't wanted to talk about it. Rachieli didn't want to give herself time to worry. She scrolled through the contact list on his iPhone until she found the number, and cringed while the phone rang, knowing it would be waking Achala. A woman answered.

'Excuse me please, Ma'am,' said Rachieli, ridiculously polite from anxiety. 'I apologise for calling so late. This is Rachieli, Araj's . . . friend.'

'Yes,' Achala interrupted. 'Rachieli, I know who you are.' She sounded indignant. Maybe she was someone who sounded angry when they were worried.

'Araj has been hurt,' said Rachieli. She put her finger over her other ear to try and hear Achala more clearly. 'He is at Colonial Memorial Hospital.'

'What's happened?' said Achala, and then Rachieli could hear her shouting for Sudesh. 'He's had a blunt force trauma to his back, which has caused a kidney bleed. They are doing an ultrasound now, but it's possible he could need surgery tonight. He's lost consciousness.' Through the glass window, Rachieli could see the full moon. She heard Achala breathe in sharply on the line.

'Sudesh, Sudesh!' she called, and then there were raised voices speaking in

Hindi. Rachieli had never heard Araj speak in Hindi. She didn't know whether he could. She thought she should ask him about it, when he was okay, when he recovered. She wondered if she'd completely lost her mind to even be thinking about this, especially as she was probably running out of phone minutes. She prayed that the call wouldn't drop out. A man's voice came on the phone.

'Hello. Rachieli, this is Sudesh. I am Araj's brother. What is happening?' She told him what she'd told Achala, and explained that because Araj was unconscious they would need his mother to sign a form as next-of-kin. Sudesh sounded calm and capable, not at all the way Araj had described him. He said they would come straightaway.

Half an hour later Rachieli was still waiting to hear about the ultrasound results, even though the procedure should have only taken ten minutes. Maybe there was only bruising, and it looked fine, and they'd been busy with other patients. Rachieli's mouth was dry, and she searched in her purse for some coins. She walked over to the green plastic table where there was a box of teabags and a jar of instant coffee. She scooped coffee into a Styrofoam cup and poured in hot water from the zip. There was no milk.

A junior doctor called Nisha walked into the waiting room, a cheerful smile on her face.

'Oh, hi Rachieli,' said Nisha, glancing around the room and out the doors. 'I'm looking for the partner of the guy with the kidney tear, Araj –'

'I'm Araj Singh's partner.' Nisha looked at the form on her clipboard.

'Oh yeah.' She laughed. 'Silly me. I presumed his partner would be Indian.'

'He has a kidney tear,' Rachieli prompted, impatient to hear the news.

'Yes,' said Nishra. 'We saw a cut on the ultrasound, so we've taken him into theatre. He should be out in under two hours.'

'Okay thanks,' said Rachieli, already mentally scouring medical articles on kidney trauma and surgery, trying to recall the statistics for mortality, or scarring, infection, and permanent injury. Nisha was still standing there, and Rachieli looked at her, confused. What else was there to say?

'I think it's really cool that you are in a bicultural relationship. I really admire your bravery,' said Nisha, her voice earnest. Rachieli tried to think of how she could respond without being blatantly rude. She thought of Tiny, and how she would just tell Nisha to fuck off.

'I'm sorry,' Rachieli said. 'Araj being in surgery is all I can focus on right now.'

'Of course,' said Nisha putting her warm, French-manicured hand on Rachieli's back as though they were friends.

'Let me know if there is anything I can do.'

Nisha walked back through the swing doors into the emergency department, and a wave of sickness surged through Rachieli. She sat down on a brown vinyl chair, wondering what bothered her so much about Nisha's comments. Aside from the lack of comprehension about what it was like to have a loved one hurt, what grated was the sense that Rachieli had done something admirable by loving Araj, when it was the same as loving anybody. Glad she was the only person in the waiting room, she lay down across three vinyl chairs. The hard metal base of the chairs pressed against her shoulder and hip. From where she was lying, she could see cigarette burns and initials cut into the grey lino. She wished she hadn't encouraged Araj to come out to Traps. They would be at home now, sleeping, if she hadn't.

Rachieli wrote a text to Tiny, telling her about it, and then deleted it because it was too late to send. She looked at the oversized plastic wall clock and decided that Tiny wouldn't mind. She tried again, 'I'm in SMH waiting for Araj to get out of surgery, he was in a fight with Tomasi. It's serious. I'm okay. Please send prayers tho. x'

When Sudesh and Achala arrived, Rachieli recognised them straight away. Achala was immaculately dressed in a green salwar kaameez. She was still a beautiful woman in her mid-sixties, with dramatic almond shaped eyes surrounded by kohl.

Rachieli had long imagined meeting Araj's mother. In her head, she'd seen herself wearing a long skirt and baking an impressive banana cake. Achala would be charmed by her domestic prowess. Who could have imagined this situation instead? Sudesh, taller and broader than Araj, quietly steered his mother down the hospital hallway. Achala was sobbing, and Rachieli was filled with dread. Bubu, please help me through this, she thought. She didn't want to cry, because on a deep level – less conscious than her pragmatic medical self – she was afraid that crying would mean she'd given up hope. Rachieli walked up to them, self-conscious in the clothes she had worn nightclubbing, self-conscious about her broad frame. Perhaps Achala might not think she was physically attractive enough for her son.

Sudesh kissed Rachieli on the cheek. She lent down to hug and kiss Achala, but Achala stayed rigid instead of moving towards her. Rachieli backed away awkwardly. Araj's mother must be in shock.

'What happened to Araj?' said Achala.

Rachieli explained that Araj had gone into surgery and Achala started wailing like a siren, sounding out the injury to her child. Rachieli tried to console her, afraid that Achala's helplessness would catch like bushfire. But Achala sobbed on. Maybe all mothers felt this when their children were hurt. Rachieli didn't know. She hadn't been raised by her own mother.

'We show a lot of emotion in our culture,' said Sudesh, clearly noticing her discomfort.

'So do we,' replied Rachieli. 'When someone passes.'

As soon as she said it, she regretted it.

'It must be frightening for you, too,' said Sudesh.

Rachieli nodded, but she couldn't answer. Her phone beeped with a message from Tiny: 'OMFG that's crazy. I just woke up and read your text. Do you want me to come to the hospital? It's no problem x'. Usually in this situation Rachieli would call Tomasi. 'Come' she quickly typed so Achala didn't hate her for being distracted by something as trivial as a phone.

'How did it happen?' Sudesh asked. He and his mother had sat down, side by side in plastic chairs. He had his arm around Achala. She'd stopped crying, but her face looked bleak and drawn. A cleaner came into the waiting room with a mop and a wheelie bucket and started mopping the floors. The smell of bleach was overpowering. Rachieli felt sick. How could she tell them it was Tomasi? They would hate her. She took a deep breath.

'We went to Traps,' said Rachieli.

'Traps? It's usually safe, isn't it? "said Sudesh, "It's a nightclub, Ma.'

'We went with my brother, Tomasi,' said Rachieli slowly. 'He and Araj were drinking a lot.'

Sudesh was shaking his head. 'But Araj doesn't drink much. I mean, he's a lightweight.'

'Okay,' said Rachieli, wishing she hadn't mentioned the drinking. 'I was on the dance floor. Tomasi and Araj got into a fight. I didn't see it.'

Rachieli felt her body tensing, waiting for them to react. To blame her. Maybe it was her fault. The sliding doors of the emergency unit opened and closed as some ambulance officers arrived with an elderly man on a trolley.

Sudesh stood up and started pacing, his arms hugging his chest as though he was cold. The clock on the wall read 2: 25. Achala was standing now too, leaning against the white plaster wall, and muttering under her breath with her eyes closed. She's praying, thought Rachieli, and felt oddly comforted by it.

'Your brother got into a fight with Araj?' Sudesh's voice was louder now, more abrupt.

'Io,' said Rachieli. 'Sorry, yes.' She stared down at the lino. She couldn't remember ever feeling this wretched and betrayed. She'd counted on Tomasi her whole life, and hadn't understood she could feel this let down by him. Well, maybe once, when he was a teenager. When she looked up again, Sudesh had tears in his eyes.

'I don't know where things are at, with you and my brother, but I can tell you that my brother is not a fighter. He wouldn't –' Sudesh couldn't finish his sentence.

Rachieli was trembling with shame. She wiped away the tears that had started drifting down her face.

'I'm so sorry,' she said. 'Tomasi is not a fighter either. I don't understand. I'll do whatever I can to make this right. I –' Achala opened her eyes and looked at Rachieli.

'Why did your brother do this to Araj? Why did he hurt him?' she said, and began to sob again. Sudesh walked over to Achala and put his arms around her. Rachieli stayed frozen in her seat.

'I don't know what happened,' Rachieli said, looking down at the floor. 'I have no idea.'

She felt her stomach flip because it was a lie. She didn't know what was going on with Tomasi, but on a deeper level, she knew the argument would be because Araj is Indian. Tomasi was protective and dismissive about them being together. This was the last thing she could tell Sudesh and Achala right now. The glass doors opened, and it was Tiny, wearing a faded red tee-shirt showing Cloudbreak, the surfing spot, with black leggings and flipflops. Rachieli stood up and they embraced. She introduced Tiny to Achala and Sudesh, but they just looked bewildered.

'What the fuck happened?' whispered Tiny. They sat down next to each other a small distance from Sudesh and Achala. Rachieli retold the story, gripping Tiny's hand, ashamed. Tiny winced as though she was physically hurt.

'Did Tomasi say anything about why?' said Tiny.

'Sega,' said Rachieli. 'He was too smashed to talk. It's not like him. I just don't understand.' Tiny was rocking on her chair and covering her mouth with her hand. She looked frightened. It felt surreal to see Tiny so upset, and Rachieli felt guilty for inflicting this on her. Tiny said she needed to get some air, and when she came back in Rachieli could smell cigarettes and menthol. Rachieli could see she had been crying. She wondered if Tiny was taking this so hard because of what Tomasi represented. Their childhood was well and truly over. Maybe the adult Tomasi had shattered Tiny's memory of him as a kid with a big grin.

Something about Tiny's expression in the waiting room reminded Rachieli of how she had looked the other day at the church, too. Uncomfortable in her skin.

'Is something . . . going on with you?' Rachieli asked her. Tiny shrugged and tucked her hair behind her ear. She smiled wanly. 'Let's just focus on Araj tonight, okay?'

'Io.' Rachieli felt tears welling in her eyes, and turned her head to look at the moon, visible through the glass panes of the tall outer doors. It was behind clouds, leaving the barest luminescence in the sky. The doors to the emergency department swung open and Shabeena walked towards her. Sudesh and Achala hurried over to hear what the doctor had to say, and Rachieli stood up to introduce them. Her voice sounded calm, but inside she felt terrified. Just a few hours ago she was telling Araj that she loved him. Maybe they had some kind of curse.

'The surgery was successful,' Shabeena told them. 'Araj had a tear to his right kidney, and we've put in six stitches to stop the blood loss.' She explained that Araj would need to be on bed rest for a few weeks, and monitored in hospital for the first week, because of the risk of kidney failure or infection. Rachieli felt overwhelmed with relief. She wanted to see him, but Achala was asking Shabeena questions about why the surgery was necessary, if it put Araj at risk of infection.

'If we hadn't operated, your son would have died.' Shabeena sounded frustrated and tired. 'When will we be able to see him?' Rachieli asked her, and Shabeena glanced at her watch. 'He'll come out of the anaesthesia in an hour, but he needs rest. He'll be exhausted. Why don't you all go home and see him tomorrow?'

Rachieli felt crushed. She wanted physical evidence that Araj was okay, even though it was probably childish. She thought about his goofy smile, and about how he often seemed aloof and alone like a solitary star. 'I'll stay,' she said, her voice louder than she'd intended.

When Araj woke up, she wanted him to know that she was there.

NO SPEAK ENGLISH

By Lani Wendt-Young

When Gina got the phone call from her nephew's school, she was at the salon getting her hair and nails done. It was her once a month self-care treat. She would take the day off work and go to the mall. Have a massage at the Chinese place by the escalator. Be beautified. Then virtuously enjoy a fruit and vegetable smoothie from the health bar. And meander through shops. Her day off always made her feel better. Revitalized her for the exhausting office politics at her university. So she was especially unhappy about the school asking her to please come in right away so they could 'discuss Fatu's situation'.

What's that boy done now?!

She got her smoothie to-go and breathed deeply on the drive to Fatu's school. By the time she got there, she was calmer. Ready to engage with palagi's. Glad for the extra confidence that salon hair and nails gave her.

Okay, let's do this.

The meeting was with the Principal and Fatu's homeroom teacher. And another woman who taught the ESL class. Fatu waited outside in the reception area for the meeting to be over.

"This is Val who works with our students for whom English is a second language," explained the Principal, Mrs Collins, a tall woman with greying hair and the ugliest cardigan Gina had ever seen. It was brown with embroidered red sheep. She welcomed Gina with a big smile and a firm handshake. She smelled strongly of lilies. It made Gina sneeze.

Val bobbed her head in greeting, but stayed in her seat. She was tiny. A petite mouse of a woman. All dressed in green. *Like a leprechaun?*

"And this is Fiona who spends the most time with Fatu." The homeroom teacher was young and bubbly. Brown curls, pink lip gloss and glittery red spectacles. She leaned forward in her chair with earnestness, and nodded enthusiastically at everything the Principal said.

"Fatu is just a delight, a real gem," Fiona gushed. "Ever since he came from Saa-mo-wa, he's made friends with everyone and really thrown himself into all our activities. The other children love him."

So what's the problem then? Why am I here?

"Which is just amazing considering the language barrier. That he's able to bond so well with the other children. If not for his struggles with English then everything would be fine, I'm sure," said Fiona.

Language barrier? E a? What struggles with English?

Gina looked from Fiona to the Principal and back again. Confused.

Val joined in. "We are concerned because he's just not showing any progress at all in my class. Barely makes a sound. Doesn't even attempt to verbalize words in our activities. I can see him enjoying the games with the other children, but when it comes to speaking, he is afraid to try. I feel it's his self-confidence that's really lacking here. His self-doubt is paralysing him!"

All three women nodded in unison, while Gina raised an eyebrow in disbelief. *Fatu lacks confidence? Are we talking about the same boy? The kid who won't shut up at Sunday School? The one who always hogs the limelight at White Sunday, and shouts his tauloto the loudest?*

"Ummm, I'm not quite sure what you mean," said Gina cautiously. "And I'm confused. Why is Fatu in an ESL class?"

"Well, because he can't speak English," said Mrs Collins. "We have an excellent program for new migrants. It's usually the children of our refugee families who come to us with no English, but sometimes children from the islands will need that extra help. It's just that we've never seen a child with quite a language deficit like Fatu."

"Yes. This long with us and he's still not able to speak a single complete sentence in English," added Val.

Not a single sentence in English?! I'M GOING TO FASI THAT BOY! JUST WAIT TILL I GET MY HANDS ON HIM.

"Oh really," said Gina. A taut smile on her face. "This is a shock to me."

Val rushed to assuage the situation. "Oh please, don't feel badly! It's a real asset that Fatu speaks his native language. You must be very proud that he's fluent in Samoan. So many of our Pasifika children can't speak their indigenous tongue, which is a real shame. We only want to help him acquire English as well."

"Yes, this is not any deficit in your guardianship. Rest assured, you're doing a wonderful job with Fatu," said Mrs Collins with magnanimous reassurance. "Together we can work on what Fatu needs to support him through this and get him on that path to adding English to his language bank."

"We are here to help Fatu. And help YOU," assured Fiona. She pushed her glasses further up her nose as she nodded again. With added enthusiasm. "Together we can boost his confidence and get him on the road to English language fluency. I mean, your English is beautiful. You're so articulate! With the right help, Fatu can be too."

I'm articulate? Are you kidding me lady? What fresh hell has this boy gotten me into? Where do I start? Breathe Gina.

"I appreciate that you all want to help my nephew," said Gina. "And I know you mean well with the reassurances about my being his guardian. And my *articulate* speaking. But as I said before, I am shocked to hear about Fatu's language struggles. Because English is his first language. That's what we speak at home. Even back in Samoa with my sister and her husband, all their children, Fatu was speaking English. Everyday. Everywhere. He's gotten the school prize for First in English in his class for the last two years in a row."

The three women were taken aback. Bewildered.

Gina continued. "Yes, he speaks Samoan. As a second language, acquired through attending pastor's school regularly and learning to read the Bible in Samoan. In fact, his grandmother back in Samoa is always lecturing everyone about not speaking Samoan to the children enough; that their Samoan isn't good enough for her liking."

The palagi's were puzzled.

"Wait, you're saying Fatu can speak English?" asked Val. Disbelief.

237

"Are you sure?" demanded Fiona. "I've never heard him utter a word of English."

Mrs. Collins gave Gina a look of doubt. Mingled with pity. As if to say that Gina didn't know what she was talking about. Or maybe she did but she was lying to herself. And to them. A kindly smile. "We know that the education standards in Samoa can be quite different than in New Zealand. So it's understandable that while he may have been a star English student in the islands, it would be a struggle for Fatu here."

Oh, you didn't just say that. No. You did not just look me in the face and say that.

There was a loud sound in Gina's ears. Rage. A horde of screeching flying fox, disturbed from their esi patch. A swarm of black flies, fat and furiously feasting. A pack of Samoa dogs attacking, rabid and wild. A force that would not be stopped.

But with great restraint, Gina stopped it. Because that's what you do when you're talking to palagi. Swallow the words, Choke on the anger. You ignore the flying fox. (They're a protected endangered species in Samoa anyway.) Fan away the flies. Scatter the dogs with a rock and a HALU. And sometimes, you even smile while you do it.

A deep breath. Clenched fists. Manicured nails digging into her skin.

Through gritted teeth, Gina replied, "I'm telling you that Fatu speaks fluent English. He could have tea with the Queen of England and awe her over crumpets."

Gina wanted to say '*the **fucking** Queen of England*' but she was too polite.

"Well, this is a surprise to us," said the Principal. "I'm not sure how to take this. It doesn't make any sense. Why would Fatu be concealing his English proficiency?"

Oh yes, I wonder why?

Gina was grim. "Val, can you tell me, what do you do in your ESL classes?"

"We have plenty of games that encourage the children to speak. There's also computer activities for language as well," said Val.

"I see. So instead of doing the regular assignments in Fiona's class, Fatu gets to play games in ESL? And go on the computer a lot? That explains it," said Gina.

"It does?" asked Fiona.

"Explains what?" asked Val.

The women were still befuddled and Gina shook her head at their slowness.

"My nephew figured out that if he wanted to play games all day and avoid any real schoolwork, all he needed to do was pretend he couldn't speak English. It's actually rather brilliant of him." Gina stood up and went to the door. Opened it and snapped an order for Fatu to come. He was sitting on a couch in the reception area, reading a comic book.

Her tone and the look on her face told him all he needed to know.

You are in so much trouble boy. And your kuluku game is over.

Fatu's shoulders slumped as he followed his aunt into the office.

"Fatu, stand over there," snapped Gina. To the women she said, "What I find surprising is that it's taken this long for you to contact me about my nephew's apparent lack of English. He went four whole weeks faking it? Perhaps if you hadn't been so willing to believe that a kid fresh from the islands was so pitiful with his English, then you would have clicked on much sooner."

Fiona's mouth gaped and the Principal frowned. Val didn't meet Gina's eyes.

"Now here's where I give you ladies some advice for when you have other students 'fresh' from Samoa. Most children from home are bilingual and can speak SOME English. Many, like Fatu, speak perfect English," said Gina. Her head swivelled so she could glare at the boy in the middle of the room. "Isn't that right Fatu?"

The boy who couldn't speak English, nodded.

Which infuriated his aunt.

"Gagu maia!" *Speak in English or else...*

"Yes," whispered the boy as he stared at his shoes.

Gina spat out a lacerating tirade all in Samoan. One that ripped her nephew to shreds. She ended it with a command in English. Spoken through gritted teeth.

"Now you will apologise to your teachers and to your Principal."

"Oh no, humiliating Fatu is unnecessary . . . " Mrs Collins started to say, but her protest trailed away as Gina glared at her with the barely contained rage of a very ticked off Samoan auntie.

Stay out of it lady.

Fatu gulped and then straightened up. He stared directly ahead as he delivered a flawless speech. Like he was giving his very best performance on White Sunday.

"Principal Collins, Ms Fiona and Ms Val, I humbly offer you my deepest apologies for my deceit over these past weeks. You welcomed me to your school and treated me well and I have repaid your hospitality with lies and false pretence. All so that I could be lazy and not do any school work. It was wrong of me. I have wasted your time, efforts and valuable resources, and for that I am sorry." He paused, darted a glance at his aunt, then continued. "I have also wasted my parents' sacrifices on my behalf to send me to New Zealand for better schooling, and a better life. And the generosity and sacrifice of my aunty. My behaviour has shamed them and the name of our aiga. I hope you can forgive me. If given another chance, I will endeavour to make restitution. I will work hard to make up for the assignments missed, and I will strive to be an exemplary student."

The palagi women gaped at the boy who couldn't speak English.

Gina grabbed her handbag. "Right. Fatu will be participating fully in his regular classes from now on. In English. Mrs Collins, I take it this meeting is over? Thank you for your time."

Gina was glad none of the women could speak Samoan as she muttered dark threats at Fatu all the way out. "Aikae. Faakali oe pe a ka o'o i le fale."

Yes. Her nephew could speak perfect English. But sometimes, for some things, only Samoan would do.

For the learners of Gagana Samoa – O se faʼamanatu mai le Matāmatagi

By Niusila Faamanatu-Eteuati

A taili le matagi i suiga ona popoʼe lea o le tōfā

A faʼataʼutaʼu le laʼi pe matagitogaina ona fetuʼunaʼi lea o le lā

A siʼisʼii le gataifale ma souā le fogatai ona sisi le ao le lāʼafa

Le lā fala i le agi fīsaga po o le mataʼupolu nai le atuvasa

Tautai tu i le foe, mataʼalia faʼatonufolau, le tapasā lenā

Neʼi lōfia i le tuʼāoloa, pe sasi au taga e toe tau tatā

Tagoʼau i au measina, o lau gagana e oʼo oʼo ifo i le loto

Na te faʼatupu ma faʼaʼoaina lagona, logoitino, ivi ma le toto.

Utugāʼoamau ia lē tūfalaʼaia tupulaga mo le lumanaʼi

Tatou umufonotalatala, matimati le gagana, o se Faʼamanatu mai le Matāmatagi.

Unfathomable insight is dubious in times of swirling winds

Adjusting the sail when destructive southerlies blow

When facing storm surges and rough tides, raise the sennit sail

While the easterlies blow with the woven mast on calm seas

The navigator at the wheel, the sturdiest in steering and predicting

To rise above the strong northerlies and unexpected trials

Holdfast to your treasures, your language speaks to the hearts

Your language soothes the soul, is felt by your body and sensed by your bones and blood

Filling the funds of knowledge for the future so no youth is left behind

Let us engage in deeper conversations, revitalise the language, a reminder from Matāmatagi.

Any heritage language thrives within steadfastness and affirmation.

If well nurtured in the homegrown, it survives and blossoms in the peripheral

MISSING MY PITU PITU

By Rebecca Tobo Olul-Hossen

Naswaiu slings her plain large-leaf Malekula basket over her shoulder. Narrow woven pandanus shoulder straps digging into the soft flesh on her arms. Tropical winds rifling through dried leaves of the banana suckers standing like security guards on the roadside - searching for something. Searching for something missing that was there, but is now not quite there.

Fresh minty scents of the straggling nasai'i, the leaves of which are normally used for Tannese kastom dance, tantalise her nostrils. There, but not quite there. Stirring memories lying dormant for years in her mind. Memories of days spent at Ienemaha Village, Whitesands, Tanna, with Kaha Patan.

Memories in the same place as that of picking overripe mulberries with Kaha Patan. Mulberries dropped on the volcanic soil by the heavy-laden trees. She walked from tree to tree in her underpants with Kaha Patan picking mulberries from the ground and popping them into her mouth. Purply juice running down the sides of her mouth and her chin. Her little belly tight with deliciousness.

Naswaiu realises what is missing. Something is missing from her. Something that was there, but is not quite there now.

The carefree feeling of childhood. Days climbing the nabanga tree with childhood friends and cousins, lali Mary, and cuddling discarded shiny bottles dressed up in clothes fashioned from castaway calico bits. The bottle babies were lovingly bathed, fed, cuddled, and sung to.

"Iao pitu pitu

Iao pitu pitu

Iatapuli e niki nimanwahli

Narawia tahngi iao

Nuhwan tuh iao

Iatapuli e niki nimanwahli"

Songs like the "Pitu Pitu" – grasshopper - song that Kaha Patan would croon to her while boiling the blackened kettle filled with freshly picked lemon grass leaves for breakfast. The grasshopper who lies in the midst of tall grass. Sunned by the rays of the sun and watered by the falling rain. The pitu pitu lies in the grass. Content.

Naswaiu remembers going back to Ienemaha with her mother when Kaha Patan passed away. The village was the same. But not quite. Something was missing. Sitting by her Kaha Patan's grave made up with fresh flowers, calico and the best plastic Chinese store flowers, the sun rising behind her and roosters crowing to her guitar. Singing softly. Ever so softly.

"Iao pitu pitu

Iao pitu pitu

Iatapuli e niki nimanwahli

Narawia tahngi iao

Nuhwan tuh iao

Iatapuli e niki nimanwahli"

Memories of walking to Ilisi to pick up mangoes in the early hours, at only four years old. Coconut leaf-woven baskets on hers and Kaha Patan's heads laden with ripe mangoes that had fallen throughout the night. Mangoes for breakfast. Ilisi mangoes were really the best. Just a little bit of stringiness that stuck to small teeth. It was okay for Kaha Patan. She could take her teeth out to eat mangoes, then put them back in.

Arrrgh. Arrrrrgh. Sounds of throat clearing. Spit. Spit. Spit. Rudely bringing her back to the present. "Sol ia nois, Naswaiu! Saharang ia ko kino," said Kaka ordering her to keep the noise down, and move away from the grave. "O nakeruh naman kaotahwan apaha e imaiim," Kaka said. As if she sat there merely to watch the men going to the nakamal! Hugging her guitar close to her chest, she croons softly, tears finally rolling down cheeks once stained purple with mulberry juice, as the sun sets before her.

"Iao pitu pitu

Iao pitu pitu

Iatapuli e niki nimanwahli

Narawia tahngi iao

Nuhwan tuh iao

Iatapuli e niki nimanwahli"

For the first time ever, if she laid down on the ground, she could see her Kaha Iarman's legs sticking out under the sheeting that provided cover for the makeshift bathing area. She'd never seen her Kaha Iarman's legs while growing up. The story she heard was that Kaha Patan had taken a bush knife to him. She often thought that he must have a scar somewhere on his leg which he always covers with long trousers. A tall man, sometimes trouser legs were too short, only reaching Kaha Iarman's ankles. A gentleman, he was never without his beret, and his pipe sticking out the side of his mouth. She wondered if these were the hallmarks of someone who was once an indentured labourer in Australia.

She remembers the time he chased her. She had come to the village with her brother for school holidays. Kaha Patan made nawanangen, grated manioc rolled tightly in island cabbage leaves and boiled in coconut cream, for lunch. It did not help that her brother had told Kaha Patan and Kaha Iarman that doctors in town had said he must not eat pumpkin or he'll get terribly sick. Kaha Iarman stood over her pointing at her. Telling her she must not come to the village anymore if she is refusing to eat their food. She stood abruptly, pouring the hot nawanangen on his feet, then took flight! She knew he'd be after her.

Rounding the corner of her uncle's thatch roofed house, she spied a window propped open by a piece of wood. She climbed up and jumped through the window. She knew she was safe for the moment. The door had a padlock hanging on it. Heart thumping, like the sound of mangoes falling in rapid succession when the boys are up in the tree shaking the branches, she looked around. The smell of overripe pineapples mixed with something else came wafting from the dark corner. There was a barrel sitting there. She gingerly opened the lid. Homebrew! It was the smell of yeast and pineapple left to ferment into a homebrew that the boys liked to drink.

Some time had passed. She could hear Kaha Patan calling for her. "Naswaiu. Naswaiu. Naswaiu…ik ia?" She knew it was safe to come out. She climbed out through the window. It's a good thing she was wearing shorts, even though girls in the village are not allowed to. But Kaha Iarman said she could when she is at home.

"Iao apa," Naswaiu called back softly as she emerged from her hiding place and peeped through a hole into Kaha Patan's kitchen. Good, Kaha Patan was alone stirring a pot of something delicious smelling over the fire. Tanna soup with local fowl for dinner! Yes! Kaha Iarman would be on his way to the imaiim.

Later that evening, stomach full of Tanna soup, Kaha Patan rubbed her forehead crooning softly as they lay on the rough coconut woven mats laid out on the carpet grass, the Southern Cross up above:

"Iao pitu pitu

Iao pitu pitu

Iatapuli e niki nimanwahli

Narawia tahngi iao

Nuhwan tuh iao

Iatapuli e niki nimanwahli"

She fell asleep knowing she'd wake up on the big bed with Kaha Patan to the smell of praying marigolds.

Now, Naswaiu sets off for work thinking of Kaha Patan and Kaha Iarman long at rest.

To my Kaha Patan, Rachael Nawase Namu (1936 – February 2004), and Kaha Iarman, Namu Ialeko (1930 – May 2004)

TALES OF TAILS

By Lauren Keenan

Troy's car splutters as he parks in front of the ATM. He pulls the key out of the ignition and turns to the boy sitting in the back seat. Jeez. How did Benji get chocolate all over himself already? It's only been ten minutes since Troy picked him up. Troy narrows his eyes. Where are Benji's shoes? He was wearing them when he hopped into the car. And is that *chocolate* on his feet?

Benji catches Troy's eye and grins. "Thanks for the chocolate fish, Dad. Are we at the zoo yet?"

"Bloody hell, son. Your face."

Benji's eyes widen. "You just said the 'b' word. That's a bit naughty. Doreen and Brian say so."

"No," Troy says. "I said muddy, not bloody. I said your face looks muddy. Because of the chocolate."

Benji reaches for his foot, contorting his limbs to lick a smear of chocolate on his heel. Troy sighs. Lucky Doreen and Brian aren't here to see. He can just picture what their faces would look like if they were: hard eyes; mouths like cats' bums. Stuck up gits, the both of them. They talk to Troy like he's a half-wit, always asking stupid questions. Did Troy have a car seat? Did Troy have a water bottle for Benji? Did Troy agree that he shouldn't take Benji to see Kaylee, under any circumstances? Would Troy remember to carry Benji's giraffe bag at all times, as it contains Benji's spare pair of undies? Nag, nag, nag. It's enough to give you a headache, especially when you've had a hard night. Which Troy had last night. Not that he'd ever tell Doreen and Brian that, though. Their silent judgement would make him want to hit things.

Troy glares at the car seat he'd bought. Bloody expensive piece of crap. It lies upside down beside Benji, who sits on the seat Doreen said she supposed Troy could borrow, as we don't have any other options now, do we? It wasn't fair. How was Troy supposed to know toddlers need different seats to babies? And what was that flash of fluorescent green underneath the bloody thing? Ah. That's where Benji's shoes are. At least they'd turned up. If Benji was returned to Doreen and Brian without shoes, Troy would never hear the end of it.

Benji grins. "My shoes have their own cave. That's so cool. They have to stay on my feet when I'm in Brian and Doreen's car."

"Yeah, that's why I got it," Troy says. "For your shoes."

Benji peers out the window. "This doesn't look like the zoo. Where's the picture of the Red Panda and the zed-oh-oh?"

Zed-oh-oh? Of course. Zoo.

"Not yet. Hang on a sec, I'm just gonna check my bank balance. We'll be at the zed-oh-oh soon."

"Is there a gelada at the zoo?" Benji asks.

Troy raises his eyebrows. "A what?"

"A gelada."

"That a sort of ice cream?"

Benji laughs. "No, silly. It's an animal."

"An animal? What sort of animal?" Troy frowns. Why couldn't Benji talk about normal animals, like lions and tigers and bears?

"It's a scary sort of monkey with a big mean face. Is there a gelada at the zoo?"

"I don't know," Troy says. "Guess we'll see when we get there. Stay here a minute. I'll just check my balance."

Troy slides out of the car and shuffles toward the cash machine. Shame he doesn't have any data on his phone. If he did, he'd look up whatever the hell a gelada was. Then Benji wouldn't think his old man was thick. Troy slots his card into the machine, keys in his pin, and squints at the screen. $0.51. Uh – what? Aren't there some numbers missing? He looks again. $0.51. Troy feels cold. He's supposed to have fifty dollars, not fifty cents. He'd had fifty dollars yesterday; he'd saved it especially for the zoo. He'd just stopped once on the way to Brian and Doreen's to get a pack of smokes, some chippies and that chocolate fish. The money shouldn't be gone. He grips the edge of the ATM and exhales slowly.

"Dad!"

Benji waves at Troy from the back window of the car, hands dripping with melting chocolate. Troy's shoulders slump. Poor Benji has such a loser for a dad - the sort of dropkick that promises the zoo but can only deliver a chocolate fish. A man who doesn't even know what a gelada is, he's so stupid.

Troy takes a deep breath and climbs back into the car.

"Dad?" Benji says.

"Yeah?"

"Do geladas have tails?"

Troy pinches the bridge of his nose. His headache is getting worse. How should he know whether geladas have tails? He'd never heard of the bloody things until just now. Brian probably knows. Brian probably has an entire encyclopaedia about weird animals with names that sound like ice cream.

"Yeah, nah, I don't know," Troy says. "But all the animals I can think of have tails. So I reckon all animals have them. That sound right to you?"

"No," Benji says. "People are animals and they don't have tails. Chimpanzees and gorillas don't have them either. Brian told me that when he took me to the zoo."

Troy clenches his fist. "Oh."

"Why?" Benji says. "Why don't you know? Do geladas have tails? Why don't you know? Why?"

"I just don't, okay?"

Ooops. That was louder than Troy intended. Benji inhales and closes his eyes. He rocks back and forth in his seat, rhythmically banging his head against the back: thud, thud, thud. Troy frowns. What the hell is Benji doing?

"Benji?"

Benji's eyes remain closed. Thud, thud, thud. Troy feels his pulse race. Benji needs to stop that, or else he'll hurt himself. Think, Troy, think. What can he do with fifty cents? How can he make Benji happy?

Troy pats Benji on the knee. "I'm sorry for snapping, bud."

Benji opens his eyes, sits upright and sniffs.

"Are we going to the zoo now?" Benji says in a small voice.

Troy blinks. *No, because your thick loser dad only has fifty cents.* He then forces himself to smile.

"We're not going to the zoo anymore. You know why?"

Benji's lower lip quivers. "Why?"

Troy leans as close to Benji as the small space between the front seats will allow him. "Because we're going on an adventure."

Benji's eyes widen. "Really?"

"Really."

"What sort of an adventure?" Benji holds his breath.

Troy smiles. "A gelada hunt. Let's go on an adventure to see if geladas have tails."

A bubble of laughter bursts from Benji's throat. "Really truly?"

"Okay, not really, but it'll be fun to pretend."

"A pretend galada hunt?" Benji claps his hands.

"A pretend galada hunt. But first, we need our weapons."

Benji's eyes swivel around the car and pulls his shoe from underneath the baby car seat. "We can throw my shoe at it. The shoe will knock the gelada to the ground, then we can sneak up to it and see if it has a tail.

"Great idea," Troy says. "Maybe this is a magic shoe with special bommy-knocker powers. And what else do we need?" His eyes rested on the baby car seat. "Lucky I brought a gelada cage, eh?"

Benji shrieks with laughter. "A gelada cage!"

Troy nods, corner of his mouth twitching. "A gelada cage. What else do we have?" He reaches over and rummages through the glove compartment, pulling out old unpaid bills, a lighter, a pen that doesn't work.

"These papers will be part of our gelada trap," Troy says. "This lighter will show us the way when we're in the dark."

"Can we go now?" Benji says. "Can our adventure start now?"

"Yup. Let's go."

Troy pulls on his seatbelt and turns the key, stealing glances at Benji in the rear-vision mirror as he pulls into traffic. Benji hums under his breath, bopping his head from side to side. Troy's eyes sting; Benji deserves so much better than him and Kaylee for parents. Maybe Benji living with Doreen and Brian wasn't all bad. They were brainy. They probably did crosswords, and made a bottle of wine last two nights. They probably knew what to do when Benji bangs his head against things. Maybe they'd even lend Troy some money.

Nah. Troy doesn't need a loan. He can wait until payday; he'd done a double shift last night, so he'd be paid extra this week. It was worth today's headache if it meant some money to get some more data on his phone so he could look up whether or not geladas have tails before his visit with Benji next weekend.

Troy blinks back a tear.

"One day I'll do better than this," Troy says. "We'll go to the zed-oh-oh next time."

"Brian and Doreen always take me there." Benji screws up his nose. "I'd rather go on a gelada hunt. Are we there yet?"

"Soon, son. We'll be there soon."

Benji laughs. "I like going on adventures with you, Dad."

Troy drives toward the trees in the distance.

"Me too, son." Troy smiles. "Me too."

SUPO MOA

By Salote Vaai-Siaosi

The speckled chicken lies at my feet in a crumpled heap. Glassy eyes wide open and staring. At me. At the sky. I had purposely picked this one, knowing it was a slow runner unlike its' friends. I should feel bad. But I don't. I feel nothing. Just this morning with the sunrise, it was living carefree and loud in our backyard, and now, one swift stone throw from my expert hand has sent it to meet its' maker.

Well at least I think so - I mean, do chickens go to heaven?

There is something comforting in that. In ordinary everyday things. Making it to paradise. Moa Sa, Sa moa, I laugh to myself. Sacred chicken.

"Salafai! Le afi!"

My little sister Mele's warning about the fire startles me back to reality. It is no time for theological questions. The soup has to be made and ready before the sun sets, otherwise the belt will be my only dinner.

I dash to the umukuka where the embers of the fire I started earlier have raged into a brilliant masterpiece of angry orange hues and the pot of water has started to boil. I work quickly on the chicken, pulling feathers, exposing the shiny pink skin, then scrub it clean under the tap. Done. Into the boiling water it goes, with onions and salt. Chunks of kumara and eggplant will follow soon.

The chicken is a skinny tough thing and it shrinks even more as it boils. I have a sinking feeling I may still be beaten for this soup - but it's not my fault that the tomatoes have been stolen again. Those village kids sneaked into our garden with their basket. Again. I saw them run off with Faitala - the faifeau's son. I recognized his broad behind struggling to keep up with his friends. I don't know why he does it. It's not like he needs the food. At church, he sits there righteously with his white shirt and buttons about to burst, no doubt from all the food the village sends to their house on Sundays. No skinny chicken soup for them. Faitala must enjoy salted beef and mamoe dripping in juices, while the rest of us go home to eat soup and elegi.

Elegi would've been faster today but at least stirring this soup is calming. It reminds me of the swirling water in the pool at Mama's village in Savaii. Far away from here. If we ran away there, would he find us? Would he bother? Would the police really chase after us and bring us back, like he always says they would? But if they did - maybe then I could tell them about the beatings? I could never say anything about the Room in the Fale palagi. The Room has walls so no one can see.

Just thinking of it makes me feel sick, the way I feel on the boat to Savaii. When the waves roll and everything goes up and down. When my stomach heaves, and I vomit over the railing into the blueness far below. I don't want him to take me into the Room. Not again. But I don't want him to take Mele. I promised Mama I'd look after her.

The smoke from the fire stings my eyes. Time for the rest of the vegetables to go in. I stir. Hunger growls deep and low in me. I hope he leaves us some of the meat. Not just bones and sua like he usually does. Mmmm, the aroma is rich and rising now. Wisps of smoke are a delicate dance in the air, a magical pattern with the sun peeking through the banana trees as it prepares for bed.

The sun falls quickly here. Dusk doesn't hang in the sky. The soup has to be ready soon. Soon there will be little to no light and the chicken is still too firm! I try to think of what Mama would do. Ah yes, she once said that adding green papaya can make the meat cook faster. I run for the closest papaya tree as I pray for mercy.

Mercy and effective papaya from Mama's garden.

Kalofae ia Mama - she was my shelter. When Papa died, Uncle became the boss of our home. At first he was nice to Mama. He said he would look after her and us for love of his older brother. When Mama tried to talk to him like a younger brother about his drinking, he wasn't so nice anymore. He said this was his family's land, so it was his house. He beat Mama and many days we would huddle and cry together after he had thrown her outside and dragged her through the dirt where the chickens feed. One awful night, he punched her so hard, her smile lost a tooth, and for some time that smile was gone too. Mama didn't go to church for three weeks and when the faifeau came to visit and ask why, she lied to him that she had had a bad fall. I watched that faifeau, a big man with his belly hanging over his belt and a small peek of brown skin between buttons, just like his son Faitala. He carried his Bible tightly, even as he sipped tea. And wrinkled his nose at our meagre offering of bread and jam. Then he was on his way to sip tea at the next house. Still clutching his precious Bible that could not save us.

Mama could not be saved when a month later, just as the palolo rains began, she became very ill. Shaky and weak, she put on her second best puletasi, the yellow one with white flowers, and got on the blue bus to go to the hospital. But first, she pulled me into a soft embrace, one arm holding me close, while she held her black umbrella in the other, saying "Salafai, vaai tamaiti, vaai fa'alelei Mele, I will be back".

So I did, I looked after the little ones, but Mama never returned. Not on the blue bus anyway. Instead, a white pickup came to our house the next day, bringing news. The neighbour looked at me with wide, sorrowful eyes and muttered, "Aue kalofae, I am sorry".

What was he sorry for? For being the one to tell us that Mama had died? For not walking over all those times he heard Mama scream? Or when us kids cried and got beaten too?

The faifeau came to say he was sorry. I wonder if he was sorry that we smiled at church and came home to old fears and new tears? I wonder if he was sorry that he smelt alcohol on Uncle when he shook his hand at church but chose not to see the fear in our eyes.

He could say hand before God that he didn't know our plight.

What he did know was that our Mama had died at the hospital. His daughter was waiting there to see a doctor, when a crowd formed around a woman who had collapsed outside. Mama in her yellow puletasi and still clutching her worn purse with its precious contents of 10 tala and 50 sene.

The doctor said it was a heart attack, but I know Mama was heartbroken. I was heartbroken too. Our mother was gone and we had nothing of her. Someone had taken the purse, someone even took her umbrella.

I hoped this meant she was now with Papa. Aue Papa, soft and gentle, he used to return from the plantation daily with a dirty shirt but a light face. He would beam at baby brother and say this was his twin. Then I would prepare his dinner, Papa's favourite of taro and fish, as he always said chicken was too hard to chew.

The chicken! I forgot about the chicken!

I run back to the pot. My heart beats faster, more panicked, more afraid, to see it has boiled over and the fire has died. So careless! I start to cry. Already feeling the pain of his rough heavy hand and the sharp burn of his belt on my back. I scramble to relight the fire, and it is harder now with darkness setting in and wet wood. My hands shake.

Suddenly, I hear the smash of dishes being thrown in the umukuka. He has returned and is surely angry the food is not ready. I can see my siblings peering out from beside the house. They know what is to come. The nights are the worst. We hate the night. Brother's shoulders are shaking as he struggles to hold his tears and Mele has her hand over his mouth. The more we cry, the heavier the blows. Mama is not here. Papa is not here to see what his twin has become.

Oh how I hope it is only the belt. Please give me just the belt.

He walks towards me, swaying and unsteady, and I can see his eyes, bloodshot from the Kava at the Billiard House, are hungry as he looks at me.

No please, just beat me. Please.

He fumbles with his belt as he lurches closer, stumbles, and his lavalava comes off. There is a heavy stone in my stomach. And the Savaii boat rocks up and down in the dizzying waves.

He grabs me and I cry out. Try to break free and run. But his grip is too tight. I struggle and he is angry. He throws me to the ground and then reaches down to pull me by one foot. My face is in the dust as he drags me towards the house. I look up and see my brother crying as Mele holds him close. I see the umukuka. The red glow of the embers. The soup pot is still open and I can see the soup bubbling angrily, steam rises. Rising as my hope falls. My hand scrabbles on the ground, and I grasp a rock, a smooth round stone fits perfectly into my palm.

I kick and shout, trying one more time to break loose, to angle my body to throw.

A chicken runs across the yard. It squawks as he trips. Falls. A thud and a sickening sharp sound. Like when a stubborn coconut is cracked open. Then, silence. I struggle to my feet and peer into the shadows.

"Uncle?" I whisper. "Uncle?" Silence.

He is still. A dark shape on the ground.

The chicken squawks again. I look over to see it struggle out from under his leg. It seems no worse for wear.

I move to crouch beside him. There is blood pooling on the rocks beside his head. His eyes are open, glassy eyes wide open and staring. At me. At the sky.

I should feel bad. But I don't. I feel nothing.

There is a rustling of leaves from the nearby mango tree. I stand. Look up and see a feathery cluster of chickens, roosting for the night. They stare down at me. At the man lying in a crumpled heap at my feet.

I unclench my fingers and let the stone fall harmlessly by my side.

I walk back to the soup. I remove the pan carefully from the afi. There is something comforting in ordinary everyday things.

MUSINGS TO CHRIST WHILE BABY NAPS

By Courtney Leigh Sit-Kam Malasi Thierry

Imperfection realised. Trying to keep everyone happy. God knitted this human in my womb. Make sure she has all the right names. Multicultural babies. Which culture will play the strongest part? The Lord is my shepherd. I lack nothing. Don't offend parents. Husband comes first. Priorities, priorities, priorities. Communication, communication, communication. Numb, numb, numb. Prayed for an easy birth. Prayed for a peaceful mindset. Prayed prayers no one knows. Prayed and forgot past tense or present tense. Talking to God about my culture. Spend time with older sibling. Yumi mas givim preis igo long God. Send photos of child regularly. Keep everyone in the loop. When did she last eat? What is for dinner?

Blessed are the meek for they shall inherit the earth.

Rock this bubba to sleep. My milk is enough for her. Breast is best. All creatures great and small. All creatures God made them all. What happens when I go back to work? Don't worry too much. He makes me lie down in green pastures. He leads me beside quiet waters. God is sooo good. God is sooo faithful. I remember when God did that. He saved me from myself.

Are we going to travel home ever again? My home country is changing. I may never see my haus meri again. I loved her. Should I brush her hair? What is the time? I need to eat. Did I take my vitamins? This radio station is making her sleepy. No routine with this kid. Are veggies enough? Rice is a healing food.

Does her che che feel neglected? Does her che che feel loved? I'd love a massage. Where does time go? Kairos, Kairos, Kairos. He refreshes my soul. He guides me along the right paths. God pours into my cup. I don't belong here. I am a citizen of heaven. I need to be present in every moment. My future generations will be blessed.

Do my children know where they come from?

Na lukautim yumi olgeta taim. Yumi mas givim preis long Jisas. Em i rot na tru na laip. I can't remember it all. Is she sleeping enough? God is my refuge and strength. Not my will but your will be done. Gethsemane stoicism. Christ's blood is thicker than DNA. What is the time? You prepare a table before me. In the presence of my enemies. Who are my enemies? Father God bless my husband. I am flesh. I am soul. I am spirit. No good or bad. Avoid judgement. Noken bisi. No expectations. But do expect God. Could it get any better than this? Could it get any better? Could it get any better?

How many hours do I sleep?

God made everything beautiful in its time.

PĀREU

By Stacey Kokaua

I stop on the path and pull the note from my pocket to check it again – Pāpā's wobbly swirls written over the back of a power bill:

Church Hall 7.00

Corner of Cable Street and Sidey Street by dairy

Go up ramp to green door

At the time he'd said, "Now Bella, make sure you get there at *7 o'clock*. Don't be late. I told Mama Grace you'll dance at the pākoti'anga next weekend. Good girl."

I don't even remember the name of the boy whose hair's getting cut.

But I'm pretty sure I'm at the right spot. The sun's still up because it's nearly summer. I still have to wear a jacket though. The church has one of those pointy roofs. It cuts against the pink sky. It's quiet now, everyone's home for dinner, but next weekend it'll be different for the pākoti'anga. The boy's family will arrive from all around, dressed in their best dresses, 'ei katu, tīvaevae made especially and food, so much food. I can't remember how we're related to the family but the food will make it worth it.

I look around trying to find the entrance. At the top of a concrete ramp I see an open door. It had probably been green once. There's no music yet, just a voice speaking over some children laughing. Hopefully they've started late. I can see two or three girls standing barefoot, in t-shirts and pāreu. They're listening to someone I can't see.

"…And also, Nga and Jasmine, can you make sure you don't spread your fingers out like this? You know…?"

They've definitely started.

I move as quietly as I can and come to the door. It's one of those halls that all the churches have, a high roof with windows too high to see out of. The wooden floors have those little pock marks from high heeled shoes and the lines that if you look closely, you can see they are full of grime, like a hundred years of gatherings stuck between the floorboards.

I try to sneak along the wall without anyone noticing me, but I drop my bag too fast. The sound of my bag makes one of the dancers look over but she doesn't really see me. She's listening. It's Māmā Grace talking. They call her Māmā but she's still quite young. I met children at White Sunday last weekend. She might be a bit older than she looks, or it might be because she's a great dancer, a beautiful dancer. Even people who aren't even Cook Islands know her. She's standing in the middle of the circle of dancers, talking, and she's short, so it's hard to see her. I can just see flashes of her hands, dancer's hands, pointing, extending and articulating in the gaps between the girls.

"And make sure you finish your actions. Extend your arms right out to the end and finish with your fingertips. None of these short actions. Slow, graceful movements, 'inē."

I'm trying to slip my jandals and jacket off quietly and get ready so I can just join the group. I pull out my pāreu from my bag. It's an old blue one with a white tipani print and 'Palmerston' printed all over it. Dad got it for me ages ago, but my other ones were in the wash because I'd been doing some gardening for Pāpā. I wrap it around me and tie it at my left hip over my clothes, and then roll the top so it sits above my knees. One of the kids bangs on the wall beside me before running away laughing.

"Ē! Māniania tikai kōtou! ‹Aere mai!"

The kids walk slowly back across the hall so they can get told off by an old man at the big drum. The rest of the drummers and a few older women sit behind different drums, chatting and waiting. Now that the children have stopped, Māmā Grace's voice seems louder. I creep over to join the circle of dancers.

"And you all need to watch your shoulders more. Keep them still. I'm still seeing too much of this..."

Mama Grace brings her fingertips to her shoulders and shimmies while she waggles her hips. Everyone giggles.

"Ē Bella! Kia orana!"

This is what I was trying to avoid.

"Just before we start, girls, this is Bella. You know Pāpā Mou? Mou Tuavera? 'Aē, Pāpā Mou is Bella's grandfather. She's just come over from Rarotonga, eh girl?"

I nod, trying to make myself small. I really don't want to talk. The girls look at me and it's hard to read what they think.

One girl looks at my pāreu, "Palmerston eh? We gotta Marsters! Auē."

I should have worn one of the other pareu.

"Ritea!" Māmā Grace says but she doesn't mean anything by it. "Right! Get into your lines!"

Māmā Grace looks over at the drummers and nods. In response they straighten their backs and hold their tokere over the drums. She turns back to me and asks, "You know '*Enua Mānea*'?"

That's an old one. I can't remember the last time I danced to it. Before I get to answer she says, "Ok, then you go behind Ritea."

I want to say I know the song but I don't because I want to learn their actions for it. Plus I don't want to be in the front row on my first practice.

So I get in line behind the girl, Ritea. We're facing Māmā Grace and the other māmās who were sitting are now standing and the drummers. Then this one, Ritea, turns back and just looks at my pāreu and then turns around again. What does that mean? She places her hands on her hips, and carefully arranges her feet. Even with her back straight, Ritea's hair drops to the top of her pareu. I'm just staring at her when I hear the drums.

I straighten and stare ahead. I find myself looking at a banner behind the drummers – 'Happy Anniversary Mama Lani and Papa Oko!'

I don't smile. It's just a practice.

"*Enua mānea, te vai nei, kā vai ra...*'

I drop my knees, roll my hip across to the right, in time with Ritea. The actions are pretty different, but I like seeing how other groups and dancers interpret 'īmene. These actions are more complex and interesting. There's a lot of step work.

"Katakata mai!" Mama Grace calls loudly.

I stretch my lips into a dancer's smile. Even when I'm not happy, I know it looks like I really am. I've seen it in videos.

'Kua rau rupe te tiare…'

I follow as Ritea extends out her arms and lowers to the ground. They're singing about a flower growing on the porch of their home. I slowly lower myself to the ground and hold my right hand out to symbolise the flower. In Rarotonga. I miss home.

'Tāku i akaruke mai…'

Ritea comes back to standing and I try to follow her actions. I was thinking about Raro so I lose my balance and fall over. I could almost cry. Because a part of me hates it here. It's cold and smells weird and I hate seeing my Papa sick when the doctors here are meant to be better than back home. And it's weird because I was born here but I feel nothing. I get back up quickly and find my place as the other dancers are turning. From the corner of my eye, I see Ritea watching me. She's smiling.

You can never trust a dancer's smile.

'Auē Rarotongaaaaa…'

We finish the last action and raise our hands above our heads on the last drum beat. The drummers don't start into 'ura pa'u so we just stand there in our finishing pose.

Māmā Grace steps forward. "'Āe. E no'o ki raro girls."

We sit on the spot waiting for her criticism.

"Ok. Ah, when you go down at 'Kua rau rupe…' put your right foot slightly behind your left so that when you stand up you don't lose balance. Then push off more with your right foot when you come back up. And keep your backs straight. And don't tense your shoulders. Soft arm movements 'inē."

I'm so embarrassed. I feel my guts suck up into my chest like an anemone. She's saying this because I fell over. I want to say that I wouldn't normally fall over, but it's just hard being here and having Miss Rarotonga Ritea staring at me. And I'm glaring at the back of her head and her perfect hair, and it's like she can feel it. She turns her head. I can see her ear and the curve of her cheek.

After the third time, I've got it. And Māmā Grace is happy with how it looks.

"Bella, I want you to do 'Mou Piri' for us. Your papa showed me a video of you at Aunty Jane's wedding. Kua manea tikai koe. If it looks alright, we might get you to do it for Saturday. Ok?"

I knew this was going to happen, but I feel more nervous about it now. The other dancers sit to the side and I am alone in the centre of the hall. I should at least say hi to the drummers.

"Kia orana kōtou," I say. Even though I've been in Raro five years, I still have a New Zealand accent. It's a bit embarrassing.

"Kia orana!" they all shout. It makes me laugh.

Ritea takes a place right beside Māmā Grace by the drummers. Both of them have the same expression: half smiles, eyes unmoving.

I straighten my back, place my hands on my hips, carefully arrange my feet. Breathe in, smile on the exhale, crinkle my eyes and eyebrows raised. Ukulele play the opening music…

"Mou piri…

…mou piri au ia koe…"

Mouth words, reach out arms and bring them to embrace myself, lift chest for drama.

"I te kimi ma'ana"

Pa'u come in at 'amiri', lower knee, roll hip down to the right. Add some drama – not the tourist stuff but things I know Māma will appreciate, more subtle, eye movement, fingers, foot work.

As I dance, I forget my stomach in my chest, forget the cold, forget how sick Pāpā seems, forget Mama Grace and Ritea. I ride the swell of the song and imagine I am the girl they sing about, get lost in the drums and harmonies. The voices were strong and the drummers very sure. Next thing, the song's coming to an end…

"…Motukore te 'openga, tā taua i papa'u."

I stand in my last position, arms raised and left leg straight, serene smile. Everything is quiet. One of the dancers looked at another, raises her eyebrows. But everyone waits for the opinion of Māmā Grace.

"Mānea tikai, Bella. That was nice. Who taught you? Mama Tepaeru and

Mama Vai, eh?"

"Hmm," Bella nodded.

"Meitaki, my girl, makomako rai," She turns to Ritea, "And you? What did you think?"

But this one just sits there like before with her half smile and says, "Yeah."

"Ok, good," Māmā replies like she had something more than one word. "Ok, girls, I think we'll finish then. Kids to feed, eh? Pāpā Henry can you do the pure?"

We bow our heads. An older man stepped up from behind the drums, shifting his weight on each foot before speaking, "Te 'akameitaki atu nei mātou ia Atua…"

I closed my eyes but I find myself thinking about other stuff. I've got to pick up some milk, and things for Pāpā on the way home. Hopefully the supermarket will be open. I need to check my phone to find the closest one…

"…Aaaaamene."

" 'Āmene," I say.

"Ok, meitaki ra kōtou. Ritea, what time are the performances?"

Ritea stands. "Yeah, the performance will be at 11.30 before the kaikai. The pākoti is at 11 o'clock so can you all get there at 10.00 to get in your costumes? I don't want you guys to miss out on Leo's big moment. Bella, I'll have something for you, ok? So everyone - 10.00! Ok ra?"

"'Āe!"

I stand up and start taking off my pāreu. My feet are black with hall dust. While I'm folding up my pāreu, Ritea comes up to me. I pretended to not see her until she's really close to me.

"Bella," she says. Up close, she's actually older than I thought. Lines brush out from her eyes and she stands differently than a girl. "Thanks for coming today."

"All good."

"Hey, I'm sorry your Pāpā is unwell. Tell him me and Gracie are praying for him."

"Yeah, I will. Is Māmā Grace your aunty?"

She throws her head back and laughs. "Girl, don't you tell her that! Nah, she's my older sister. Although she's been bossing me in this group so long, she probably seems like my aunty." Again the laugh, "She said you were coming today to practice for my boy's pakoti'anga. Thanks for doing it eh. Your pāpā will love it too. You know you're related to us. Your pāpā's sister is married to our mama's brother."

"Oh, who's that?"

"Do you know Papa 'Uapa? And his wife, Māmā 'Ine? Yeah, she's a Tuavera too."

It turns out I know her people. I see the resemblance. Māmā 'Ine is also beautiful and laughs with her whole body.

"Well, see you Saturday eh. I've got an outfit I'll get you to wear. I wear it when I do solos but it should fit you. And don't be late this time!" Ritea had turned away.

I laugh.

"Ka kite ra!" Ritea called over her shoulder, waving her hand. Those dancer's fingers.

"'Āe, ka kite ra."

Most of the other dancers have already left. Māmā Grace is talking to Ritea and another woman while children tug at their legs, sucking thumbs, rubbing eyes, calling, "Mamaaaaa". The drummers bang and shuffle as they pack the drums into bags and onto trolleys to put back into storage.

I put the pāreu in my bag, slip on my jandals and twist my hair into a topknot. Outside is dark and I feel cold looking out the door. So I put my jacket on, fold my arms around me and go out into the thin night air.

Aiga Fausiga

By Sisilia Eteuati and Lani Wendt Young

It is a truth beyond space and time that every Samoan child is taught from birth, from their mother's breast, that their own aiga is intrinsically better than any and all other aiga. Other aiga they must look down on. And that each had to do their best to be part of this grand tradition.

Masina sighed. It felt like in the year 3022, we should be over all this already. That some of these traditions would have been left on the old planet. But as her parents constantly told her Fa'aSamoa stayed important even when you moved to another solar system, even when you moved to another galaxy.

We figured out intergalactic travel and still couldn't escape she thought gloomily as she looked down at the zaflan body paint with an "Eh!" In the old stories you could read about adjusting your clothes. How novel. Nowadays once you walked through the Arizalator and talked to Ari about your outfit and it was sprayed on, if there was a kink in the application there was no fixing it!

She had chosen for her arms to be fully covered so she looked a little less bare. Today the plain dark purple paint she had chosen only just covered her arse. She stared down at her bare legs. They shone at her, iridescent.

Masina was a great name. When you were on a planet with only one moon. Now they were on a planet with eight, you would've thought her parents might have come up with something slightly more unique. Oh but no, it was your great grandmother's name and it is important to honour the ancestors! They called her Sina for short. Just the most common Samoan girls' name of all time. In all the eighty-nine known galaxies. Eh.

She stretched out and the hologram in front of her did a full pivot so she could see exactly how she looked from each angle. It was unusual to see herself without any pattern or adornment. Normally her zaflan was whirls and swirls, each pattern unique to her. The solid colour block she wore today reflected none of her personality.

In this light the gill slits on each side of her neck were clearly visible. Usually she wore eight strands of red lopa close to her neck to keep them covered while moving about above water. It made for fewer stares and whispers as she walked the corridor. Gave them less to look at and mutter darkly about. But today's ceremony called for no jewellery. No extras. Just her and the tufuga's 'au.

"Sina, are you ready? We can't keep Tufuga Feke waiting."

It was Mother at the door. Lines of tight worry on her face. A frown when she saw Sina's choice of zaflan. "That's not what we discussed. Where's the 'ie sina?

Masina grimaced. "Mother, it doesn't matter how fine the artifacts you have the constructor devise for me, it still won't make me something I'm not. They're not going to accept me."

Mother's dark eyes flashed. Lightning on the night water. "It's ridiculous. They do not honour old ways with their stubbornness. We are a people of change, how else would we have navigated the great vanimonimo. Their prejudices hold them back and will drown us all." She strode across the room, angry and defiant, as she shifted into the role she wore like a second skin. Planetary Commander. Mother had ascended to the Tagaloa position before Masina was born. Most people found the Tagaloa intimidating. But her anger only made Masina, beloved to Tagaloa and knowing it, roll her eyes. Because no matter how powerful or threatening Mother was Masina knew she couldn't change people's minds or hearts when it came to her generation. Sure the fausia children were the prophetic future of their race on this planet. But it didn't make them seem any less of a threat to the ones they would replace.

She watched Mother stalk back and forth, as she ranted a familiar tirade about the small-mindedness of ignorant people. Masina had heard it many times before. It gave her a headache. She told herself she must be patient.

Onosa'i. There was something about the four syllables of that word on her tongue. Maybe it was the time it took to say it. It was like the low slow beat of a lali and it always calmed her. Onosa'i, because she knew the true cause for Mother's mood.

She was afraid for what Masina would endure today.

"People fear what they don't understand. That which is different." A soft voice spoke. A welcome interruption.

"Mama!" Masina's smile was one of relief. Her other parent would soothe Mother on this most important of days. Mama was the gentle lull of the lagoon to the Tagaloa's black stone resolve. The sweetness of orange esi to the Tagaloa's bitter lime. They were perfection in combination.

It was Mama who had been the vessel to carry Masina to term, omplanted in the safety of her alofa, after Masina had been fausia in the Apaula Laboratory. Tagaloa had banned, not just the use of the word engineering as hate speech, but the concept itself. It was foreign to them, Tagaloa would say, when Masina was their very own treasured measina. But sometimes Masina would think it still. Sometimes she would turn its ugliness around in her mind and weigh its heaviness, knowing that even the mighty and fierce Tagaloa couldn't stop her thoughts. Mother certainly hadn't stopped others thoughts even though they never had the ake to say it aloud.

Mama had first cradled her in her arms, when Masina slipped into this world in a rush of amniotic fluid and warm blue. And it was Mama who had willingly descended into the ocean with Masina when she was but a new infant, donning the necessary protective suit and breathing apparatus every day so that Masina would not be alone as she frolicked and explored. As she delighted in the fins that feathered the ridges of her arms, at how lightning fast she could move through the water.

While Tagaloa ruled their water planet, it was Mama who swam with her, risking death daily in the ocean where creatures of the deep were more dangerous even than shadow and song.

"How are you our daughter?" asked Mama as she gently ignored Tagaloa's scowl and crackling anxiety. She reached out to place a gentle hand on Masina's.

"I'm fine. Ready to get this done," said Masina, with a confidence she didn't have to pretend. She had been looking forward to the day of her malu ever since she was a small child and first noticed the patterns scarred on both her mothers. She had traced the markings with pudgy fingers, in wondrous awe at their beauty, at their permanence. Unlike the zaflan they all wore, these markings were immovable. Mother had explained the malu was a sign of her womanhood, of her strength and courage. It marked her as one with her sisters.

"Will I get a malu one day?" Masina had asked. Eager and hopeful. "When I grow big and strong like you?"

Her mothers had exchanged a look. One heavy with words Masina could not understand. Not then anyway.

"Of course," Mother had promised her. "You are our daughter and one of us. When you turn eighteen and reach the age of the warrior, you will go to the Tufuga Feke and be tattooed with your malu, as is your birth-right."

Had Mother known then that her promise would spark so much hostility and resentment in her people? Probably not. She had thought that by the time Masina was grown, the people would be ready to accept the Moana generation.

She had been wrong.

The malu was not simply adornment. It contained power. Once a woman was ka she came into her loloto. The most powerful among them like Tagaloa could draw on it to hold back water, which is how they had settled the planet Ometa in the first place. They had combined their power to claim back 2% of the planet surface for fanua, and used that to build platforms that skimmed over the ocean in spirals and arcs into buildings of grace and beauty. The malu contained power. And though many would not admit it, that was the actual problem.

The fausiga children of the Moana generation were powerful beyond anything they had imagined. The elders had thought they had understood the need to adapt and change. Samoans have always been diasporic since days immemorial. So arriving on Ometa, and knowing the platforms could only ever be a temporary solution, they had thought ahead and they had come up with a cunning plan.

They would adapt to the deep just as they had always adapted. They thought they had understood the need for their descendants to change, to use the Oronian's gift of their DNA to create that which was stronger, faster, better. To create true children of Tagaloa who could survive in the moana as pure humans could not.

No-one anticipated the children would take on the Oronian's life cycle and age through childhood and puberty eight times as fast as one of the pures, so that in three years they had reached their maturity. Once maturity was acquired, the fausiga children's biological aging slowed to one-eighth of that of a pure human. The elders had thought they had time to adjust, that the change might be gradual, instead they had three years and the Moana children were adults. Adapted and agile adults built for a water planet and strong in ways the elders had not anticipated. Strong in views as well as body. And alien to them in a way they hadn't expected.

The elders found they had been ready for these descendants in theory. But not in reality.

To all Samoans great shame, many had rejected their own children in that first year after ga ola when in the space of sixteen months that made up the Ometa year, the children had grown from baby to infant to child at astonishing pace. In the second year many had quietly claimed their fausiga children had left of their own accord while their pure children remained. And now Masina was one of only very few fausiga left on the surface. And no-one knew what had happened to the children cast out into the deep. Did they swim there still? Or had the creatures of ocean nightmares consumed them?

Masina had been the first of the Moana generation. She was now three years old, twenty-four in pure human years, and would be the first and maybe the only of the fausia children to go under the 'au. The elders had argued against it.

"These new ones have Oronion, who knows if they can be trusted with our ancient powers and secrets?" the elders had tried to play on people's prejudices.

"We do not know how the powers will interact with their Oronion DNA," they said slyly, "we are only thinking about them." They would draw the ipu kava up from a bowl and tip it first to the Gods before placing it to their lips. "Also the patterns just don't make sense with gills."

But Mama and Mother had been fierce in their determination, just as they had been fierce in speaking out against those who had rejected their own.

Mama nodded at her. In understanding. "I am so proud of you Sina."

Mother quieted now, drew in a breath. "You honour the old ways Masina Moanatumau," Mother said, using her whole name, responding formally to honour their daughter's mana and courage. "Lele, beam us to Tufuga Feke."

They arrived barefoot so as not to soli the sacred space where the malu would be ka. A xanython bubble surrounded completely by the Moana meant Masina almost felt at home.

Tufuga Feke had been formally adopted as a tama fai into the Sua aiga, and the deftness of his touch with all eight of his arms was known throughout the galaxies. It was a supreme irony, Masina thought, that those who would stop her from having this malu ka respected Tufuga Feke, who was not even human let alone Samoan for his great skill with the 'au.

Tufuga Feke's ka was well known to channel strong malu powers. And surely that was a sign that his ka was blessed by Atua. Of course, he had never been any threat to the pures. Until the Sua aiga had agreed that he, as the most skilled among them, would be the one to ka Masina.

Tufuga Feke greeted them in the language of their ancestors. Mama responded with the oratory of old. Tagaloa was Ali'i and too important to speak. Mama's words soared as she praised Tufuga Feke and all the Sua ancestors, acknowledging the family line all the way back to the small but important village, on the small but important island, on the small important planet. in the small but important galaxy, that they all acknowledged as the Amataga. Masina listened knowing that one day she would be expected to be able to both know how to use these words of oratory.

When the greetings were finally done Masina lay down on the fala and rested her head on the ali. She marvelled at the feel of them. They seemed so like natural objects. Surely not. Then the 'au bit in to her leg and she knew they were real enough.

Mama and Mother's voice both raised in perfect harmony.

"O le mafuaaga lenei na iloa

I le ta'aga le tatau i Samoa

O le malaga a Fafine e to'alua

na feausi mai fiti i le vasaloloa"

The words and their rightness washed over Masina to the rhythm of the tap, tap, tap as she was marked. Her ancestors were Atua who swam the ocean in the old planet, who traversed the deep.

Masina looked out the xanython bubble at the expanse of water surrounding her. The ocean that splayed as far as the eye could see. Slowly she saw dark blue shadows rise, their features becoming clear as they surrounded the bubble.

Fausiga children- Samoan and alien both, who had been born the best of their worlds, children who could not only survive the harsh conditions of this water planet, but thrive in it- had come to the chant. They had come to tapua'i. Mama's soft gasp held both fear and wonder as the women caught sight of them.

Masina could feel the vibrations as the fausiga children joined in the song. The bubble thrummed with it. Their chant reverberated in her very bones.

That is where she belonged. It's where she wanted to be.

She could feel the force of the malu swelling in her like a wave.

The 'au hit her knee and she breathed in. Oxygen felt harsh in her lungs. It prickled and bit at her chest. She looked out knowing that the ocean would flow through her gills with silken ease.

The wave's power curled within her.

Those who were here to tapua'i this most sacred of their ceremonies, Mother Tagaloa, Mama, and the fausiga children, these were her aiga. As the 'au took its last bite, she felt the Tsunami rise in her.

It is a truth beyond space and time that every Samoan child is taught from birth, from their mother's breast, that they are intrinsically better than any and all other aiga. Who they must look down on. And that each must do their best to be part of this grand tradition.

Masina smiled.

She would honour tradition.

THE STORY OF MY LIFE

By Momoe Malietoa Von Reiche

The story of my life goes like this:
My father was a product of the
Aftermath of the colonial era
And the Second World War
His father was a colonial left over
With Aryan overtones
His mother was a Polynesian princess
Who had more vanity than pride
I was the product of the baby boomers
Of the sixties
Made in the back of a Chevrolet truck
To the Beatles' 'Love Me Do'
And 'Hard Day's Night'
My mother was a Poly-eurasian bar girl
Of the Matai Club
That made music without strings
She was never accepted by my father's family
Because of her villaged colour
When I was three days old

My mother left me on the front doorstep
Of my father's house
Where their part Chinese house-girl
Found me.
The note pinned on my nappy read:
"Here is the extension of our penis. Feed it."
(Lou ga'au lea. Tago e fafaga)
He saw his green eyes reflected in mine

ROOTS

By Sisilia Eteuati

"Alu ai gi ou kae!"

She shouts at his car once it was a safe way down the street. It felt good to let the ball of pain that lived between her stomach and her chest well up to her throat and be unleashed. The words reverberate around the empty street giving her a moment of release before the ball reforms and resettles hard and burning and tight. When she was a child she used to think a lot about where her soul was. She'd worry about where the space for it was among bone and blood and organs. Now the pain was a beacon and it was always there. The pain seeps through her and bends her back. It slows her feet, her arms and thickens her body, and wells up into crashing migraines that blind her. She can see the justice in that she supposes. What thou chooseth, that also shall be revisited upon thee. That was biblical, right? She had chosen blindness and so now it would be visited upon her, her own personal plague. She never worries anymore about where her soul is. Now she worries about containing it. Ensuring it doesn't take over her whole body, until she needs it released from long vertical slashes that would run from wrist to elbow.

She looks back to see her son standing at the door defiantly, his little knuckles white, his hand is so tightly gripping his spade. She'd told him to stay inside. She had been proud at the pleasure he'd taken in the simple gift when she had given it to him on his sixth birthday. "It's a real one, not a toy, ay mum? Now we can do that garden, ay?" He had danced around with it and she'd laughed as he'd used it as an ailaoafi, spinning it around and around and around. It had been a gift of hope.

And now he stands there brandishing it as a weapon. She desperately wants to say something silly or funny; something irreverent, to wipe the fierce expression off his face. She needs the light of his smile. But she has nothing. Nothing.

"Alu i totonu bub," she says quietly. "It's okay. It'll all be okay."

"He comes again, I'll smash him," he says fiercely, "Like a watermelon." He stretches out his arm, his fist expanding in slow motion. His other hand, still white knuckled, grips the spade.

"You know watermelons crack themselves, hey bub? You just have to leave them in the light for long enough. They can't take it. They expand slowly and blow up from the inside."

She uses both hands miming a huge explosion, and he almost cracks a grin.

"So never you mind old watermelon head." She sticks her tongue out. That does it. She sees an actual smile.

"I promise you bub. These things take care of themselves." She is not lying to him. She will make this the truth she vows to herself. And this to her is the holy, the sacred and the divine. This is smooth round wooden beads of the rosary, that she rolls between her fingers, reminding herself over and over and over, the mother too is divine.

She straightens her back and walks to the door. She grabs the spade from his hand and brings him close to her. His pulse is still racing under her hand. She holds him close. Slows down her breath, so he feels the rise and fall of her chest and his body follows hers.

"Can you help me dig out some of the weeds? Those baby tomatoes can't protect themselves."

"I hate weeding," he grumbles amiably as he allows her to steer him towards the garden.

He grabs the spade back and thunks it into the soil with satisfaction, cutting into the vine that had begun to spread. He leans down and pulls hard. It comes up dirt and all. "Hmmmmppphhh!" he grunts. He shoves it to the side and repeats.

It is not yet summer and the weather is still turnable. For now, the rain holds off, though the sun does not quite make it through the thick storm cloud grey. The heat weighs down oppressive. She whips off her shirt. The stretch marks on her stomach are almost the exact colour of siapo before it is printed. The mulberry trees take a beating too. You take it to the sea and bury it in the shallows. You put coral on it to make sure it doesn't rise up and float away with the tide. It ends up beautiful. Treasured.

She kneels down and puts her hands into the soil he has turned over. No gloves. She imagines the tomatoes a few months from now . . . ripe. She imagines carefully choosing the reddest firmest one straight from the vine and giving it to him. He will be seven by then. She imagines taking another. She imagines them counting 1, 2, 3 and then, in silent agreement, popping them into their mouths simultaneously; the burst and warmth of them filling their mouths with sweetness.

She feels the dirt pushing into her nails, and she starts pulling at roots left behind.

A LOVE THAT ONCE WAS

By Rebecca Tobo Olul-Hossen

She could see his head over the crowd of people.
Past the neat rows of broccoli and cauliflower laid out on multi-coloured cloths spread on the volcanic black soil. Orange vt100 carrots, so bright they hurt your eyes to look at them. Lenakel market bustling with activity. Friday being its biggest market day.

Their eyes meet. Sparks fly. Memories are re-lived. Even for a second.

He is not the young man she had known. The young man whose arms she once craved. He still looks good in his Vanuatu Mobile Force khaki uniform. Beside the other officers, he is a giant. A *nabanga* tree towering over the other trees in the forest.

Her heart is thumping. Can her colleagues hear it? Thud. Thud. Thud. Thud. He brushes past her in uniform and grunts.

"*Rahak patan…*"

Hearing the familiar voice calling her his woman, her heart tightens with a sense of longing so deep, it's like an ancient call.

"*Raham patan ia?*" she responds. She knows that he had moved on with his life, just like she did.

"*Natapuli ia?*" he asks. She tells him where she is staying and that she is only here for a few days for work.

"*Bae mi kam pas,*" he says. Her skin tingles all over with longing, as if he had touched her. That afternoon she is sitting on her bed at Lenakel Cove, only in a singlet due to the searing heat, responding to e-mails. A voice calls out her name softly. She looks up. There he is.

"*Mi kam jekem yu nomo*", he said.

Her heart flutters to her throat. She grabs her cardigan and throws it on. She goes outside and there he is. She had not the time to say one word and like an apparition, he is gone. Just like that.

The next day, walking to Western Union with her friends, she spies him, standing, talking with some other men. He nods acknowledgment when he sees her. She waves back.

And just like that, the longing was no longer there. He was just another tall, strong, good-looking man from Tanna Island, with whom she once had a fiery passionate relationship. Today the feelings have gone, leaving only a sense of familiarity, like the feeling you get looking at a photograph of a mango and your tastebuds remembering the deliciousness of it.

She thinks about all of this as she sits at the departure lounge waiting for her flight back to Port Vila. Writing, writing, writing . . . amidst the hum of voices and the lilts of laughter. A baby cries to her left. Another coos to her right.

The man on the crutches is fast asleep on the hard-wooden airport stool, his salt moustache moving up and down in time with his breath. His crutches laid to rest beside him as if ready to spring to action at his command.

A man in a neon vest walks purposely past. The back of his vest is inscribed "Air Vanuatu Operations" to remind him where he works in case he forgets.

The ATR 42 landed. A procession of passengers is making its way out. Lining up at the soap-bereft handwashing station to do the needful. Or at least a show of it.

There she sits. Bent head deafened with the sound of the aircraft. And a heart full of a truth and a hard realisation that a love that is once lost is never regained.

KARANGA

By Cassie Hart

Eventually, you have to answer the call.

I'd avoided it when I was a child. Hidden inside. Ducking below the line of the windowsill, so that they couldn't see me. Hiding behind trees or in bushes, when I was out on the farm, I was careful not to follow the muted silver flash of a ponga frond that may lead to other worlds.

Part of me yearned to go. Part of me ached.

And the rest of me was terrified by the prospect. I loved my whanau, but I never felt like I belonged. Feared I was a changeling. Which was why the Patupaiarehe called. They wanted me back.

But this world, this land. This farm at the foot of Taranaki Maunga, it was what I knew.

I grew up, closed my ears to the lure, moved away. Endured life. That's the only way to describe it. Sure, there were moments of great joy, but more moments of sorrow, of not belonging. Of disconnect.

Which is why I'm here now, back at the foot of Taranaki. I'm ready.

The mist swirls along the ranges as though Ranginui has sent it. His fingers gently tracing the curves of Papatūānuku. It is beautiful. It is sad. A love that deep, only to be separated forever by the force of your children. I've never experienced anything like that. I can't even say that I love myself. But I'm here now, in the mists, ready to hear that song, and be called home. I have a pack with a few supplies. I have a change of clothes, and good walking shoes. A jacket, of course. The chill of an Autumn evening is coming in and I don't want to freeze to death before I find them. Before I am found.

I have a torch, too. No slipping from a cliff for me. Too many have died on this maunga, and I don't intend to be one of them - although, that might be what's said about me when they can't find my body. I wonder if there were others too, collected in such a way. Disappearing into the mists with the fey of this land.

Taranaki Maunga has always been my shelter. He stood watch over me as I grew, witnessed it all. If I have a god, it is he. I will always worship at his feet, on his tracks, in his goblin forest. Even in appreciation of the way he shrouds himself with a korowai of cloud.

It feels as if it was always going to be like this. That I would give up on the life I had, and give in to that call. No, it's not a giving in. That feels too passive. It's more like this perpetual aching longing has ground me down over the years. This is my last resort.

It's not. I could go on, living my same old mundane life. Never feeling like I belonged unless I was here, beneath Taranaki's protection.

But I don't want to. It's not enough.

I put my car keys on the top of the rear driver's side wheel, and move away from the vehicle. It's time. I shiver a little as I step onto the track, but I don't glance back. There is nothing left for me there.

It's very hard to find information on Patupaiarehe. Most people think they aren't real. The knowledge of them may have been lost to time for some, but I know in my blood that they are. My people are from this region, and we have our own stories. So, I come bearing offerings for them. Some food to share, a song in my heart, a willingness to meet in mist.

I flick on the torch and let the beam of light play over the ground. It's not full dark yet, but the mist is so thick that it might as well be. A haze of white, darkened further by the shadows of the trees looming over me. The torch does nothing to help, and maybe that is how it's meant to be. I turn it off, shove it into a pocket in my backpack. I let my feet guide me.

Trust is what I need. Trust, and that song in my heart.

I begin to sing. The words don't really matter, just the intention, so I sing the song that comes to me, a warbling melody that isn't exactly pleasant, but doesn't sour the air.

"I come to you, my heart willing, my soul ready, to break free from the bonds of this world. I yearn for more. I ache to walk the paths that twist between realms., I want to belong, to be, to live, in harmony with all things. I know that you know my name. I know that this is the place. This is the time."

There is sound in the trees around me. They rustle like the wind is blowing, even though it's completely still. It sounds a little like laughter. My heart thuds harder. Anticipation making my hands shake.

Someone has heard me.

The mist ripples, swirls in eddies, a small space clearing around me. And it's no surprise at all to find that I am standing in a rough circle of stones. I freeze, sudden panic racing through me like fire in my veins. The urge to run overwhelms me, but I'm rooted to the spot. Because I chose this. This is where I wanted to be.

A melody I don't recognise comes from the mist. Then it changes pitch, and I recall it from my childhood. That unspoken sound that used to vibrate in my chest. A male voice, low, lyrical and lulling. Te reo Māori, words I do not understand, but long to. The language of my people has always evaded me, slipped from a mouth that feels like it's shaped wrong to hold that beauty. Unworthy of those words, and the way they intertwine with the very soil of Aotearoa, with the hills and valleys, the rivers and sea.

He comes closer. Steps into the clear space, looks down on me. He has pale brown skin. His face is like mine, but not. His limbs seem long, too long, but firmly muscled. I get the sense that if he wanted, he could destroy me, tear me from my skin and leave this meat sack here to decay, to feed the forest.

It wouldn't be so bad. Would it?

I'm sure he would make it quick.

Shrugging my backpack from my shoulders I rummage inside for the offerings I've brought. Freshly baked bread, the way my nan used to make it. It smells yeasty and warm, even though the heat has left the loaf. A bottle of elderberry wine that a friend gifted me over summer. I couldn't bring myself to drink it alone. That never goes well.

I place them on the ground between us, and then the Patupaiarehe and I stand there. Not moving. His chest rises and falls as he breathes. I guess mine is too, but I am more fixated on this being before me, one I have been imagining my entire life.

His skin is not blue like some people say, although it is such a pale brown that I can see the veins tracing his limbs. His hair is red and wild. His eyes bright and dark, all at the same time. I could get lost in those pupils, find other worlds, swirling universes.

But then, that is what I came for.

"Once, your kind called me. I'm here to answer that call," I say. The words are hard to get out. It feels like my throat is a barren desert, a wasteland. Full of ash and dust.

I want this. I do.

Then why is there a small ache in my belly?

"Ko wai tō ingoa?"

"Pania," I say. I might not know my reo, but I know enough to understand his question. "Ko wai tō ingoa?"

He shakes his head, as though names are meaningless to him. Or maybe just negating my desire to know. He ignores my offerings as well. His gaze boring into me, his head tilting this way and that, like a bird. Like he can see through my epidermis to the layers of me.

It makes my skin crawl. It makes it feel like something wants to come out from inside me, but I don't know what.

What else do I have to give?

He paces around me, the mist swirling away from him as he moves. Inspecting me. Does he find me lacking? Worthy? How the hell will I know?

Other voices call to me from the mists, te reo Māori and another language I cannot define. Is it that of the Patupaiarehe? Something else, beyond that? A universal language. The voices sound desperate, yearning, and my insides clench in recognition of that feeling. Goosebumps prickle my arms. I close my eyes, try to inhale, but it feels like the mist has invaded my lungs, clogged them with liquid.

The Patupaiarehe stops before me, closer than he was before. No longer separated by the gifts I brought with me, I can feel his breath on my face. When I open my eyes, he is peering directly into mine. I can see galaxies inside them, swirls of blue, purple and jade, flecked with silver like the paua shell, and that inky darkness. Te pō. Ngā whetū. I don't know how I know these words, but I do.

He presses his long fingers to his ihu, then to mine. Kanohi ki te kanohi. And I understand. I understand that somehow he is infusing me with his knowledge, our language. The one that should have been mine. I nod, I lean in, and we press ihu. Whakahā. Whakangā. Te hā, Te hā, Te hā, the breath, it moves between us in the inhale and exhale, floods my senses, shoots through my synapses. It settles in my belly and explodes through my body as I expand like his lungs, like mine.

And I know. This is the gift he gives me. It is not a retreat from this physical realm to another. But a stepping from one understanding to the next. The disconnect, that sense of not belonging sat inside me, but this whole time it was a thing that could be healed.

This gift, my language, dissects me, cleaving me like the atua did when they separated Ranginui and Papatūānuku, and it weaves me back together like a kuia with her harakeke. It opens a new path for me to tread: one that is connected with the mountain and the rivers and the sea; one that offers me a world threaded with the pain of my ancestors.

I didn't know.

I didn't know.

I shudder, my breath leaving me on a sob. "It would have been easier if you'd just taken me with you," I said, laughing, crying, not knowing whether I should be grateful or not.

"Easier, yes, but not better." He offers me a subdued smile. "This was the call we made. This was the call you answered."

"But I didn't know!" I want to stomp my foot like a toddler. I clench my fists, and then release them. It's uncomfortable in my skin as the new words find their home.

"How could you?"

His voice is kind, but I feel that old lack: feel like I should have known, should have searched harder, worked harder, found a way to claim this earlier - before I was willing to give everything else away.

"Do you wish you hadn't come, moko?" he asks.

I look at him again, recognize my nose on his face, the way the shape of our eyes is the same, acknowledge that the red in my hair doesn't come from my father's people, but my mother's. From the people here on this mountain.

"I wish I'd come sooner, tipuna." I nod to him and chew on my lip feeling both younger and older at the same time. Ageless. Timeless. Like we all are.

I came up this path onto the mountain with a half full backpack. And I will walk down it with overflowing kete held inside me. I may never divulge myself of the baggage that comes with the trauma of my people, but I can walk out of these mists knowing that I have answered the call.

Eventually, we all must.

In the Beginning

By Kiri Piahana-Wong

Sometimes I go back to where it
all ended for me, to where it
all began. They named the
cliff face after me — Te Āhua-o-
Hinerangi. The gulls still circle
there, the rātā still blooms,
all the threads of my story
still cling to the grasses and
tuapuke.

You might be wondering if
you should feel sorry for me —
after all I lost my husband
and my life. I want you to
understand, I chose my destiny.
When I sat on the headland
and did not move, there
was power in it. And
certainty. Not just my grief,
I *knew*.

What I didn't realise is how
powerfully that knowledge
would grow into the ground
there, would seep into the
earth. I never intended
that my decision sway
others despairing of life.

Now I exist in kōrero
and waiata and yes
pakiwaitara too. My
very likeness is scored
into the cliff, cascading
down into the sea. But
I have grown bigger
than the life I had. I
can be everywhere
now. And nowhere.
Sometimes, on the
right day, with the
wind in the west and
the sea gleaming,
I even catch myself
on the edge of song.

LEMON BERRY IS BITTER SWEET

By Isabella Naiduki

The Departure

The ruby-brown soil of my childhood days was still the same as I remembered it. When I was younger, I used to imagine that the hints of red were from the bodies of my ancestors buried deep beneath the land that our forefathers had first discovered. The soil so fine that it reminded me of the freshly ground Morobe coffee that I loved. Its intoxicating aroma like the smell of the earth, swollen from heavy rain. I have missed my early morning routine these past few weeks. I looked down at my feet, my leather slippers looked out of place, like an intruder claiming spaces it had no business being inside of. I had arrived into the country about a month ago but hadn't been able to summon the strength to make it to my final destination. The superficial everyday chatter and empty laughs that I was putting on as a front to friends and family who came far and wide to visit, could no longer hide the yearning that called for me. The side-stepping of questions about the son I hardly ever spoke of, the only link between a life that was and the life that was forced onto me. I found myself awakening at night thinking I had heard a voice calling out my name in the dark. Reminding me of the limited time I had, only to slowly fall back into sleep. The darkness rolling me away into patched up dreams of yesterdays.

It's funny how I had always thought that coming back to where my life started would have begun with me having a come-to-Jesus' moment. My ancestors singing from the heavens, heralding my return. A joyous return of the prodigal daughter. But there was no fanfare, no happy reunions, no rekindling of relationships left smouldering over time. Just recurring dreams that would bring me back to the shadows that covered the paths. There was an overwhelming sadness about the place now that pulsated through it, reaching up through the fertile soil to cling to the hem of my skirt. Tenderly tugging at the whimsical tail end of my childhood, hanging but by a delicate thread to my soul. I dream-walked through the now silent plantation. I slowed my steps down to hear the youthful raucous of teenagers husking coconuts by the shed. Their excited conversations intermingled with the harmonising of female voices from inside the drying shed. The beautiful voices that belonged to the women who were laying the white, fleshy coconut meat onto the blackened smoking kilns. Their arms moving in military unison as their bodies gently swayed in rhythm to their singing. There was a heady scent of fermented coconut infused with smoke that was drifting through the air. A few steps further and I began to hear men's voices. The communal laughter giving life to tired limbs piercing through the silence of the plantation. Their glistening bodies working the land of our forefathers. I strained my body to listen out for a specific voice as I continued to walk through the overgrown path. It was a voice that had shaped my childhood. The frustration of not being able to hear the voice that had called for me in a distant dream, willing me to return, made me stop and throw myself onto the soft, grassy pathway. I forced myself to conjure up the image of the person that the voice came from. It came fleetingly, teasing me with the hints of stolen sun-kissed moments. I held my breath, willing it to stay.

I felt the pins and needles begin to sting from the awkward kneeling position I was in. I arose with grinding knees as if from prayer. A prayer that had me pleading to the land before me to return my stolen memories as a soft breeze lifted the strands of my greying hair. There's someone there on the path ahead. A radiant glow on his dark, luminous skin from the setting sun behind him. I reached out to touch his cheeks. Running my hands across his high forehead and down the sharp bridge of his nose, through the frizzy curls of the beautiful black crown that adorned his perfectly shaped head. The tentacles of sleeping moments spinning me tighter and tighter into a whirlwind that was a kaleidoscope of images of what my life could have been. I choose not to awaken from this dream.

The Arrival

A young man sits by the glass window overlooking the tarmac of the runway. He seems to be staring intently at something happening down below where they were unloading the luggage from the plane parked at the terminal gate. He stands up and adjusts his suit before picking up his luggage and to walk towards the exit. He looks around the heaving crowd at the front of the terminal, there's a man with a red hat, holding up a sign and waving at him. He smiles at the misspelt name on the sign. They shake hands and exchange pleasantries before walking towards the entrance and out to the carpark. The heat from outside hits him square on his jaw as the doors slide open. The young man feels out of place with his suit. They get into a battered Toyota pickup truck, the man in the red hat places his luggage in the tray of the truck. The windows were those wind-up ones which refused to wind any further when he had opened it halfway. He felt the engine come to life and they moved forward. "Are we going straight there now?" he asks the man in the red hat. The man nods and reaches out as if to pat his shoulders but changes his mind midway through and places his hand on the gearshift that separates them instead.

They drive out of the airport carpark and join the traffic. It's afternoon and people are rushing back home from work, school or wherever they seem to be coming from. They stop at a traffic light and the young man looks up at the bus stopped beside them. There is a little kid who has her forehead pressed against the window staring back at him. She's sucking on a yellow lollipop whilst fiddling with the oversized pink, gauzy bow in her hair. He raises his eyebrows at her as if to say hello, she sticks her tongue out at him in response before ducking her head down so that she and her bow completely disappear from his view. The lights change and the truck begins to inch forward. The young man looks back at the bus to see if the little girl with the pink bow is still there and sees her sitting in the same position from when he first saw her. She offers a conciliatory smile and a wave as the bus turns into a street, going off in the opposite direction with a belch of black smoke in its wake.

295

The man in the red hat says he might as well get comfortable as it would be a few hours before they'd arrive to their destination. The combined heat and dust coming in through the half-opened window makes it a little difficult to do just that. The buildings start to give way to greenery and the hot air becomes a little easier to bear. The sun still beats down mercilessly however and it feels like they're travelling in a tin can. The man in the red hat points up ahead at a service station and asks if he would like to stop and stretch his legs, the young man nods. They pull in and park on the side. The man in the red hat says that he's going to go in to get a few things and asks if the young man wants anything. He shakes his head and says he's going to go find a toilet to use instead.

The young man gets off and stretches his body. He could feel sweat patches on his shirt as he takes off his blazer to lay carefully on the seat. He looks around for a sign to show where the toilets were, he spies it hanging off the side of the building. The toilet smells of ammonia and gardenia flowers mixed together. He notices the mirror above the washbasin has spiderweb

cracks throughout it. He sees a dozen eyes staring back at him as he washes his hands. It was strangely comforting to have them for company. He wonders what it would be like to pry one of the slivers of the mirror from the wall, would it dig into his skin as he tried to remove it from its glass web? He's startled out of his daydreaming with a loud bang on the door. It's the man in the red hat yelling at him that it was time to go. They drive out from the service station and carry on with their journey. The young man wonders if he should try to make conversation but struggles to find the words to say anything. They seem to be stuck in the back of his throat and he can't pry them loose. The silence settles around them like the dust coming in through the window.

The truck turns down a gravel driveway. The drive is surprisingly level and apart from the crunching sound of the tires going over the gravel, the ride remains the same as if they were still on the highway. It's lined with towering trees whose branches reach over to the other side creating a green canopy for cars to pass under. The air has turned from a furnace like blanket to a cooler, welcoming breeze. They stop in front of a large, white wooden house that had a wide veranda running right around it and disappearing to the side of the house. The man in the red hat gets out without waiting for him. He takes his bags out of the tray and places them at the bottom of the steps of the house. The young man gets out and reaches for his blazer still neatly laid on the seat between him and the drivers' seat. He hears the driver's car door slam shut and looks up just in time to see the old man tip his red hat at him before driving out again, leaving him on his own in front of the house. The young man takes a deep breath and walks towards the front door. He stops at the entrance and notices that the front door is open. He was unsure whether he should knock or call out.

He hears his hello echoing down through the long hallway before him. He spies a pair of slippered feet at the top of the stairs that he can partially see from where he stands. It's a young woman whose face he can see through the gauze of the screen door. It reminds him of the spidery reflection from the service station toilet. She hesitates at the landing when she sees him before walking towards the door, "Come in, we were expecting you a little earlier."

She takes him by the crook of his elbow and he is forced to place his luggage by the door. He just has enough time to grab a package that is strapped to the top of his suitcase. There are voices coming from the back of the house and the clink of glasses over the faint murmur of voices. The young woman pushes open the screen door that led to the back of the house and announces to the group of people before them, "Papa, he's here!" A man in a white polo shirt and khaki trousers turns to look at them. He slowly puts his glass down on a nearby table and walks towards them. There is a familiarity in this old man's face.

The old man takes the young man back into the house and they sit down at the kitchen table. The young man passes him the package he's been holding onto. He notices that the old man has begun to cry, silent tears streamed down his face, as he opens the plain brown packaging and lifts out the urn, the final remains of a daughter returned. The young man has travelled far to bring her home to Waimoro. The moment is broken by the banging of the back door. The young man looks up to see a familiar pink, gauzy bow and the smell of lemon-berry lollipop.

WHAEA FIRE

By Ria Masae

We were a fruit salad of colourful Primary School kids. Our previous choir teacher, had been a mousy woman who had a tendency to spray tunes of saliva during her lessons. We were always arriving late to her class, hoping to avoid sitting in the front row. Mousy liked us singing merry songs like '*She'll be Coming Round the Mountain*' (Yeehaa!). By the time she left we were all over 'whoa-ing back'.

I remember how Whaea strode in. Back straight, take up space, ignoring our curious whispers.

"Why do we have to learn Maori songs? I'm not Maori."

"Yeah, how am I gonna sing Maori songs when I can't even *speak* Maori?"

"You guys can't even say it right. It's not *Marry*, it's *Mah-oo-ree*."

"Does this mean we have to get those scary tattoos?"

"You guys should – to cover up your ugly faces."

"I can't get a tattoo! My mum goes mental if I even use the lick-and-stick-on ones!"

Reaching the front of the school hall, Whaea faced us and took a stance.

Big. Everything about you was big.

Whaea's upper arms spilled from her sleeveless floral dress, spreading like lumpy peanut butter over her underarms. Her legs were thick like kauri tree trunks planted into pale leather thick-heeled shoes that looked twice the size of my dad's. She wore fishbowl glasses that distorted the shape of her eyes, yet did nothing to dull the fierceness in them. Whaea. I tried to get my tongue around it. Fai a. Fire. It seemed right to call her that as she stood up there radiating warm confidence.

Whaea stared intently at each child, until one by one we hushed, silenced by her silence. I rolled my eyes to the left, then right, every kid's face was stamped with a mixture of awe and fear. I bet my own foliga was the exact same. I pretended to study the slated floor as Whaea's eyes glided towards me. I sensed her stare slide to the next cowering child and only then did I feel safe to look up again.

Then came the unexpected. Whaea put her hands on her hips, and started to waiata. I was dumbstruck. *"Faaarrr, didn't tell us who she was first. Rude!"* Her booming voice was deep and feminine, as if Mother Earth herself was serenading us. Her song swept over us like the tide, bounced off the wooden walls, and then washed over us again and again. *Did her bigness never end?!*

From that day on our choir became a Kapa Haka group. We practiced eagerly for the end-of-the-year performance. Whaea taught us to get our tongues around the reo. I learned strength and passion. Whaea taught poi and stick dances; I learned grace and beauty. Whaea taught songs from the heart of hapu and iwi; I learned respect and acceptance. Whaea showed us how to see beneath the surface of everyday life. How to discover and understand the flesh and bones under the skins of different customs.

By the end of the year we thought we were sweet as bro. That practice had made us perfect like the palagi saying promised. We were supposed to be at the hall by 6pm for the 7pm start. My parents arrived home at 6.30 p.m from work and started to get ready in their island-time. 'I paced back and forth, biting my nails down to the skin in frustration. 'Bet if we were going to boring church they wouldn't be taking their time.'

When we finally pulled into the school car-park it was 7.20pm. I had watched the clock and silently counted each minute that passed after start time. I shot out of our jaffa-red mini and zoomed towards the classroom where the Kapa Haka group were to meet.

My stomach clenched when I peered through the curtain-less windows and saw it was empty. I opened the door just to be sure and the silent room became blurry as tears welled in my eyes. Then, Whaea suddenly whooshed into view from the adjoining cloakroom. 'I almost mimi'd myself in excited relief.'

Banging my palms against the glass, I called out, "Whaea! Am I too late?"

Her head jerked up. The tight lines on her forehead relaxed in relief. Rushing over to unlock the door, Whaea jumped aside as I burst into the room.

"Sorry Whaea, it was Mum and Dad's fault! They're *always* late. You know what, Whaea? I started walking all the way home all by myself because they kept picking me up from school late."

"It's okay, girl. But we've got to move quickly," Whaea said, as she swiftly pulled off my coat. "The others are already in the hall and we're on soon."

I didn't resist as Whaea worked her magic, transforming me from a pudgy-nosed school girl into an enchanting daughter of a Maori chief.

"Be still, girl," Whaea smiled, as she applied the final touch. I giggled as the tip of her black vivid marker tickled a moko onto my chin.

As we hurried through the night to the school hall I delighted in the swaying of my piupiu. Swish-slap-swish-slap-swish-slap. I was giddy with enthusiasm.

As I walked into the dark lobby past the double-door entrance, I tripped. The gaping doorway seemed to swallow me as I stumbled forward. I looked up at the looming black ceiling. I felt a large hand in mine.

"Whaea," I asked, in a small voice, "why is it darker in here than outside?"

"So that tonight, all you kids on stage can shine brighter than whetu in the sky."

I breathed in the beauty of Whaea's words. They wrapped around me as she pulled my hand and we crept towards the back of the hall where the Kapa Haka group were waiting for us. Rounding the corner, we saw them lined along the wall in single file, their piupiu chittering with worry and impatience.

"There's Whaea!" Breaths sighed and shoulders sagged.

"Everyone hush," Whaea said, softly. "Come now, get into your lines and correct positions."

"Yes Whaea," we chanted back in a collective whisper.

We shivered in anticipation as we waited for the new-entry class to finish bellowing '*Kookaburra Sits on the Old Gum Tree*'.

"Amateurs," we scoffed.

Finally, the littlies ambled off the stage. Whaea flurried down our lines making last-minute adjustments. When she reached the front of the line she faced us. She clasped her hands and we bowed our heads. She murmured a soft karakia. At the end we joined in whispering ferociously "hui e, haumi e, taiki e" and we felt those words of binding deep in our hearts.

"Go now," Whaea instructed, "show them what you can do."

We marched down the aisle towards the lights of the stage. We piled onto the platform and measured ourselves into our positions: feet apart, backs straight, shoulders squared, arms straight down our sides, and heads bowed. We waited for the command.

Junior called out, "Hope!"

Simultaneously, our heads snapped up and our hands slapped onto our hips. A wave of heavy stillness rolled over us. The bright stage lights prevented us from seeing the crowd, but we sensed their presence. It was unfamiliar and daunting. I was supposed to lead the first waiata-a-ringa by singing the first few words to cue the class into action.

Silence filled the room as I imagined rows and rows of lizard eyes staring at me.

Then I heard Whaea's forced cough from the back of the hall, "Utaina... mai... nga waka...toru, wha." I croaked out.

The whole kapa haka group followed that lead. We didn't sing, we squawked. We didn't harmonize, we rasped and mumbled. I hung my head, trying to hide my whakama. In Samoan shame is just ma. Whakama seemed to be an exclamation mark! We were dishonouring everything we had worked on. Whakama that our fear was eclipsing our brilliance. Whakama we were disappointing our Whaea.

Then, we heard the click-clack-click-clack of Whaea's big shoes against the wooden floor. Forcing my head up, I waited with dread for Whaea to emerge out of the shadowed aisle.

Whaea stomped into view. I heard shuffling as even the audience shrunk in their seats in her presence. Just like the first day she came to us, she planted her hands on her hips and took her stance.

Her silence now was a wero. *Kia Kaha! Be strong!*

One by one, our voices became clearer. Her intense stare bore into us. Bit by bit, our lyrics become louder. Whaea stood her ground, demanding more with the very force of her presence. We lapped up her challenge until our suppressed nervous energy burst from its cage! Our song harmonised with feeling; angels stopped to take notice. Our actions took on meaning and purpose; grace swayed with power. When we blended into the finale, the powerful Haka, we roared. Warrior ancestors quivered with nostalgia. The audience whooped and cheered, and we thundered right back! Oh, the breathtaking glory of it all – ordinary eight-year-olds bathing in wondrous, unpretentious glory! We blew Whaea's challenge to the four corners, north, west, east, south of Aotearoa.

Then, the sudden calm after the storm spread over the stage.

We were spent. But, not yet complete. For still, Whaea remained silently watching us. And we watched her – trapped in stillness until judgement was passed. At last, something softened in her gaze, and we knew. Whaea had provoked; we had conquered; Whaea was defeated. With her spreading grin, we were complete. And all was well in our world.

She was proud.

FACE RECOGNITION

By Nafanua PK

The it's ok I'm used to it face/ you can stuff your job face/
no, you go first face/
The Resting Brown Bitch Face//
God-fear Sunday face/
typeset/typecast face/
The Placeholder Diversity Face/ solemn lies on Fridays face//
The Side-eye Squad Face/ white space/ down face/
Les Mills trained face/ start us with a song face//
The Sidekick Sista Face/ brown card carrying face/ you think you're smart
face/ smart is not enough face/ The Bruised Face//
The Gauguin Face/Disney face/Porn Hub search face/ crunk face/selfie face/
make a tea for Aunty face//
The dusky face/rape face/
you know better face/
gossip face/gone native face/ we've been here before face//
the fight face/the brown face/
the shame face/the brown face/
the crime face/the brown face/
the drug face/the brown face/
the gang face/the brown face/

The FUCK YOU Face/the brown face/

the brown face/

the brown face/

the brown face/

the brown/ face/

the brown/

face/ the brown/

face the brown/

face the brown/Face//

NAILED IT

By Ashlee Sturme

Blossoms flutter around my face as I clutch a pile of papers to my chest. I imagine I am one of them, dancing in the sky.

Sure beats being me, today. *I'm going to nail it,* I reassure myself.

I am left outside waiting, waiting. Watching the petals fall from the tree and spiral to the ground. I pick at the vintage lace on my dress. I reapply lip balm four times until I can taste it, caked to my teeth.

The panel is made up of two men and a woman. The woman leading the parade has a dozen bracelets on her wrist, a song of metal as she gestures. I think the others are becoming agitated by them. One man glances at her arm darkly every time she speaks.

"It says here you have travelled? What was your favourite place?"

"I sure have," what an easy question to start. "Twenty-six countries in Europe. Parts of the US, four Pacific islands, Australia, some of Indonesia. My all-time favourite destination was Vancouver Island. I worked in an art gallery. Absolutely loved it." I am talking too fast.

The men nod. "You've got an impressive resumé," one says. "Banking, project management, marketing campaigner, grants and funding operations. Is there anything you haven't done? Represented us at the Olympics, perhaps?"

He leans back and laughs, his belly shaking, unset panacotta. My tummy rumbles.

"Well, funny you should say that," I am pretending to laugh. "I competed in Norway in a three-day adventure race," I say. "Not quite the Olympics. Although I did go to Beijing, for the horse riding and the gymnastics." He gapes. "To watch," I clarify.

His neighbour elbows him in the ribs, then straightens his glasses. "Miss uhhhh," he peers down at the papers in his hands willing them to tell him my name. "Miss. You don't appear to have held a position in project management. How do you feel qualified to undertake this job?"

I nod. "I understand your concern." I flick nervously at the corner of my notes. I have practiced for this question. Bracelet woman clears her throat and stares pointedly. I sense she is impatient and demanding. The men look at her with varying degrees of distaste. Interesting dynamics.

"I have not had a project management position, per se," I begin. "However, I am a fast learner."

"We've heard that before," I hear her mutter under her breath. "I'd be interested to know your take on shared office spaces?"

I draw a breath. "If you don't mind," I say, voice shaky. "I'd like to finish answering the previous question. Although I haven't had a formal project management role, I have organised no less than forty courses, ranging from one night to six weeks. I have arranged two expos in support of the local lifesavers' group which gave away thousands of dollars in prizes, there were over thirty-five stallholders at the second. I have project managed minor property projects, including a multi-million dollar rebuild; in addition to sourcing funding and executing a number of other events, fundraisers, and theatre productions."

One of the men is nodding. The other is rubbing his hands.

"That's something," says the woman. I can hear the "I guess" although she doesn't say it aloud.

"I have also done all of that while raising my four children," and I look down at my notes, "including my daughter with disabilities. I am committed, and I go over and above every time."

"Four! Will you have any more?"

Even the men look at her.

"Another question," she says quickly, shrugging off the offence. "Do you usually dress like this? It's just we have a strict dress code, proper office attire you know," she winces as if it is difficult for her to tell me this.

I look at her heavily made-up eyes and down to her red blazer. Her black pants hugged large thighs and ended over tight red stilettos, chipped and dirty.

I pulled my lips into a smile. "It's been a pleasure," I say. "Unfortunately, this is not the job for me."

They're too shocked to speak, and one attempts to stand as I walk out.

My shoes clatter on the lino as I step out into the Spring sunshine. I look down to the shoes, peeking out from the lace of my dress, tiny horses on a carousel forming the chunky heels of glittering pink pumps and whisper, "Nailed it."

RAINBOW CLUB

By Lani Wendt Young

"Mama, I'll be late home after school today. Only an hour later. Still enough time to help with the dinner." Moana's face was earnest. She really really wanted her mum to be okay with it.

Sosefina was fixing her youngest daughter's hair. She tugged the brush through tangles with vehemence while Tina winced and tried not to cry out. All the girls knew that if they complained, then their mother only intensified her efforts. Hair brushing and braiding was a war they engaged in every morning.

"E a? You be late? What for? You doing a extra study?" demanded Sosefina, as she frowned at a particularly tough knot in Tina's hair that dared to defy her.

"Sort of," said Moana. "It's a meeting for Rainbow Club. Remember I gave you that information form about the clubs I'm in?"

Sosefina couldn't remember. But she wasn't going to say so. "Ia okay. Hurry home quick after. And be careful." She tied off Tina's braid with a rubber band and then pulled on it once, twice to straighten it. And just because. "Uma. You girls go now. Don't miss the bus."

The sisters said goodbye to their father, who was washing a frying pan at the sink in the kitchen. Whenever Sosefina made eggs for breakfast, she always left the pan to soak and Farani scrubbed it. That was their unspoken deal. She cooked and he cleaned.

"What she say?" Farani asked as he watched the girls go up the drive.

Sosefina bustled about the kitchen, wiping benches and putting away mess. "Where she go after school?"

"Rainbow Club."

"O a ga mea o Rainbow Club?" asked Frank. "What's that?"

Sosefina didn't know. But she wasn't going to say so. "It's about painting. Colours. Art class."

Farani snorted in disgust as he dried his hands on a towel. He wasn't impressed. How many times did he have to tell his kids what subjects were important at school and which were a waste of time? Art was right up there next to Music and Dance on the useless list. Their eldest daughter had completed her university degree in a subject that Farani deemed the most useless of all – Performing Arts. What was the point of all that money spent to go to school, when now she was always in between gigs and going to auditions, and she had to work at Countdown so she could afford to pay her rent?

Their second daughter had chosen only marginally better in Farani's opinion. She had a Master's Degree in Museum Studies. Which sounded impressive on paper and whenever they announced it to people at church.

A Master degree?! Oi aue, manaia! Oka le poto la'u fanau!

But in real life, the only job she would ever be able to get, was at the museum. And what kind of job was that anyway? Looking after all the rubbish that palagis stole from other countries?

No, it was subjects like Maths, Science and Accounting that mattered. Farani was hoping for wiser choices from his two younger children. To have a doctor, engineer or accountant in the family? Now those were careers a Samoan parent could be proud of. Moana was a clever girl and she worked hard at school. She had already won several science awards and the teacher said she had a good chance of not only being accepted into the Civil Engineering program at university, but also getting a full scholarship.

"Maimau kaimi i ga painting club," muttered Farani as he followed Sosefina out the front door. "What a waste of time." They had to get a move on or else they would be late for their shift. Farani was a packer at a warehouse and Sosefina was a forklift driver for the same company.

Sosefina shushed his complaints. "I already tell you before. She needs to do those clubs so she can put it on her applications for the scholarships. They like when the kids do different things besides schoolwork."

Another snort of disgust from Farani. That made no sense to him either. Why make a child do other activities different from schoolwork? When what they should be doing, is focusing on schoolwork? Of what use to Moana's schoolwork was kicking a ball around, singing songs or painting pictures? *Eh.* Sometimes the palagi's ways mystified Farani. *Valea.*

But Sosefina was already in the car and waiting for him. Impatient. A discussion about their daughter going to Rainbow Club would have to wait for another time.

"Mum, Dad – can we talk please?" Moana was nervous as she faced both parents at the same time.

"What is it?" asked Sosefina. "We don't want to be late for your plane."

"There's plenty of time," said Moana. "This shouldn't take long." *I hope.* "There's something I need to tell you before I go. And I want to tell you in person. Please?"

It sounded serious. Both parents exchanged a look. Then they sat down at the kitchen table and braced themselves.

Sosefina looked at her third child. Eighteen years old now, graduated from high school and ready to go to university, Moana looked to her mother, like a little girl who thought she was all grown up and ready for the world. But Sosefina worried that she wasn't. And now she was leaving, going all the way to the other island. Where there was snow, and only many palagi, and where crazy gunmen killed people when they were praying at church. *Oka. Why must she go so far away?*

A pang of something . . . sadness. Mingled with pride. And so much alofa. Where had the time gone with this daughter? It seemed like only yesterday Sosefina was combing knots and uku's from Moana's tangled hair while she squirmed and wriggled, impatient to get back to her books.

How is it possible she's old enough to go be an engineer? She's just a baby still.

Farani looked at his third child. A bit lapo'a this one. She liked to eat, and would miss her mother's panipopo and sapasui for sure. He didn't envy her having to live in a student dorm and eat palagi food. Porridge probably. And sausages for dinner. With mash. Only exactly enough food calculated and allocated for each person. No spare for sharing with unexpected visitors. No leftovers for the next day. But he knew she would do well at her studies anyway. She was a smart girl. A hardworking girl. And she had plans that Farani approved of. To be a engineer. To work for Fletcher Construction. To travel overseas and do big projects. Make big money. Then one day, to go to Samoa and work there. Give back to their homeland.

What a blessing this daughter is!

Farani smiled at Moana. Encouragingly. "What is it? What you want to tell us?"

Now that she had their attention, Moana's courage fled. She wavered. "Ummm, well it's not easy for me to tell you this. I know you're going to be upset . . . and I hope that, no matter how disappointed you may get, that you'll try to remember that I'm still me. I'm still your same daughter . . . "

Dread was a stone in Sosefina's chest. *Oi aue. God, no. Please!* "Are you pregnant?"

It was like she'd thrown a firecracker onto the table. Moana flinched backwards. Farani jumped to his feet, his chair a harsh scrape on the floor. "What!? Pregnant?! How? You don't have a boyfriend! We never see one. You always too busy doing your schoolwork! No Moana, how could you?"

Moana was alarmed, panicked as she tried to calm the explosive situation. "No, no. I'm not pregnant. Mum, Dad, I promise you. I'm not."

"You're not?" Sosefina was suspicious. Doubtful.

"No, I'm not."

Farani sat down again, one hand on his chest, muttering to himself about the stupidity of youth, and the foolishness of daughters. Even as he breathed a huge sigh of relief that, no, his third daughter was not pregnant. "That's good. You going to study engineering. Be a very busy, very smart engineer, and make plenty money. You can't do that if you pregnant now."

Moana corrected him. "Actually, I could Dad. My friend Sharon is a single mum and studying at Uni and she's doing great . . . " Her voice trailed away as she saw her mother's warning glare. Now was not the time to try and convince her parents that single mothers could still go to university. Not when she should be convincing them that no, she wasn't pregnant. "I mean, you don't need to worry. I am not pregnant. Not even a little bit."

Sosefina bristled. "Okay. So, if you not pregnant, then what's wrong? What did you do?"

"Is it drugs?" demanded Farani. To Sosefina he said, "Remember Tino and Mata's son? That one whose head went cracked because he do many drugs?"

Sosefina nodded. "Yes, yes, their Alfred. That's right. Poor Tino and Mata. Alfred used to be such a good boy. Always helping to clean the church and make the flowers with Mata. Then after he started that stuff, he wasn't the same. Stealing money from them, even took their television and sold it for drug money. Finally, got locked up. It's very sad." To Moana she said, "Is that it? Are you on that stuff too?"

Moana shook her head. Frustrated now. "No, I'm not on drugs. Never touched the stuff and never plan on it either. You're the ones who told me, remember? My brain is too smart and too precious to waste on taking drugs."

Sosefina and Farani nodded in unison, grateful for the recognition of their good parenting.

"Alright, so what did you do then?" repeated Sosefina. "Hurry up, we gonna be late to the airport."

"It's not something I've done. It's more something about who I am that I want to tell you. Moana took a deep breath. *Here it goes.* "Mum, Dad, I'm bisexual."

Blank looks. Questioning.

"What's that?" barked Farani, gruff and uncomfortable, because he was embarrassed to be having a conversation with his daughter where the word SEXUAL was being mentioned.

"It means, I like girls and I like boys. Heavily leaning more towards girls, actually." Seeing they were still puzzled, Moana forged ahead. "I like girls like a lesbian does. Do you understand now?"

Understanding dawned. "Like a gay?" asked Farani. "You're like a gay?"

"Sort of. Yes."

Sosefina was bewildered. "You a fa'atama?" That made no sense. Moana didn't look anything like a boy. She always had to oke Moana to pull up her top because this daughter liked to wear tight ofu's that showed her big susu. "My cousin Salote in Samoa is fa'atama. When we kids, she stronger than all the boys. Always fighting. Getting mad when her mother don't let him cut his hair short. Now, he is called Tony. He talking, walking, looking like a man. Nobody call him Salote anymore. You not like that?"

"No, I'm not fa'atama," said Moana. "I'm a girl. And sometimes I like other girls."

Farani and Sosefina looked at each other. An electric wire of questions raced between them. *Our daughter is lesbian? A gay? Why? How did this happen? Since when? Did you know? Why didn't you tell me?*

Moana appealed to her mother. "Didn't you suspect something when I was in Rainbow Club all those years?"

Farani looked accusingly at his wife. "I thought you said that was a painting club. For doing Art."

Sosefina shrugged. Helpless. "Ia, that's what I thought. Rainbows. Colours. Painting stuff."

Moana couldn't stop the half-smile on her face. "Is that really what you thought? No, it wasn't for Art. It's a club for LGBT kids to come together and get support. Lots of lesbian and gay and bisexual kids like me."

The kitchen was very quiet. So quiet they could hear the tick tock of the Jesus wall clock. And the droning hum of the old fridge. Sosefina and Farani both stared at the table. Thinking. Processing. Absorbing.

Finally, Farani spoke. "Does this mean you not going to university? You not going to study to be an engineer?"

"Dad, my being bisexual has nothing to do with that."

Farani winced when she said the S word again. He didn't think kids and parents should talk about SEX. Ever. It wasn't right. He didn't know why his daughter thought she had to tell them these things.

"So you still going to Otago for school? You still going to be a engineer?"

"Yes Dad. Of course. You know my plans. We discussed them together."

"Okay," said Farani. Relieved. "Everything alright then." That was sorted. He stood up. Looked at his wife. "Let's go. Everybody will be waiting at the airport to say goodbye."

Sosefina nodded as she got up and hustled about the kitchen, checking for her bag and the house keys. "Where's your sister?" She raised her voice to a practised yell. "Tina! Kope mai! We going now to take Moana."

Tina appeared from where she had been unobtrusively hiding in the corridor. She darted a wary questioning look at her big sister. *How did they take it? Everything okay?*

Impatient with Tina's distractedness, Sosefina flicked her ears. "Eh, don't stand around. Help Moana with her bags. Hurry up."

Moana looked at her parents. Surprised. "So, you're alright with it? Really? You're not upset?"

Farani was halfway out the door with the larger of Moana's suitcases. He turned back. Serious. "You go to university. You work hard. You be a engineer. When you graduate then you can have a boyfriend. Or a girlfriend. Whatever you want." *End of story.*

The sisters followed their parents out to the car, Moana still shaking her head in disbelief.

Tina nudged her, whispered. "You told them you like girls? And they're okay?"

Moana nodded. "I guess so."

In the car, Farani turned the stereo on loud. He hummed along all the way to the airport. Moana was a good girl who had worked hard, got a scholarship, and now she was going to university to study to be an engineer. She wasn't pregnant. She wasn't getting a cracked brain doing drugs.

It was a good day to be a father.

Late that night, Sosefina was about to drift off to sleep when Farani sat straight up with a sudden jolt.

"O le a?" she asked. "What is it?"

"I just think of something," said Farani. "If Moana is a gay who likes girls, then that means we don't have to worry about her getting pregnant while she's at university!"

Farani lay back down with a big grin on his face. It was a *very* good day to be a father.

THE SEI AND THE BLADE

By Amy Tielu

Nina was hungry and the adults were boring.

"Mummy..." She sulked, sagging under the hardship of it all in a twisting sprawl over her mother's arm and thigh.

Her mother startled with a sharp look, sucking in a sound of exasperation behind her teeth, eyes narrowed. *"Nina."*

From their seat on the floor, Nina was pushed back upright, legs crossed, back slumped. The four-year-old swayed into the knee of her elder cousin, Carla, who barely glanced up from the light of her cell phone clutched low against her side. Sandwiched so close in the small space of Grandpa Ropati's living room, rows and rows of cousins, aunties and uncles would usually be the highlight of Nina's week, clustered around a table with music, laughing and *talk talk talk*. And food.

Today, Grandpa Ropati was lying in a long box with a glass lid at the front of the living room. Everyone sang like they did on Sundays. No one was laughing. No one was playing. Only one man talked and that was her uncle Carlos, Carla's father. They had all dressed like they were going to church, and that would have been okay because there was morning tea after church, but Uncle, with his saggy black suit and his little black book, had droned for the longest ever, and Nina was *hungry*.

In the other room, the sounds of a busy kitchen and the fragrance of a steaming lunch called to her. Nina had slept so well, there had not been time for breakfast. Her mom had lifted her out of bed, wiped her face with a hot flannel, stripped her and dressed her in her i'ila white dress, and then handed her off to Carla to pull a hairbrush through her tangles. An orange juice box had been shoved into her hands as her mom bustled them into the car.

Her tummy growled and she smushed her face into her mother's arm, whining. *"Mummy."*

Soft, pillowy arms closed around her, lifting her up - her heart soared, turning her face up for the hug - and she was swiftly deposited on her mother's other side, nudged to the door. "Alu i fafo. *Alu."*

Her mother's eyes had already returned to Uncle Carlos when Nina looked back, disappointed, chest tight. She glanced to the door leading to the balcony and round to the kitchen. She looked back to her mother.

Hunger won out.

The door clattered shut behind her and Nina tensed, wincing, counting one… two… but her mother didn't come crashing through the door, with a scowl and eyes blazing. Nina's shoulders dropped in relief.

The scent of barbequed meat and fa'alifu kalo was stronger from out here, and maybe if she was lucky there was some fried--

A tall woman slumped against the balcony's railing, broad-shouldered and draped in black like everyone else. But on her, it looked like a cape of queens: long sweeping robes, loose, heavy and free; and, around her neck, wrists and fingers, gold. Her hair was coiled high atop her head like a raven crown. A white sei tucked over her ear, its petals falling tired and limp. Her rich, red lips pressed in a grim line as she stared at a long, thin object of wood in her hands.

Nina's eyes widened with a gasp, hunger forgotten. "Auntie Siliva!"

"Oof!" Siliva swayed with the full impact of the little one suddenly wrapped around her thigh, and twisted around in surprise.

Nina's beaming face emerged from the curtain of her auntie's robes, her arms tightening in delight. "Mummy said you weren't coming!"

Arms splayed high and wide in surrender, Siliva blinked at her once . . . twice. The wooden thing in her hand was held carefully aloft. "Hey… kid!"

Nina's shoulders dropped at the blank look. "You don't remember me."

"No! Of course, I…"

She scowled. "It's Nina."

"Nina! Yes!" A nervous, weak smile. "Hi, baby."

Nina's voice pitched to an indignant squeal. *"Auntie Siliva, you forgot my name!"*

That hurt because... Auntie Siliva was just... the prettiest, the coolest, the most ... never around, and even when she was, she did things like this, hanging to the sides away from the rest. And that was sad because she and Mummy were sisters but Nina never got to see her.

"Shhhhh." Siliva cast a nervous glance back to the open door of the kitchen behind her. To her apparent relief, only steam came billowing out. "Nina, baby, why aren't you inside for loku?"

"Ou ke fia 'ai." Nina looked hopefully around to see if Siliva had a bag, as a bag may contain snacks. Nina's gaze snapped to the wooden object balanced carefully in her aunt's hand. She stepped back, bouncing on bare heels. "What's that?"

Siliva's shoulders tensed and she looked at the offending item, her grip delicate. "It's... it belonged to your grandpa Ropati. It's one of his shards."

Shards?

Nina peered curiously as her aunt brought it closer for her inspection. When she reached out to touch, her aunt made a disapproving noise and shook her head. Briefly stung, Nina obeyed and used only her eyes, hands tucking obediently behind her back.

What she thought was a long stick was in fact a long *knife* with a wooden handle as long as her arm, braided in weathered afa and tape faded brown with age.

Nina's eyes widened in recognition. "I know this! Carla has this in her siva! You light on fire and--" she waved her arms in great arcs mimicking what she'd seen of her cousin practising on the lawns of their grandparents' house. Of the cousins who knew how to dance with fire, Carla was the one Grandpa Ropati always asked to demonstrate, her thin wrists twirling as the fire danced in whistling whorls of light and black smoke.

Nina leaned in, eyes closing with pleasure at the trace scent of kerosene on the long, wooden stick.

"It's an 'ailao afi," Auntie Siliva said, balancing it in her two hands. "This one is very old. Very sharp. So we have to be careful. Ua e iloa?"

Nina squinted. "*Eye-lah--*"

"Aila--" Her auntie gently corrected. "Ah-ee--"

Ailao afi.

"But you said 'shard.'"

"It…" Siliva sighed, hand curling tightly around the blade's handle. "You're a bit young to…." Her mouth twisted, conflicted.

"Shard like a glass?" Nina pressed. She wasn't dumb. After all, she was four-and-three-quarters.

Siliva studied her face carefully. "I mean like… agaga. Soul. Have you heard of that before?"

A memory spilled to the fore and passed Nina's lips before she could consider the implications. "Agaga… pa'ia?"

Siliva's face broke into a broad smile. "That's right! But… just soul."

Nina fumbled with her hands, glancing from her aunt's pleased expression to the ailao afi in her hands, then to her feet, suddenly awkward. What was idle curiosity had spilled into too many words at once and she was not understanding at all.

Her auntie's smile turned rueful, and she leaned against the wooden pillar of the balcony, ailao afi lying tall against her shoulder. The sea breeze coming up over the cliff ruffled her robes and the petals of the pale sei against her temple. A grey shroud of a storm was approaching from the sea, and the wind pushed harder, bending the tall banana trees in the back lawn.

"In every one of our souls, there's a forge. And over our life, we collect shards."

Nina hummed politely, mouth pressed thin.

Her aunt chuckled softly at whatever she saw in Nina's face. "They're the pieces of other people we pick up along the way, baby. Some of them we grow ourselves. And some, people leave behind… they don't always mean to."

Nina glanced into the kitchen at the fresh smell of what was definitely fried chicken. She hadn't imagined it!

"You want to see a cool trick?"

That caught Nina's interest.

Auntie Siliva smiled, nodding for her to take a few steps back. "Give me some space."

Nina giggled, bouncing back in anticipation. A trick! She loved magic tricks.

"Where do you think your soul lies?"

A soul lies? "In a bed?"

Her aunt gave a startled bark of laughter "Oi se teine… Count me in." Siliva's hands pressed together, as though in prayer, before her chin. "Tasi…."

The familiar tone Nina had heard over many a siva and pese practice made her light up.She was delighted to help. "Tasi… fa!"

Siliva bowed her forehead to the steeple of her fingers, eyes sliding closed, perfectly still. Nina held her breath. The cool sea wind whipped at them, drawing strands of hair loose from the coil at Siliva's temples. Her shoulders sank with a slow exhale. Her hands lowered.

A flare of light erupted. From where Nina could not tell. She gaped as Siliva's expression tightened to one of stern concentration, and her right arm lashed with tight motion. Something whistled as it cut the air. When the light faded, Siliva stood before her with Grandpa Ropati's ailao afi in one hand and in the other . . .

Nina squealed with excitement, clapping. "Another one!"

Siliva stared at her, eyes narrowing gently. The two blades - one long and weathered; the second paler and smaller, as though for a child - lowered to her sides. It was like she had anticipated some other reaction. "Have you seen someone do this before?"

"Yeah! Mummy does that when she reads bedtime stories. The letter from Daddy, before he died."

"… Oh … "

"Then she saves it in her special place."

Siliva glanced away in thought, mouth shrugging. "Spe- . . . okay." She nodded. "Okay."

"Do you have stories in you, too?"

Siliva's expression softened with surprise. "I… I don't know. I haven't… we don't always know what we carry, you know, until we… dig."

"You wanna see what I have?"

Siliva's eyes widened. "You can do it already?"

"Yeah!"

Nina's hands clapped before her eyes, and she didn't wait as her aunt had. Focusing inward for the seed of stillness her mummy had trained her to find when she needed a quiet place, that beat between breaths where her dad used to tickle her under her ribs. It was a spark and utter dark. She felt the pull from low in her belly zipping up like a rush of breath when she winded herself on the playground. And then her hands were opening. Light fading. Air spilled in.

She grinned, looking up at her aunt, and offered her treasures. "Ta-da!"

Siliva stared at the red sei in her tiny hands and the broken segment of an ula fala.Her expression unreadable. Siliva's fingers hovered above the two, curious, but not daring to touch. "Oh, sweetheart. That's beautiful."

Nina held out the sei, red petals of the hibiscus crisp and perfect. "You want this?"

Siliva's eyes widened in alarm. "Oh, no that's . . . "

"Your sei is floppy and dying. Mine's prettier."

Her aunt's shoulders shook with a helpless snort of laughter. She looked from the offered flower to the little girl's hopeful face, that strange, rueful smile curving her mouth again, her eyes soft. "How about a trade?" She held out the two ailao afi, brandishing the larger and older first. "Grandpa gave me this."

"Wow," Nina breathed, then squinted. "It's all rusted."

Siliva's smile turned brittle, visibly swallowing, and her eyes shone with tears. "Yeah, I… I didn't take the best care of it."

"This one is my size!" Nina pointed excitedly to the smaller of the two blades. "It looks new."

"It's as old as me." Siliva's smile thinned with regret.

Not waiting for her aunt to change her mind, Nina bounded up to the smaller of the blades, arms outstretched. Her sei was proudly offered with a broad grin.

Siliva rolled her eyes but her smile held, and she lowered to her knees, removing the pale, limp sei and turning her head for Nina to slide the new one in place. Siliva tensed at the first touch of the red hibiscus upon her skin, shivering as it slid into place. The flower pulsed with an inner light, recognising its new owner. Gold forked from the hibiscus, racing like lightning upon the highway of Siliva's veins, up the coils of her hair and across her temple. Her eyes leapt wide as the shard's power and memory infused into her being, pupils briefly seized by the inner glow.

Nina watched her aunt briefly sag to brace herself with an arm on the rail, chest heaving.

"I always forget," Siliva's voice was strained, breathless. "How much power you kids pack in those tiny bodies." Her gaze met Nina's with trepidation. "How do I look?"

Nina clasped her hands together fondly, her father's broken ula fala dissipating out of mind and sight.

"Oh sweetheart, that's beautiful," she parroted, voice thin and high, and her aunt laughed.

A rueful laugh and strong arms encircled her, pulling her close, mindful of the two blades still clasped in each hand. Nina gratefully threw herself forward, burying her face in her aunt's neck. Siliva smelled like fresh towels and sweet, stationery paper and Nina burrowed closer into the scent. Auntie Siliva never allowed hugs.

"Thank you, funny girl," Siliva murmured against her hair, squeezing her gently. She drew back, the flat of the smaller blade bopped Nina's forehead and shimmered out of sight, the young girl's vision dancing with the afterimage of fireworks in shades of straw and sun.

Impressions surged through her mind – the soft prickle of grass beneath bare feet – the whistle of a blade whirling and cutting the air – Grandpa Ropati, but his hair was dark and his face stern, pointing with the tall ailao afi in Auntie Siliva's hand ("Toe fai mai!") -- the howl of the wind cresting the cliffs as Siliva practised for hours and hours, muscles burning as her face streaked with tears because she couldn't get it right and she was going to embarrass Tamā . . .

Nina blinked as the images faded from her vision.

Auntie Siliva was watching her with concern, murmuring under her breath. She reached out to thumb at Nina's cheek, and Nina realised she was crying.

"Auntie…" Nina's voice shook with the ghost of feelings that were not her own. "Can . . . can you practise with me?"

Siliva stalled, staring at her, eyes abruptly shining again, and her lip threatened to quiver.

"Are you crying?" Nina squinted, voice sharp with judgement, sniffing through her own tears.

"Mmm." Siliva's gaze darted away, rapidly blinking. She cleared her throat suspiciously, and Nina swiped at the incriminating smears on her own face. She knew the truth.

The screen door to the kitchen swung open behind her with a whine of rusted hinges and Nina looked back. In Siliva's hand, Grandpa Ropati's gift dissolved from sight.

On the threshold stood Nina's grandmother, back bowed, eyes squinted and, tucked against the side of her billowing black church dress, a tall bucket of fried chicken.

Nina gasped, heart singing, mouth drooling.

"Who brought this?" Nina's grandma crowed, voice cracking, brandishing the bucket with offence. She hobbled, leaning against the door frame for support. "I said no *KFC*."

"*Chicken!*" Nina cheered, charging ahead, and dragging her aunt along by her hand.

Stumbling after the little one, Siliva muttered from the corner of her mouth. "Sorry, mum. My bad."

"Eh." Nina's grandma relinquished the bucket to the ravenous four-year-old, and motioned the two inside. Siliva was tugged down for a firm peck on the cheek. "At least you're here."

A shy smile found Siliva's mouth, eyes downcast.

The screen door smacked shut behind them and the glass door followed, sealing out the approaching storm.

HER GARDEN

By Vanessa Collins

She put the last strawberry plant into its pot, her hands covered in dirt and happiness as she stood back to admire her handiwork. It was November, so it was hot like a motherfucker beating down your back. Aucklanders get fooled by the consecutive hot weathered days, thinking, 'Yay! Summer's coming early!' Then the sky opens her legs and soaks the earth, reminding they still needed to wait for January. But still, it was the best time to start your summer garden, turn the soil, descend on Mitre 10 and get strawberries.

The day had been hard, her body was broken, sore, tired. Her mother's garden was on the to-do-list that was a mile long. It felt good to get it done. She had spent the whole day working, cleaning out the weeds along the fence and in the potted plants; emptying out the old soil and renewing the compost. Her fingers ached, nails full of dirt, but she was happy with what her hands had created. The dreariness of winter was all cleared out and the garden was ready for summer. She could already imagine it in full bloom, hear the heavy buzz of honey bees amongst the flowers, and taste the sweet redness of ripe strawberries. It would be beautiful.

Her thoughts were interrupted with the call of her name.

"Maria?". Her mother stood by the back door, walking stick in hand, looking over her garden. A frown on her face. "You know, we shouldn't have anything up against the fence."

"What?" replied Maria, confused and somewhat bewildered. All the potted plants against their side of the fence were her mum's.

"We shouldn't put anything against the fence, so you don't disturb the neighbours, it's just being respectful". Her mother had that tone in her voice.

"You mean you want me to move all the plants away from the fence?" asked Maria.

Her mother made a familiar sound of annoyance. "Ahhh, Maria! I mean the other things! They don't belong there. Just be mindful when you put plants near the fence!"

Her mum came down the steps, slow and careful, the walking stick now her constant companion. She made her way through the garden inspecting Maria's work. She pointed to a pot Maria had moved to a better space, "This shouldn't be here, the lily needs its own space". Jabbed with her stick at a rose bush, "Why would you put this here for?"

And on it went. The soil wasn't turned properly, Maria hadn't pulled out enough weeds, this compost didn't look right, and where did all the old soil go?.

Maria sat on the back steps trying to enjoy the late afternoon sun which wasn't hot, it was just the right warmth for the ending day. She sat with her knees up, resting her arms across them, watching her mum. She felt the familiar weight of disappointment and defeat as every flaw was pointed out. She looked over to her stacked pots of strawberries, hoping for solace. And it dawned on her.

All her mother's plants along the fence; the potted palm trees; the mini lemon trees with their fruits the colour of summer; the flowering rock orchids; the Japanese maple elegant with her reddish brown leaves; the bamboo tall and steady; the trimmed down veggie bed, out of all of this greenery and perfectly designed beauty, Maria's strawberries stood out like a sore thumb, the outsider, just newly added.

The strawberries didn't belong. Like Maria.

As her mum, the woman who birthed her, continued her critique, Maria thought of the woman whose garden she did belong in, her nanalevu who had nurtured her in the inbetween years.

The garden down from their bure, on the land that ran up to and along the river. The garden that looked up to the mighty Nakauvadra, where they say

Degei sleeps. The garden with the sweetest pineapple, skin peels boiled with water to make the sweetest of juices. And when she had time, her nanalevu would make pineapple jam, over the wood stove.

The garden filled with red juicy kavika, weleti and if you went to the very edge maybe you would get lucky and find guavas the size of your fist, flesh ripened red.

As a child she would get sent to gather bele, ota and sometimes when the leaves had grown well, rourou leaves for the evening meal. But the best thing was nanalevu's hydrangeas, the blue and purple ones. Planted alonside the bure, always kept neat.

In nanalevu's garden, there was always space. In nanalevu's garden, she was home.

Maria picked up the pots of strawberries and moved them, onto the footpath further down the end of mum's garden. To the side of the shed. Out of sight. Out of her mum's way.

"I'll water you later," she said gently.

One day, when her duty here was done, she would return home. Where she would plant strawberries alongside the hydrangeas. In her garden.

ON COLONISING KUPU

By Sisilia Eteuati

There's a poem in this

My friend Mere says

There is a poem in this
a poem in how people equate kindness
to aroha

But kindness is not our concept
and aroha

Aroha
Is a real living breathing giving taking way of being
    and life
it is mutual obligation, and understanding
we are all part of the whanau
But not in the tokenistic
Way you say it.

And kindness

Kindness
is just
Some voluntary

White saviour
Bullshit.

SHUT

By Nichole Brown

"It's just a three-hour flight, darling," she excitedly told her brown eyed, brown haired, brown skinned tamahine.

And then the borders slammed shut.

They'd driven around the edges just to check. And by the time they came close to the end of the second inspection of all the edges and coasts and rivers and highways, they were sure; Aotearoa had run out of room for them.

They were only two. They had always been only two. But their creeping suspicion that they'd outgrown home was being realised sooner than their hearts had anticipated.

They tried moving from the top of the north to halfway down, and as east as they could go before Tangaroa interfered. And then they tried swapping islands and burying themselves in the snow and whiteness of Te Waipounamu. They checked all the corners and then they checked the edges again.

And still, they felt the walls closing in.

Technically and literally, there was enough space for them. After all, they were only two.

But they could feel the haunting whistles as Tawhirimatea whipped their cheeks, the hands of Papatuanuku holding them too close to her chest, and the drag from every awa drawing them into spaces they had outgrown.

"It's just a three-hour flight, my little adventurer," she promised her brave and eager-eyed daughter, as they condensed their entire lives into two suitcases, kissed goodbye their favourite, most comforting cheeks, and embraced for one last hug, and then two.

The plane doors closed, sealing tightly, with tears on both sides of the curved white walls.

Tears on the outside from those left behind that they loved.

Tears on the inside for those left behind that they loved.

She looked over at her pink-cheeked daughter, golden brown hair tumbling down to her waist, with her full-bodied smile that ran from her eyes all the way to the bottom of her legs that were nowhere near long enough to reach the plane floor. She watched as she unwrapped the plastic wrapped cake and set it down next to her plastic wrapped Mainland cheese and crackers, taking careful nibbles between little sips of water with a dramatically satisfied, "ahhhhh," in between.

With each little ahhhhh she felt a sense of something gentle. Some strange mix of relief, calm, and maybe hope? Yes, hope. Small, flickering hope. Slow burning hope.

Suddenly wheels touched tarmac. Concrete. Lights. An overwhelm of lights. Documents. Checks. More lights. Warm, sickly city air that somehow felt joyful in their lungs.

They were somewhere new.

It was only a three-hour flight, but that flight had made space for them again. Space to think, space to wander, space to wonder, and space to be. They made splashes on new golden coasts that faced the lands where they began. They grew accustomed to the harshness of the concrete and found softness in its once menacing embrace. They befriended the tall towers that reached beyond the clouds, bridging the cavernous distance between their beloved earth mother and sky father.

And then the borders slammed shut.

Suddenly, home had a different meaning. Home became two places; where they were, and where they began.

And the home where they were was still theirs. But the home where they began? It didn't belong to them - they belonged to her.

She noticed small changes in her little girl. Her pounamu - Hei Matau -

slowly crept out from the inside of her t-shirt. She had always worn it close to her heart, wanting to keep it warm, and wanting to feel it against her beating chest. But now she wanted it seen. She wanted the whole world to see her pounamu in an act of defiance to a world that didn't recognise her brownness.

She drew a moko kauae on her chin. In bold, brave black. And she wore her moko kauae to school with poi hung at her sides, with steps so fierce Tumatauenga would recoil.

She embraced the words and hauntingly beautiful melodies of wahine like Maisey Rika when she hosted her closed-door, concert-for-herself nightly shower. And the sound was so achingly beautiful that it reminded her of the thick, weighted sadness from the kaikaranga standing on the mahau welcoming the manuhiri blanketing in cloaks of sadness and grief.

"It's just a 3hr flight," she repeated like a mantra, whispering into the wind, hoping the wind would carry her words home, and home would reach back to find her.

Soon, darling, she soothed her brown-eyed wonder. Soon we will be able to go home.

And together they traced the outline of the coast their hearts knew without looking. They shared favourite memories of home to each other in fits of giggles that often turned into rivers of memories pouring down cheeks. They tried as hard as they could to use words no one else around them understood; simple words that felt like home. Kai. Homai. E noho. Kia tu pato. Kei te pehea koe? Mamae. Mamae. Mamae.

Mamae. Mamae. Mamae. That's what sound their hearts made.

Soon, darling, she soothed her brown-eyed wonder. Soon we will be able to go home.

But the slammed borders made no such promises....

The slammed borders paid no attention to tears...

The slammed borders buckled for no one...

The slammed borders with invisible barriers with strange names stayed shut . . .

The slammed borders stayed shut.

ATUA LOA

By Sisilia Eteuati

The old ways are not easily forgotten.

No matter what people think. The old ways are not dependent on these ridiculous humans. Pffft! The old ways do not rely on their own remembering.

People and their thoughts are so … limited.

I think about the things they say about me. Atualoa. The long God.

Ha!

How unimaginative. It is unbecoming of an Atua to eyeroll. But hard eyeroll.

I am a God of hundreds. I am a God of household and home. The God of small and many. I am a God of multiplying things unnoticed, unnoticed, unnoticed.

Which is why I love Fua. Just Fua. Not named for the fragrant pua tucked as sei lovingly behind a precious daughter's ear; or the strong relentless teuila that stands up defiant red to the island heat; or the vibrant unashamed aute; or the exotic introduced rosa - just Fua, a non-descript not named flower.

Fua loves the salu. Always sweeping that one. Early morning and late afternoon. No one notices she wipes down all the louvres each day. No one notices the government house Siaki rents for them is always spotless, it is expected that it will be spotless. As if the pefu from the road never comes in and settles and, but for Fua's vigilance, would cover everything in the house. No one notices when the grass doesn't get long because she spends hours bending over the grass with the sapelu. Swish, swish, swish. The cuttings are swept up with a salu tu. No one notices when she does the kagamea and hangs it in the sun to dry, and then folds it and puts it away neatly in the drawers. No one notices when she goes to church to worship the new god. Everyone goes to church. Nothing special. No one notices when she stays home to prepare the toʻonaʻi. No one notices Fua cooking, although that is no task for women. Fua makes faʻalifu faʻi in the umukuka at the back, the peʻepeʻe always thick from the popo she has scraped. No one notices Fuaʻs arms sinewy from doing men's and women's work both. Perhaps it would have been different if they had stayed in the village. Where everyone notices everything.

I am the God of the everyday, the ordinary and the always. I am not flashy like Isumu with his tricky ways and his sharp teeth. He loves being in the stories. Hero or villain. Either. He's not bothered as long as they are told. Isumu likes it when he hears people tell about how he tricked the octopus. No matter how many times he hears it he always stops and laughs his raucous show-off laugh. Isumu loves it when kids still call for him to take their teeth. He roars with laughter when he hears songs sung to his cleverness and tenacity. Oh, but he is the trickster God indeed, and I am the God of stories. I am not bothered about featuring in them. The worship is in the way the words are woven, in the tongue of the teller, and in the slow inevitable unfolding.

The person who notices Fua the very least is Siaki. He has the isumu flash, but not the isumu smarts. Smarts was not even necessary for Siaki's high high government job. He is ACEO of the Ministry of Revenue and Customs, compliments to his Isumu charm, the way he was always at the Reef Bar and strategically sent over cold bottles of Vailima to anyone of influence. And most importantly, that his dad was a former MP and their aiga have been very loyal to the SATP, Samoa Aia Tatau Party.

Sometimes Fua thinks Siaki only noticed her long enough to tell her she should run away with him. That once was enough. He had a fancy Apia job and could get them a government house away from others he whispered. Away. That was all she needed to hear. She was seventeen when she followed him like a fool, in the deep of night, rolled her clothes up in an ie lavalava and left without a word. An avaga needs no explanation. What is there to say? Running away has always been the traditional way to show unhappiness and dissent. It is the speech of the silent. Sometimes Fua wonders if her family had paused that morning to try to work out what exactly was missing. That was over dramatic of course, she had been an extra set of hands and a useful set. And they would have had to get another. But cousins were in abundance. They hadn't come looking.

I have watched Fua for twenty-five years now so I know the way of things. Toalua. That was how Fua had thought of herself. She had moved in with him. Nothing was less reversible. No wedding could have made it more formal. Toalua. One of two. One is insignificant of course. It had always been insignificant among the many. But toalua made you part of two and surely two together could be something Fua had thought. But here she was more housegirl than wife.

The man she ran away for, out every night. She had thought he wanted a simple village girl like her, but he was out chasing the pa'uguguku rich town girls, dripping Hawaiian gold jewellery with their names engraved black in Old English letters. If Fua was willing to bring out her hopes and ka them clean, if she was willing to hang them like Siaki's shirts, in the wind and strong sun. If she gathered those hopes from the line to iron out carefully, it was perhaps that she thought there might have been a crispness to being twenty years younger than Siaki. That he might wear the age difference with pride, like his collars she starched. Not to show affection in public. No one did that. But just enough so she could claim, at least to herself, that some of the deep creases on his face were from it crinkling into a smile of approval. For her. She keeps this secret so close it is a hush beneath the rise and fall of her breath. She does not betray it in even the slightest upturn of her full lips. She withholds no words from Siaki, lest he think she is musu or fa'ali'i. Neither does she give them freely. These things are always finely balanced.

Isumu is not so observant, nor does he have to be really. He would not claim such a buffoon as Siaki anyway. Isumu has many faults, but he despises bird brains with all the passion of one who has crushed them between his powerful jaw. His own cleverness and quickness mean he has no onosa'i at all. He would know better than to interfere anyway. We have dealt well together Isumu and I over the millennia.

I am not the God of patience either. Ah, but I do understand that stories take time to uncoil. This one has been a tight roll of afa and needs to be unrolled before it can be used to bind. I am Atualoa, the God of long and the lingering, I am the God of the unending and enduring. I am the God of persisting and prevailing. Foolish humans, I did not exist this long because I am the same. I am the God of stories and stories grow and change.

Fua's smooth brown brow does not betray how her thoughts have begun to scurry and creep. The advantages of being deeply unnoticed have begun to occur to her. I like to think that is all my influence, but Fua knows nothing of my ways, not consciously at least, and so I must acknowledge some credit to her. We Gods are flawed, and humans take after us in that at least.

Fua begins to notice that in the long evenings when Siaki is wherever-the-hell not-for-plain-Fua-to-dare-question is, no one notices if her hands aren't busy, busy, busy. She doesn't have to su'i another new ie faitaga for Siaki in the hope that he will be pleased. He has five that are all beautiful as new and always neatly hung for him to choose from. She doesn't have to quietly weave fala lili'i for Siaki to give away carelessly as if they grow abundantly in the garden, to be harvested without thought or care.

On a full moon night Fua can sit outside and look to the masina. I have never really got the human fascination with her - God of soft glow and stolen kisses. Bah so what?! God of the pull and tides, she pulls Fua outside to bathe in her light, but Fua is one of mine.   I am not a jealous God. Masina has nothing on me - moonlight is not half as beguiling as a tale. There is more romance in a story than in any of her enchantment. She is a minor God at best.

"Ah!" Fua cries as she slaps away one of mine. O le tama'i maigi and a little sting never hurt anyone. At least not someone as beloved to me as Fua. She will only be nursing it a few days, and let that be a useful reminder about mooning away at night when she should be plotting revenge.

I am the God of venom and bane. Do they not know that nothing can poison quicker than a tale told? Oh, and do I have a tale for you my friends. Or perhaps it is Fua's tale. I need not claim it when I claim her as my very own.

The cyclone comes suddenly in the night. The winds lash and rain batters down. Fua works, leaning the plywood up against the windows; propping it as best she can with other pieces; a nail in her teeth and one in the hand pressed to the plywood; hammer in the other. Bang, bang, bang. This is a two-person job but there is one of her, and she must make each hit count. There is not much time. Her sinewy arm muscles are taut, slick with rain and sweat. She struggles and swears in frustration as the wind blows at the plywood and she tries to angle it in with her hip. The government issued Santa Fe sways down the dirt road drive that should be familiar enough for Siaki to drive straight even when blind drunk. Fua turns her head. The Reef must have closed early when the meteorological office started blasting the cyclone warning on 2AP; a bit late as the violence of wind and rain had made it obvious to all of them, before the radios started to crackle. Even an afa wouldn't have seen him home at this time otherwise. She turns back to her task. The plywood needs to be fixed in place. It blows at her and she drops the nail and clutches that piece.

Siaki gets out of the car and stands there in the rain and wind. Like the imbecile he is. He stands there, his fiafia shirt drenched, watching Fua or perhaps just drunkenly trying to puzzle out the working of his legs. One foot forward. Then the next.

Fua feels the wind tug, tug, tugging at the piece of plywood heavy in her hand. She turns and looks at Siaki, looks at him not under lashes but straight in his stupid eyes, and slowly uncurls her fingers. The plywood is whipped up by the wind and flies straight into his face, the corner catching his eye. A deep red welt opens. He yells out but the wind catches that too, as he falls to the ground.

Blood streams down his face as she walks into the hurricane towards him. The rain stings her face but she keeps her eyes wide open. She is the tempest and the tumult. She is squall and the storm. I am Atualoa, the Long God and I have waited long to watch on, a proud mother, as Fua walks towards him unafraid. Fua reaches him. "Fia ola!" he cries.

"Ia ola pea oe," she says, disdainful, as she takes his key, walks to the car and slams the door. She backs it back down the dirt drive.

Running away has always been the traditional way to show unhappiness and dissent.

It is the speech of the silent.

"The old ways are not easily forgotten," I laugh. Siaki lies there like a fool.

Isumu looks on from the eaves. Tucked away safely. He is a trickster God indeed. I see him laugh although I cannot hear it. It reverberates in my bones.

I am the God of many, and many do I call now.

The little ones come, atualoa swarm a dark red brown blanket over him, so not a drop more of water touches his skin. I smile. And they sink in their teeth.

I am the God of stories.

The worship is in the way the words are woven. In the tongue of the teller. And in the slow inevitable

unfolding.

The End.

Which is also, our beginning.

VI'IGA
From the Editors

An acknowledgement is so dry, so palagi, so let us sing to you a vi'iga- a song of praise.

We sing of our mothers Lynne-Marie Dillon and Marita Aroha Johnson who left their own places in Aotearoa so we could grow up in Samoa.

We sing of our fathers Leiataualesa Tuitolova'a Dr Kilifoti Sisilia Eteuati and Tuaopepe Dr Felix Wendt, who brought us up to understand our power and strength and value as tamaita'i Samoa.

We sing of our children who are joy and light to us and make us fierce in our determination to ensure they see themselves in story.

We sing of the men of the moana who support and uplift women, Lani would especially like to sing of her husband Darren and Sisilia would especially like to sing of her brothers Tigiilagi, Kilifoti and Mose.

We sing of the women of the moana, Tamaita'i Tusitala, Wahine Writers, who are our village and who trusted us with their faagogo.

We sing of the Brilliant and Amazing Mothers and Writers who have been a community and support to us.

We sing of those who have supported us generously and without any expectation of acknowledgement:

- Lalovai Peseta, the artist whose beautiful painting adorns this cover, and his muse Nikki Mariner-Peseta who supported us without hesitation when this book was only a crazy creative idea

-Lynne-Marie Eteuati, our amazing Copy Editor who has committed much of her life to literacy in Aotearoa, Australia and Samoa through her work in education

- Fiona Ey, Founding Partner of Ey, Clarke and Koria Lawyers in Samoa, a great supporter of the Arts and of many Samoan community initiatives, who believes in Pacific business women supporting Pacific women creatives, and who insisted on donating a $1000 so each of the 38 writers could be provided with a physical copy of Va.

Fa'afetai, Fa'afetai, Fa'afetai le alofa.

O le tusi lea o le taumafaiga vaivai e fa'amoemoe e tali atu ai lo outou agalelei ma le lagolago mai -
ua outou seu i le vateatea lupe o malama.

Sisilia and Lani.

EDITORS

Lani Young

Lani is an international bestselling author of YA fantasy, contemporary romance, speculative, and literary fiction. The 2018 Pacific Laureate, her work is inspired by the diverse mythology of Oceania and the richness of her cultural heritage as a Samoan and Maori woman. She is the author of the Telesā World books, the Scarlet Lies series, the Afakasi Woman collection, Mata Oti, and the non-fiction book Pacific Tsunami Galu Afi. She's also a writer of stories for children and has worked as a script writer for Disney. Born and raised in Samoa, she attended university in the USA and New Zealand before returning home to work as a high school English teacher. An award-winning journalist, she is the former Chief Editor and Co-Founder of Samoa Planet. Lani is an advocate for Oceania writers taking ownership of every aspect of their storytelling, including publishing and distribution. Connect with her on her website at https://laniwendtyoung.co To find more of her books, check her Amazon page at https://www.amazon.com/Lani-Wendt-Young/e/B005BK5EXM%3Fref=dbs_a_mng_rwt_scns_share

Sisilia Eteuati

Sisilia is an award winning writer and poet whose work has been published in various publications across the Pacific including Landfall, The Sapling, Blackmail Press, Samoa Observer and Samoa Planet. Sisilia Eteuati, her children and her poem Mauga features in Mana Moana: Pacific Voices series to amplify and support the Pacific to drive global action to reduce greenhouse gas emissions. Sisilia has a Masters of Creative Writing from the University of Auckland where she was the recipient of the Sir James Wallace Scholarship based on the strength of her writing portfolio. To support her writing habit Sisilia currently works as a Chief Legal Counsel in a Government Department in New Zealand and is very grateful to have been able to serve the public as a lawyer in Samoa, Australia and now Aotearoa where she lives with her two children.

VĀ ANTHOLOGY CONTRIBUTORS

Amy Tielu

Amy is a Filipino-Samoan woman based in Ngunnawal and Ngambri country (Canberra), Australia. A writer, business analyst and researcher, Amy currently leads the Service Design team at the Australian National University. She studied Arts and IT as an undergrad at the ANU before extending this interest into her research Masters at the Auckland University of Technology, "Searching for the digital fāgogo: a study of indigenous Samoan storytelling in contemporary Āotearoa digital media". During her Masters, Amy wrote for her University about the postgraduate experience and volunteered her time as the Story Lead in a cross-institutional physics project celebrating the United Nations' International Year of Light (Beambox Interactive, 2015). Upon graduation, she served as Cultural Adviser to theCoconet.tv's inaugural season of Legends of Polynesia (2017-18). Amy remains an advocate of LGBTIQA+ rights in the Pasifika and faith community and is passionate about stories that uplift the flawed humanity, diversity and dignity of her intersecting communities.

Arihia Latham

Arihia is a Kāi Tahu Māori living in Te Whanganui a Tara, Aotearoa. She is a writer, facilitator, rongoā practitioner and māmā to three beautiful tamariki. Her work has been published among others by Huia, Oranui, Te Whe, Landfall, Pantograph Punch and The Spinoff. She has been a regular arts columnist for Stuff and loves an opportunity to celebrate other artists whenever possible.

Ashlee Sturme

Ashlee (Ngati Awa, Te Arawa, Tuwharetoa) is an experienced non-fiction writer but her heart lies in fiction. Her dream is to make a career out of crafting words while raising her whanau in the beautiful Bay of Plenty. She is a qualified health coach with an interest in mental health, and works in a school, passionately fighting to ensure her students are provided with best outcomes. Ashlee holds several writing qualifications, is a Pikihuia Short Story awards finalist and is published in Huia Short Stories 14. Her first novel is due to be released in 2022. Find her on:

https://mlt.org.nz/?s=ashlee

https://www.facebook.com/ashleesturmewriter

Audrey Teuki Tetupuariki Tuioti Brown-Pereira

Audrey is an innovative poet who plays with text on the page and words in the air/ear. Poetry collections include 'Threads of Tivaevae: Kaleidoskope of Kolours' with Veronica Vaevae (Steele Roberts, 2002) and 'Passages in Between I(s)lands' (Ala Press, 2014), available from Amazon. Her work appears in several anthologies including 'Whetu Moana', 'Mauri Ola' and 'Upu' an Oceanic poetry performance curated by Grace Iwashita-Taylor and directed by Fasitua Amosa. Audrey has performed at the New Zealand Fringe Festival, where she won the joint award for 'Best Spoken Word' (2002), Poetry Parnassus in London (2012) and features alongside other poets, orators, activists, youth and community leaders in the digital poem 'Our Ancestors Speak' (2021) written by Dr. Karlo 'Ulu'ave Mila for the Mana Moana: Pacific Voices series to amplify and support the Pacific to drive global action to reduce greenhouse gas emissions. Audrey wrote the script for the short film 'The Cat's Crying' produced by He Taonga Films (1995) and the experimental film inspired by her poem of the same name 'The Rainbow' (1997) directed by Veronica Vaevae. Audrey is of Cook Islands Maori and Samoan descent born in Rarotonga and raised in South Auckland. She is a graduate of Auckland University and the National University of Samoa and lives in Samoa with her family.

Caroline S Fanamanu Matamua

Caroline S Fanamanu Matamua is Tongan with Sāmoan, Fijian, and Niuean heritage. She is the direct descendant of Kavaʻonau, the daughter sacrificed by her parents Fevanga and Fefafa, resulting in the production of the Kava plant and sugar cane at Faaʻimata ʻEueiki. Her clan are the shark people. She is the mother of four, the pearls of her heart. She no longer writes to share the thoughts of a diagnosed dyslexic but because writing is beauty. Caroline was born in Neiafu, Vavaʻu and migrated to Aotearoa in the 60s. Home is Painituʻuua, Havelu, Tongatapu and she currently lives in Whau, Tāmaki Makaurau. An entrepreneur, she owns Vavaʻu Carving House based in Tāmaki. She is also currently finishing her Masters in Pacific Studies and her law degree at the University of Auckland where she guest lectures on women in Sports. Caroline is a former rugby league player, coach and sports developer. She was the first and only Tongan woman to have coached a district representative team in New Zealand, the (Auckland Vulcan) and the Tongan women's national rugby league team. Caroline co-created the Auckland girls grade with Tasha Davie and coached the first U18 girls champion team. She is the co-founder and board member of Tonga's first female only women's Rugby League Association.

Cassie Hart

Cassie Hart (Ngāi Tahu) is a writer of speculative fiction. Her short stories have appeared in several award-winning anthologies and she is a Sir Julius Vogel winning author, and a Hugo and Shadow Awards finalist. She has self-published over ten novels and novellas under her pen-names, Nova Blake and J.C. Hart, and her first traditionally published novel, Butcherbird, was released by Huia in 2021. A fan of coffee, cats and zombies, Cassie lives in Taranaki.

Courtney Leigh Sit-Kam Malasi Thierry

Courtney was born in Bougainville, Papua New Guinea to PNG-Chinese parents. She moved to the mainland when the civil war broke out and spent most of her multicultural childhood in Lae, PNG. She came to Australia for boarding school, and currently resides in Brisbane with her husband and two daughters. Courtney has a B.A of Environmental Science and works in the water industry but has always loved writing. She had an opinion piece published in the PNG Courier Mail when she was 11 years old, and has published articles as an adult mostly for water industry newsletters. Courtney is a God-centric woman of faith and her contribution in Vā is her first creative piece published in the public arena.

Dahlia Malaeulu

Dahlia is a passionate educator, author, publisher, and is the creator of Mila's Books – Pasifika children's books that help our tamaiti to be seen, heard and valued as Pasifika. Since 2019, Dahlia has written children's stories and is the first Pasifika author to have authored stories that have been published across all schooling levels (pre-school, primary school and high school). In 2021 she authored Te Papa Tongarewa's first Samoan bilingual board book, Asiasiga i le falemataaga i Te Papa / Going to Te Papa, which won a Storylines Notable Book Award. Dahlia also created the Mila's My Aganuʻu Series – the first Pasifika children's picture books in the world written, edited, illustrated, designed and published by an all-Pasifika team.

Find further information about Mila's Books here:
Fb:@MilasBooks
IG: @MilasDM
Website: www.milasbooks.com

Denise Carter-Bennett

Denise is a Cybersecurity Analyst by day and night. Takiwātanga and Aroreretini. Advocate for her fellow neurodivergent people. A wāhine whose whakapapa is both Māori and Kanaka ʻŌiwi, she straddles a link that ties her closely to the moana. A Northerner at heart (Ngāpuhi, Ngāti Hine and Ngāti Whātua Ōrākei), she resides in Tāmaki Makaurau with her tama and ngeru.

Her work has been published by The Spinoff and NZ Drug Foundation. Find her on
Instagram: @neurodiverseaf
Facebook: same as Instagram
Twitter: @Dram_Of_Sleep

Emmaline Pickering-Martin

Emmaline is a Fijian Marama ni Veiqia, Matriarch and Māmā of three exceptional humans of Fijian, Māori, Samoan and Tuvalu descent. She is a passionate advocate for all things Pacific and has a deep love for her Vanua. She resides in Tāmaki calling Te Atatū home. She is an activist at heart and feels most at home in the wasawasa Te Moana nui ā Kiwa. Emmaline is the creator of Tabu Tok, an online platform for Pacific peoples to unpack Tabu topics. She is a Pacific thought leader - she holds an MA with first class honours in Pacific Studies and frequently appears on TVNZ as a Pacific commentator.

Filifotu Vaai

Filifotu is a Samoan mother to two daughters, Lili'uokalani and Idania, and currently lives in Ewa Beach, Hawaii where she works as an Executive Director for Consumer Product & Sales for Hawaiian Telcom. For the past 17 years, she has worked management and executive roles in providers of Phone, Internet, Wireless and TV service in Samoa, American Samoa, Cook Islands and now, Hawaii. She was born and enjoyed a typical Samoan upbringing surrounded by a big family, church, and going to the beach, before leaving Samoa to pursue University studies in New Zealand and later, the USA. She was inspired to write after reciting the poem "Identity" by her Uncle Lemalu Tate Simi, in a school talent show when she was 7. Aside from personal journaling and blogging over the years, Fotu has written for The Frank Book, a youth culture publication in New York City, USA, and she published a book chapter for an Information Technology textbook about the findings of her research on Measuring Success of IT investing in Small Businesses in Samoa.

Gina Cole

Gina COLE (from Tāmaki Makaurau, Aotearoa, New Zealand) is a writer of Fijian and Kai Valagi descent. Her collection Black Ice Matter won Best First Book of Fiction at the 2017 Ockham New Zealand Book Awards. Her work has been widely anthologized and published in literary journals. She is a qualified lawyer and holds an LLB (Hons) and an MJur from the University of Auckland. She has a master's degree in creative writing (MCW) from the University of Auckland, and a PhD in Creative Writing from Massey University. Her forthcoming SFF novel titled Na Viro is a work of Pasifikafuturism.

Isabella Naiduki

Isabella Naiduki is an Indigenous Fijian scholar and writer whose interest is in the study of the Fijian identity, diaspora identity and traditional knowledge within contemporary societies. She completed an LLB International Law & Globalisation from the University of Birmingham and is currently pursuing a postgraduate LLM International Business Law degree. She has had work published in the Mechanics' Institute Review, for the Birbeck Centre of Contemporary Literature, University of London and recently had her collection of essays, "A Season of Soliloquies" shortlisted in a call for submissions by The Emma Press Publishing, UK.

Karlo Mila

Karlo is a New Zealand-born poet of Tongan and Pākehā descent. She is currently Programme Director of Mana Moana, Leadership New Zealand. This leadership programme is based on her postdoctoral research on harnessing indigenous language and ancestral knowledge from the Pacific to use in contemporary leadership contexts. Karlo received an MNZM in 2019 for services to the Pacific community and as a poet, received a Creative New Zealand Contemporary Pacific Artist Award in 2016, and was selected for a Creative New Zealand Fulbright Pacific Writer's Residency in Hawaii in 2015.

Kiri Piahana-Wong

Kiri Piahana-Wong was born in Taumaranui. Her Chinese grandfather emigrated to New Zealand from Maktin Village, Xinhui (Sunwui) District, Guangdong, China in the early 1930s. He met Kiri's Māori grandmother working in market gardens in Tauranga. She was the daughter of paramount chief, Te Hare Piahana (Ngāti Ranginui). After their marriage, Kiri's grandparents moved to Auckland. Kiri's father was the eldest son of nine children; her mother is NZ-born of English heritage. Kiri is a poet and editor, and she is the publisher at Anahera Press. Her poems have appeared in over forty journals and anthologies, most recently in *A Clear Dawn: New Asian Voices from Aotearoa New Zealand*, *Ora Nui 4*, and *tātai whetū: seven Māori women poets in translation*. Her first poetry collection, *Night Swimming*, was released in 2013; a second book, *Tidelines*, is due out soon. Kiri lives in Whanganui with her family.

Laura Toailoa

Laura is a high school teacher, writer, and rom com enthusiast. She has work peppered across the internet including in e-Tangata, Pantograph Punch, and Blogger.com. Normally a columnist, personal essayist, and art reviewer, Laura has ventured into fiction writing for the first time in the Vā anthology.

Lauren Keenan

(Te Atiawa ki Taranaki) Lauren started writing after having children, to give herself something to think about that wasn't baby food, sleep routines, and a pile of laundry so big it ought to have its own gravitational pull. She has eight short stories published in three Huia short story collections. In 2017 she won the Pikihuia Best Short Story award, and in 2019 was a finalist in the Pikihuia Best Emerging Writer category. Lauren has a Master of Arts in History, and has worked for both central and local government in New Zealand and the UK. She calls Wellington home. Lauren's #lifegoal is to see 50 countries before she's 50, although, admittedly, she still has a way to go. The 52 Week Project is her first full-length book.

Lehua Parker

Lehua writes speculative fiction for kids and adults, often set in her native Hawaiʻi. Her award-winning published series include the Niuhi Shark Saga trilogy, Lauele Fractured Folktales, and Chicken Skin Stories, along with many other plays, poems, short stories, novels, and essays. A Kamehameha Schools graduate, Lehua is a passionate advocate of indigenous voices and authentic representation in media. She is a frequent speaker at conferences, schools, and symposiums, and mentors through the Lehua Writing Academy and PEAU Lit. When the right project wanders by, she's also a freelance editor and story consultant. Now living in exile in the high Rocky Mountains, during the snowy winters she dreams of the beach.

Connect with her on her website at https://www.lehuaparker.com . To find more of her stories, check out her Amazon page at https://www.amazon.com/Lehua-Parker/e/B009SDCHA6

Lily Ann Eteuati

Lily was born in Samoa and raised in both Samoa and Aotearoa. She is from the villages of Togafuafua and Nafanua and currently resides in Auckland with her young daughter. She is studying towards a Bachelor of Science in psychology at the Auckland University of Technology. She is a bookworm and finds writing a safe haven. She won speech competitions in Otago Girls Highschool and Otago Pasifika Perspectives, before moving to Samoa to finish school at Samoa College and LDS Church College Pesega where she graduated on the Honour roll. This is her first published work.

Mere Taito

Mere is a Rotuman Islander from Rotuma, Fiji, and moved to New Zealand in 2007. She is the author of the poetry collection The Light and Dark in our Stuff (2017), and her work has appeared in Landfall, A Fine Line and So Many Islands: Stories from the Caribbean, Mediterranean, Indian and Pacific Oceans. Mere lives in Hamilton with her partner Neil and nephew Lapuke.

Momoe Malietoa Von Reiche

Painter, writer, illustrator, teacher, poet, artist, and publisher, Momoe is an icon of Pacific Literature, one of the first Pasifika women to have a poetry collection published. The author of 5 books of poetry, her groundbreaking work is studied across the world and continues to inspire Oceania writers. Her paintings have been exhibited in NZ, Germany, the USA and across the Pacific. She has a Masters Degree in Education and in 2004 she created the first performing and visual arts curriculum for Samoan Primary schools, a foundation which continues to be built on today. She is certified in Teaching English as a second language and Translation, and has published many bilingual teaching resources and reading materials. Currently she runs her own gallery in Apia, the MADD Gallery which is a creative hub for local artists and writers. She has 9 children and 17 grandchildren who she adores.

Nadine Anne Hura

Nadine Anne Hura is a writer and activist-by-stealth. Her essays, poetry, zines and spoken word pieces seek to harness the power of individual stories to inspire collective action. Whether it be the protection of Papatūānuku or healing the intergenerational harms of colonisation, Nadine is passionate about social justice and equity, and absolutely believes in the innate wisdom and knowledge that indigenous storytellers and artists bring to the solve the gnarliest problems society is currently facing - environmentally, politically, intellectually and spiritually. Nadine is a member of the Te Hā o Ngā Pou Māori Writers' committee and uses this role as a way to advocate for better resourcing and support for all Māori writers, and in particular Kaupapa Māori-led opportunities. Nadine's work has been anthologised widely, and she is a contributor to a number of online platforms including The Spinoff, e-Tangata and Newsroom. Nadine is of Ngati Hine, Ngāpuhi and Pākehā whakapapa and grew up in South Auckland with her mother and two older brothers. Nadine is a staunch solo Māmā of three teenagers, a student of Te Ataarangi and an insatiable knitter, print-maker and reader.

Nafanua PK

Pōneke raised, Samoan writer Nafanua PK hails from the villages of Mosula and Malaela on her Father's side and Satufia, Falealupo-tai and Tuaefu on her Mother's. She lives in Mangatahi, Hawkes Bay where she raises three free-roam children, adores her 'aiga and writes about things and stuff - but mostly arts. She enjoys activating the fluidity of Pasifika naming and storytelling, and the persona shifts that come with this. Poetry is her long time introvert friend whom she has just started introducing to others as the 2020 winner of the Hawke's Bay Poetry Slam. She is proud to have Vā be the first to publish her poetry and her favourite writer moment to date is fan-girling so hard that she made it onto the back cover of an actual poetry book, by her favourite poet Tusiata Avia.

Nichole Brown

A fiery concoction of North (ngapuhi) and East (ngati porou), Nichole began writing as a way to cope with the struggles of being a single mum. Her blog, Emmy & Me, made a few small ripples which eventually led to her writing for The Spin-off Parents, and then becoming a published author when her viral essay, "I'm sorry for whitewashing your world," was published in a parenting anthology called, "Is It Bedtime Yet?" Nichole now lives in Brisbane, Australia with her daughter, now 9, stepdaughter, 15, and the love of her life who encourages her to write every single day.

Nicki Perese

Nicki was born and raised in Samoa. She graduated from Victoria University of Wellington (B.A in Pacific studies, Samoan studies and English Literature) and from the National University of Samoa (Post graduate diploma in Education). Proud faafafine. Teacher and poet. Nicki works at the Samoa Ministry of Education and Culture as the Principal curriculum officer.

Niusila Faamanatu-Eteuati

Dr Niusila Faamanatu-Eteuati has been a lecturer for Va'aomanu Pasifika, Victoria University of Wellington and the Faculty of Education, National University of Samoa for over 20 years now. She hails from the villages of Samusu Aleipata, Vaegā Satupa'itea, Solosolo, Lepā with in-laws from Sala'ilua, Manono and Ti'avea. She has been an editor, translator and author for Children's Books and Pacific Literacy in New Zealand. Niusila has also written, translated poems and composed songs for the teaching of Gagana Samoa and English literature at university level.

Ria Masae

Ria Masae is of Samoan descent, born and raised in Tāmaki Makaurau in Aotearoa New Zealand. She is a librarian by day and a solo mother of two and a proud new nana 24/7. Any spare from that she is a writer, poet, and spoken word artist. Her work has been published in various literary outlets including, Landfall, *takahe, Stasis Journal,* Cordite (Australia), *Circulo De Poesia* (Mexico), and Best New Zealand Poems (2017 and 2020). Ria's poetry has also appeared in stage productions such as, *Upu Mai Whetu: Mea Fou, Between the Pages, and Makai – Black Sand:* Ocean Bones. She won the 2015 'New Voices: Emerging Poets Competition', and the 2016 'Cooney Insurance Short Story Competition'. In 2018, Ria became the 'Going West Poetry Slam' champion, and in 2019 she was a recipient of the 'NZSA Mentor Programme'. A collection of her poems, titled, 'What she Sees From Atop the Mauga', was one of three collections chosen for publication by Auckland University Press', *AUP New Poets 7* in 2020. Ria is currently working on a poetry collection for her first sole anthology...in her spare time.

Rebecca Tobo Olul-Hossen

Poet, short story writer and editor, Rebecca co-edited Vanuatu's first women's anthology, *Sista, Stanap Strong!* (VUP, 2021) and first non-fiction children's book, *Taf Tumas (2020).* Her poems have been published in *Sport 47*

(VUP, 2019), *Sista, Voes (AF, 2020)*, and the anthology *Rising Tides (SPC, 2020)*. A collaborative work was recently published in the anthology *A Game of Two Halves: The Best of Sport 2005–2019* (VUP, Nov 2021). She lives in Port Vila, Vanuatu, with her husband, sons, and daughter.

Salote Timuiapaepatele Vaai - Siaosi

Salote is a General Practitioner in Samoa with her own medical clinic, Health in her Hands. She is the second youngest of six siblings and her villages are Lepea, Moataa and Sataua, Savaii. She started writing a blog in 2016. Her favorite author is Pastor Lisa Bevere and her favorite part of any day is early morning coffee on the couch with pure silence to think. Her possible dream future is to retire early to write and teach, run a Cafe with husband Lubuto and invest in Real Estate.

Shirley Simmonds

Shirley is a descendant of Raukawa on her koro's side, and of Ngāpuhi on her nanny's side.

She lives in Tauranga moana, with her two sons Tamihana and Raukawa and her partner Puruhi. She is dedicated to raising her sons in their native language, te reo Māori, and living the values passed down from our tūpuna. As a whānau, they have strong goals to journey towards a self-sustainable lifestyle.

Shirley attributes her love of words to her mum, she loves the lilt and curl of them, their beauty and power. She spent much of her childhood reading, and much of her adult years thinking about writing. It is only in recent years she has ventured into putting words on paper and has found writing a creative outlet that helps her make sense of the world. Shirley was a participant in the Te Papa Tupu writing programme in 2016 where the story in this anthology first came to light.

When not at her computer, Shirley spends much of her time in the kitchen or garden, at the beach or at the marae. She loves learning new things, exploring new places, and hanging out with her favourite people.

Stacey Kokaua

(Ngāti Arerā ō Rarotonga | Pāmati | Pākehā) Stacey lives in Parihaumia, Ōtepoti. Her writing interests include Cook Islands identity, environmental issues in Moana Nui a Kiva and coaxing the personal from the political. Her work has been published in Landfall, Turbine, Fresh Ink and Pantograph Punch. Find some of her creative non-fiction on Turbine: The Masterly Works of Pāpā John Numa.

Steph Matuku

Steph Matuku is from Taranaki (Ngāti Mutunga, Ngāti Tama, Te Atiawa). She's a mum and an awardwinning freelance writer who likes to write stories for young people for the page, stage and screen.

All her books have been published by Huia Publishers. Her novels, 'Flight of the Fantail' and 'Whetū Toa and the Magician', and 'Falling Into Rarohenga' were Storylines Notable Books, and 'Whetū' was a finalist at the New Zealand Book Awards for Children and Young Adults.

'Whetū Toa and the Hunt for Ramses' was published in 2021, along with her first picture book, 'The Eight Gifts of Te Wheke', which was also translated into te reo Māori by Kawata Teepa.

Recently she completed a residency at the Michael King Writers' Centre where she worked on a YA novel about post-apocalyptic climate change. If she doesn't delete the whole thing out of frustration and loathing, it should be finished sometime in 2022.

Sylvia Nakachi

Sylvia is an Erub Island woman from the Eastern Islands in the Torres Strait. Nakachi was raised in a remote first people community called Bamaga and has attended both her primary and high school years in Bamaga. Reuben is an artist and writer, currently completing her Doctor of Philosophy (PhD) in Indigenous Perspective with Bachelor Institute in the Northern Territory. Her work is to capture concepts how her Erub Island, culture, way of life and practices have evolved after the 1871 arrival of the London Missionary Society Sylvia has a Master's degree in human services, specializing in childhood studies, a graduate certificate in childhood studies and an undergraduate degree in education. A passionate child advocate and educator, she also teaches and works through different schools and educational institutions to embed the Aboriginal and Torres Strait Islander perspectives.

Tanya Kang Chargualaf Taimanglo

Born in South Korea and flourished in Guam. She ventured into her passion for writing at the same time she rooted herself in her teaching career. After moving to California, and eventually Washington State, Tanya continued indie publishing stories that reflected her Chamorro and Korean heritage. *Secret Shopper, Sirena*, and a collection of short stories entitled *Attitude 13* were all homages to her parents. She contributes short stories to Guam publications including the University of Guam's *Storyboard* editions and *Kinalamten Gi Pasifiku*. She is a 3rd Dan Black Belt in Tae Kwon Do, with the hopes of being a Master to honor her late mother. She wants to be Wonder Woman some day and can be regularly found at Marvel movie premieres and Comic Cons. She continues to inspire students, currently 6thgrade ELA. Tanya is passionate about equity and diversity at her school and instilling this with youth. She launched the Asian Culture Club and Pacific Islander Culture Club at her middle school. She blogs, on occasion, at Guam Goddess in Training. She is a certified introvert.

Tulia Thompson

Tulia Thompson (Fiji/ Tonga/ Pakeha) has a Ph.D. in Sociology and an M.CW. Hons (First Class) in Creative Writing. Her first book Josefa and the Vu, a fantasy-adventure for 8-12s was published by Huia in 2007. ://huia. co.nz/huia-bookshop/bookshop/josefa-and-the-vu/https://huia.co.nz/huia-bookshop/bookshop/josefa-and-the-vu/

Josefa and the Vu was made into an audio version for Storytime by RNZ, narrated by actor Madeleine Sami.

https://storytime.rnz.co.nz/book/josefa-and-the-vu/

Tulia primarily sees herself as an essayist; she (jointly) won the 2018 Wallace Foundation Award for Creative Nonfiction, and her critically-acclaimed essay 'In the Under' was published in 'Life on Volcanoes' https://beatnikpublishing.com/products/life-on-volcanoes (and online by Pantograph Punch). https://www.pantograph-punch.com/posts/in-the-under

She has an essay on the relationship between the Moana and Aotearoa in BwB's 'Beyond our Shores' https://www.bwb.co.nz/books/beyond-these-shores/ an abridged reflection is printed at https://e-tangata.co.nz/reflections/i-am-doing-this-for-our-seas/

She has a piece of speculative fiction in Scorchers, an Anthology of climate fiction https://fivedogsbooks.co.nz/scorchers-climate-fiction-9781990000621

Her writing has been published in JAAM, Overland, Pantograph Punch, The Spinoff, Blackmail Press and The Big Idea.

Tulia is working on a collection of personal essays, and procrastinating by writing a sitcom. When she is not writing she is walking her three-legged dog or playing with her 8-year-old stepson.

Vanessa Collins

Vanessa was born in Fiji to Fijian and New Zealand parents. While growing up in Suva she spent most of her early teens and 20's working and campaigning with the Fiji Women's Rights Movement, an experience that has helped shape her strong commitment to women and social issues. She's a single mum to a daughter who she credits as a strong influence in her work with children. In her spare time she runs educational programs for young children. Her and her daughter call West Auckland home. Her short story for Vā is Vanessa's first attempt at writing for a publication.

Tatou Publishing: About Us

Tatou Publishing was co-founded in November 2021 by Sisilia Eteuati and Lani Young because of a deep belief that our stories deserve readers and readers deserve our stories.

We both benefited immensely from growing up in Samoa immersed in our own culture and values.

We knew that too many of our Moana stories were being lost because too often our people are overlooked by Western publishers who

- have failed to understand the appeal of our stories
- have an individualistic approach (often characterised by gate keeping, and running things like competitions where there is only one winner)
- are part of a system that prioritizes profits over people and over story.

We knew there was a better way, a Samoan way, a Moana way, which would harness the collective strength of ALL of us.

We want to bring together our writers, both those who are award winning published authors and those who are new to being published, to inspire and help each other.

We want to work with writers who share our vision, and who want editors and publishers who can, because of our shared cultures and values, truly inhabit their stories.

It is no surprise to us that when we approach projects using our own aganu'u and our own kaupapa that prioritizes people and the va between us, the richness that results.

We deeply believe that people are orators, and storytelling is our inheritance.

We publish stories from the Moana, written by us, about us and for us.

Our goal is to help Moana writers worldwide, take ownership and control of how our stories are marketed and distributed, as together, we take our stories to a global audience.

E pala ma'a, ae le pala upu.